Acknowledgments

I owe the realisation of this book to the following people, for without them it would not have been possible.

Many thanks to my group of "expert readers" Graham, Malky, and Kenny for helping me keep Thoroughgood real! Thanks also to Michael Brady who designed the cover for this e-book.

My eternal thanks to my late grandfather, David Jones, for giving me a set of values with which to start my life and to one day try and live up to.

Thanks to my late stepfather, Martin Kaney, for never judging me when everything seemed a mess. I hope he will look down from above and see that I have done my best.

My gratitude to my mother, Margaret Kaney, for all her encouragement and love.

My undying thanks, love and devotion to my wife, Arlene Mitchell, for her belief in Parallel Lines when no one else seemed to, her endless hours of admin, doing the boring stuff and so, so much more.

Thanks to my daughter, Ava, for helping to make me a better human being.

And finally, to you the readers.

Reviews

"They call Scottish crime fiction 'tartan noir' - and if that's the case, then the thread of red that runs through Parallel Lines is a river of blood, and the blacks and greens are the bruises on a battered corpse. This book doesn't pull any punches in its depiction of a deadly cops-and-robbers feud that strays far beyond the procedural into the personal. At the core of the story is a traditional love triangle - the hero, the villain and the girl that gets between them - but it's Mitchell's first-hand knowledge of what goes on behind the police station's closed doors that sets the book apart. This is a real page-turner: once that plot is set in motion, like a car with its brake pipes cut hurtling down a steep Glasgow street - and that's an image from the book you won't forget - it carries the reader right through to its bullet-strewn climax."

ALAN MORRISON, Group Arts Editor, Herald & Times

1

"CODE SIXTY-THREE, armed robbery in progress, Smith's Pawnbrokers, 11 Argyle Street. Any station to attend." The hiss of the radio jolted the two men into action.

"Bloody hell, Gus, that's just round the corner!" exclaimed DC Kenny Hardie.

"Go, it's the corner of Robertson Street at Argyle Street, we must be about a quarter of a mile from it. Straight down Wellington Street, Kenny; I'll stick the light on the roof. Come on, man, put yer fuckin' foot down or we'll miss the whole shebang. DS Thoroughgood from Wellington Street, any descriptions, reggy numbers for motors involved?"

"That's a negative," crackled the voice from the control room. "All we've got is the raid alarm. Treat with utmost caution. The Tactical Firearms Unit has been alerted but ETA is five minutes. They're coming from the other side of the Clyde, that's a big shout this time of the afternoon. So you're the nearest station, DS Thoroughgood." The controller warned again: "Treat with caution, repeat, treat with caution!"

"Thanks for your concern, mate," said the DS out loud.

Kenny Hardie's temperature, as well as his heart rate, was rising fast. The veteran DC blurted out from behind the steering wheel: "Gus, there it is the other side of Argyle Street. You're first out. Watch your arse, son."

Hardie's words of warning could have been coming from the dark side of the moon for all the likelihood they had of making an impact on Gus Thoroughgood; he was surfing a whitewater adrenalin ride and the DS wanted bodies.

Immediately taking in the key elements of the scene before him, Thoroughgood sprung out of the Ford Focus in one fluid movement. A green Mondeo parked at the corner of the pawnbroker's looked decidedly dodgy. He could see it was one up with a male behind the wheel, but by then the detective was halfway through the pawnbroker's door and the shit was about to hit the fan, big time.

The first shot rang out before Thoroughgood had taken one step inside the premises. His subconscious registered the sound of the shooter as a shotgun even as his blood ran cold. The impact on the roof brought a fall of plaster and a chorus of screams from the shopgirl behind the counter.

Standing inside the door was armed robber one, complete with balaclava; for a vital split second he paused, surprised to see Thoroughgood diving through the door. The DS threw himself at the criminal and managed to knock the sawn-off out of his grasp with the impact of the collision. It landed on top of the counter, drawing further screams from the petrified girl. Right at that moment, though, her welfare was not top of Thoroughgood's agenda.

Detective and villain hit the ground with a thud, Thoroughgood just managing to get his hands round his opponent's neck. This was a fight to the death, and

2

Thoroughgood had no intention of coming second. Over and over they rolled, smashing into the counter and bringing the shooter down, conveniently into the grasp of the criminal.

Thoroughgood moved his grip from flesh to firearm as he attempted to stop it being levelled at him. The acrid smell of whisky and smoke almost knocked him out as it seeped from the ned's balaclava. The two tightened their embrace on the sawn-off until it was forced upwards, and another shot into the roof brought a deluge of plaster down on the pair.

It was the criminal who was on top now, and he rammed the firearm down onto the cop's jugular until slowly the air seemed to seep from his lungs as the constriction mounted.

Where the fuck is Hardie when you need him? Thoroughgood thought. He forced himself to scan the walls of the shop for anything that could help break the ned's killer grip. There it was, a foot to the left of the counter, a fire extinguisher mounted on the wall. Thoroughgood aimed his size ten at the catch holding it to the plaster and the contact brought a shudder, but nothing more. It was time to gamble.

Thoroughgood put all his power into a left hook to his assailant's ribs and surged his body weight upwards. It wasn't enough to knock the thug off but it allowed the cop to grab the neck of the extinguisher, which promptly came crashing down onto the ground. That moment also allowed the robber to regain his breath, and he was once again using the sawn-off to crush the oxygen from Thoroughgood's throat and lungs.

Flicking at the catch on the extinguisher, Thoroughgood could feel consciousness slipping away from him fast.

With one final supreme effort from what was likely to be his last breath, the DS concentrated his fast-fading energy on firing the extinguisher at his assailant. Everything went white. Caught off-guard, the villain was snow-blinded.

Thoroughgood smashed a right hand off his jaw; at last, movement. Stunned, the robber lost the grip on the firearm and Thoroughgood's forehead met the bridge of his nose with sudden impact. A satisfying crack resounded as bone, blood and mucus burst forth in a froth that produced a raspberry ripple effect on the surrounding foam. This time all of the robber's momentum was going backwards, and the cop seized his moment.

Thoroughgood rolled free and turned on his man with his police-issue baton. A swift left jab with the point of the implement meant the robber was left more than momentarily breathless. It was game over as Thoroughgood smashed on the cuffs, making sure that they were tight enough to turn the skin on the criminal's wrist red.

"You're nailed, fucker," growled the gasping DS as another boot from his size ten took the last remnants of the air from the gunman's lungs.

Meanwhile, Hardie was otherwise engaged. The green Mondeo had sped off almost the minute the driver had spotted the all-too-obvious form of the CID Focus in his rear view. The lookout posted on the corner opposite the pawnbroker's was now fleeing on foot towards Clydeside down Robertson Street.

A foot chase was not one of Hardie's favourite activities. He was forty-two going on fifty-two and had a bronchial problem brought on by his thirty-a-day habit, while "a bevvy" was his favourite method of relaxation. Hardie was no favourite to catch a spring-heeled criminal twenty years younger and at least two stone lighter than him.

Caught up in his own thoughts and focused on the disappearing back of his quarry, Hardie was snapped from his reverie when the crack of a gunshot whistled over his right shoulder before ricocheting off a parked car five yards to his left. Thoughts of self-preservation were brought firmly to the forefront of his mind: the distant but still comforting wail of sirens meant back-up was on its way. Hardie grabbed for his airwave radio before bulleting in an update:

"Code 21, CID officer engaged in foot chase south, down Robertson Street towards Clydeside. Suspect armed with handgun, wearing black hooded jacket and what looks like a stocking mask over his head."

Delivered in one huge breath, Hardie gulped another before attempting to take stock of his situation. Looking ahead, he saw the suspect change direction along Clydeside, weaving in and out of the late afternoon traffic. He bolted down the steps to the front of the Waterfront Pub, making for one of the nearby footbridges that would take him over the Clyde and into Carlton Place, on the south side of the river that flowed through the heart of Glasgow.

Hardie barked into his PR: "He's making for footbridge leading into Carlton Place. Unit to attend south side of footbridge immediately."

By this time, Hardie was descending the steps at the riverside boozer. As he reached the bottom tread he saw the robber turn towards him. The hunter had become the hunted. The stocking mask was pulled up on top of the criminal's head, and Hardie guessed his target was in his late twenties. The gap between them was around thirty feet, and the handgun was levelled at head height.

Behind it the villain, flashed a feral grin as a glint of late afternoon sunshine caught on the pistol.

Time stood still and Hardie wondered if it was another one of the alcohol-fuelled nightmares that plagued his sleeping hours.

Instantly a crack rang out and Hardie hit the deck, rolling under a nearby bench in one desperate movement. The shot hit woodwork and Hardie let out a gasp of relief that was almost over before it had begun. The DC hazarded a quick glance from under the bench. The ned was off his mark once again.

Hardie staggered to his feet and made for the bridge. As he looked along the foot span he had to blink to shed his disbelief at the scene now confronting him: the ned was bolting at full speed straight towards him.

At the other end of the bridge a Tactical Firearms Unit vehicle had just screeched to a halt and two black uniform-clad figures were taking their first steps on to the bridge. Hardie could see, even from the opposite end of the bridge, the levelling of the Heckler and Kochs belonging to his armed colleagues. The robber had decided, presumably without much thought, that the portly detective was by far the easier option when it came to his own survival.

His pistol was out again and assuming its familiar position: pointing straight at Hardie.

Oh fuck, thought Hardie. This is it.

In the distance he heard "Stop, armed police!" A shot cracked across the bridge and Hardie jumped. But as the DC hit water he found he wasn't alone in the drink, for the gunman broke the surface almost simultaneously.

The grimy fluid of the Clyde closed over him as Hardie's first thought was Fuck, I've been shot, is this what it feels like?

6

The murky depths continued to envelop him and he sank deeper, panic beginning to seep through. He tried to decide whether he would die of the bullet wound or drown first.

Come on son, give it a fuckin' go, he told himself and kicked for the surface, wondering if he had enough oxygen in his nicotine-stained lungs to fire him through. Piercing flickers of the bright spring sunshine made him realise that he was almost there.

Keep going, the voice in his head said.

The cool air hit his face and Hardie knew he'd made it. Breathing hard and trying to stay calm, he spat out the gut-wrenching contents of the river. Hardie looked down at the cold fluid splashing around his torso and gritted his teeth, fearing the worst. But there was no red liquid spreading out from his substantial midriff.

A voice from the bridge punctured Hardie's thoughts.

"You all right, mate?" Can you make it to the side?"

Hardie almost surprised himself when he heard his voice shout:

"Nae bother, bud." And sure enough his arms worked, one in front of the other as he swam to the riverbank. Then smack, his leading hand rapped against a solid sodden object bobbing in the water to his right.

Fuckin tyre, this shithole is full of them, thought Hardie. Wrong. Seeping from the floating form of the now-deceased robber were his vital fluids, mingling with the putrid water in an ever-widening ruby pool. Robber number two was indeed dead and belly-up in his watery grave in the Clyde.

Well, fuck you, matey, thought Kenny Hardie.

2

"LUCKY BASTARD," grinned Thoroughgood as he looked at the opposite bunk in the ambulance.

Hardie raised his eyebrows in mock indignation. "I hardly think two lungfuls of that sewer of a river is what you'd call lucky. Fuck only knows what germs have worked their way into my system. You wait and see: before you know it I'll have pneumonia, that's how fuckin' lucky I am!"

The two detectives were on their way to the city's Royal Infirmary Casualty department, Hardie to have checks done after his unplanned dip in the Clyde, Thoroughgood because Detective Super Tomachek insisted that a cautionary check-up was needed.

Rather than any genuine fears over his officer's health, Tomachek needed to ensure that Strathclyde Police would avoid assuming liability at a later date for any claims from their employee. The political correctness sweeping through the police and, in particular, Scotland's biggest force, made Thoroughgood wince with disgust.

Hardie was even more vehement and vocal in his anger at the politicians who now seemed to be turning a cop's life into a bureaucratic nightmare of endless paper mountains.

"Anyway, it's okay for you. A few scratches and a keeker, big deal. I've 'ad bigger cuts shaving," mocked Hardie. "Looks like I'm in here overnight for tests and observations when the only medicine I need is a pint of Stella. So what's happened with the rest of the gang?"

"Well, your man is in the morgue waiting on his post mortem. Mine is being interviewed at Stewart Street and the green Mondeo was found abandoned halfway down Meadowside Street, in Partick. So I guess you could say two out of three ain't bad, old son."

The ambulance drew to a halt, and the driver and his mate padded round to open the doors.

"Okay, lads, welcome to your hotel!" said the chauffeur.

Sixty minutes later Hardie was reclining in his bed with the GRI's medical staff fretting over him and various tubes attached for company.

Thoroughgood was ready to go, the X-rays revealing that his cranium was fully intact, something Thoroughgood thought was sure to disappoint Divisional Commander John Brown when he made the regulation welfare visit to his wounded-in-action officer.

Materialising at Hardie's bedside, the DS radiated sarcastic concern:

"You'll be okay, faither, just take it easy and let them do their stuff. Fancy a small wager on who gets here first, Tomachek or old 'Grizzly' Brown? They'll be falling over themselves to get here and check on their injured hero."

Hardie was unimpressed. "It's always the fuckin' same. The minute you do anything good, the uniform want to pat you on the back as well as the CID brass. For ninety per cent of the rest of the time they treat you like a leper, unless they get the chance to boot you in the balls. I'll need to get the nurse to put a sign up on the ward door: 'Out to tea or unavailable for comment.'"

The rising voices alerted Hardie's nurse, a burly red-headed sister who Thoroughgood thought should have had three stripes on her shoulder. The sister didn't disappoint: "How, I ask, is Mr Hardie to recuperate with you raising his blood pressure by encouraging him to lay bets, DS Thoroughgood? You know where the door is."

The DS nodded sheepishly at the fiery sister and winked at his colleague: "I'll look in tomorrow sometime, Kenny. Hopefully a few days off the sauce will see you come out of here good as new, probably better."

"Fuck off, arse!" was the mild-mannered reply from the poorly patient, and as Thoroughgood headed off he could already hear the admonishment from the sister.

Thankful to be making his way down one of the GRI'S grimy corridors, Thoroughgood tried not to dwell on the events of a shift that had been anything but just another day at the office. Sure, it had been a close call, but then he'd had plenty of those during his service. It was at times like these that he wondered what might have been if he'd managed to pursue his preferred career as a historian.

Thoroughgood's entry into the police had been a distant second choice, but one borne of necessity after a youthful mistake had seen him almost leave Glasgow University without a degree or a future, back in 1988.

The previous summer, Thoroughgood had worked as a bartender when the city enjoyed its year as one of the UK's five national Garden Festivals. With licensing laws permitting the hostelries of the West End to open until two a.m., Thoroughgood had found himself regularly spilling in the front door of his student flat in Lawrence Street as dawn broke. This had a disastrous effect on his degree and, in particular, the dissertation he was attempting to write for the start of the new term in October. The simple answer had been plagiarism.

Great wads of Thoroughgood's paper on the Peasants' Revolt of 1381 were lifted from existing books. The naïve nineteen-year-old was hauled up in front of the University Senate and humbly accepted his punishment. The dissertation had third class slapped on it: in layman's terms a fail, and Thoroughgood's dream of a PhD spent studying private archives in France was to be no more than that. His failure meant that within twenty-one days of his graduation, with the world at his feet, he found himself on the end of the drill sergeant's Doc Martens at Tulliallan.

And the rest was indeed history.

What a fuckin' day! Kenny was right, I could do with a beer, thought the DS.

Home for Gus Thoroughgood was a large ground-floor tenement flat in Partickhill Road in the West End. But that could wait a while. First he had to get back to Stewart Street nick and uniform were, for once, only too happy to give him a lift.

Jumping into his pride and joy, a gleaming blue RX-8 Mazda, one of the few luxuries he allowed himself, Thoroughgood switched on the ignition and switched off one of the more frantic days he could remember in his service. The voice of Fish sprang to life on the CD player. Sometimes Thoroughgood thought he'd been caught in an Eighties time warp when it came to music. The music of Marillion provided a comforting security blanket of happy teenage memories.

Parking his car outside the flat he headed across Highburgh Road and up the steps of his local, the Rock. One pint of Kronenburg later and the world already seemed a better place. The DS fingered his mobile and placed his delivery order with the local Chinese, the Amber, down in Byres Road.

"Forty minute," said an Oriental accent at the other end of the phone.

Time to finger the sports pages of his favourite paper, the Telegraph, unwind a bit and then enjoy the delights of a weekend off before nightshift. Maybe a visit to Firhill to watch the latest torturous instalment of Partick Thistle's quest for promotion from the Scottish Second Division. Perhaps a game of squash and then a hospital visit to check on Hardie's progress.

Thoroughgood thought ten to one his portly sidekick would be back in harness for the ten p.m. start on Wednesday night. Not that much to look forward to, he mused, for the events of the last twelve hours had planted a seed of doubt that his life was indeed arse for elbow. The old cop's saying "You don't live to work, you work to live" was, Gus Thoroughgood admitted to himself, all too true. But maybe at the age of thirty-seven he was starting to get it the wrong way round.

3

WEDNESDAY NIGHTSHIFT, 2200 hours: Thoroughgood watched the ambling shape of Kenny Hardie framed in the doorway of the DS' room at Stewart Street nick. Sure enough, Hardie had discharged himself from the GRI on Saturday, leaving half an hour after Detective Super Tomachek had made the second senior officer visit that afternoon, to check on his welfare.

The first evening on the nightshift was always a hard one to call. Quieter than the weekend for obvious reasons, sometimes dead, but at times surprisingly explosive. Thoroughgood finished trawling the notes left for him on the crime management computer system by the backshift, but looked up long enough to nod in the direction of the kettle. Hardie's eyebrows shot up.

"You're supposed to be looking after me, rather than me nursemaiding you. What is it anyway, one lump or two in yer coffee?"

"That dip in the Clyde addled your brains where all that Stella Artois failed? You know damn fine, you old jake, now get on with it and then we can take a look at an enquiry left for us by these lazy gits in Group One CID," said Thoroughgood.

As he considered the back of his burly partner, Thoroughgood admitted to himself that hats had to be taken off to Hardie. The DS was well aware he had been paired up with Hardie in order to benefit from the forty-something's considerable experience and the gut-instinct approach which had brought Hardie an erratic stream of spectacular successes over his twenty-three years of service.

Okay, Hardie might not be in the best of shape, but he made up for it with a brain that was alert to the slightest clue. The problem with Hardie was a loose tongue which landed him in hot water with a growing regularity.

They both knew that was exactly the reason why Thoroughgood was the superior ranking officer.

While Hardie looked at the world with a cynical gaze, Thoroughgood followed a much more measured and almost analytical approach which in turn had irritated some of the dinosaurs above him in the CID chain of command. However, after eighteen months of working together, the two had smoothed out the kinks in their relationship, at work and at play. In short, they were comfortable in each other's company.

Top of the agenda tonight was an enquiry over a serious assault outside one of Glasgow's ever-increasing number of pubs. Happy now his coffee had been slammed down in front of him, Thoroughgood briefed his colleague.

"This is one of Declan Meechan's boozers. Some kid went and got bevvied up on the cheap booze on students' night, then picked a fight with one of the doormen, or according to the backshift note, the lot of them."

"The boy, an eighteen year old called Terry Devlin, went outside to continue his altercation and ended up with a fractured skull. The CCTV tape shows him getting laid into by one doorman in particular, a Franny Hillkirk. Unfortunately, he did one before uniform got to the scene.

So far address checks have come up with hee-haw. The boy had a knife in his possession but one of the witness statements from another student says he saw Hillkirk punting Devlin drugs earlier in the evening. We need to get a hold of Hillkirk, and that won't be easy. Meechan won't want one of his boys doing time or, more like it, the adverse publicity that would attract. Meechan's whole operation is as slick as tanker spill and this might be a way in. So, let's just go for a nice little chat with the management and see where that takes us."

The red CID Focus pulled up outside Babylon, in Sauchiehall Street. The market Meechan was catering for was obviously young. Cheap booze nights for students during the week, then the kids from the city's schemes at the weekend. Assaults at places like Babylon were ten-a-penny, especially at the weekend when they acted as a release for all the testosterone that had built up over the week. Babylon catered for all the needs of its young clientele, drink or drugs, and was the perfect launchpad for a night's clubbing.

Thoroughgood was forced to admit to himself that Declan Meechan had done pretty well for a young ned from Belfast, graduating from teenage gang member to all-too-efficient steward on the doors of some of the toughest pubs in the area. And now he was number two to Jimmy Gray, the Partick and West End crime overlord.

Gray had been particularly grateful for the way his young lieutenant had ruthlessly cleared up a small outbreak of trouble with a Maryhill mobster called Archie Gallagher. He had subsequently been found minus his limbs floating down the Clyde last October. The reward for Meechan's clean-up job was control of Gray's burgeoning city centre pub and club operation.

All very cosy, thought Thoroughgood, but how long would it take Meechan to turn on the hand that had fed him so generously?

As the two detectives made their way past one of Meechan's stewards, both officers found their attention drawn to the bar where a dark-haired young woman was holding court with the staff.

Celine Lynott was a real looker, as Hardie might describe her: thirty-three years old, of mixed parentage with coffee-coloured skin that glowed in the fluorescent lighting of the bar. Her luxuriant hair was curled in a series of unruly tresses cascading over her shoulders, and her chestnut eyes could burn a hole in you. She may have run Meechan's three toughest city centre bars, but Celine Lynott's style of management was almost regal. She had been brought up in Hayburn Street, Partick, and then found herself a place as a croupier at Jimmy Gray's Riverboat Casino before being snapped up by Meechan as the extremely glamorous face of his club empire.

Meechan trusted her implicitly and knew everything about her, or so he thought. Everything but the fact she'd been one of Thoroughgood's informants years back in his early days as a Detective Constable, that and a little bit more besides. Kenny Hardie, aware of the undercurrents that would soon be at work, arched his left eyebrow in (he thought) a fine impersonation of his hero, spaghetti Western star Lee Van Cleef.

There may be trouble ahead, thought the DC.

"Good evening, officers. We don't usually welcome gentlemen as distinguished as yourselves to Babylon on a Monday night. I assume you are here on business, not pleasure?" asked Celine. Playing to her audience of staff and hangers-on, Celine failed to betray the slightest

16

acknowledgement, either in her expression or in the timbre of her voice, that she had any familiarity with Thoroughgood.

Ten years can pass so quickly, he thought.

Thoroughgood was keenly aware there would always be some way that Celine Lynott could get to him. It was a chapter in his life he had found all too hard to close.

"Hi Celine."

Unusually for him, Kenny Hardie, perhaps sensing his gaffer's reticence, took the lead.

"We're here to see Declan Meechan, you know, about that business of your over-enthusiastic door policy. We hate to disturb him, but—"

"I'm sorry, Declan isn't here tonight. In fact, he's out of the city, but if you'd like to come up to the office we can discuss things there."

Celine gestured at one of the staff.

"Jimmy, make sure this bar is sparkling and keep the security on their toes. I don't think our guests would appreciate being disturbed. Okay, officers, if you'd like to follow me …"

Thoroughgood shot his sidekick a glance. After almost two years of working together the two detectives could operate without the use of words, and Hardie was aware his boss was telling him to button it. But the burly DC couldn't help indulging in a mischievous wink as the pair made their way up the stairs behind the curvaceous shape of Celine Lynott.

Upstairs in her office Celine wasted no time.

"So, how can I help you? You've got the whole incident on one of our CCTV tapes, which were taken by the officers who were first here last night. And I guess half a dozen witness statements from a group of drunken students. You'll be hoping the student fails to pull through and then you'll go after our licence. I hear he's in intensive care?" Her eyes never left Thoroughgood's.

"What if the young guy pulls through? I reckon you're struggling to make anything stick. Why the visit, Gus? Just for old times' sake?"

"Look, Celine, I'm not here to play games. The bloody gorillas you keep on the doors are the worst in the city; every weekend the streets outside your pubs are a war zone. Outside your pubs means it's on our streets, and that's gotta stop. When a kid is lying in hospital with a fractured skull and a head covered in boot prints, something has to be done. How convenient your doorman Franny Hillkirk has gone walkabout and you don't seem to have a current address for him. Either that, or your chargehand gave the uniform boys a bummer.

"So why don't we start with a current address for Hillkirk. Did you know that we've also got a witness statement saying Hillkirk was seen supplying the kid with ecstasy an hour before the assault? How do you like running a pub staffed by thugs and drug dealers?"

Celine's lips curled almost into a sneer. "I don't know what you mean. All our staff are hired in accordance with the company policy of Gray's Leisure. Mr Meechan takes a personal interest in their suitability."

Her forthright delivery brought a surge of anger through Hardie's veins, and before he could stop himself the DC butted in. "Well, that's a real endorsement of your door staff. What about you, Celine? Did Meechan take a personal interest in your suitability?"

There was no reaction on her features, but the temperature in the office seemed to have dropped five degrees.

"Perhaps it's time you left, gentlemen. As I said, Mr Meechan is unavailable and he has instructed me to tell you that he has provided all the co-operation he needs to through our lawyer, Charles Coyle.

"You've been very quiet, DS Thoroughgood, and I'd prefer it if your colleague also stayed that way until he has left the premises."

Thoroughgood decided the best form of defence was attack.

"Listen Celine, the bottom line is that we have an out-of-date address, and a check with the council housing office shows Hillkirk hasn't stayed in Springburn Way for over a year. So you are either wasting police time or attempting to pervert the course of justice. Have it your way. Do you want to come down to the station to help us with our enquiries? Then we can get Mr Coyle to join us and it will all be quite cosy. It's your call but I've got a search warrant for Hillkirk's address here."

The DS produced the legal document and laid it out on the desk. "So why give yourself grief over the home address of a jumped-up thug?"

Celine seared Thoroughgood with a stare of unrelenting ferocity, but her hands dropped to the PC keyboard and she brought up the employee details for Franny Hillkirk. "Springburn Way is the home address we have for him but there's a second address for his mother, an Iris Hillkirk, at flat 21c, 12 Eccles Street, Springburn. That's all we have. You can look at the computer for yourself if you don't believe me."

"That wasn't so painful, was it? If your chargehand had been more cooperative in the first place it would have been unnecessary; seems like your staffing problems aren't just on the door, Celine. See you around."

As an afterthought Thoroughgood added, and instantly wished he hadn't: "Oh, and tell Declan I was asking for him, would you?"

Celine said nothing, but her eyes met Thoroughgood's, holding his gaze in a moment that said more than any words ever could. And again, Thoroughgood found his emotions going through the mixer.

The two officers headed back out to the Focus. The silence between the two was almost deafening: it was Hardie who was first to break it.

"Look gaffer, I'm sorry about back there. The words came out before I could help myself."

"Listen, faither, this business can be used to make life extremely difficult for Meechan. It doesn't help matters, you upsetting his staff with your throwaway lines. Let's just see if we can get a hold of this Hillkirk character. Eccles Street, that's up opposite Springburn office, isn't it? Let's go and see if Franny's home."

The Focus swung off onto the M8 before taking the Springburn turnoff and there was silence once again, except for the sound of the pouring rain which seemed to provide a continual soundtrack for life in Glasgow.

Thankfully the lifts at 12 Eccles Street were working, much to Hardie's relief. Four flats on the level. As they scanned their way round each one the officers' attention was immediately drawn to the doorway of flat 21c, which lay open. Thoroughgood turned to Hardie and signalled to his mate to draw his baton. The DS took a step into the doorway and reached for the light switch, flicking it on, but the hall remained in darkness. Fortunately, the light from the landing offered some help. Thoroughgood gave the whistle that had been the universal warning used by neds in the city ever since he had joined the cops. A simple three-note shrill, first up and then down and up once again.

Still silence.

By this time Thoroughgood had reached bedroom one, Hardie right behind him. The DS turned on his mini-Maglite and poured the torchlight over the walls of the room. The bed was smashed against a wall and there were obvious signs of a disturbance. A cup of coffee lay half drunk on the table next to the bed. Thoroughgood shook his head as he reached Hardie in the hallway. Bedroom two empty. The kitchen showed signs of use, although the fridge had milk dated from two days ago.

That left the lounge at the front of the flat. The lounge was empty, but an icy draft was coming from the door leading out to the small balcony. Thoroughgood strained his ears and thought he could hear a screeching noise coming from outside.

The DS made his way out through the balcony door and took in the spectacular skyline provided by the twenty-first floor view. The shapes and silhouettes of Glasgow's skyline, shadows in the spring night. Then he took hold of the metallic railing boxing the small utility area in and felt his hand catch on fabric. Automatically he glanced down and there in the dark night sky he saw the inert form of a body swinging gently in the midnight breeze. Franny Hillkirk had been home all right, but someone else had got to him before the detectives. Someone who had made sure his silence would be eternal.

Was it, pondered Thoroughgood, the same someone who may have been watching the detectives?

4

SCENES OF Crime were soon present and with the locus secured, the late Franny Hillkirk didn't have to hang around for long. An exhaustive search for fingerprints was then conducted as Strathclyde's finest hunted for the smallest clue that could help them put together the pieces which would tell the story behind the erstwhile doorman and small-time drug dealer's final hours.

Thoroughgood and Hardie had found Hillkirk at 0050 hours on Thursday morning, and the time of death had been estimated at less than ninety minutes prior to that. The Scenes of Crime Team had confirmed the body was still warm. The life had been strangled out of Hillkirk by a leather belt, which turned out to belong to the deceased.

The lack of a forced entry implied Hillkirk had known his murderer, or murderers. Preliminary door-to-door enquiries, started by Thoroughgood and Hardie, were being taken on by local uniform from Baird Street and Easterhouse Offices, as the murder locus was in E Division. Unfortunately, and much to Thoroughgood's frustration, the CCTV covering the entrance foyer to the high-rise was on the blink. But as he headed out the front door of 21c, Thoroughgood was confident that the exhaustive searches and door-to-door enquiries would provide some crumb of a clue despite the lateness of the hour.

Pulling up the collar of his Barbour jacket, Thoroughgood followed Hardie onto the chilly landing and was immediately confronted by the scowling features of Detective Chief Inspector Henry Farrell.

Farrell was the senior detective on duty in the East, as E Division was known, and he made no bones about his dislike for Thoroughgood.

The DCI, at five foot seven inches, wasn't physically intimidating. What he lacked in bulk and size he made up for with a meticulous inquisitorial appearance, exuding an unhealthy menace. Farrell's unsettling habit of peering over small rectangular glasses which he clearly felt were the epitome of high detective fashion, only added to the feeling that everything you said was being noted and would one day be used in evidence against you, whether you were a criminal or a copper.

"So what, Detective Sergeant Thoroughgood, are you doing in E division, without even having the courtesy to inform our local CID that you are conducting enquiries on their patch?"

At six foot two inches Thoroughgood was able to look down his nose at his superior, and it was a physical advantage he was not about to pass up. Boring his almost feline green eyes into the top of Farrell's head, Thoroughgood was equally curt.

"You know full well that if we had a penny for every time an enquiry from another division is pursued over a border without notice given, we'd both be comfortably retired." Gesturing at a shivering Hardie, Thoroughgood continued: "Both Hardie and I have completed statements detailing our reasons for visiting Springburn. If you take the time to read them you'll find it was perfectly legit, boss.

"Now if you don't mind, I have court in five hours' time and you now have a murder enquiry to run. Good luck to you, Detective Chief Inspector." Thoroughgood drawled Farrell's full title in an obviously sarcastic mark of disrespect.

This terse exchange was clearly making the uniform officer stationed outside the door uncomfortable. But Farrell was determined to have the last word. Taking his designer glasses off and rubbing the lens on the immaculate pin-striped suit, which made him look more like a bank manager than a DCI, Farrell spoke:

"Listen to me, Thoroughgood. You will give me the respect I am due. If you think I'm going to let you come into my division pursuing enquiries that could have caused this murder, and then put up with your cheek, you'll soon know all about it.

"I'm sure Detective Super Tomachek will want the full details of your little jaunt into the East, and of course your conduct and insolence tonight. I, be equally assured, will enjoy informing him."

Thoroughgood, tired, jaded and ready to blow, looked over at Kenny Hardie and, for a change, it was Hardie who attempted to defuse the developing confrontation between his two superiors.

"Gaffer, you know what it's like first night on. We thought we were onto a right good lead and maybe had a chance of getting something on Declan Meechan, but that avenue is blocked now. Like Gus says, it's all in our statements, including the preliminary door-to-door results. We're sorry if we've trodden on any toes, but neither of us expected it to pan out like this. Please accept our apologies."

Appeasement wasn't something Farrell did readily,

and it wasn't on his agenda that morning. Placing his glasses back on at the most precise of angles, in a gesture that only expanded his sense of self-importance, Farrell said,

"Nevertheless, there are procedures and they must be followed. Now if you don't mind, as you so precisely put it Detective Sergeant, I have a murder inquiry to run. You can both go but this won't be the last you hear of this, believe me."

Two minutes later the detectives were exiting 12 Eccles Street when Hardie grabbed his DS's arm and pointed upward.

"Look at that camera. It's pointing at the bloody ceiling; what good is that? I thought they had concierges for the flats 'round here, or at least a janny. What's the point in security cameras if these twats don't bother to maintain them? What fuckin' chance dae you have, gaffer?"

As the two detectives left the high-rise with the rain beating in their faces, a shrug of the shoulders was all Thoroughgood could muster in reply.

Going to court was one of the things Thoroughgood hated about his job. Giving evidence was one thing, but the time wasted hanging around, and the often illogical and at times utterly shambolic way in which the judicial system was administered, could play havoc with people's lives, and not just those of the public.

How many times had a holiday been ruined by a witness citation to return home and give evidence? It was an occupational hazard, but one that brought constant grief to every relationship he had ever been in.

In all probability Thoroughgood would not be required to give evidence, but it could mean a whole day spent hanging around the Sheriff Court witness rooms on the back of less than three hours' sleep. Resigned to his fate, the DS unfolded a Daily Telegraph and started to read. The sports pages first, as always. After ten minutes, the newspaper was grabbed roughly from him.

"All right, big man?" said a deep voice.

Ross McNab had been in the city's Eastern Division CID for as long as Thoroughgood had been in City Centre CID and their paths had crossed frequently over the years.

Thoroughgood got on well with McNab. The DC tended to dress as if he was straight out of the pages of a glitzy fashion magazine. His suit, shirt and tie always conformed to the current vogue, brown hair gelled to perfection, apparent rude good health glowing from his perma-tan, and everywhere he went a trail of aftershave followed.

"Fuck me Gus; you're looking a bit rough there. You been a naughty boy again?" asked McNab.

Thoroughgood, despite his initial inclination to answer this opening gambit with an expletive-laced reply, couldn't stop a smile coming to his face.

"The fuckin' job, of course. I don't have a personal life. You should know that, Ross."

McNab had already heard the rumble of the jungle drums, and was well aware of the DS's confrontation with Henry Farrell, his superior officer. A smile soon crept over the Detective Constable's face:

"It's none of my business, mate, but you need to watch out for Farrell. We've heard all about your run-in with him up at Eccles Street. He is a vindictive little shit who takes great pride in ruining careers and he treats the boys at London Road as if they were fresh out of nursery: you

26

need permission to fart with him. So a word of warning: just make sure that you and Hardie are watertight."

But McNab couldn't help his interest in his colleague's trip across the border from surfacing.

"So, Gus, what were you boys doing up in Springburn anyway?"

Thoroughgood, usually the last detective who would share even a grain of information with a colleague from another division, had no qualms about explaining the nature of the enquiry at Eccles Street. McNab was well aware that the DS had a longstanding animosity towards Declan Meechan that stretched back to his time as a young DC in Partick. As rookie detectives back in the early Nineties, working out of the old Partick Marine station, Thoroughgood and McNab had been mates on the book, as the CID roster was known, and drinking buddies off-duty. Indeed, the duo had done more than passing damage in the boozers and clubs of Glasgow's West End.

McNab wasn't one to miss an opportunity, and he thought this might be just the time to be helpful.

"Listen, mate, I might have something for you on Meechan. I've been sitting on it for a week wondering whether I should turn it over to the SCDEA. But fuck me if those bastards didn't ignore my application. Anyway, I know how much you'd like any info that would make that wanker squirm."

Thoroughgood almost dropped his Telegraph, his fatigue forgotten for a moment.

"Go ahead, big man, make my day."

McNab was only too happy to oblige.

"On the nightshift last week, I got a phone call from one of my touts, said he had some information about drugs coming into the country. He mentioned the drop-off point was somewhere near the West Coast, maybe from a yacht, and more to the point he said the whole deal was being run by one of Jimmy Gray's men.

"As you know, Gray's main man is Meechan. Tommy Briggs is much more the muscle side of the empire, strictly enforcement and extortion, plus Briggs is getting on a bit. Never been quite the same since that shotgun blast took half his face away. Nope, my guess is it's gotta be Meechan. This one sounds as if it involves a bit of imagination. What do you think, Gus?"

Thoroughgood was stunned. "Look, Ross, you know as well as I do that Briggs is as subtle as a whore with no knickers on. It's got to be Meechan. My guess is he's trying to up the ante as far as taking over Jimmy Gray's operation when the old boy finally pegs it.

"Gray's not been well for a while now. He must be pushing seventy and he's turning more and more over to Meechan. I'd bet dear Declan is looking for a really big turn to impress the old man and get him to abdicate his throne or make the case for a coup d'état compelling."

Thoroughgood continued, "So, when can I meet your tout?"

All good favours deserve a return, and although McNab was undoubtedly doing one for Thoroughgood he wanted one back, and big time.

"Right, here's the deal. Your old boss at the Marine, Derek Nelson, has been given the Commander's job at the Serious. The SCDEA might have knocked me back, but you and I both know the favour he owes you. You want Meechan? Get me in the Serious and I'll have you one-on-one with my tout within twenty-four hours. What do you say, pal?"

Before the two detectives could continue with their own peculiar form of plea-bargaining, the Sheriff Court intercom system sprang into life:

"DS Thoroughgood to court seventeen, DS Thoroughgood please attend court seventeen now."

"Listen, mate, I'll give you a call tonight. What are you, backshift at London Road?" asked Thoroughgood.

"Yep, fire away, Gus. Always remember: 'We're a self-preservation society!'"

5

TOP OF Thoroughgood's agenda was some kip, but a late afternoon call to Nelson would do no harm and he'd probably be delighted to have his card marked about McNab's interest.

Tuning the Focus' stereo to Radio Two, he turned into Ballater Street before hanging a right into Tradeston Street and then back round onto the Kingston Bridge flyover that would take him onto the Clydeside Expressway.

Thoroughgood's mind was on automatic pilot, half-listening to the debate on the Jeremy Vine show on the dying days of Tony Blair's premiership but thinking more about the all-engulfing need to get home and catch some shut-eye. He turned onto the flyover, enjoying the effortless way the Focus held the road despite the tight bend and the wet greasy surface on the bridge. But his admiration of the Ford's smooth driving was rudely interrupted as a loud bang warned him something had just collided with his vehicle.

Instantly the cop car was shunted off the barrier encasing the outside lane, protecting vehicles from the hundred-foot drop over the side into the murky volumes of the river Clyde below.

What the fuck was that? shuddered Thoroughgood, as he looked across his right shoulder to see a white Ford Transit prepare to ram him for a second time. He pulled hard to the right as he anticipated the impact, and wasn't disappointed. He managed to straddle the white lines dividing the two lanes in preparation for a second, but still the blow shunted him against the rails for a second time. A flurry of sparks and the piercing wail of metal on metal sounded out.

Straightening the Focus up, Thoroughgood put his foot down only to find himself blocked in by a middle-aged female in an Espace people carrier, who was blissfully unaware of the drama unfolding behind her. The white Transit continued to parallel the detective's Focus as the driver grinned from underneath the peak of a black baseball cap.

As the gap between Thoroughgood's vehicle and the car in front closed to fifteen yards, a sighting in his own rear view registered the imposing presence of a Scania artic truck. The detective realised he was now at the mercy of his tormentor in the black baseball cap.

The detective hit the horn repeatedly and signalled frantically with his hand to try and elicit some reaction from the glazed features pictured in the Espace's rear view. But as he desperately attempted to gain her attention, the vacant look on the motorist's untroubled features remained intact and she carried on at thirty mph, oblivious to the flashing lights and the detective's frantic actions framed in her mirror.

This time the van smacked home diagonally into the right-hand-side, to the rear of the Focus. The impact drove Thoroughgood into the back of the Espace at an angle. At last a shocked look was solicited in the mirror from the female driver; her face now enveloped in disbelief as she finally became aware of the events unfolding behind her.

Checking his rear mirror, the DS clocked the van was two up. The passenger was also sporting the requisite baseball cap, this time white with a black Nike tick.

As the Transit readied itself for one more swoop on the badly battered CID Focus, Thoroughgood thought frantically as he tried to bring about an immediate escape strategy that would help him avoid being forced right through the fly-over railings and a death plunge into the fast-flowing Clyde beneath the Kingston Bridge.

Taking immediate stock of the facts, he realised that the Espace was lurching on in front of him at roughly the same speed as before it had been hit. Checking in his rear view, he saw that the Scania continued to push up behind him, as the artic driver had little or no option but to continue forward on the flyover off-ramp, with traffic probably jamming up behind him. So there was no point ramming on the anchors and creating merry hell and a possible pile-up behind him.

Thoroughgood looked back at the driver in the white Transit. His tormentor raised his right hand from the steering wheel and using his index finger and thumb, made a gesture as if to pull the trigger of a gun at Thoroughgood's head as the Transit sailed past on the outside lane.

There was no time for relief to register in Thoroughgood's mind. His primary concern was avoiding an immediate impact with the Espace, whose brake lights were now glowing. The driver had finally panicked into an emergency stop. With the back of the people carrier now approaching the front of his battered Focus, Thoroughgood yanked his steering wheel hard down to the right, and managed to squeeze the cop car out into the overtake lane. Simultaneously the Scania surged up into the space previously vacated by the white Transit, which had now disappeared down the off-ramp and was shooting along the Clyde expressway in the direction of the Clyde Tunnel.

The full blare of the artic's horn and the flashing lights now scorching Thoroughgood's mirror left the DS in no doubt as to the anger felt at his sudden manoeuvre by its driver. Pulling back just in front of the now-stationary Espace, he rapped out a lookout call for the white Transit on his car radio system, posting direction of travel, vehicle and passenger details as best he could.

What, thought the detective, the fuck was that all about?

One hour later Gus Thoroughgood sat in Detective Super Tomachek's office, a piping mug of coffee in hand.

"Well, Gus, I did want to see you but you appeared to be in an even bigger hurry to see me!" Tomachek grinned benevolently. "You'll be glad to know the female witness is okay and down at the Royal, but the Focus is pretty badly banged up." Then, as an apparent afterthought,

"How are you?"

"I've had better twenty-four hours, boss," admitted Thoroughgood.

Tomachek was keen to accentuate the positive from his subordinate's latest run-in with misfortune.

"As far as I see it, Gus, this was more of a warning than anything else. Let's face it: if the Transit driver had really wanted to, you would have been through the crash barrier and at the bottom of the Clyde about ninety minutes ago. I think the wee hand gesture, pulling the trigger on you, was the final proof that this was more about sending a message than any real attempt to put you out of your misery, young man."

Content at his summary of the facts as he saw them, Tomachek took a long drag from his pipe, and his office was enveloped in a shroud of Condor-laced smoke. The fact that every ounce of property owned by Strathclyde Police was strictly under the nationwide no smoking ban in public places bothered Tomachek not a jot when it came to what went on in "his" office.

Thoroughgood agreed. "Yes, boss, but it's when that warning starts to put members of the public at risk that you've got to wonder just what lengths whoever is behind it will go to before he gets his message across."

Silence ensued as Tomachek enjoyed his Condor moment and fiddled with the buttons of the tweed waistcoat forming part of a natty three-piece number. The Detective Superintendent appeared more like a member of the Perthshire gentry than a senior detective officer in Scotland's busiest policing division.

The quiet, as Thoroughgood expected from past experience, never lasted long with Tomachek. Behind his genteel façade, the workings of a razor-sharp mind were apt to be in overdrive.

"You're right, of course, Gus. So just what the fuck are you doing to make Declan Meechan so angry he threatens you with a watery grave and puts the punters at risk, as well as bringing the possibility of a major incident on the busiest feckin' bridge in Scotland?

"Now, I know you and Meechan have history, but tell me why would he go to such extremes to warn you off an enquiry that started with a serious assault on a kid at one of his clubs and has now moved on to the murder of one of his doormen? Especially since, as I've seen from the enquiry notes, you haven't even interviewed Meechan."

Taking another moment to enjoy his pipe, Tomachek leant across his desk, and with the pipe now clenched in his right fist he gestured at Thoroughgood.

"I think it's time you filled in between the lines on this one before things spiral any further."

Thoroughgood met his superior's enquiring features with a steady glance and a nod of the head

"I just don't know what it's all about, gaffer, other than the fact it's personal. To be fair, the enquiry with the kid is, if you pardon the pun, at a dead end now that Franny Hillkirk has met with an untimely demise; if we don't get anything with SOCO, and have no witnesses from the murder scene—and the CCTV being out doesn't help—then we're struggling to go anywhere with this one.

"No doubt about it, Meechan is a bastard, but even by his standards this is a bit heavy-handed unless Franny Hillkirk could have led us to something far, far bigger than some routine assault enquiry. And that's it, boss. I just don't know any more than that."

Tomachek was far from convinced.

"You sure you aren't giving me a highlights-only version here, son? Maybe you should be taking some leave? Because right fuckin' now everything around you is turning into a twenty-four carat war zone. I want you to give that some serious thought. Take the rest of the night off, go home and get some shut-eye. Report back to me at midday tomorrow and by then we will have the SOCO results from the murder scene up at Eccles Street.

"Let me tell you this. If they don't reveal a shred of evidence, then the Hillkirk enquiry will stay with that arsehole Farrell in the East. You can tie up the loose ends of the assault on Devlin, the student, and then I'll probably be signing your annual leave application. Unless there's anything else, Detective Sergeant, that you want to get off your chest, I'll see you tomorrow. Now can you get home without all hell breaking loose around you yet again?"

Thoroughgood nodded in obeisance.

"I'll do my best, boss."

6

IT WAS nearly five-thirty when Thoroughgood's phone finally rang and the voice of Ross McNab crackled into life. "All right, Gus, had any sleep? I got your message about Nelson and I suppose you'll be wanting a little something in return?"

Thoroughgood responded, "Took your time, Ross. I thought you were going to leave Nelson dangling; remember he's got a reunion dinner tonight?"

"No worries, mate, but I wanted to get in touch with my informant just to touch base and make sure we can get things moving between you two as soon as. So how's a three way hook-up sound for tonight?

"How about ten p.m., Glasgow Green? If you go to the front of the People's Palace you'll see the Doulton Fountain. It's forty-six feet high and seventy feet wide, so you cannae exactly miss it, mate! Me and the tout will be standing there bang on ten pm."

"You've got a deal. Mind if Kenny Hardie tags along on this one?" asked Thoroughgood.

"Rather he didn't; my man's a bit nervy about meeting you, never mind a crowd. Hope that's okay."

The opportunity to meet with an informant who had anything on Declan Meechan was, however, too good to be true for Thoroughgood to object. The handling of informants was now supposed to be run through Division under the centralised grandly-titled Covert Human

Intelligence Source Units, or CHIS as they were known for short. But there were still plenty of cops who felt they needed to retain some kind of personal control over their informants, rather than handing both the tout and the information that came with him or her over to a CHIS Unit.

The relinquishing of a tout who could bring you to the attention of the brass and help launch an ambitious cop or detective on the promotional ladder, was something that more than a few found unpalatable when it came to mapping out their career paths. Thoroughgood had no intention of getting sticky on the matter, doubly so when the informant concerned was tried and trusted by McNab. So he answered in the affirmative:

"Okay, son, I'll see you then."

After a shower, and a dinner of last night's leftover Chinese, Thoroughgood made it to Glasgow Green in less than a quarter of an hour. Traffic was dead at that time of the night; in fact, if anything, he encountered more traffic on the green itself than in the city streets, albeit human traffic.

The People's Palace was Glasgow's social history museum, telling the story of the city and its people from 1750 onwards. But Glasgow Green had long been a popular place for the city's vice girls to ply their trade and tonight was no exception. Every couple of hundred yards a shadowy figure would teeter awkwardly, the lack of balance a symptom of the endemic drugs habits of Glasgow's working girls.

Sitting outside the People's Palace in his own private car made Thoroughgood feel damned uncomfortable, especially given the conspicuous Winning Blue of his RX-8. As the DS got out of his vehicle and took in, for the first time, the magnificence of the Doulton Fountain, he had to admit a certain appreciation for McNab's rendezvous location.

The Fountain had been gifted to the city by Sir Henry Doulton and first unveiled at the Empire Exhibition held at Kelvingrove Park in 1888. The largest terracotta fountain in the world, its five tiers were bedecked with an assortment of sculptures representing Australia, Canada, India and South Africa: the Doulton undoubtedly brought back the full imperial grandeur of those bygone days of the British Empire. But the DS swiftly re-focussed when he saw McNab arrive in a dark blue Peugeot 409.

The diesel engine groaned monotonously as it telegraphed the message to whores and punters alike that there were CID on the green. McNab immediately jumped out of the driver's seat and made his way over to Thoroughgood, offering his hand in standard greeting.

Looking over McNab's shoulder, the DS tried to sight the shadowy figure seated in the back of the Peugeot. He looked small and bald but beyond that, the darkness offered a more than adequate concealment.

Thoroughgood was determined to make sure the conversation took place on his verbal ground, even if the location and time had been of McNab's choice. The DS immediately steered the conversation around to the subject of McNab's call to Detective Superintendent Nelson, in order to ensure his colleague would not forget the favour he had been done which had ultimately brought them to this evening's meet.

Pulling the collar of his brown Barbour jacket up to his jaw to deflect the spray coming off the fountain and keep the spring chill at bay, Thoroughgood asked,

"So, Ross, are you in then?"

"Straight to the point as ever, Gus! Aye, I made the call, as you knew I would, and you could say there's a fair chance I'll be part of next month's intake. I'm meeting Nelson next Monday for a pint and hopefully that'll cement it, but first thing tomorrow the application will be going in just to keep Personnel happy."

Gesturing back at the lane leading up to the People's Palace, McNab complained,

"Fuck me, the tarts are out in force tonight. I had to threaten one of them with the jail before she would believe we weren't punters." Then he nodded his head in the direction of the Peugeot and added with a mischievous wink: "Not much chance of that, though, with Gerry boy in tow?"

Thoroughgood's attention, as McNab had intended, was immediately drawn to the male sitting in the back of his pool car.

"So Ross, you going to introduce us or has yer man lost the power of his legs?"

"He's a wee bit on the nervy side about coming forward. Must be worried he might upset you, Gus! You remember back in our Partick days, the Western Hospital was being screwed for drugs, morphine, Temazepam, Diazepam etcetera, and they caught the McIlroy brothers for it? Well, my friend here provided more than a little assistance in helping us clear that one up. I believe you'll know him all right, but take it easy, okay?"

"Come on Ross, put me out of my misery. Who is it?"

"All right, Gus," said McNab, and with his right hand he pointed an index finger at the Peugeot and called,

"Time to get out, wee man. Gus, meet Gerry McIlroy, Mick and Johnny's wee brother."

"Gerry was a charge nurse in the Western back between

1995 and '97. Yep, and a very big help in securing the arrest of those two Partick worthies who also happened to be his big brothers."

McIlroy's uncertainty at the whole situation was all too obvious to Thoroughgood. A little over five foot three, the tout shuffled over to the fountain, studiously averting his eyes from the gaze of both detectives.

Plainly enjoying his introduction, McNab continued with some relish,

"Oh, but of course, Gerry was completely innocent of any involvement in his brothers' drug operation, if you pardon the pun, at the Western."

"Well, that's not strictly true Gerry, is it? Nope, Gerry here used to leave the fire doors open to selected wards and if he could manage it, the keys to the drugs cabinets were always placed at the fire exit end. Quite often on the nightshift, he was in charge, so it wasn't hard to offload the keys once the drug round was over. All very simple, wasn't it Gerry? Still, there's nothing like paying your debt to society by grassing your own brothers up!"

This last remark seemed to provide McNab with endless mirth, and his shoulders heaved in unashamed self-appreciation. This only served to heighten McIlroy's discomfort; the air of hopeless vulnerability surrounding the diminutive figure was almost palpable.

Burrowing his face in his zipped-up leather jacket, McIlroy bit on the zipper while his baseball cap almost completely obscured any of his facial features from the CID officer's scrutiny. Sensing he may have overplayed his hand, McNab quickly changed tack:

"Look, Gus, I know you never liked the McIlroy brothers but to be fair, Gerry here was forced into it by them. You see, the wee man's got a secret."

40

"His big brothers figured it was a piece of cake really. Blackmail Gerry with his secret sexual tendencies, an outing embellished by just a hint that there might be paedophile tendencies in their kid brother's make-up as well, and Gerry didn't have much option but to cave in. The alternative? Gerry loses the single thing he values most in life: his position as a trustworthy and hardworking nurse, and the self respect that he'd made it out of the gutter legitimately. So don't be too hard on our Gerry."

McNab added with a wide grin: "Oh, one last thing I'd better tell you. Gerry here is one of Celine Lynott's closest friends! Must have been your bedside manner that won her over, eh Gerry? I suppose she felt quite safe with you; you weren't exactly likely to jump her, were you?"

Despite the immense enjoyment this little introduction in the moonlight had given McNab, it was obvious the East detective was fully confident Gerry McIlroy could be the key to pulling Declan Meechan down. Thoroughgood took the bull by the horns.

"Look, Gerry, I know you and Ross have obviously had a good working relationship over a few years and you trust him, but all I want from you is one thing: Declan Meechan. He's the guy who is supplying Partick, the north-west of the city and most of its clubs with their drugs. If you work as a nurse you must have some compassion for people, care in the community and all that."

"Partick, even Drumchapel, used to have a sense of community until Meechan started flooding them with heroin. Old Jimmy Gray would never have dealt in drugs if someone that bit younger hadn't made him wise to the profit margins. Declan Meechan is everything that is wrong with Glasgow; cut him down and a big part of the cancer eating into this city dies. I believe that and I believe you can help me. It's up to you, mate."

"If you want to get back in the car then fair enough, I won't try and bullshit you. Once you've gone, you've gone, no comeback. Mr McNab has finished with you so it's your call. Can we give it a go?"

For the first time McIlroy looked the DS full in the face and said,

"Mr Thoroughgood, the whole of Partick knows you'd give your granny for Declan Meechan. You don't need to convince me of that, and anyway, Celine has told me enough.

"You're right about one thing. I need to be able to trust you and I think I know enough about you to do that. But what's in it for me? This is serious shit; nobody grasses on Declan Meechan and walks away. If it comes off I'll need out, money and a new start big time. Can you guarantee that?"

Thoroughgood was in no hurry to promise his newly acquired informant the earth. The DS thought honesty was by far and away the best policy at this stage in their embryonic relationship. "Look Gerry, it's early days to be making big promises; you gotta show me the goods or at least give me a flavour before we start talking new starts."

McIlroy was nonplussed. "All right, but first I need a small favour from you to establish some trust here."

Ross McNab could no longer keep out of the conversation between his soon-to-be former star tout and his colleague. His impatience clear, McNab rapped:

"Look, for fuck's sake Gerry, I told you what the script was, so stop fuckin' about. You're workin' for DS Thoroughgood now and that's it, you wee poof. Just do as he says and cut the bullshit."

Thoroughgood, less than impressed with his colleague's indelicate summary of McIlroy's situation, sought to pour oil on waters that were becoming increasingly troubled.

"Gerry, I'm not going to force you into anything here. What's the favour?"

"It's simple really. I want ma maw moved out of her mingin' tenement, away from the damp and the junkies that don't give a fuck whether they tan the house if she's in or out. A nice two in a block with a front door and a wee garden, that's what the old bird needs. Can you do that? If it's arranged then we can get to work."

Caught off-guard, Thoroughgood answered the request with a question:

"Councils have waiting lists for that sort of thing, and anyway, how's old Ma McIlroy being tormented by junkies with your brothers on the scene?"

McIlroy, impatience showing for the first time, played the straight bat.

"The junkies down the Drum are so smacked up they don't give a shit who her sons are. When they're inside Bar-L for a ten stretch, the bastards know they're more likely to be dead than to meet either Mick or Johnny."

Fair play, thought Thoroughgood.

"Okay, Gerry, leave it with me. I'll get on to it as soon as. Where can I get you?"

McIlroy's outstretched paw shoved a piece of paper towards Thoroughgood.

"That's my mobile number; give us a bell any night this week between six and seven and hopefully we can do business."

McNab decided it was time to interrupt the beautiful beginnings of this new working relationship.

"Will that do for now, big man? Got enough to start the ball rolling?"

Thoroughgood decided if he wasn't to lose face in front of his colleague, he needed a wee olive branch from McIlroy.

"Listen, Gerry. I don't doubt I can help your mother out, but you'll need to give me a wee sweetener to take away. Then the better homes scenario can happen all the quicker for your old dear."

"All right, Mr Thoroughgood, how's this: Celine told me to say hello!"

Watching the Peugeot disappear down the lane and out of Glasgow Green, Thoroughgood turned on the RX-8 and gunned the engine. The CD player was just finishing Whitesnake's Still of the Night and as he shut his eyes, David Coverdale's voice sparked into life once again with the anthemic refrain to tortured love:

Fool for your lovin' no more.

How appropriate, thought Thoroughgood, and as he shifted into first, it was not police work occupying his mind.

7

THE WHITE Transit cornered the top of a hill which provided a beautiful view of the Milngavie Reservoir, and the vista below that took in the City of Glasgow. It pulled up opposite a gleaming black Range Rover, already stationary in the car park that was the final stop for the vehicles of walkers of the West Highland Way, and locals exercising their dogs.

The driver, a massive individual sporting a black baseball cap, jumped out and made his way over to the Range Rover driver's door. The smoked window of the huge four-by-four, a menacing vehicle resembling a hearse on wheels, slithered down and the rough Glaswegian voice of the Transit's driver asked in deferential tones:

"All right boss? You'll be wanting a word with our friend in the back?"

"Open the doors and keep him in place; then maybe I can make Mr Johnson understand what it means to break his word," ordered the Range Rover's incumbent.

With the stinging April rain falling horizontally, the car park and the countryside it gazed over were empty, except for the two newly arrived vehicles. The immaculately dressed driver jumped out in one languid movement.

Resplendent in a bespoke suit, with his sandy red hair reaching almost to his shoulders, Declan Meechan made his way to the rear doors of the Transit. Inside a male, his arms bound behind him and his mouth gagged, was pushed into a kneeling position on the floor of the Transit, in line with the doors. The second male in the Transit, topped in a white baseball cap and wearing jeans and an Adidas tracksuit top, removed the gag from the captive's mouth.

Meechan stood opposite his prey and glowered:

"I trust you know why you're here, Johnson? Treacherous you maybe but stupid you are not. Or do I have that one wrong as well?"

The captive could not help his voice betraying the fear wracking his body and soul:

"You have it wrong, Declan, believe me. There's only been a delay in the supply, no more. I know better than to cross you."

Before the sentence could be finished, Meechan's right hand slashed down in a vicious motion that harked back to a past obsession with the sweet science. The blow crashed off Johnson's jaw and his body went limp. The black cap snapped Johnson's head back to meet the merciless gaze of Meechan's slate grey eyes. Eyes with no soul.

Blood trickled down the side of Johnson's jaw and a tooth dropped out of his slack mouth as the captive regained consciousness. As he did so the sound of liquid became audible, as urine darkened the tormented drug dealer's trouser leg.

Meechan's grin was feral.

"Fear has a way of focusing minds, I always find. When I enter into a business agreement with anyone, I must be able to trust them. When that trust is broken, the relationship ends."

A pause, to let the ramifications of such an ill-starred course of action sink in, Meechan added:

"I find myself forced to make an example of my betrayer so that future business relationships are not similarly blighted. Do you understand me, Johnson?"

Johnson nodded in the affirmative but did not trust himself to words. Meechan continued his summation of where it had all gone wrong:

"You guaranteed me that a month's supply of the product would arrive in Glasgow to the agreed inlet without fail. This is April the tenth and we are still waiting for the March consignment. You made your excuses for the delay in March, but you have now run out of them, and time, in April. Your dear brother has; sorry, I should say 'had,' a mouth on him. It is your misfortune, Johnson, that you can choose your friends and not your relatives. I have always made it my golden rule of practice when it comes to business to trust neither friends nor family."

Johnson's face crumpled in a mix of pain and surprise as Meechan's left hand came up in a hook that seemed to almost snap the captive's recoiling body in two. Johnson doubled up and vomited, gasping for air, his midriff constricting in convulsions of agony.

The thin smile etched across Meechan's face was, for a moment, replaced by a frown as he observed a trace of vomit spattered over his gleaming Peter Barker shoes.

Meechan reached into his raincoat and pulled out a leather glove from an inside pocket before fitting it with painstaking meticulousness over each finger of his right hand. From his other pocket came the handgun.

Reaching into the outside left pocket, he pulled out a cylindrical metallic object and fitted it onto the barrel of the gun. Raising the handgun to the left-hand side of

Johnstone's head and pausing to savour the raw fear in his prey's eyes, Meechan said:

"How does it feel to know that the last thing you will see in this life is the face of the man who made you rich, and yet the one you betrayed for your own greed?"

Again the pause.

"Naw ..." was all Johnson had time to scream and then there was a dull thud as his life was extinguished and his body dropped onto the Transit floor. A dead weight.

Tossing the gun to the Transit driver, Meechan rapped:

"Destroy it. Dump the body in the reservoir and then torch the van. No fuck ups, just do the job."

Meechan added in the direction of the Transit driver:

"So tell me, Frankie, did our copper friend get a fright on the Kingston Bridge yesterday?"

Frankie Brennan's indelicate mean features were temporarily masked in a smile.

"Aye boss, that's a copper who knows he's lucky not be finishing his days at the bottom of the Clyde. I'd say the polis' garage would have a fair bit of work to do on Thoroughgood's motor into the bargain!"

Reaching for his wallet, Meechan removed a fifty pound note and, extending his arm, stuck it behind his huge underling's ear. Turning his gaze to white baseball cap, Meechan tucked another fifty pound note inside the top of his henchman's tracky top.

"You do well for me, boys," Meechan said, "and you will enjoy health, wealth and happiness. You let me down and I will take the type of personal interest in your welfare that will make purgatory seem like a holiday camp."

"Tomorrow the papers will be full of the corpse in the reservoir story. That corpse will be dismembered. Finish your jobs, boys."

Pulling his raincoat collar tight around him to protect from the driving wind and icy spray, Meechan climbed back into the Range Rover and took the cell phone from its holder.

"Yes boss?" said the voice at the other end.

"I want you at the office in one hour, Tommy. I have work for you." ordered Meechan.

Sitting back in the luxurious leather interior, Meechan surveyed the scenery unfolding across the valley, from the eyrie's view afforded by the reservoir car park. The temporary setback caused by the mixture of personal greed and treachery that had let to Davie Johnson's untimely demise had cost, Meechan estimated, around a quarter of a million pounds in cocaine and heroin. But the islander's brother, whose loose tongue had led to the end of both himself and his elder sibling, had ensured that business should resume as normal in April.

Yet Meechan was concerned that not all the loose ends had been tied up at the far away end of his business empire, the beautiful, rugged and windswept Western Isle of Barra.

Meechan's main office was situated in Dumbarton Road, opposite the Western Hospital, the irony of which had not been lost on Meechan himself when he took over the former Exchequer bar premises. Split over two levels, Meechan's personal office was located on the first floor. As he sipped his latte, the buzzer on his massive mahogany desk crackled.

"Mr Rankin for you, Mr Meechan."

Meechan's office door opened and in stepped Tommy Rankin.

"Afternoon, boss. The trouble sorted to your satisfaction?"

"Very much so, Tommy. What concerns me now is making sure there is no repeat. That means you need to be taking the first available flight up to Barra."

Rankin smiled and nodded his head in affirmation.

"I've never been up in the Western Isles, but they say if the weather is good they're beautiful. No worries, Declan. A flight from Glasgow Airport in one of those Twin Otters only takes an hour anyways."

Meechan quickly continued: "It's time we used the softly, softly approach with our island associates. Make them aware how beneficial it will be if they continue with our relationship. I want you to offer them a five percent increase in their cut. I think a sweetener would be wise to help avoid a lingering bad taste in the mouth after the passing of their two fellow islanders.

"If you have any doubts, tell them we're pulling the plug and leave them with a permanent reminder of what happens when they fuck with Declan Meechan. I don't give a sweet FA if there is some of my family's blood flowing up there. You make them aware that nothing gets in the way of business, Tommy."

The scar down the left-hand side of Rankin's face appeared to offer a second smile from his chiselled features. Rankin swept a hand over his bald dome and tapped an index finger on the gold tooth at the centre of his mouth.

"Aye boss, you have it right as usual. Do you want me to take an interest in every aspect of the island operation?"

Meechan nodded. "I want to know everything, but most importantly of all, I want to know that when you come back from Barra there'll be no more trouble for us up there. I'll expect a call from you on my mobile by early evening tomorrow night, with your initial impressions."

Rankin nodded. "Consider it done, boss."

No sooner had Rankin departed than Meechan's buzzer sounded again. Jimmy Gray, the man he nominally called 'boss,' was on the line. Meechan took the call and a gravel-sounding voice crackled into life at the other end:

"Aye Dec, is that you? Call me back mobile to mobile." Meechan returned the call immediately.

Picking up, Gray cut to the chase: "Have you sorted things with our friends from the Islands, Dec?"

Gray was the only man who Meechan allowed the implied familiarity of the shortened form of his Christian name. Meechan replied,

"Yes, Jimmy, both Johnson brothers have been suitably rewarded for their disloyalty and greed. Tommy Rankin is taking a couple of the boys up to the Western Isles on the first flight tomorrow to make sure there will be no repeat. It's vital we can trust these bastards not to make an arse of things second time around."

"That's good, Dec. We can't afford any weak links in the operation. This business is just too lucrative and the more we make from it, the more property and business ventures we can diversify into, all of which will take us one step further away from the prying eyes of the polis. But tell me, what happens if Tommy Rankin goes up there and doesn't like what he sees?" queried Gray.

"You could say that Tommy has been briefed on how to respond to all eventualities."

Gray may have been in his seventh decade but his mind, if not his hunger, was still in full working order.

"Now, I am going to be taking a wee break for the next fortnight. Me and Senga are heading off to the villa in Mallorca. I just wanted to make sure you were on top of things. But remember, you jeopardise fuck all. If the Western Isles' business is dodgy at all, we pull out. There's no way I am risking everything because these island fuckwits can't see the bleedin' woods for the trees. You understand me, Declan?" Gray demanded.

"Take it as read, boss. You takin' the clubs with you?" Meechan attempted some banter.

"Aye well, that's the only fuckin' way I'll be gettin' any birdies when I'm over there. Goodbye Dec." The mobile went dead.

Meechan smiled with satisfaction. He'd known all along that Jimmy Gray was intent on a short break to his Mallorcan villa. The one thing he took pride in, above all else, was having informants everywhere, including his boss's office. Jimmy, dear old Jimmy, I probably know when you want to take a piss before you've arrived at the bog!

8

FRIDAY MORNING, nine a.m., and the rain pissed down once again. The black Range Rover pulled into its bay in the car park outside Meechan's office, and the crime boss jumped out of his vehicle. The clock was already ticking and Meechan had just a fortnight to put his plans into action and settle a series of scores that would place him virtually unchallenged in Glasgow's underworld circles on the north side of the river Clyde.

But Meechan had problems closer to home that needed dealing with some immediacy. Encroachment on his turf was something that could not be tolerated, and had to be put down in the most compelling fashion. Examples must be made.

It had also come to his attention that a doorman at one of his city centre clubs, by the name of Franny Hillkirk, had been peddling drugs, firstly without his permission, secondly from a supply that was not in-house. Hillkirk's overzealous ejection of a student had hospitalised the latter and brought the unwanted attention of the cops. This had granted Meechan the excuse to terminate his services and his life with immediate effect. Unfortunately, the enquiry had also brought the figure of the copper Meechan hated with a most personal ferocity, DS Gus Thoroughgood, back into the crimelord's stratosphere.

The two had first crossed swords in the mid-nineties when Meechan had been graduating from his school of hard knocks and Thoroughgood had been bursting his arse to make Detective from the Dumbarton Road beat of Strathclyde Police's old 'B' Division, a.k.a. 'the Marine.' The first time the two met had centred on a beating Meechan handed out to a drunk around the back of the Volcano nightclub.

The young Meechan had been doing his best to catch the eye of the West End's unchallenged criminal overlord, Jimmy Gray, by turning a financially haemorrhaging boozer-come-nightclub with a dodgy clientele into one of the West End's most happening hangouts. The fractured skull suffered by the lowlife had seen Meechan ending up in the dock at the Sheriff Court for Attempted Murder. Thoroughgood had been the reporting officer. Needless to say, Meechan had escaped when the victim developed a timely bout of amnesia in the dock. The little jolt Thoroughgood had been given at the beginning of the week would serve as a reminder to the copper that he hadn't forgotten about him.

Meechan's mind had already prioritised his most pressing business.

First things first, thought Meechan as he sat down in his office chair. It's time to sort the Browns out.

As he picked up his mobile, Meechan's secretary, Jenny, arrived at his desk with his early morning latte, the steam still rising from the froth. Meechan surveyed the curves of his pretty young employee with personal satisfaction. Handpicked from a city centre agency, Jenny was immaculate in a coffee-coloured silk blouse, a moderately tight and short cream skirt, and heels that were lofty but not ludicrous.

Her blonde hair may have been of the non-natural variety but it was immaculately cut in a bob, and everything about Jenny was perfection. At twenty-four, Meechan had hopes that Jenny might yet grow into a role as something a little bit more than his PA.

"Morning, Mr Meechan," said Jenny with an understated smile.

"How are you, Jenny? And how busy is my day looking?" replied Meechan.

"There are some papers for you to look over regarding the planning permission for the new club, and then at eleven a.m. you have your meeting with the Council Planning department. Plus there are new contracts to sign."

"Okay Jenny, that's fine, leave them here and buzz me back at ten-thirty," said Meechan before signing off with a wink and then wolfishly appreciating the rear view as Jenny left his office. His mobile went off.

"Boss, it's Frankie here. Are you okay to talk?" enquired the voice at the other end.

"Go ahead, Frankie," suggested Meechan.

"Thought you'd want to know Gazza and I have taken care of Johnson. I think the Milngavie punters are going to find they have a bit of a problem with their water supply sometime soon today! But I just wanted to make sure you want us to move on the Browns tonight as planned," queried Frankie Brennan.

"Aye Frankie, it's as arranged; text me when both hits are completed, the same when the pub is done. Until then, no contact, Frankie. Do I make myself clear?" Meechan warned.

"Aye boss, by the time we've put the lights out on these fuckers there is no one this side of the river who will fuck with you on your ground. Just the way you want it boss. Cheers." And Brennan was gone.

There was no doubt that Frankie Brennan was a brute, both in terms of his six-foot-five-inch frame, but also in the malevolent enjoyment he seemed to take in "doing ma' work" as Brennan liked to describe it. With Tommy Rankin despatched to the Western Isles, Meechan was confident he had a more than able deputy for his absent lieutenant, who at the same time was expendable if it all went pear-shaped.

A former fully paid-up member of the IRA, big Frankie boasted a grandfather who had fought alongside Michael Collins in the Easter uprising, he was also avidly homophobic. But what mattered most was that both Brennan and his sidekick Gaz Reid were ambitious, ruthless and utterly without pity. Meechan had always liked his "boys" cruel and these two, he thought with some satisfaction, were crueller than the grave.

Standing in front of the full-length mirror on the wall behind his semi-circular desk, Meechan surveyed his own image with some satisfaction. At thirty-four and six foot plus, he showed no sign of piling on any excess pounds. His sandy-coloured hair, parted in the middle and swept down at the sides, almost collar-length at the back, was immaculately groomed.

For today's meeting with the City Planning Department he had donned a Hugo Boss suit of the most sumptuous quality, lined in pink silk and sporting his initials DAM … Declan Aloysius Meechan. His middle name betrayed his own strong Irish roots and upbringing in Belfast. The sharp white shirt and cerise tie hinted at nothing but the best. His brown Peter Barker shoes were of the softest leather. Meechan could not stop himself looking forward with increasing confidence.

By the time today ends, thought Meechan, the city

north of the river will be another step closer to being mine and there will be nothing anyone can do about it.

Twelve-fifteen and Meechan, Celine and Charlie Coyle, the crimelord's lawyer, in his customary grey double-breasted suit, the epitome of slippery politeness, stood back on the pavement outside the City Chambers. As Coyle had promised, the well-oiled mechanism of the city planning department had indeed been well oiled. Permission had been granted for the redevelopment of one of the handful of derelict churches in the Hyndland area of the West End. The resulting permits would allow it to be converted into an exclusive nightclub, bar and theatre complex that would cost Meechan and Jimmy Gray the best part of ten million pounds.

But Meechan's attention was wandering from business matters and he had to admit he could hardly keep his eyes off his business manager, for today Celine dazzled. The Afro curls in her brown hair appeared to have a new crispness to them, but still there was something unruly there. The scarlet jacket of her two-piece Chanel suit was cut to reveal a silk camisole top. As usual, Celine used a minimum of make-up; with skin which resembled the colouring of his favourite morning latte and was as smooth as silk, she needed none.

Seeing the smile on Meechan's face, Celine asked, "So, Declan, where are you taking us for lunch?"

"The Rogano. The table is booked for one o'clock. That'll give us time for a wee toast. Eh, Charlie? To a job well done!"

"Nothing would give me more pleasure, Declan," agreed the lawyer.

Holding his upturned palm out in no particular direction, Meechan added,

"Now, since the rain seems to have stopped, let's walk over to Royal Exchange Square. You could do with the exercise, Charlie, to be sure. What do you say, Celine?" asked Meechan.

The trio began to make their way across the road to the inner pavement that rings the very heart of George Square. Minds lingering on the first bottle of champagne, and a lunch that was bound to include the renowned lobster thermidor, not even Meechan paid any attention to the private hire cab hovering on the other side of the road until he heard the first bang. The whistle of the bullet and the rush of the air accompanying it missed Meechan by a matter of inches, embedding itself fifteen feet past him in the rear of a black hack dropping passengers just outside the Chambers.

"Down Celine, Charlie, get the fuck down," ordered Meechan as the second bullet skimmed off the pavement and pierced the rear tyre of the black hack. Its passengers, an elderly couple of American tourists, let out a scream.

The private hire was now crossing towards the pavement onto which Meechan and his colleagues had dived flat, as certain death closed in.

At that point Lady Luck saved Declan Meechan. With all his focus on getting off a third shot and this time hitting his target, the driver failed to check his rear view and sight the approaching open-top double-decker tourist bus. The Mondeo passenger pointed his barrel straight at Meechan, less than ten feet away, and the crimelord saw the sneer of delight on the shooter's face as the flash from the barrel took light, just as the impact of the bus threw the private hire into a forty-five degree skid and onto the pavement it had just pulled away from. The driver desperately tried to regain control of the steering wheel while the shooter tried to gain an upright position in an attempt to get a final shot off.

The badly dented Mondeo was soon straightened, but with the double-decker providing a busload of witnesses and a twenty-foot obstacle between the would-be assassins and Meechan, the driver thought better of it and accelerated straight through a red light as he bid to get out of George Square as quickly as possible. Self-preservation rather than a successful hit was now top of his agenda.

A moment later the maroon Mondeo was gone from sight and Meechan helped Celine to her feet.

"You okay, Celine? What about you, Charlie?" asked the crime boss.

Celine, the ever-present mask of her composure momentarily gone, was first to respond.

"What the hell is going on Declan? You don't pay me enough to get involved in this kind of stuff!"

Coyle, his cheek grazed from his headlong dive onto the pavement, was also badly shaken.

"For pity's sake Declan, I'm just a lawyer, no more. My brief doesn't include drive-by shootings. It's a bloody miracle none of us was shot. What's it all about?"

Meechan lied and did so with conviction. His face seemed to take on an icy glaze and the slate-grey eyes hardened.

"I don't know, I just don't know, but that will not be the case for much longer. I'm sorry you both got involved in this but believe me, it's something that won't happen again. Now we can wait for the polis or we can go and have that drink 'cos if anything, I think we now have double cause for a celebration!"

Coyle's eyes had taken on a wild look as his body

trembled in fear caused by his brush with death. A fear which made him forget who his master was. Before he knew it, Coyle blurted out:

"For fuck's sake, you're unbelievable, Meechan! We've just had one of your rivals try and gun us down outside the City Chambers in the middle of Glasgow and you want to go and have a bottle of bubbly to celebrate the fact we're still walking about. What if the Rogano is being watched and there's someone tailing us and this time they don't fuck up? No, Meechan, I've had enough of your company for today. I have a wife and kids and I want to see them at the end of my working day."

Before Coyle could blurt out more, Meechan had him by the lapels of his Crombie and pinned against the back of the black hack that had taken two of the three bullets intended for Meechan.

"You listen to me, Coyle. Your wife's health club, your yacht, the private school for your kids and your fancy house in Bearsden; you would have sweet fuck all if it wasn't for me and Jimmy Gray. Do you want to lose that and go back to your two-bit lawyer's shop off Partick Cross at the foot of some manky tenement with your only customers the junkies and the drunks? 'Cos you can get back to that midden tomorrow if I say so."

Meechan rattled Coyle off the back of the cab for a second time. The taxi driver, who had been standing open-mouthed next to his unbelieving American customers, advanced on the pair. Meechan turned to his left.

"Listen, friend, this is some private business so keep your fuckin' distance or your ability to continue making a living will cease. Comprendy?"

The sheer menace in Meechan's delivery was enough to stop the taxi driver in his tracks, and Meechan turned his attention back to Coyle. Brushing the trembling lawyer's coat lapels in an extravagant placatory gesture, Meechan released his grip.

"Now listen, Charlie, I think we all need a drink to help us calm down." And with a smile, Meechan added: "On reflection, a brandy might be more appropriate. We've been together for a long time and everybody reacts differently to situations like the one we have just been through."

Putting his arm around the lawyer, Meechan nodded toward the astonished Celine and then continued to guide his employee across the road in the direction of St Vincent Street just as the first sirens began to howl.

9

TURNING INTO Royal Exchange Square, they entered the cocktail bar of the Rogano seafood restaurant, Glasgow's finest art deco eatery.

Meechan selected one of the comfortable booths opposite the bar and, with his companions both seated, turned and raised one finger in the air, in the direction of the manager. The silence round the table was all-embracing. Meechan appeared to have a change of heart as he jumped up and headed for the bar, returning with three glasses loaded with the finest Remy Martin cognac.

"Celine, Charlie, here. Drink these and it will help drive the chill from your insides and stop the shivering on your outside."

Raising the glass, Meechan added: "Feel the warmth!" and downed his cognac in one swift gulp before slapping the glass down on the table.

Looking at Celine first, then Coyle, with an air of expectancy, he raised both his hands and turned them palm up as if to say what are you waiting for?

Celine immediately followed Meechan's example and belatedly, Coyle did likewise. The waiter appeared at the table just as Coyle's glass came back to its resting place on the gleaming mahogany surface of the table.

"Bollinger '53 as requested, Mr Meechan?" enquired the waiter.

"As always, Marcel."

Uncorking the champagne, the waiter proceeded to pour before leaving, almost in the same instant. Once again Meechan raised his glass and beckoned his companions to do likewise.

"To winning."

Meechan took another sip of his champagne and, looking into the glass, continued

"Look at all these tiny bubbles. Sometimes I think that's exactly what human beings are all like. Rushing about to what purpose before bursting, and no one would know we've even been on the planet. For as long as I can remember I wanted to be different, wanted to be better, and by Jesus I will."

All of a sudden a fire burned in those slate-grey eyes, and the anger in Meechan's voice raged.

"But in order to succeed sometimes you have to take a risk or two, and in dealing with people who have no scruples or qualms you need to beat them at their own game. The only way you can do so is by being more ruthless, showing no remorse and no weakness, whoever these people may be."

Meechan took another break for a third mouthful of Bollinger. In the ensuing pause Celine shot Charlie Coyle a quick glance and saw from his features that the lawyer was taking little reassurance from Meechan's words. Turning her gaze back to the crime boss, Celine ventured a question:

"What do you mean by all this, Declan? It sounds like you're involving us all in some kind of war."

Meechan, sitting opposite Celine, leaned forward and ran the fingers of his right hand down her left wrist before saying:

"A war is when two roughly matched sides go at it. What the people who were behind what has just happened to us in George Square don't know, is that they are not remotely on the same level as Declan Meechan. They had one chance and that has gone. All I want to say is, hang on for the ride because the good times are about to roll. Now, are either of you hungry?"

Charles Coyle finished his glass of champagne and, having finally recovered some degree of self-composure, he broke the silence he had kept since his outburst back in George Square.

"Declan, I do apologise for my, well, indelicate remarks after the incident. Obviously I was in shock and not in control of my emotions or my mouth. Please forgive me. You have, without fail, my continuing and unquestioning loyalty, but I don't think I'll be much good as company over the lunch table. So if you don't mind, I'll take a raincheck and head back to the office and get on with my paperwork. The planning permission for the club may have been granted, but there's still much to process and I'd like to head into the weekend with my decks cleared. The brandy was just what I needed, and the Bollinger most welcome," he concluded.

"Ah, Charlie, glad to see the drink has had a calming effect on you. That's, fine old friend, I understand completely. Unless there's anything urgent we'll speak on Monday morning as usual." Almost as an afterthought, Meechan added,

"Correct me if I'm wrong, but you and Fiona are off to Paris for the weekend for her birthday? Please give your lovely wife my best and have a great time."

The colour in Coyle's nondescript face heightened considerably as Meechan underlined the point made earlier about the lawyer's lavish lifestyle. Rising from the table and placing his Crombie over his arm, Coyle knew better than to bite.

"That's nice of you, Declan, I certainly will. Enjoy your lunch."

"So Celine, you ready to eat?" asked Meechan as he refilled her glass and then his own.

"Yeah, you could say my appetite is beginning to return, Declan," she admitted, one hand, Meechan couldn't help notice, playfully entwined in those unruly brown tresses. Their eyes locked and Celine was first to avert her gaze. An uneasy silence developed, and then Meechan stretched his right hand across the table and took Celine's left in his grasp.

"Look Celine, I know that was scary stuff out there, but you've known me for nearly ten years and never seen anything like that. The stakes have been raised a helluva lot higher, and as a result so has the danger."

His gaze never wavering as he held Celine's eyes, Meechan continued:

"You remember when I first met you, when I was on the door at the Volcano back in '95 and you'd come off your shift at the Riverboat Casino? Now nothing seems as straightforward as it did then." He paused for a while to let her appreciate where his words were leading.

"The minute I saw you, I knew you were the one for me. I don't know what happened but here we are, ten years down the line, and can you honestly say you are happy with the way your life has worked out?" Meechan asked.

"I don't know, Declan. What do you mean by that? My professional life has come a long way from flashing a pretty smile round the crap tables on the boat, wouldn't you say?" she responded.

"That's not what I mean, as you know full well, Celine. Where did it all go wrong for us all those years back? Do you know how hard it has been, watching you develop and grow in our organisation, and yet you shut me out—that is, except for that night after Jimmy Gray's do.

"But that was just a one-night stand, and would I be right in thinking you did that to punish me? What I want now more than ever is the chance to try again. Will you give me that opportunity? We all make mistakes and yes, I made a big one, but have you ever felt what we had between us with someone else?"

Celine's brown eyes seemed to become molten as they watered in the dimmed light of the cocktail bar. She took another sip of champagne in an attempt to steady her feelings and keep the wave of emotion engulfing her firmly dammed, before she could once again trust herself to speech. Setting her glass down once again, she seemed to be lost as she looked into the tiny exploding bubbles of the Bollinger, but eventually, much to Meechan's relief, her lips moved.

"I know what went before has gone, Declan, but you hurt me. We're both different people now in our thirties, and I don't have time to make the same mistakes in my personal life that you learn from when you're a kid. That night after the party was no strings and you know it. If you feel I was punishing you, then who is that down to, Declan? I just don't want someone to control my life again the way you did. I certainly don't want to be worrying every time a guy comes with twenty yards of me that he'll end up in the GRI. How can you prove to me that if I let you back into my life you won't do that all over again?"

Meechan's face tautened with tension as he considered her words.

"You're talking about Thoroughgood, aren't you Celine? I know you blamed me for his accident, but where's the proof I was behind it? What would I have had to gain from something that was only going to make you suspicious of me? He wasn't right for you then, now or never." concluded Meechan.

"But the point is, Declan, are you?" asked Celine.

Their eyes met and locked, and this time it was Meechan whose gaze was broken first. The interruption was caused by the arrival of a third party wearing a uniform.

"Mr Meechan?" asked the police constable.

"That's right, officer. How can I help?" offered Meechan.

"We've had a report of an incident outside the City Chambers, and the description of the persons involved matches both yourself and the young lady here. We believe there was also a third older gentleman wearing a Crombie involved, and that all of you were the subject of an attempted shooting?" revealed the officer.

"Well, well, officer. It's now one-thirty and the incident happened almost an hour and a quarter back. Myself and my companion found ourselves in need of some medicinal refreshment around the corner here, and you have just found us. But I can save you a lot of time because I'm afraid there is nothing I, or the young lady here, can help you with. So if I'm not mistaken, I can sign your police notebook to that effect and we will be done," suggested Meechan.

"I'm sorry, sir, but the seriousness of the incident and the fact that members of the public were involved means that I'll need to contact CID. If you would excuse me for a moment, I'll have to radio in and inform control."

Taking a step backwards, the cop began to speak into his radio handset. Meechan gave Celine an exasperated look and rolled his eyes heavenward, then groaned.

"Inevitable, I suppose, but still dammed inconvenient. Wouldn't you agree, Celine?"

"Yeah, you could say the officer's timing was less than perfect, but I guess he is only doing his job," she soothed, with a hint of a smile at the sides of her mouth, but Meechan was well aware the moment had been lost.

"Sorry to interrupt Miss, Mr Meechan, CID have arrived outside and are on their way in to see you. Just to let you know, sir."

"Thanks officer …" Meechan started to say then stopped in midsentence.

His slate-grey eyes narrowed for a moment at the approach of the two CID officers.

"Good afternoon, Mr Meechan, I came as soon as I heard you'd been involved in a shooting, but oh dear, they fucked up!" said Detective Sergeant Gus Thoroughgood.

Meechan vaulted out of the booth and shoved his face in the detective's.

"You jumped-up fuckin' plod, are you the best Strathclyde police can offer? What hope is there when there are now shootings in the middle of Glasgow in broad daylight?"

Thoroughgood smiled. "Terrible, isn't it? Just as well DC Hardie and I were detained on duty and able to come to your rescue."

But Thoroughgood's attention had wandered from Meechan to his beautiful companion. Fully aware of the powder keg situation fast developing in the cocktail bar, Kenny Hardie took charge immediately. Inserting both hands between the two males, he prized them apart.

"Gaffer, just back off a minute would you? Let me deal with this," suggested Hardie.

Turning to Meechan, Hardie continued his bid to calm the situation.

"Look, Mr Meechan, I can appreciate you've had a bit of a jolt with this incident, but I'm sure that with both your lives, and those of the public, having been put in jeopardy, you won't mind furnishing us with a brief statement?"

"Nicely put, Detective Harvey isn't it? I don't know what I can help you with, as I haven't got a description or a number plate. But both myself and I'm sure, my lady friend," this said with a gloating look over Hardie's shoulder to the bristling features of Thoroughgood, "will do everything that we can to help you with your enquiries. As I'm sure you appreciate, I am a busy man. If it's possible, can we do so here, as it's not going to take long?" suggested Meechan.

"If we can get a bit of privacy that would seem fair enough; if you don't mind, sir, I would suggest I take your statement and my colleague," Hardie turned to his superior, "Detective Sergeant Thoroughgood will take Miss Lynott's, if I'm not mistaken, story."

Looking over to Celine, Meechan said: "I'll be waiting at the bar for you when you are finished helping—DS Thoroughgood with his enquiries."

Celine smiled, stood up and made her way to Thoroughgood's side.

"What now, Detective Sergeant?"

Speechless at first, Thoroughgood nodded in the direction of an empty booth at the back of the bar, and the pair made their way to the waiting seats. In Thoroughgood's head a voice said:

Where the fuck do I start?

10

USHERING CELINE into the booth with his right hand, Thoroughgood flagged his left in the air, to catch the attention of the hovering waiter.

"Listen, mate, could you do us two white coffees?"

This said with a quick glance at Celine, who nodded her agreement, and the waiter beetled off. Thoroughgood sat down opposite her, trying with all his might not to make contact with those brown eyes, took a subconscious deep breath and got down to business.

"Well, Celine, I guess there's no better place to start than the beginning. But before I take your statement, are you okay?"

Wincing as she recalled the shooting, Celine shrugged her shoulders as if she wasn't quite sure how to answer Thoroughgood.

"Thanks for your concern Gus, if I may call you that? I guess it's not every day that you're shot at outside the City Chambers, at midday! To be honest it was pretty scary, and as you can see, my suit will need to go to the dry cleaner's."

Her smile showed she had recovered her composure and her humour. She added, almost reluctantly,

"Declan ordered a brandy and that has had a calming effect, thanks."

"It must have been pretty damn frightening, though.

I take it you had been at the Chambers for a planning meeting over Meechan's new West End complex?"

"Yeah, that's right, and it was a successful one. Declan had just told me and Charlie he was treating us to lunch at the Rogano when I heard a bang. The next thing I knew Declan was pulling me to the ground, then there was another bang and by then I was aware it was gunfire."

"Charlie? I take it that Charlie Coyle was the third member of your party? So where is he now, Celine?" asked the DS.

"Charlie was pretty shaken up by the whole thing, and after he'd had his brandy he made his excuses and said he had paperwork to get on with back at his office. I don't suppose he'll be hard to find if you need to speak to him this afternoon," she offered.

Celine explained what she had seen and heard, the maroon car, the four shots, but there was little to add to what Thoroughgood already knew.

"It all happened so fast that before I knew it, it was over. It was kind of surreal, a bit like being in your own movie."

Then she added: "The whole thing was just unbelievable. But that is really all I can tell you, Gus."

The DS kept his eyes on Celine, as if he was expecting her to continue, but it was soon clear there was nothing more to tell.

"Well if that's it, that's it. I was speaking to a friend of yours a couple of days back: Gerry McIlroy. He's an interesting character."

"That's right, Gus, Gerry told me he'd had a meeting with you. I hope it was mutually beneficial?" asked Celine.

"Time will tell on Gerry, but is this what you really want for your life?" Thoroughgood persisted.

"Sometimes you can't help being in the wrong place at the wrong time, Gus. You should know all about that. Nevertheless, I have to make something of my life and I am pretty much my own boss. It isn't a bad life."

"Not a bad life, but not a happy one either, Celine. Meechan hasn't put you in charge of his city centre operation for business reasons alone. We both know that isn't the case. Sooner or later you will have to choose, because the type of man Declan Meechan is, he won't be satisfied with you keeping him at arm's length. He will want to own your soul, just like he did before."

"I know all that, but there is good in Declan Meechan. Anyway, what about you Gus? Is your life a happy one?" she asked.

Not a question Thoroughgood was happy fielding. A shrug of his shoulders was the detective's initial reluctant reaction. Again his eyes held Celine's and Thoroughgood seemed to want to say something more, she thought, but it just wouldn't come out.

"Life's not bad," was, as Thoroughgood thought, a pretty woeful attempt at an answer and then he added, as if admitting as much, "but yeah, it could be a whole lot better."

At that, Thoroughgood was aware of a presence behind his right shoulder and Kenny Hardie's rumbling baritone said:

"All right gaffer? I've finished with Mr Meechan's statement; are you finished with Miss Lynott?"

Looking searchingly into her face as if he hoped there was something more to come, Thoroughgood eventually admitted:

"Yep, we're done here. Thanks for your time, Miss Lynott." Thoroughgood couldn't help himself, adding: "Take care, Celine."

"Of course, Detective Sergeant, and you too."

The pleasantries may have been almost banal, but the final look that passed between Gus Thoroughgood and the woman who still cast a spell over him was anything but meaningless. Celine headed over to the bar where Declan Meechan awaited her.

"All done, Celine? I hope you were able to help the Detective Sergeant with his enquiries?"

She nodded but her body language said it all. She wanted to be elsewhere and not, once more, caught in the crossfire between the cop and the crimelord.

Meechan was in no hurry to avoid Thoroughgood, and as the DS made his way towards the restaurant doorway, he mocked in a raised voice:

"I hope you intend to keep me fully updated with your enquiries, Detective Sergeant. After all I would imagine the fact that Glasgow's city centre was turned into a shooting gallery at noon will be front page news. Just like every other concerned Glaswegian, I would like some reassurance that Strathclyde police are doing their utmost to keep our streets and communities safe."

Thoroughgood half-turned back from the door but Kenny Hardie, anticipating both a parting shot from Meechan and the angry reaction it was sure to draw from his gaffer, had once again placed himself between the two.

"Let it go gaffer," said Hardie. "He just isn't worth the grief."

"I can't argue with that Kenny," admitted Thoroughgood, but before he turned away his eyes sought Celine's for a final time.

Their departure allowed Meechan to refocus all his attention on Celine.

"He's still carrying a pretty big torch for you; even a blind man could see that, but what about you, Celine? Is there still a place in your heart for Thoroughgood?" demanded Meehan.

Celine was caught off-guard, her composure ruffled; she cleared her throat to buy a few valuable seconds.

"Neither of you made me happy, Declan. So my answer to that question would be the same one I gave you before we were interrupted by the officers."

Not wholly convincing, Celine had to admit, but there was no point in trying to bullshit Meechan.

"Well, at least I know where I stand, Celine. Now, are you still hungry?"

"Yeah, I would have to say I have an appetite, Declan."

Outside, Thoroughgood and Hardie jumped into the blue Peugeot acting as back-up, after their usual Focus had been taken to the police garages at Helen Street following the "accident" on the Kingston Bridge. Hardie was first to puncture the silence:

"Well gaffer, you get anything helpful out of Miss Lynott?"

"A maroon saloon with a private hire sign above it and four shots fired: that was the lot. What about you Kenny, was Meechan much of a help?" asked Thoroughgood.

"About the same: no number plate, which is annoying, but the vehicle was two up and they were both males but nothing else to go on," admitted Hardie, before he continued:

"Did you hear about that business up at Milngavie Reservoir, gaffer?"

"It was on Radio Clyde news before we came out.

Seems some old boy out walking his dog noticed what he thought was a log bobbing up and down in the drink but when the dog goes in it turned out to be a headless torso. They've turned up some of the limbs but not found the head yet, and the reservoir has been shut down. Who does it sound like to you would be behind that type of execution, gaffer?"

"It makes you wonder. A corpse turns up in the water and then Meechan gets himself shot at in broad daylight in the city centre. I'd put good money on the two incidents being connected," said Hardie.

Thoroughgood raised his eyebrows.

"Meechan's done it before, we both know that. But he always covers his tracks. Just look at Franny Hillkirk. Nothing from the murder locus at all and surprise, surprise, no witnesses either. But listen, faither, there's something I need to bring you in on. The other night I had a meeting with Ross McNab over at the People's Palace, you know, the night after the Kingston Bridge bump.

"Well, the big fella has introduced me to a tout of his who he thinks might be able to help me with information on Meechan. I think tonight it's time I gave wee Gerry McIlroy a call."

Before Thoroughgood could continue his mobile went off. After a check on the screen to confirm the identity of his caller, the DS blurtedout:

"Fuck, it's Tomachek. He'll be wanting the whole shebang on Meechan."

A smile crept over Kenny Hardie's portly chops.

"Well, I wouldn't keep the Detective Superintendent waiting, gaffer!"

Thoroughgood answered the mobile.

"Afternoon, boss."

A powerful voice from the other end was clearly audible to both detectives:

"What the fuck's going on down there, Thoroughgood? I've already had the Chief Constable on, biting my arse about drive-by shootings in the city centre. It's all over the Evening Times and the TV crews are camped outside the City Chambers. It's a complete circus. I want you and Hardie back at Stewart Street office tout suite. I need all the details and the chief is expecting a report on his desk as soon as."

Tomachek had barely taken time for a breath before he continued unabated:

"Well, Thoroughgood, was Meechan any help or was it all bullshit?"

Then, answering his own question before Thoroughgood could get a word in, Tomachek was off and ranting again:

"Now listen to me, Thoroughgood. The Chief has to give a four p.m. press conference about this business with the headless corpse that washed up in Milngavie Reservoir. Fuckin' perfect timing, it's all we need. The press are having a field day saying we've lost control. So you get your arse back here pronto."

Thoroughgood looked at Hardie and the two detectives laughed. There didn't seem much point in doing a whole lot else.

Hardie said: "Well, gaffer, just another routine day in the life of 'A' Division CID!"

"I guess lunch is going to have to wait," said the DS, and with that the CID pool car was en route to Stewart Street cop shop.

11

SPRINGBURN WAY was fairly quiet by six p.m. on a Friday. Boasting a small shopping centre, a bank, job centre and a couple of pubs, it wasn't exactly teeming with commercial activity, serving as it did one of the poorest areas of Glasgow. The blue Transit pulled up outside the bookies at 5.57 p.m., as Brennan confirmed with a last look at his watch.

Turning off the engine, his stocking mask already covering his face, he opened the door and jumped out. He booted the bookies' door open and marched straight into the shop with Jarvis a pace behind him.

"Right you bastards, everybody except staff get the fuck oot," and to make his point Brennan pulled out the sawn-off and blasted a round into the roof

Jarvis obligingly trained his sawn-off over the shop floor. The punters, a mixture of drunks, pensioners and assorted local lowlife, made their way out without needing a second invite.

Springburn was the type of place that had more than its fair share of violent crime, and the punters in Brown's bookies had all witnessed similar incidents at one time or another. With the exodus from the floor complete, Brennan smashed the butt of his shooter into the two CCTV cameras covering the entrance and the main floor area. As he did so, he made his way to the counter, lowering the sawn-off at the girl behind it.

"Listen tae me, darlin'. Do as I tell you and it'll be all right, pet. Now, where's old man Brown?" he hissed.

While he was focusing on the girl behind the counter's glass security window, the heavy door at the side of the counter had begun to creak open and a barrel pointed out.

"Lookin' for me fucker?"

And immediately there was a flash from the barrel aimed in Brennan's direction. He ducked instinctively as the discharge shattered into one of the TV screens behind him. The door sprang wide open and the burly shape of old Walt Brown came charging out just as Chico Jarvis opened fire, spewing the contents of his sawn-off straight into the old man's guts. The bookie was thrown back against the door with the violent impact of the discharge. Brennan looked over his shoulder and gave Chico the thumbs-up, then signalled to his sidekick to start dousing the premises with petrol.

Turning to stare at the terrified assistant, he screamed:

"Get the fuck oot of here, darlin'."

This time the girl needed no second invite and sprinted out of the side door, hurdling the groaning body of Walt Brown as she escaped into Springburn Way.

Brennan was now leaning over Walt Brown. The bookie was still alive, but his breath came in torturous rasps. Pulling his mask back up onto his head, Brennan leaned closer still to Brown.

"Well, well, Walt, did you really think you'd get away with that little turn down in George Square earlier today? Looks like it's time to say goodbye."

Recognition flickered across Brown's anguished face and he managed to string together a sentence:

"Frankie Brennan, ya bog-trottin' bastard," Brown

agonisingly drew another lungful of air. "Don't worry, Meechan's gonnae get his yet."

The effort needed to make the threat had taken almost all Brown's dying breath from him, but Brennan was determined there was no way Brown was going to meet his maker without being made aware of the fate awaiting the other members of his family.

"Now now, Walt, that isn't a nice thing to be saying about Mr. Meechan. But it's just not going to be happening 'cos you ain't gonnae have any family left to organise fuck all by the time tonight is out, old man."

Brown's eyes began to assume the glazed quality of a dead man's stare. Smiling benevolently, Brennan signalled to Chico to bring the can of petrol over to him. Taking it from his sidekick, he stood up and doused the bookie liberally before producing a lighter from his jacket pocket.

"Goodbye, old man."

The lighter's flame was applied to Brown's petrol-sodden shirt. Taking a step back, Brennan waited to make sure the flames began to engulf Brown.

"Right, wee man, let's get the fuck into the van, it's done here."

Sprinting out the bookies' door, the two jumped into the Transit and headed up Springburn Way, passing the leisure centre on their left and up the hill towards Balgrayhill Road. Stopping at the junction for a second, Brennan shot over into Mosesfield Street when the first gap in the cross-traffic appeared.

Springburn Park ran up the left-hand side of the road; on the right there were flats and a cul de sac. Brennan turned the Transit into the cul de sac while Jarvis poured the remainder of the petrol all over the interior, and the lighter was once again administered. The duo exited the Transit and ran over to the waiting Cavalier. Engaging reverse, Brennan turned back into the main street and continued to head north just as the first sirens pierced the evening air.

It was 6.14 p.m.

The hit on the car showroom was about half a mile to the north west of Springburn Way. Turning off Springburn Road, the red Volkswagen Golf pulled up outside the showroom and Reid jumped out quickly, followed by Simms. Reid could already see Jimmy Brown standing on the showroom floor talking to a punter in animated fashion.

Stocking mask over his head, he headed straight across to the car salesman; the colour drained out of Brown's sharp features as recognition dawned. Gazza Reid enjoyed his work. He was a violent man who enjoyed violence for its own sake. When it afforded him the chance to settle old scores, it gave him an added sense of satisfaction.

The punter standing with Jimmy Brown also knew something was far from right, and began to back away from Brown and the closing Reid. The distance between Brown and Reid was now less than five feet, and at that point Reid reached inside his Berghaus anorak and pulled out the Smith and Wesson. Still he closed on Brown and, when he stood less than a foot away, lifted his handgun and put the barrel to Brown's head. Reid spoke.

"You know who I am, Jimmy?"

Brown said nothing but his eyes opened wide in the terror of recognition.

"You bastard, you carved me wide open all these

years back and you thought I would'nae come for ye," continued Reid.

Keeping the gun trained on Jimmy Brown's head, Reid pulled out the machete from inside his Berghaus and plunged it straight into Brown's midriff before twisting the blade deep in his guts. Brown gasped and staggered and before he could fall, Reid added:

"Night-night, Jimmy," and with that he pulled the trigger.

Brown crumpled to the ground with half his head spreading across the previously immaculate, gleaming black and white tiled showroom floor. The temporary silence was pierced by a scream as a female member of the showroom staff came out of the ladies' and started to head for her desk, only to pull up in disbelief; fear and shock etched in her face.

As she became hysterical, the screaming went on and on. A voice shouted,

"You bastards! Come and get it!"

Reid, and Simms, now positioned ten feet behind his superior at the showroom entrance,turned to see a suited male in his mid-thirties come out of the door next to the showroom coffee machine. The male, who Reid immediately recognised as Davie Brown, the second of Walt's two sons, was not empty-handed.

"You fuckin' bastards, what have you done to Jimmy? You're gonnae pay," And with that Davie Brown lowered his revolver and opened fire.

Reid and Simms threw themselves behind the nearest glistening showroom motor. Reid, peeking round from behind the rear spoiler of a Fiesta, caught Simms' eye and signalled to him to start moving round to Brown's left. Reid started to edge round his right flank.

Brown, his fury unabated but his wits still with him, could see exactly what was happening. However, with his brother lying with his brains half-blown across the showroom floor and his entrails spilling out from his midriff, he was starting to succumb to a Neanderthal bloodlust.

Reid, the killer of his brother, was the one he wanted, and as he saw the murderer attempting to shimmy across the showroom to his right, he opened fire again.

The first bullet embedded itself into the Ford Fiesta Reid was using as a shield. The second bullet punctured a hole in the showroom's glass wall. So intent was Davie Brown on avenging himself on the man who had brutalised his brother that momentarily he forgot all about the second of his two adversaries, Ricky Simms. But by that point Simms had sidled right round Brown's left flank and was standing exactly behind him.

"Hey fucker," Simms said, and as Brown turned on him, Simms emptied the sawn-off into his chest as the third and final male member of the Brown family met his maker in a salvo of lead.

Simms immediately caught the shout of "Out!" from Reid and the two made their way back to the waiting Volkswagen before they screeched off in a rubber-burning exit. They made their way up Springburn Road, turning into Possil and then heading out the back road to the village of Torrance and on into the Campsie Hills. Their intention was to rendezvous with Frankie Brennan and torch the Volkswagen in one of the myriad small country roads that were impossible for the police to patrol effectively.

*

By seven p.m. Brennan and Reid were able to rendezvous in a small lane just short of Ballat Crossing, around three miles from the village of Killearn. Once Brennan had all the information he needed from Reid regarding the showroom job, he texted Meechan that both jobs had been successfully completed.

Despite Brennan's confidence everything was going to plan, Meechan was not one for taking unnecessary chances, except when the rewards demanded. The point of taking the getaway motors out into the sticks was that the dumping grounds preferred by the gang were in a different policing area to that of Strathclyde Police.

Central Scotland Constabulary, which covered Stirlingshire and the beautiful, rugged but sparsely populated Trossachs, was one of the smallest Scottish police forces in terms of manpower. With so few police officers covering such a vast expanse of terrain, the gang's chances of disposing of "hot" vehicles successfully in the aftermath of their operations were greatly enhanced.

Meechan sat in his office chair, his hands steepled and his eyes looking straight up at the ceiling.

So far so good, he thought. But what about Tommy Rankin?

His number two was due to check in with him from the Western Isles, and so far, nothing. Then there was the call Jimmy Gray would be expecting from him over in his Mallorcan villa. Pulling his tie loose, Meechan made his way over to the drinks cabinet which was more of an ornament than a supplier of liquor.

But just tonight, thought Meechan, I could do with a malt, while he waited for Tommy Rankin's call.

Cradling the sixteen-year-old Lagavulin in his right hand, he had to admit he had been careless, perhaps even arrogant, and it had nearly cost him his life and that of the woman he supposed he loved. From now on, Meechan vowed to himself, he would take no such chances again. With the Browns out of the way, control over Glasgow, north of the river Clyde, was his. It was now time to start phase two, and that meant he needed to talk to Tommy Rankin.

12

EIGHT-THIRTY and Meechan's mobile went off, the display screen flashing up the name Rankin.

"Tommy, where the fuck have you been?" demanded Meechan.

Rankin was unrepentant. "Sorry boss, but do you know how hard it is to get a reception in this place?"

"Very good Tommy, forget the excuses and get on with it," ordered Meechan.

"Okay boss," Rankin could tell, even from the other side of a mobile, when Meechan's patience was wearing thin. "Anyways we were met at the airport—if you can call it that—by a nice little welcoming committee. It turns out that we weren't the only ones those greedy fuckin' Johnson brothers were ripping off." Rankin was gathering momentum. "It appears the main man now is an Iain Morriston. After a couple of refreshments and grub, Morriston started to put us in the picture."

"Very good, Tommy. Now, without revealing how many courses you had and what vintage the plonk was, can you get the fuck on with it," ordered Meechan, this time with some levity in his voice.

"Yes boss. Well, it turns out Morriston has had his suspicions that the Johnsons were skimming for a while, and not just at our end. The short and curlies of it is that Morriston and his boys started watching the Johnsons.

After the container truck was leaving the factory, there were unscheduled stop-off points. Morriston claims that he was about to contact us and put us in the picture but the Johnsons had already left for Glasgow. We all know what happened to them down here.

"Morriston also claimed he knew you would have to send someone up to sort things in Barra and didn't see the point of getting in a flap. I have to say, boss that would be about right for this place, nothing seems to get done today when tomorrow will do. I think they call it mañana!"

"And?" was the only word Meechan uttered.

"The bottom line is Morriston is more than happy to be your man up in the Isles, he's confident he can deliver, delighted with your offer of a five per cent increase in the island take of things, and keen to get to work on the new deal. Morriston also said to me, if we were interested, it might be time to start dipping our feet in the crystal meth market? That's for you to decide, boss."

"First things first, Tommy; we need to get the current operation up and running, watertight and efficient. Morriston needs to earn our trust. To a certain extent we need to earn the same from him. So what do you think about our new friend, Tommy?" asked Meechan.

"I'd say he's hungry and ambitious, all right. But like you say, boss, it will be a time before he's earned our trust," admitted Rankin.

"It does sound pretty promising, but you're sure there is no resentment over our disposing of the Johnsons?" enquired Meechan.

Rankin was adamant. "Naw boss, no way. I think when the other island boys found out the Johnsons had been ripping them off they were just delighted when we did their work for them."

"Okay, Tommy, so what have you got planned for the rest of the weekend?"

"Well tonight, boss, me and the boys are guests of Morriston at a ceilidh, would you believe, in the Castlebay Community Hall? Then tomorrow he's going to show us round the Barra Fresh from the Sea frozen food factory, and we're going to have a look at some of the beach drop-off points."

"If the weather holds, that should be pretty damn good, the beaches and the seas are something else." Rankin added: "It's just a pity it's so bloody Baltic."

"Aye very good Tommy, to be sure. Just remember you're no' a bloody tourist. Don't let the Teuchters hoodwink you. This is business, and they might fancy pulling the wool over our eyes and then the laugh's on us when we've fucked off back to Glasgow," warned Meechan.

"Give me a call on Sunday night if there are any unforeseen problems; if not I'll catch you at the office Monday afternoon," he concluded.

"Okay, boss, have a good one," said Rankin, and the mobile clicked dead.

Meechan afforded himself a grin. This was a far better scenario than he had hoped for. The fact that the other islanders had caught the Johnsons ripping them off as well was a real bonus. Meechan was also in no doubt Tommy Rankin would make them only too aware of the fate that befell the Johnson brothers, in graphic detail.

Meechan got up from the desk and helped himself to a second Lagavulin from the office cabinet, then punched in Jimmy Gray's Puerta Pollensa villa number, one hundred percent confident he had some music for the old man's ears.

13

BY THE time Thoroughgood and Hardie had finished de-briefing Detective Superintendent Tomachek over the shooting incident outside the City Chambers, both detectives were grateful that six p.m. was the start of their weekend off. After watching Tomachek do his best to give himself a coronary, Thoroughgood had to admit it was at times like these that the brass really earned their inflated wage packets.

Tomachek was due up at Disneyland, as Pitt Street, Force HQ, was known to the rank and file of Strathclyde police, for a three-thirty p.m. briefing of the chief constable. Meanwhile, Thoroughgood and Hardie tied up their loose ends, making sure there was a full briefing note left for the backshift. By four-thirty their main concern was where to enjoy a pint and mull over a strategy for Thoroughgood's first meeting with Gerry McIlroy, which was pencilled in for eight p.m. that night.

Hardie, ever mindful of his aching bones and the need to bring warmth into his rotund body, had clearly given the matter some thought.

"Listen, gaffer, what about the Ubiquitous Chip in Ashton Lane? It's got a fire, and a nice pint of Furstenburg would be a good place to start the weekend and help the brain to relax and function at its best. Plus, it's about the only place in Ashton Lane you can hear yersel' think, and not get surrounded by posers like a wagon train encircled by the Apache!" Hardie's grandiose case was, he hoped, compelling.

"Fair enough, you old git. Drop your motor up in Hyndland and we'll nick down and have a couple, at least. I'm supposed to be meeting McIlroy in the Snaffle Bit on Sauchiehall Street, so I'll text him and see if he can bring the meet forward to seven p.m."

By 5.30 p.m. the two detectives were ambling down Dowanside Road. The night air was bracing, and this only heightened the mounting sense of anticipation for the impending pint or two awaiting them in the UB Chip, as it was known to everyone in the West End.

Perching their pints on the mantelpiece above the small fire already crackling and spreading its warmth out from the heart of the UB, Hardie opened up the discussion.

"First thing I'd like to know, gaffer, is where is McIlroy going to be getting his information from? Celine Lynott? Forgive me if I say so, but she looked pretty bloody cosy with Meechan at the Rogano. I can't see her wanting to jeopardise the expensive pad, the designer gear and a big money management job with Meechan to help bite the hand that feeds her. Maybe I've got her wrong, but you were the one who interviewed her. Did she give you any indications?"

"I dunno, Kenny. In all likelihood, the answer has got to be no, there. I got the feeling that Celine is at a bit of a crossroads right now. I think she could be starting to think that Declan Meechan is as good as it's going to get for her in this life. But she still has doubts."

After further consideration and a mouth of Furstenburg, Thoroughgood added:

"You're right, though; are these doubts big enough to

chuck away everything she has and gamble her future on god knows what for a return? You'd have to say the odds are stacked pretty big-time on her hanging her coat on Meechan," concluded the DS.

His lips encircled his pint, as the pot of Furstenburg reached half-empty in one massive swallow that made Hardie looked like some kind of submerging whale, the DC still managed to roll his eyes over the rim in agreement. Setting the glass back on the mantelpiece, Hardie stuck his arse a shade closer to the warming hearth and cracked a fart at precisely the same time he belched from his mouth. The dual expulsion of air brought a hearty smile to his ruddy chops and left Thoroughgood wishing a hole would open up in the middle of the gradually filling bar which would allow him an instant escape from his colleague's antics.

"For fuck's sake, Kenny, do you have to?" demanded Thoroughgood.

"As my old man always said, better out than in!" retorted Hardie, and then continued with his thoughts on McIlroy.

"So, if he is isn't getting his information from Celine, where the fuck is it coming from? You said he had managed to keep his job as a charge nurse, thanks to all the help he gave McNab, and if McIlroy's brothers are both in Barlinnie then he must have some other way in. What about his ma? Have you managed to do anything on the house front for her?" he asked.

"Aye, it's all sorted with the Glasgow Housing Association. She'll get a wee front and back door with a postage stamp of grass out the back, the minute I'm sure he has something valuable for me. Certainly not before," pledged the DS.

Thoroughgood was enjoying the sight of his notoriously tight colleague make his way to the bar for the next round when his mobile beeped with a text. It was McIlroy, confirming he could make the meet at seven-thirty but not before. Taking stock, Thoroughgood consulted his watch. Just past six now, which would allow for another couple of pints, and then a leisurely walk down University Avenue into the Kelvin Way and he'd be there in good time.

Hardie handed his pint over and bleated:

"Would you believe it, five frigging pounds and ninety six pence that round cost? I can hardly get my heid round it, the three-pound pint is only a baw' hair away."

"Well, at least it hasn't gone up any since I got the first round in. Anyway," the DS added, as he surveyed Hardie's shabby, greying white shirt, outdated paisley pattern tie and dull brown double-breasted suit,

"What else have you got to spend all the overtime on? Certainly not clothes!" cracked Thoroughgood.

Changing the subject with some speed, Hardie enquired about his superior's love life, a tactic he knew that was sure to put Thoroughgood's gas at a low peep.

"So gaffer, any hot dates lined up for the weekend— apart from a visit to Firhill? Who have Thistle got this weekend?" he quipped from behind a smug smile.

"Fuck off, why don't you? For your information I have a wee coffee situation the back of eleven tomorrow morning and yes, after that I plan to head up to Firhill to watch the glorious Harry Wrags trounce Airdrie. What more could a man want?"

"You kept that one quiet, gaffer. So where did this all come from? Anyone I know? She's not a copper by any chance?"

"Well, if you must know, and this is obviously between the two of us, I've started going to that speed-dating thing down at the Corinthian and it looks like it's beginning to pay off," Thoroughgood admitted.

Barely able to conceal his amazement, Hardie spluttered out a mouthful of foam from the head of his Fusternburg.

"Yer fuckin' kiddin' me on, gaffer!"

"As it happens no, I'm bloody well not. For your information I had three lines of enquiry in my inbox from the other night's meeting, and coffee tomorrow morning is with a pretty brunette civil servant called Sara," Thoroughgood replied.

Hardie, his head shaking in a mix of disbelief and shock at the hidden depths to his gaffer's love life, was determined to get the full story.

"Come on, gaffer, you can't keep an old dog dangling for his bone. How does all that speed-dating shit work?" he demanded.

"Look, faither, there's no way I am gonnae let you know the ins and outs of my love life just so you can piss yourself at my expense. The bottom line is, at thirty-seven I'm not getting any younger and I just thought it was time to explore all the avenues. Anyway, it's nowhere as painful as it's made out to be," claimed Thoroughgood, far from convincingly.

The truth was that after a string of meaningless encounters, Gus Thoroughgood was beginning to feel the passing of the years with more than a little trepidation. Much as he tried to deny it, he had never recovered from the rollercoaster relationship with Celine Lynott back in his early twenties, over ten years ago.

Sure, there had been other relationships. One in

particular, with a primary school teacher called Ellen, had even resulted in her moving in with her four-year-old daughter Aimie. But it hadn't worked. Thoroughgood had found himself comparing Ellen to Celine at every instant, or telling himself that there was surely someone more suited for him round the corner. The fact that Ellen had a kid from a previous relationship also freaked him out. Thoroughgood had found it hard to take responsibility for someone else's child or impose the type of moral authority on the little girl he felt was needed.

When Aimie's father, a lieutenant in the Navy, had returned to Scotland, his reappearance had placed fresh doubts in Thoroughgood's mind. After six months Ellen had moved out of Thoroughgood's flat, both agreeing that a steamy love life wasn't enough. Since Ellen, and that had been the best part of six years back, there had been plenty of women in his life. Certainly enough to keep his neighbours amused, but none had lasted.

Becoming increasingly frustrated at his inability to find a woman who matched up, it had taken an ill-starred romp with a probationer at the end of a drunken coppers' night out to finally make Thoroughgood realise he had to take concerted action. All of which had led him to speed-dating.

Hardie winked knowingly. "So is the Sara bird a bit of a looker? Decent chassis, and all that?"

"Listen, Kenny," said Thoroughgood, his irritation starting to show, "I'm not going to be wasting my time with any old slapper am I? She's in her early thirties, single and definite Premiership class. But we'll just have to see how coffee goes."

Hardie was still in a state of disbelief at Thoroughgood's determination to kick-start his love life, having always considered his gaffer pretty straitlaced.

"So, gaffer, what happens if your wee coffee morning goes into extra time? Does that mean the Jags will be deprived of your support?" "Fuck off faither," was the terse reply.

Thoroughgood was saved by the bell of his mobile. The surprise caused by the display of Ross McNab's name was so obvious, he let Hardie see for himself.

"This should be interesting," said the frustrated Hardie.

"Hi Ross, how's it going?" answered Thoroughgood.

"Not bad, but yer never gonnae believe this big man. Walt Brown got blown away at his bookies up in Springburn Way, and his two boys Jimmy and Davie were done in the car showroom half a mile away at around six p.m. just there. Who's yer money on, Gussy boy?" asked McNab.

"Fuckin' hell! It's got to be Meechan. Whatever else that bastard may be, he doesn't waste any time letting revenge go cold," the DS admitted.

McNab was keen to continue.

"Listen, Gus, I was going to call you anyways to let you know we had a turn up in Springburn, and that the information was, the Browns were behind the attempted hit on Meechan earlier today." He outlined the gruesome details of what happened to the Browns.

"How bad is the fire damage to the bookies, Ross?" asked Thoroughgood.

"The fire boys got there pretty quick, but the shop floor where it all took place is pretty well done. SOCO are going to have a problem lifting anything from there. It seems a blue Transit van was used for the hit, and we have a lookout for it on the go. But at six p.m. most of the shops are shut, and up in Springburn Way that just leaves the boozers To be fair, on a chilly April night the punters are inside no' givin' a fart about what's going on out in the teeth of a howling gale."

Sensing his colleague's mind was going into overdrive, McNab, it seemed, had saved the best for last:

"Aye, the whole thing is a fuckin' shocker all right. But here's another one for you, Gus. They've put that fuckwit Henry Farrell in charge of the enquiry! Knowing that little wanker, he'll have been up bleating at the Detective Super's door to let him have his big chance the minute the shit hit the fan. The frightening thing would be if he manages to nail anything down; then his career will go back into orbit," speculated McNab.

"So what did your informant say about the George Square turn? What's the script there?" Thoroughgood asked.

"Well, we had a pretty good idea that the Browns wanted to extend their influence right the way over from Springburn and Possil into the West End and, according to our tout, there's been a bit of a turf war waging. You won't believe it, but our informant is claiming Franny Hillkirk was one of Brown's men who had got in under Meechan's radar, and it was only when he brought himself to Meechan's attention that the bog trottin' bastard took a closer look at him and discovered Franny was dodgy.

"Then you go stumbling about in the east looking for Hillkirk and find him all strung out hanging from a veranda. Well, Hillkirk was a cousin of Walt Brown's, and he went for the jugular in terms of revenge by trying to take out the organ grinder himself. So there you have it. All of which I am bound, as you know, to pass on to Farrell and the boys at the CHIS unit. I just thought it was important to tip you the wink first," concluded McNab.

"All very interesting, I appreciate it. And your tout is one hundred per cent?" checked Thoroughgood.

"Absolutely bulletproof," claimed the DC.

"Ta again, Ross, and for your info, I'm meeting McIlroy tonight. You want me to give him your love?" enquired Thoroughgood sarcastically.

"You're all right, Gus. Listen, that's Farrell on the way over, I'll need to shoot. All the best, mate." McNab was gone.

Checking his watch, Thoroughgood saw that it was nearly seven, and with one eye on the fact he had a twenty-minute walk ahead of him to meet McIlroy, the two detectives made their way down the stairs and out past the two recently added bars which seemed so at odds with the original 1960s lounge.

Then it was into Ashton Lane and the cold night. The place had become the very heart of the West End, its streetlights spanning the twenty-foot gap from one line of pubs to the opposite. Thoroughgood always thought it felt like it was permanently Christmas in the lane. Walking round into Byres Road, Hardie asked:

"Are you gonna be taping this McIlroy, boss? Considering it's the first meet, it might naw be a bad idea."

In answer, the DS produced his pocket-size Dictaphone before adding:

"Spot on, faither, but I thought you'd probably want to listen in on what he is bringing to the table anyhow."

Hardie hadn't finished.

"Before you go, Gus, can I ask why the Snaffle Bit?"

"That was his choice. To be fair I've got to respect that, given the wee man is coming over close to the West End. Turns out the boozer is owned by an old Teuchter who McIlroy helped nurse back from a brain op in the Western and he's been a welcome regular in there ever since. So it's safe ground for him and handy enough for me. If he's spotted by one of Meechan's boys speaking to me he won't get through the night," summed up the DS.

"Fair play, gaffer. I'm just gonna head off home now but you could give me a call later on the moby. You know I'll be all ears, Gus!" assured Hardie.

"Will do, faither," agreed Thoroughgood, and with that he shoved his hands deep into the brown Barbour that seemed to have become part of his body, and trudged off down Byres Road right into the teeth of the gale.

14

IT DIDN'T take Thoroughgood long to sight Gerry McIlroy. The informant was seated with his back against a wall almost opposite the entrance, his presence partly masked by a copy of that day's Evening Times, his shiny pate still evident.

Thoroughgood approached the informant and asked McIlroy if he wanted a drink. The lager shandy suggested was, Thoroughgood thought, quite appropriate.

Returning to join McIlroy, the DS placed the drinks on the table, seated himself and suggested a toast to "New beginnings."

A large mouthful of Stella Artois later, Thoroughgood, his Dictaphone silently clicked on in his trouser pocket while he was waiting for the pints to be served, got down to business.

"Okay, wee man, there's no point in us getting started without me putting you in the picture about what's been happening up in Springburn in the last ninety minutes or so."

"You mean the Browns getting wiped out," retorted a deadpan McIlroy.

Struggling to keep his irritation from becoming obvious, the detective's eyebrows instinctively shot up and before he could stop himself, he blurted out:

"How the fuck did you know about that?"

"Isn't that exactly the type of thing informants are supposed to know about, Mr Thoroughgood? I wouldn't be much good to you if I didn't know. After all, what you specifically want from me, so Detective Constable McNab told me, is information on Declan Meechan."

"All right. So tell me about Meechan then, since you seem to know everything else that is happening in this city," snapped Thoroughgood.

McIlroy's darting eyes met the detective's and held his gaze in a flinty stare. Thoroughgood had the distinct feeling he was being summed up in more than a professional capacity by the tout he had obviously underestimated. The informant spoke.

"When we met down at the People's Palace I asked you a favour regarding my mother's housing predicament …"

Thoroughgood, with an increasing sense of unease developing as he began to feel he was becoming the interrogated rather than the interrogator, said,

"Listen, Gerry, there are no problems on that count. The GHA have a back and front door house waiting for her with a bit of a garden down in the Hardgate. You just give me something to start oiling the wheels of the housing department and we'll be off and running."

"I thought you would say something like that, Mr Thoroughgood, and it isn't too difficult. Did you know Franny Hillkirk was taken out by Meechan after he found out he was undercutting him and moonlighting drugs sales for the Browns from one of Meechan's city centre pubs?" volunteered McIlroy.

It was the detective's turn to take his companion by surprise.

"Actually, Gerry, that's old hat I'm afraid. I took a call

on that one about an hour ago. I believe Hillkirk was a cousin of Walt Brown's, that right?"

"So you aren't so uninformed yourself, Mr Thoroughgood. What do you need me for then?" asked the informant.

"A way into Declan Meechan that will help me bring him down," was the DS's bald request.

"Believe me, I have just such an opening, Mr Thoroughgood, but on the way to establishing mutual trust, you must start small to go big. Do you have any idea where the people responsible for tonight's two hits are holed up?" asked McIlroy.

"Not a fuckin' Scooby," Thoroughgood admitted.

"By midnight tonight I'll have a pretty good idea. For that information I must have your word that my mother will be in her new house no later than next week, Mr Thoroughgood," demanded the tout.

Thoroughgood's mind raced. It was a huge turn given the severity of what had just happened at six p.m. that night. But the triple murder enquiry was being run in E Division by DCI Farrell, the copper he hated more than most of the neds he'd ever jailed. It was information that Thoroughgood knew he had to handle with kid gloves. So he stalled.

"That would be some starter for ten, Gerry. But as you know, the Brown murder enquiry is not being run in my division. So I have to ask myself, just how much benefit I would derive from supplying others with information which would allow them to land and interview people I wouldn't necessarily get access to?"

McIlroy was not going to be mucked about over information which he knew full well was red hot.

"You're the detective, Mr Thoroughgood. Don't

you talk to your colleagues? Surely by placing the four persons involved in a triple murder, you would not only get a hell of a lot of gratitude from above, but what a bargaining tool it would be to interrogate your suspects on their relationship with Declan Meechan."

"The latter will take some work Gerry, but yeah, you have a point. There are a couple of other things we're going to have to clear up. Obviously I don't know what it is, but do you want to remain registered under the pseudonym DC McNab gave you? Or do you want it changed when I re-register you?"

McIlroy shrugged his shoulders. After all, it wasn't his problem. Thoroughgood continued:

"These days touts also have to be kept above board with the Central Human Intelligence Unit but they don't need to know the juicy bits. I suggest we just keep you under the same moniker if it's all the same to you. Secondly, I'm sure you will have a payment figure in mind. Turns like the one you're offering me don't come cheap after all, and nor should they," admitted the DS.

Again the darting eyes seemed to be assessing all the angles before McIlroy would commit anything to words. A mouthful of shandy and a scratch of his shiny dome and eventually the informant's face broke into a surprising smile:

"My pseudonym is Morse and if it's all the same to you, I'd be quite happy to keep it that way."

Thoroughgood was both surprised by the admission and filled with a desire to burst out laughing. Eventually he raised his pint of Stella Artois and saluted.

"To Morse." One swallow later and the DS continued:

"There you go, one of life's great big coincidences. My favourite TV detective, Morse, by the way. If that isn't a good omen then I don't know what is. I'd be delighted to re-register you under that name with CHIS, but what about payment? I am assuming you aren't just doing this out of a sense of altruism." asked the detective.

"No, that's correct, Mr Thoroughgood. Well, I guess it all depends on just what the information leads to. Given that there were four men involved in the two hits, that would mean a figure being put on each one's head, should my information lead to their capture."

A pause for another mouthful of shandy and Morse, as he was now to be known, continued:

"There's no point in me playing it down, given that these men have just carried out three murders. And in the current climate, Strathclyde Police are not exactly getting a good press as we both know, Mr Thoroughgood." Morse stopped again.

Thoroughgood was in no mood to mince his words:
"So, how much?"

"Twenty thousand pounds for the four males or five grand a skull, I'd say that was a pretty good deal. If you fail to make any apprehensions, my information is likely to lead you to a safe house routinely used by Meechan's men in their various activities. For the house and the evidence you would likely be getting along with it, but without the males, I would be looking for, say, two and a half grand. I don't think, Mr Thoroughgood, that you could begrudge me any of that."

"There lies the problem, Gerry. I certainly wouldn't begrudge you any of it but the brass, who have to authorise all payments to registered informants, can be a bit sticky about big bucks like this. You probably knew that anyway. But I'll do my damnedest," vowed Thoroughgood.

"I'm afraid you'll have to do a lot more than that, Mr Thoroughgood. I take it you didn't see the Chief Constable on Scotland Today or Reporting Scotland earlier tonight? I saw his conference just before I left the house and he looked very uncomfortable. That was at four p.m. and was about the corpse that washed up in Milngavie Reservoir yesterday and the attempt on Meechan's life at twelve p.m. today, outside the City Chambers. I would suggest your Chief is under a helluva of a lot of pressure in the wake of the gangland war that erupted less than two hours after he vowed to make Glasgow's streets safe again."

Morse continued: "Within four hours I will be offering you information that could, sorry, should lead to the arrest of the murderers. I think the Chief Constable, if he has a brain, will want that information, don't you?"

It was a statement of fact rather than any search for confirmation.

"So, how do you want to play this?" asked the DS.

Again Morse had all the answers:

"When you leave this meeting I want you to make the necessary calls and I'll expect a call back from you confirming the money is available at ten p.m. When that's done I'll elaborate a bit more. It'll be a case of me providing the information as soon after midnight as possible. Then, Mr Thoroughgood, it will be up to your colleagues to make sure they act with the necessary speed to make the arrests. Does that all sound reasonable?" queried Morse, more as an afterthought than anything else.

"Fair enough."

"Well, if that's all Detective Sergeant, I will be on my way and look forward to our next chat at ten p.m.!' said Morse.

He pushed his seat back and began to rise, only for Thoroughgood to grab his right wrist in an iron grip:

"Sit down a minute, Gerry. I want to ask you something." Taken completely by surprise, there was a startled look on the tout's face. Clearly the last thing Morse had expected was for Thoroughgood to get physical. Morse sat down but said nothing.

Damn it, the little blighter makes nothing easy, not even intimidation, said the voice in Thoroughgood's head.

"Listen Gerry, there's something else I need to ask you. But for personal, not professional, reasons. Please tell me that your source inside Meechan's organisation isn't Celine Lynott."

Relief enveloped Morse's stony face.

"Of course not, Detective Sergeant. You had me worried there but I don't respond to heavyhanded stuff, as DC McNab will tell you."

15

THOROUGHGOOD WAS in no rush to make his call to Detective Superintendent Tomachek. Whenever you put your faith in a new informant there was an element of doubt. Sure McIlroy, or Morse as he was now to be known, had been run extensively by Ross McNab, but his relationship with Thoroughgood was embryonic. For their relationship to be kicking off with such significance made the DS more than a bit jittery. When you put your head above the parapet and informed a senior officer you had the type of information Thoroughgood, via Morse, was going to be providing, there was always an element of "show me yer money." Checking his watch, it was now nine-thirty p.m. Thoroughgood knew he had to bite the bullet and call his boss.

Detective Superintendent Valentino Tomachek, the son of a Polish wartime RAF pilot, wasn't the type to berate a junior officer for calling him at home. Especially when the interruption to his evening was of this nature. Taking a long sip of his Shiraz, Thoroughgood punched in the number.

"Gus, my boy, to what do I owe this unexpected pleasure?" boomed Tomachek from the other end.

"Evening, boss. I know you've finished for the night but I have something you need to hear. Ross McNab let me know all about the Brown hit, and I had a meeting with a tout earlier tonight who could be very helpful in that respect," revealed the DS.

A momentary silence, as Tomachek digested what he desperately hoped was a glimmer of hope at the end of a forty-eight hour period in which he'd felt he'd been so far up his own arse, he'd been working in darkness.

"Fire away, son, we've got fuck-all to lose at this stage," admitted Tomachek.

"Okay, boss. My man claims that by midnight tonight he may well be able to house the two teams who carried out the Brown killings. But for the information he wants five grand a skull, and we're talking four shooters here. He is confident that if we don't get the shooters, then at the very least we will get their safe house and whatever evidence is in it. No shooters, but the house and evidence, and for that he wants two-and-half grand.

"The tout also says the trail ends at Declan Meechan's door but it's going to take time before we're in a position to chap it."

"Go on, Gus," instructed Tomachek.

Thoroughgood obliged.

"I left him about an hour back and I'm convinced he's for real. Ross McNab used to run him, so he's registered with the CHIS boys and the turns he has put up in the past will all be on record. I know that Ross and he enjoyed a working relationship that was very fruitful for McNab.

"If you don't mind, gaffer, I'd rather run him myself and see what we can do, and we can square it all with the CHIS Unit afterwards."

Thoroughgood quickly added:

"Anyway boss, he's made it clear he wants to deal with me and me only."

It was a necessary lie, thought Thoroughgood, as the last thing he wanted was to lose control of Morse and, more importantly, the information he hoped would help him land Meechan. Taking Tomachek's silence as approval, he continued:

"He wants me to call him back at ten p.m. with the green light. That's it all, boss."

"Fuck me," was the two-word exclamation from Tomachek's end.

The Detective Superintendent was never one to let himself get carried away, and he was soon focussing on the job at hand:

"What I'll have to do now is call the chief. Before that, I need to make a call to Pitt Street, and the Force Intelligence Bureau; they should have all of your informant's previous turns on record. Hopefully they'll be good quality, because that'll strengthen my hand with the chief constable. But Salmond is desperate, and it probably won't take too much to convince him to put the money up and run with it."

"After all, as we both know, Gus, he wants his knighthood and the way things are going, if we don't make a breakthrough soon that will be up shit creek in no time. So what's the informant's handle?"

"Morse," replied the DS.

"Very good, Gussy boy! I know you have a sense of humour but that's taking it a bit far," said Tomachek.

"That's it, boss, and you can blame McNab. The wee man just said to me tonight he wanted to stick with it. You not a Morse fan? I thought he would have appealed to a copper of your generation!"

Tomachek let out a chortle.

"That's enough of your cheek, pup. Time is marching on and I have calls to make. It's nine-forty now, and you say you need to call your man back by ten p.m.?"

Thoroughgood confirmed that was the case.

"Right, I have fifteen minutes to check Morse's credentials. But before I go putting my arse out the window on this one, I think I'll hold off calling the chief till we have all the information in place. You are one hundred per cent on it?" Tomachek demanded.

"Yes, boss. I believe it's a runner all right. The wee man is definitely for real."

"Okay then, I'll speak with you in fifteen minutes," and with that the call was over and the game, Thoroughgood hoped, afoot.

He put down his phone and stood up, crossing to his window and staring out at nothing in particular. The dark shapes of the surrounding tenements were grey and forbidding. The combination of the wind and rain rattled and shook the frame of his lounge window in an intimidating combination. Thoroughgood walked over to his CD player and took a look through his discs.

Ah, Blondie. 'Parallel Lines,' aye, Debbie Harry's finest hour, he thought and slipped the digitally re-mastered classic into the CD player.

Pacing the carpet floor, the DS looked at the clock on the mantelpiece: nine-fifty. His phone went off:

"Gus, it's a goer," said Tomachek. "After I'd checked some of the turns your man put up for McNab, it's a pretty compelling case."

"Well, I'll give Morse a call the minute you are through, boss. From what he says he'll speak to whoever it is he's got on the inside and call me back as near to midnight as he can. Hopefully I'll be on the blower to you again before one a.m. and with a bit of luck it will be lift-off," said Thoroughgood.

"All right, Gus. So I suppose I'd better stay off the hard stuff. Just make sure you call me the minute you have something. Oh, and Gus, you don't need me to tell you that if this comes off it will be a big boost to your career," added Tomachek benevolently.

Thoroughgood still had to deliver the sting in the tail:

"There's just one thing more, gaffer, before you go," he intoned.

"Yes Gus, why do I get the feeling I am not going to like this?" was Tomachek's wary reply.

"As you know, boss, this is an E Division enquiry and one being run by DCI Henry Farrell. Ultimately, you know how badly I want Meechan. If everything goes to plan and Morse's information leads to apprehensions, then these captures could provide crucial information in that respect.

"I want you to see what you can do to convince the bosses in the East that I can get access to any 'bodies' we may get. I know Farrell isn't going to like that, you know we don't exactly get along, but I don't see him doing much to move the enquiry on. So if my tout provides the information that helps us forward then I think my request is reasonable."

"You know I have no time for that tosser Farrell, so I'll do what I can for you, son. But it's really in the hands of the East brass. However, I'll see what I can do to bring some pressure to bear further up the tree. That's all I can promise for now, let's leave it there and see where we are after you've spoken to Morse."

"Fair enough, boss," said Thoroughgood, and hung up.

No point hanging about, thought the DS, and lifted the phone once more, punching in the numbers of Morse's mobile.

"It's me,' said Morse's voice at the other end. "Are you ready for this?"

"You've got my undivided attention," admitted Thoroughgood.

"There are four of them, and they headed to the Trossachs after both hits on the Browns were done. I don't have the exact location, but the safe house they are using is somewhere close to Loch Ard. It shouldn't be too difficult to find; after all, it's not as if there are hundreds of them. You don't need me to confirm they're all armed. They split up earlier tonight to dump one of the vehicles used on the second hit at the car showroom. So, at the moment, there are two in the farmhouse and two on the way back," revealed Morse.

"A farmhouse near Loch Ard in the Trossachs does cause a bit of a complication, and I don't mean because we don't have the exact locus," admitted the detective.

"That's outside our area and in Central Scotland territory. They aren't going to be too happy if we go stomping all over their patch, especially if a firearms incident kicks off. More importantly, have you got any identities for our four shooters?" asked the DS.

"What do you think? Are the names Frankie Brennan and Gaz Reid familiar to you, detective?" asked Morse.

"Nasty bastards both," admitted Thoroughgood, "But what about the other two?"

"They're both kids. One is called Jarvis and the other Simms, I don't know any more than that. But the vehicle you are looking for is a dark blue Cavalier."

"Anything else I need to know?" asked Thoroughgood.

"Just that if you want to be sure of getting them, you need to move now. They'll be gone by dawn," said Morse.

"Now I've provided the information and if it's acted upon you will get your 'bodies,' as you like to call them. If you don't mind, I'm going to get some sleep.

Can I expect a call from you at, say, one p.m. today, Mr Thoroughgood?"

"Yeah, I'll do that; say your prayers, Morse."

The DS ended the call. His mind raced. The location of the farmhouse in the beautiful wilds of the Trossachs was a definite problem.

Tomachek was far from happy with developments.

"This is all getting a bit messy, Gus. I would need to call the chief and probably the ACC Crime, and then we need to make contact with the country bumpkins at Central Scotland polis; as you say, that's all going to take several hours. On the other hand, how can I authorise you and Hardie to head out into the wilderness to suss out a four-man gang, all armed to the teeth, who have just gunned down three males in cold blood?

"But what I don't know doesn't hurt me. If you and Hardie were to act on a tip off from an informant, there might be mitigating circumstances.

"Anyway, the less I know the better until you phone me at, say, ten thirty this morning. But whatever you do, just be careful. We haven't had a police officer killed since the nineties: I don't want your blood on my conscience. Now forget this conversation ever happened and do what you have to do, Gus, and good luck son."

"Cheers, gaffer."

"Yeeeeeees!" was the reply from Kenny Hardie's bedroom phone when Thoroughgood interrupted his slumbers at twelve forty-five a.m. As the DS had known, after the usual bout of cursing and moaning that Thoroughgood was putting his marriage on the line again, the old boy would soon be ready to rumble.

Thirty minutes later Thoroughgood picked up his portly partner from his semi-detached in Knightswood. Thoroughgood could never understand why his mate had remained in an area the DS had always viewed as dodgy, a belief that was only reinforced when Hardie's home had been tanned two Christmases back and emptied of a house full of presents. Both Hardie's kids were grown up, one at university in the US, the other working full-time; with the mortgage paid up it seemed a peculiar choice to stay in an area that was far from the traditional middle-class suburbs usually chosen by cops of his vintage.

When Hardie jumped into the RX-8, the DS moved into auto-pilot as he briefed his sidekick on the content of a night spent constantly on the blower. While Hardie expressed reservations, he knew full well that the quality of the turn and the lack of time meant something had to be done. As Thoroughgood had pointed out, if they didn't make any arrests tonight, at the very least they would be able to locate the safe house, and a future surveillance operation might well lead to bodies.

There was only one real problem concerning Hardie as the RX-8 wound its way out of Glasgow and passed Milngavie Reservoir:

"Just how are we going to find this farmhouse in the pitch-black?"

Thoroughgood had been waiting for the question.

"According to Morse it's on the north side of Loch Ard. There's only the one road in, so basically it's a case of working out which farmhouse it is from a choice of maybe half a dozen. We have one clue in that there will be a dark blue Cavalier parked outside."

"Mmm, shouldn't be that difficult then. But, it's gonna be a long cold night. You bring a Thermos with coffee or anything?'

With a wink and a nod of his head backwards, Thoroughgood said:

"Look in the back seat, faither."

16

THE SMOOTH purring of the RX-8's Renesis rotary engine was the only noise that punctured the silence as the two detectives made their journey of discovery. Loch Ard was around fifty minutes from the outskirts of Glasgow, but at one-thirty a.m. on a Saturday morning traffic was a non-issue.

Loch Ard was situated in the foothills of Ben Lomond, dominated by its imposing presence which loomed large, high above. As they approached the area known as the Great Forest of Loch Ard the RX-8 slowed to a crawl. Thoroughgood had opted to take his own vehicle on this unofficial spying mission, partly because the diesel engines of the CID pool cars would have alerted any self-respecting criminal to the presence of cops.

Given the isolated nature of the terrain they were now exploring, the only other alternative was really a four-by-four. With Loch Ard being a tourist spot, Thoroughgood felt his own vehicle was more likely to be taken for one of the holidaymakers who had chalets on the loch-side.

Noticing a passing place in the road looming ahead, he decided this was the end of the road in car terms. The DS opened his boot, and Hardie had to admit he was impressed by his gaffer's forward planning. The Maglite police torch was, naturally, present. But Thoroughgood then pulled out a rucksack which contained waterproof leggings, woollen bob hats, a powerful zoom lens camera and nightsight binoculars.

More important, thought Hardie, were the selection of cheese and ham sandwiches, earning Thoroughgood a thumbs-up from his mate.

Thoroughgood believed the farmhouse they were looking for was in the shadow of Edinample Castle, on the south side of the loch. As the two detectives began to make their way on foot along the loch road, he started to fill Hardie in on its history. The castle had been built by "Black" Duncan Campbell of Glenorchy in the sixteenth century.

Campbell, so legend had it, demanded the builder put a tower on the top from which he could enjoy a commanding view of the loch and the local area. The builder failed to do so, and when he tried to convince Black Duncan that the view was just fine from the roof, Campbell pushed him off the top and so avoided payment. From that day the ghost of the murdered builder was reputed to haunt Edinample.

"A bloody ghost story to put me at my ease, just what the fuckin' doctor ordered," moaned the DC.

"Just trying to paint a picture for you," said Thoroughgood. "It's a bonus for us that the farmhouse is near the castle, as it certainly cuts down on the process of elimination. If we sight the blue Cavvy, then bingo."

"How long is the hike gonnae last anyway?" demanded Hardie.

"Well, Loch Ard is only four klicks long by two wide. I reckon we're starting to turn onto the south side now so I would say maybe another ten minutes or so. Anyway, what are you complaining about? Fresh air, beautiful countryside and it's your weekend off, what's the problem?"

"I'll tell you what the bleedin' problem is, it's pitch bloody dark, I'm frozen and you dragged me out the warmth of my bed on some fool's errand that could easily get us both killed. That's what's the fuckin' matter," growled Hardie.

It was then the detectives heard the sound of a car engine slowly approaching and, with a glance between the two, they headed off the road and behind a nearby knot of pine trees.

As the vehicle drew close, it proved to be a dark-coloured, possibly navy blue, Cavalier, registration mark F189 JUS.

"Chances are that's our motor, two up if I'm not mistaken," said the DS.

Hardie agreed. "Aye, I don't see it being an innocent coincidence; let's hope we're not far away from its destination."

Sure enough, about a quarter of a mile down the lochside, there was a fork in the road. Up the hill to the right loomed Edinample Castle while about five hundred yards down to the left was situated a whitewashed farm steading, and parked outside was the Cavalier.

The detectives continued down the track for about two hundred and fifty yards, all the time training their eyes on the front door of the steading. Lights were on in two of the ground-level windows. The Cavalier was parked in a yard with a couple of outhouses, which Thoroughgood thought may have been used for housing hens, while there also appeared to be a pigsty. With the steading almost on the banks of Loch Ard, there was plenty of tree cover.

The detectives moved into the fields to the right of the track and headed down towards a pocket of birches almost twenty feet from the Cavalier and the steading's front door.

Thoroughgood and Hardie took up crouching positions while they laid out the plastic sheeting the DS had also brought with him, and then assumed a prone position. Thoroughgood took the night-sight binoculars while Hardie had the zoom lens camera to hand. They waited in the knowledge that their unauthorised observation operation was breaking almost every dictate of the Force rules governing surveillance of suspects.

After a further ten minutes, with his watch showing it was now five to two, Hardie, growing cold and impatient, signalled to his gaffer he was going to open the Thermos for some much-needed warmth and refreshment.

Just then the steading's stout wooden door opened, and out stepped the hulking figure of the brute the two detectives knew to be Frankie Brennan. Immediately behind him appeared a second male, considerably slighter than the six-foot-five-inch Brennan. The second male, Thoroughgood guestimated, was perhaps around the five-foot-seven-inch mark, sporting a white baseball cap with what appeared to be a black Nike tick on it.

Thoroughgood immediately whispered to his mate:

"That's one of the fuckers who tried to ram me off the Kingston Bridge. He had a white baseball cap with the black Nike swish. I'll bet you it was the pair of them. Bastards."

Brennan made his way to the Cavalier's boot, opening it before bringing out a canvas-wrapped bundle which he handed to baseball cap, who immediately returned inside the farmhouse. Then Brennan removed a huge petrol canister which led to both detectives exchanging a knowing glance; shortly afterwards the giant followed his mate back inside.

Both had been captured by Hardie on the special

police surveillance zoom lens that provided pictures of superb clarity in conditions of pitch darkness. This time it was Hardie who broke the silence:

"What now, boss? We've got a definite ID on Brennan, and the snaps I got of the other male may help us make him. But you don't have to be a rocket scientist to work out the canvas bag contained the shooters and the petrol canister was the one that covered old man Brown at the bookies. So here we are, two in the morning, miles from nowhere, unarmed, no back-up, takin' observations on a farmhouse that possibly has four highly armed killers inside. Come on, gaffer, what's your call?"

Thoroughgood replied, "I told you, Tomachek warned me that our brief was only to house the suspects, try and get an ident on them if possible, and then get home safe and sound. I'm not gonnae be calling him at two a.m. to provide a report when it can wait 'til ten a.m. as he requested. But we could do with getting all the guys on film."

Hardie, whose spirits had been soaring at the thought of packing up and heading home to the warmth of his bed, now experienced a sinking feeling in his gut.

"With respect, gaffer, just how the fuck are we gonnae be doin' that?"

"We need some kind of diversion to draw them out. Pass me a coffee and a sandwich, this is something we can't be rushing into," Thoroughgood attempted to reassure.

"Yer chuffin' right there, Gus."

Although they had come dressed for a long and cold night's open air surveillance work, the damp of their lochside vigil had begun to penetrate into the very core of their beings. Even thermal gloves could only keep frozen, motionless digits warm for so long.

The lazy spirals of smoke billowing out of the steading's chimney indicated, along with the light from the main room, that the inhabitants were still enjoying the heat of the hearth, and after sporadic bouts of whispered conversation a semblance of a plan was hatched.

Thoroughgood suggested: "We need to check the two outhouses and see if there are any ladders kickin' about, or anything that would help us up on the roof. It's not as if it's any great height. But if I'm going to get onto it and block the chimney before they're alerted then it's got to be bloody quiet. So you take the pigsty and I'll check the other hut and see what we come up with, then we'll meet back here in ten minutes. That's 2.45 a.m.," Thoroughgood suggested.

Every footstep felt like it was magnified one hundred-fold, as it echoed into the night. While the search for ladders proved fruitless, the detectives were able to uncover items which would make their diversion possible. An empty keg and a giant fork Hardie found pitched into a pile of decayed hay meant the plan could be carried out.

"Okay," said Thoroughgood, "The chimney is situated towards the back of the main room and I walked round the perimeter when I was over at the byre; fortunately, the only door is the one at the front next to the Cavalier. So you'll need to get the barrel round the back. I'd say the roof is ten foot off the ground, and the chimney another five feet up on the roof.

"If you can get close enough to the chimney without actually climbing onto the roof, you can hopefully thatch the top of it with the hay and block the smoke in. Give it a couple of minutes, and they will all be chokin' and will come out the front. Then I can get the snaps taken and it's a case of an RV back at the Mazda ASAP. That all crystal?"

"Fair enough, gaffer. Is the fork long enough to get at the chimney? 'Cos I had a look at the roof from the henhouse side, and I'd say the minute any weight is on it I'll be right bleedin'through it."

"That's what's made my mind up on you takin' care of the chimney. You aren't going to need to climb onto the roof, and by doing it this way you're going to get an extra couple of minutes grace to get tae. Know what I mean?

"It's going take me a couple of minutes to get all the shots I need of the gang, and then I'm going to have to find a way through the woods to get back to the Mazda. I'd say my chances of doing that are better than yours, with respect, old friend!"

With that, Thoroughgood reached into his pocket and tossed Hardie the car keys.

"I reckon we can do it okay. But all this chat is gettin' us nowhere fast. If you're okay with it, on you go round the back. Just take care, faither, and I'll see you back at the Mazda."

"Okay gaffer, just remember a reel of poxy snaps isn't worth your life. I'll have the RX-8 purring for you, facing home for Glasgow. Don't be late."

And with that, Hardie made his way round the back of the steading, armed with the pitchfork. Thoroughgood strapped the rucksack over his shoulders, checked the camera was ready and placed the solid steel Maglite torch at his side. A moment passed and Thoroughgood thought he heard some kind of scraping coming from the back of the steading, but there was no reaction from within. It was nearly three a.m. and the inhabitants had probably been drinking for the best part of two hours.

Still the smoke kept streaming out of the chimney. Gradually, it seemed to reduce until all but a trickle was evaporating into the night air. His eyes straining into the night sky, Thoroughgood thanked God there was no full moon lighting up the whole yard like the floodlights of his beloved Firhill shining down on the Jags.

Momentarily his thoughts strayed to Thistle's home game with Airdrie later that day, when the door burst open and the giant figure of Frankie Brennan rushed out, coughing, spluttering and swearing in anger.

Thoroughgood immediately took another couple of snaps of the giant to make sure his identity was caught on camera. Next out was White Baseball Cap, who helpfully lifted his lid to allow the DS a clear shot of a podgy, unremarkable face topped with short dark hair.

The smoke was fairly billowing out of the steading by the time the third and fourth males burst out; they were notably younger, perhaps even in their teens.

Thoroughgood now had all four on camera, but curiosity was taking a grip on him and he hovered to see how the drama would unfold. Would the gang assume they had been rumbled or would they take a more practical approach to the mishap that had brought an end to their little reverie?

Thoroughgood refocussed his gaze on the front of the steading. The monstrous Brennan was, as he expected, taking control of proceedings. Pointing at White Baseball Cap, Brennan sent him round the back with one of the teenagers; then he gestured to the second kid to come closer.

Thoroughgood, less than twenty feet away, easily overheard Brennan's instructions:

"Right Chico, we're gonnae split up and take one of the outhouses apiece. You find anything, shout me. If naw, meet me back here when we're finished and then we'll make a sweep around the building. Fuckin' move, will ye!"

Thoroughgood wanted to wait until the two males sent round the back had returned. If they came back and had seen nothing untoward then the chances were the gang would be none the wiser until they got up on the roof and checked the chimney. If Hardie had been more interested in getting off his mark than concealing his tracks then they had a problem and, more imminently, he himself would have to be on his way sharpish.

Thoroughgood tried to paint a mental picture of the terrain that had led him from the roadway where the Mazda was parked to the steading. Brennan and shellsuit soon returned to the front of the farmhouse, and a moment or so later they were joined by Baseball Cap and his teenage crony.

Thoroughgood clearly heard mention of the words "barrel and fork" while Brennan could be heard confirming that the hay in one of the outhouses had been disturbed. Brennan was soon barking orders:

"Right Simms, get up on the roof and unblock that fuckin' chimney. Gaz and Chico, you're comin' with me. I don't like the look of this, I think we might have had company. We need to split up and take a look around just in case anyone is hangin' about who shouldnae be. You get a hawd of anythin' you bring the fucker to me," growled Brennan.

Time to get going, thought Thoroughgood with a smile. Useful though, he thought, the little snatches of conversation he'd heard. The mention of the names Gaz, Chico and Simms were all very helpful, thought the DS.

The hulking figure of the sour-faced Brennan reached inside his Berghaus and removed the sawn-off shotgun from inside. He turned round and started to pace towards the knot of birch trees hiding Thoroughgood.

But Thoroughgood was off. He had already scouted out an escape route for the worst case scenario now unfolding, and he warmed himself with the mental promise of the verbal roasting he was going to give Hardie for being careless enough to tip the gang off that they were not alone.

Thoroughgood's plan was to make his way back along the loch shore-line, just keeping within the tree cover that conveniently hugged the banks. He reckoned if he did that for about five hundred yards or so, then cut up to his right through the woods, he would come into pastureland just before the main road that had brought him and Hardie into the Forest of Loch Ard.

There was no way he could use the Maglite to illuminate his progress and in the dark, in a wooded area, he was likely to find himself stepping on debris, twigs and fallen branches, all of which would give his pursuers plenty of warning as to the progress of their quarry.

That thought, the DS admitted to himself, was far from comforting, especially given the savage rage which had lit up Brennan's face when he had been informed of the evidence pointing to intruders.

Thoroughgood had to focus all his concentration in making his way through the wood without alerting his pursuers, and that was proving no easy thing to do. His hopes of escape were not helped by the fact that Baseball Cap was wielding a torch in a sweeping arc, lighting up the ground ten to fifteen feet in front of him. Thoroughgood took a quick look back over his shoulder as he heard a curse, and saw that the progress of the three silhouettes pursuing him had come to a temporary stop amid a volley of profanity.

"It's me fuckin' ankle. I never saw the branch. I cannae move it."

Shellsuit had come a cropper. While Baseball Cap shone his torch down on his fallen mate, Brennan punched in his mobile and raised it to his ear.

You'll be fuckin' lucky getting a signal here mate, thought Thoroughgood.

But Brennan was soon barking orders down his mobile:

"Right Simms, what's the score with the chimney? Hay stuffed down the top, fuck, so it was company. Will you shut the fuck up and listen? Chico's fallen over a branch in the wood, about a hundred and fifty yards along the shoreline. Get yer arse along here and pick him up and return to the farmhoose. Then just sit tight 'til I bell ye. We have the scent all right."

Brennan turned round and with a theatrical sweep of his massive right arm he stared out into the wood and shouted,

"Aye, the hounds are well on to the fox trail, you could say."

The giant looked down:

"Look Chico, you prop yersel' up against the tree here and Simmy will be along for ye in five minutes. Use yer lighter to flash him in. Now me and Gaz have got to go and find our uninvited guests," he said before adding with a menacing chuckle in his soft but somehow harsh Irish brogue, "and I fuckin' hate gatecrashers."

17

HIS PURSUERS only thirty feet away, Thoroughgood felt a chill surge through his body but he had no time to linger. Using the night-sight on his binoculars, he took a glance through the wood and along the lochside to make out a path that would be less challenging in the density of scrub and trees. His assessment was interrupted when he heard a crashing from the undergrowth behind him and noticed the spherical glow of torchlight on a tree to his right. Thoroughgood toyed with the possibility of making his way down onto the shore. That could only be done if he put enough distance between himself and his pursuers, but he would be breaking cover and then it would be a straightforward foot chase and stamina test.

Thoroughgood was unperturbed; a more than decent squash player in the West of Scotland First Division, he fancied his chances on foot against any ned. Of greater concern if he took that option was the mix of pebble and shingle on the shoreline, an even more precarious footing than the grassy banks underfoot in the wood. One misplaced step and he wouldn't stand a chance. The voice in his head warned, Stay where you are and keep to the cover.

He continued to make his way in and out of the trees, but as he stopped to check on his pursuers' progress Thoroughgood noticed Brennan and his mate had split up. The second male, with the torch, was now moving off to the right and it looked like he was going to try and cut Thoroughgood's escape route to the road, while Brennan was now hugging the very edge of the woods just above the shoreline.

Thoroughgood estimated that he had been going for about four hundred yards or so, and it was time to start striking up in the direction of the road. The gap had not been significantly closed, but the DS knew, if he wasted time on a ninety-degree dog leg forced on him by the rapidly shortening stretch of available woodland, he ran the risk of being intercepted by Baseball Cap. Picking his footing as carefully as he could, while trying not to sacrifice any momentum, Thoroughgood started down into a gully and then disaster struck.

The bank descending into the dip was steeper than he had anticipated, and the combination of total darkness and slippery underfoot conditions caused by recent flooding made for treacherous ground. Thoroughgood was attempting to use his stronger right foot to keep the brakes on his descent when it gave way and he landed on his back, skiting down into the depths of the gully, a drop of maybe fifteen feet.

The crash was immediately picked up on by Brennan and his sidekick Gaz Reid. Thoroughgood saw the telltale sweep of torchlight slicing through the surrounding trees. He was definitely winded, but as he checked his right ankle, he breathed a sigh of relief, there was no damage. Putting pressure on it, he suffered some discomfort but nothing to stop him moving.

A dozen feet to his right he noticed movement, and spotted Baseball Cap coming into the gully from the side. Immediately Thoroughgood ducked behind the nearest tree, just as the torch shone into the bottom of the gully where he had been lying prone moments earlier.

Brennan's voice, coming from behind him and still a way off boomed:

"You okay Gaz?"

"Aye, ah'm doon in the brae thirty feet in front of you. Someone's had a fall by the look of it. I don't think I'm far off them …"

Thoroughgood slammed the Maglite down with as much power as he could render, and heard a crunch as it impacted on Gaz Reid's skull. Reid crumpled to the ground, taking a savage knee in the privates as he did so.

"That'll teach you to try and run me into the Clyde, you little arsewipe," spat Thoroughgood.

Reid was out cold and Thoroughgood quickly rifled his pockets to see if there was anything useful inside.

Nice, thought the detective when he uncovered a particularly wicked six-inch flick-knife tucked inside the waistband of Reid's trousers. He had no time to waste and, grabbing his pursuer's torch, he quickly started making his way up the far side of the gulley just as Brennan entered from the other side.

Thoroughgood reassured himself that the odds had been evened up now Brennan was no longer able to shed any light on his movements.

The DS began to build up some speed as he moved away from the forest, which was beginning to thin out as he approached the meadowland flanking the main road.

An enraged shout pierced the night and the giant's voice filled the night air:

"Whoever you are I'll find you, track you down and kill ye. Upon my wean's soul I will."

Obviously Brennan had located his fallen comrade.

Thoroughgood briefly found himself nursing concerns over the crunch which had emanated from Reid's skull when the solid mass of the Maglite had smacked into it. He immediately dismissed them. For years he had found the Maglite plenty more effective than the police issue batons. Even now that Strathclyde police were using telescopic batons, the solid reassurance of the Maglite and the years of trust built on the consistently effective results of its wielding, made it Thoroughgood's preferred hand weapon.

Making his way up through the meadow, Thoroughgood jumped the fence and glanced down the road to the flashing headlights of the RX-8. Hardie was already installed in the driving seat and the veteran detective gunned the engine, which drew a thumbs-up from Thoroughgood.

The DS leaned on the fence and looked back down the meadow into the darkness. Gradually, a shadow started to merge into the solid mass of Brennan's huge frame as the giant strode through the field. Thoroughgood put the nightsight to his eyes and saw with perfect clarity in the tarry blackness, the giant advancing with the sawn-off shotgun held waist-high in front of him. There was, he estimated, maybe fifty feet and closing between them.

Thoroughgood switched the full beam of the powerful Maglite on Brennan's features. He shouted:

"Listen to me Brennan, you fucker. I hope your friend has one sore head; maybe that might make you think twice about trying to ram me off the Kingston Bridge. You tell your boss the net is closing."

Brennan continued walking, his giant strides eating up the ground, and then the night air was shattered by the sound of his discharging sawn-off. The woodwork in the fencing propping up Thoroughgood was splintered by the spray of its pellets. The DS quickly dived to his right, rolled and then got back on his feet before sprinting along the road to the RX-8, which he was delighted to see Hardie had turned round and was now facing their only escape route.

Thoroughgood could hear the engine of another vehicle, and as he reached for the Rex's passenger door he saw Brennan jump into the front of what appeared to be the blue Cavalier that had been parked outside the farmhouse.

"Okay faither, let's get a fuckin' move on, eh?" demanded Thoroughgood.

Hardie, unused to the highly responsive engine of the Rex, overdid the accelerator in his desire to tear off, and the RX-8 choked on the surge of fuel caused by his heavy-footed efforts and stalled.

"For fuck's sake, what's the matter?" groaned the burly detective.

"You idiot, you've flooded it. We are not talking about your bog standard sports car here, this engine is sensitive. You tickle the accelerator, not flatten it to the floor. You've drowned her. Get out, we're swapping," raged the DS.

Thoroughgood jumped out the passenger door and sprinted round the bonnet, opening the driver's door before Hardie had barely undone his seatbelt.

"Come on man, they're nearly on us," muttered Thoroughgood with a hint of panic in his voice, caused by the sound of the Cavalier shifting through its gears as it closed. With the aid of his colleague's clawing hands, Hardie managed to get out of the low-sprung sports car and made his way as quickly as possible to the passenger side. By the time he had got there, Thoroughgood was already trying to tease the RX-8's engine into action.

At last the engine responded and Hardie managed to park himself in the passenger seat although the door remained open. As he reached out to pull it closed, the sound of metal on metal and the bright spark of a bullet catching the inside of the door warned the detectives that time and distance were fast running out for them.

"Close that fuckin' door, will you?" screamed Thoroughgood.

And they were off. Shifting through the gears to bring the coupé's lightning acceleration was not an option, the road was just too tight and bendy, but Thoroughgood knew he had to put some kind of distance between the two vehicles or risk having both Hardie and himself shot to pieces or, even worse, his pride and joy, the Rex, pockmarked by bullet holes.

The Cavalier remained dangerously close to the RX-8, hovering on its left shoulder as the two vehicles turned into main street Aberfoyle and another shot rang out, this time smashing into a postbox five feet to Thoroughgood's right. He glanced in his rear view and saw that Brennan, like some bizarre outsized cartoon character, was shoehorned into the front passenger seat with the youngster. The DS had no worries about being able to outdrive any teenager, even one like Simms, who had been one of the most prolific juvenile car thieves in the city in recent years. What worried Thoroughgood was the handgun Brennan kept firing off from the passenger side.

Brennan, the type of man who would leave a badly injured mate lying unconscious in a wood to gain revenge, undoubtedly had a psychopathic intent. Still, as the RX-8 surged out of Aberfoyle, Thoroughgood took the pressure off the accelerator and let the Rex slow.

"You fuckin' mad? How many times do you want to get shot at in the one night?" screamed Hardie.

Thoroughgood's eyes and his attention were fully engaged by events in his rearview. The RX-8 was now going back down the gears and crawling in first as the Cavalier surged forward. He lowered his electric window and stuck out his right arm before raising his middle finger in the time-honoured traditional insult.

At last he shifted through the gears into third, 189 bhp surging through the Rex as it snaked along the A821 on the way back to Glasgow. The Cavalier, a moment before only twenty-five feet away, soon faded into the background. For the first time that night, Thoroughgood found himself starting to relax. Their escape complete, he began to have some fun over Hardie's clumsy getaway attempt.

"Fuck's sake faither, you sure you've passed your driving test? And you wonder why I'm not falling over myself to let you drive the Rex? For a minute back there I thought you'd got stuck in the driver's seat!" grinned Thoroughgood.

Hardie was still shaken by the events of the last few moments.

"These bloody bucket seats are murder tae get oot of. With my dodgy hip it's like getting sucked into a bucket of bleedin' sand. Anyway, now we're on the way back home, are you going to tell me exactly what happened back there before the Wacky Races? I heard the sawnoff getting discharged, you okay?"

"Fuckin' wonderful, what do you think?" answered Thoroughgood. "Never mind that, what the bleeding hell were you doing leaving the barrel and the fork out for Brennan and his boys to work out they were being watched?"

Hardie was clearly uncomfortable with his negligence.

"Ah, that. Well to be truthful, I slipped and fell off the barrel and when I heard the door opening I thought the noise had alerted them so I just got off the mark."

Thoroughgood shook his head and met Hardie's explanation with an incredulous:

"Sham-bloody-bolic."

Thoroughgood's alarm went off at nine twenty-five and, after taking a moment to come round, he headed for the shower. Feeling lightheaded, like he had just come off a nightshift and been woken up in the middle of his sleep, the DS wondered if the previous hours' events had all been a dream. The warm jets of the shower burned into his back, gradually helping to relax the knots in his shoulders and down his spine, which felt like it had a piece of plyboard inserted in it. He soon had coffee rustled up and rapped Hardie's door before entering.

"Rise and shine Schumacher!" quipped Thoroughgood, and got a "Fuck off" from somewhere under the duvet.

Leaving Hardie to come to, he headed back for the kitchen and, after devouring a slice of toast, called Tomachek.

"All right, so let me get this. You've been shot at half a dozen times, done God knows what kind of damage to one of their men, and then been involved in a high-speed car chase through Aberfoyle with more lead flying? Balls and buggery, for fuck's sake Thoroughgood, I asked you to play it safe and just concentrate on getting them all on camera.

"Now they know who we are, and more importantly, that we know who they are. That's a big plus. It's not as though I can get on the blower to Central Scotland polis and let them know two of our officers caused a spot of bother on their patch in the middle of the night involving a running gun battle and high speed car chase through Sleepy fuckin' Hollow."

"Sorry sir," was the best Thoroughgood could come up with before attempting some mollification.

"At least we'll be able to make every one of them, and surely a Section Fourteen shot would be a good move with two of them kids."

"Aye aye, I know all that but we have no evidence, man. It's not as if I can have the house searched when we weren't even supposed to have been there. I just hope they don't go making a complaint to Central Scotland polis!" said Tomachek with some levity at last creeping into his voice.

"No boss."

Thoroughgood knew better than to try and hijack a rant from his superior. The wheels of his mind continuing to turn, Tomachek continued to share his assessment of precisely where last night's events had left them.

"So, we know we have good-quality film of four murder suspects which we didn't previously have. The circumstantial side of things is certainly pointing strongly to them all being up to their necks in it, but none of that is going to be admissible in court.

"Aye, and I would imagine yer man Morse is going to be pretty pissed that we have blown their safe house but got no arrests to show for it. You'll need to explain the way things are when it comes to operating outside of our turf. But don't worry on that front, Gus. Morse will get paid; I'm sure we could squeeze a couple of thousand out the kitty for him." Tomachek took a breath.

"Right, get IB to sort the pics and then I want them delivered on disc to Henry Farrell. He will Section

Fourteen 'em all right, if I have my way with it. The fact that two of the gang were rookies is just too good an opportunity to miss. Och well, you and Hardie are both home safe and sound and we have something that will cheer up the chief."

Thoroughgood had another call to make: Morse. Another slice of toast and a fresh coffee were badly needed, but before he could he rise from the kitchen table he was startled by an apparition now in front of him and framed inside the kitchen doorway.

There, in his full Seventies glory, was Kenny Hardie, resplendent in thick gold rope necklace, medallion dangling on the end, vest trailing down over tight red briefs and what appeared to be last night's pair of odd socks still on his feet.

"Jeez," said Thoroughgood, with a wink, "lookin' at you makes me feel a million dollars!"

18

"MR THOROUGHGOOD, a successful night's work, I trust?" enquired Morse's clipped tones.

"I'm not going to bullshit you, Morse, the answer to that one is a bit of yes and a bit of the other," admitted Thoroughgood.

Silence from the other end of the mobile, then Morse said:

"Why don't I like the sound of that? Surely you found my information to be accurate?"

"There was no problem with that. We found the farmhouse, no problem, and when we were making our way in on foot the Cavalier passed us, so we couldn't have asked for much more."

Thoroughgood then launched into a full Lock, Stock and Two Smoking Barrels recount of the night's action.

The DS had been describing how he had dealt with Baseball Cap, who he thought Brennan had called Gaz Reid, when his account was interrupted by the informant. Morse had quizzed the detective on that particular part of his story to such an extent that Thoroughgood began to feel like he was under interrogation.

Morse fired off a whole batch of questions, asking for a rough physical description of Baseball Cap which, because of the darkness of the forest, was impossible to give. The tout wanted to know just where he had landed the Maglite on Reid, and the extent of the damage Thoroughgood had done. Such was Morse's appetite for information on his battle with Baseball Cap that Thoroughgood challenged Morse on the reasons behind his questioning.

"Look Morse, what the fuck is goin' on here? Maybe I should have left this bit out 'cos to be quite frank, the way I clocked him and the noise of the impact, he could well have a fractured skull, hopefully no worse. So pardon me if I'm a bit fuckin' touchy about it, but why do you want to know every little detail?"

"Because, Mr Thoroughgood, and this must remain between you and me, Gaz Reid is my man on the inside."

"Ah," was all Thoroughgood could manage by way of a reply.

"If you've done Reid in then we may have a real problem with our information flow," admitted Morse.

Thoroughgood could not help curiosity getting the better of him, and before he knew it the question was popping out of his mouth:

"So how the fuck did you get to know Reid?"

"Like I said, that will have to keep for when you hand over the money. But if you value the working relationship we are building here you will keep that piece of information between us," instructed Morse.

Thoroughgood lied to get off the line and end a difficult call he had had his fill of:

"Listen, wee man, I gotta go. I'm absolutely knackered and I think I've got the flu comin' on after my night out rolling about the freezing ground in the middle of nowhere. You have a good weekend."

"Likewise, Detective Sergeant," was the distinctly unimpressed reply.

Once again Morse had knocked the DS off balance. How the fuck had he managed to get one of the gang on side? More importantly, had the blow he'd landed with the Maglite meant the source of information would be stopped either temporarily or permanently?

By the time he'd completed his call to Morse, Hardie had managed to pour himself into his clothes. Thoroughgood quickly brought his number two up to speed with the details of the call, including the sidebar about Gaz Reid.

Hardie was impressed, but less so when his gaffer asked him to hotfoot the surveillance camera into Force HQ, Pitt Street, so that the pictures of the gang could be put on disc for Tomachek.

"Come on, gaffer, I'm just off the blower to the missus and she's naw happy. That's nearly eleven and by the time I get into Disneyland and back to Knightswood I'll be late for lunch, and that will mean a major row after last night," groaned Hardie before adding:

"Anyway, gaffer, what's to stop you?"

Thoroughgood smiled. "Well, you may remember I have a coffee date down at Tinderbox in roughly half an hour."

"Och aye, Sara the civil servant, naw we couldnae have you missing out on that one, not after all the trouble you've gone to with the speed datin'!" A huge smile washed over Hardie's ruddy chops.

"Consider the camera delivered, gaffer. In fact I'll just get my jacket and get tae. You'll be wantin' to psych yourself up for your big date, no doubt. Get in front of the mirror and all that!" winked Hardie.

Hardie headed out into the hall and clicked the flat's front door off its latch before turning and adding:

"Now remember gaffer, I'll be expecting a full debrief—pardon the pun—on sexy Sara!"

It had been a long night, and although Thoroughgood had managed over four hours sleep, he was tired. The calls to Tomachek and Morse had forced his brain to engage and managed to banish the fatigue temporarily, but now it returned.

It would take him five minutes to walk down Hyndland Road to the Tinderbox, and maybe the fresh air was just what he needed at this stage, though God knew he'd had enough of it last night. It was hardly ideal preparation for a first date he'd tried to keep low-key but couldn't help but approach with more than a bit of hope.

Sara the civil servant, as Hardie had described her, had immediately struck him when they'd their four-minute meeting in the Corinthian. Aged thirty-one, she was six years Thoroughgood's junior, the perfect age bracket he thought. Her chestnut hair was shoulder-length with a slight kink in it that, Thoroughgood thought, was not unlike her personality.

A ready smile and kind deep brown eyes had helped put the DS at ease in a situation he was anything but comfortable in. So when the speed dating agency had emailed him to say she was one of the four interested parties who had ticked his box, Thoroughgood had been pleased, to say the least.

He found himself at the junction of Byres Road with Hyndland, and standing outside the Tinderbox's front door. It was only eleven twenty-five and even the badly out-of-practice DS knew that in the dating game, punctuality, one of his trademarks, was a no-no. Bearing that in mind, he crossed the street and headed for one of the small newsagents dotted up and down the West End's main street.

Paying for his Telegraph, Thoroughgood felt he was now ready for his date. It was one of the idiosyncrasies of his nature that he would never, if at all possible, enter a bar, coffee shop or Bar Mitzvah without having his favourite rag tucked under the arm of his Barbour jacket.

Entering the Tinderbox Thoroughgood immediately noticed Sara, perched on one of the stools parked along the coffee bar, lining the full-length window looking out onto Byres Road. He was annoyed he hadn't noticed her when he had crossed from the newsagents, but now he did, he liked what he saw. Tight jeans and a snug turtleneck topped by a fur-trimmed velvet hat presented a very alluring picture to him. And those brown eyes: what is it with you and brown eyes? asked the voice inside his head. He hoped the fatigue in his face wasn't too obvious, but doubted it.

Thoroughgood leant down to greet her with a polite kiss and felt awkward doing so. Relax, said the voice in his head.

"Hullo Gus, have you been on nightshift?" asked Sara.

So she missed nothing.

"Well yes, I guess you could say that; something came up and as a result it was a long, cold night. But you look great, Sara. I could have done with that hat last night!" Thoroughgood reached out a playful hand to pat the top of it.

She giggled, and he found he liked the sound of it; a girlish quality, full of innocence, maybe some mischief, all at the same time.

Back to small talk.

"Have you had a good week?" he asked.

"Yeah, but a long one. What do you fancy coffee-wise?" she asked.

They ordered two lattés and shared a hot Danish while looking out at the busy figures hustling and bustling up and down the street outside. The chat was relaxed and Thoroughgood found himself feeling no pressure to fill any holes. A good sign, confirmed the voice.

Gradually Thoroughgood began to draw some information from her. She'd been in the Civil Service since she had left Cambridge some nine years ago, and had enjoyed stints at home and abroad before being posted north to Glasgow.

An anecdote recalling how she had organised a reception at number eleven Downing Street for the-then Chancellor of the Exchequer, Gordon Brown, soon had the DS analysing whether that one was thrown in to impress or to let him know that she was ambitious.

Thoroughgood was determined to avoid asking any questions about how long she might be staying in Glasgow. She did admit she had been looking at buying a flat—he took that as promising—and without trying to sound pushy, offered his services vetting any potential buys.

Time was flying, and by twelve-thirty Thoroughgood suggested they move on for a bar lunch, and he knew just the place. Her smile, from a mouth of perfect white teeth framed in luscious red lips, somehow seemed fuller than he'd noticed previously.

It's the fatigue hitting you man, be careful, no bevvy over lunch, answered the voice in his head, but he immediately ignored the warning.

Thoroughgood held the door open for her; manners were as much a part of him as punctuality. Both were legacies of a childhood in which the biggest influence had been a grandfather who had fought in the RAF during the Second World War.

"Thank you," she smiled and they walked up Byres Road in the direction of Bella Pasta.

"It's nothing fancy but the food is great and I love Italian for lunch. Oh, I forgot to ask, is that okay with you?" Thoroughgood enquired, rolling his eyes to the heavens.

Again that smile, "I love Italian, Gus," she said.

Two p.m., lunch and a bottle of Chianti were finished, and a furtive glance at his watch betrayed that Thoroughgood's mind was wandering.

"You have to be elsewhere?" asked Sara.

"Eh, well I do and I don't, if you know what I mean," blushed an embarrassed Thoroughgood.

"I meant to tell you earlier, but I didn't know if we'd be doing lunch and now we have and, well, I don't want to finish up right now, if you don't mind me saying so."

Sara was intrigued. "You're a bit of a dark horse, Gus Thoroughgood. You have me at a loss; is it business or pleasure that's worrying you?"

Again she had noticed the colour had risen in his complexion, and then his right hand ruffled through his jet-black hair and Sara's eyebrows shot up.

"No, it's nothing like that. I'm just a bit embarrassed to talk about it, but I don't get many Saturday afternoons off. When I do I always try and go up to Firhill to watch Thistle play if they are at home."

"So that's a three o'clock kick-off then? But Firhill is within walking distance, isn't it? Fifteen minutes walk up Queen Margaret Drive and along Maryhill Road, if I'm not mistaken?"

This time it was Thoroughgood's eyebrows that shot up in barely concealed shock.

"You've heard of Firhill?"

140

She nodded in the affirmative and, encouraged, he continued:

"I've supported the Jags, sorry Partick Thistle, since I was a kid, and it's just become part of my life that when they're at home on a Saturday and I'm off, I go to Firhill. But I don't want us to finish up right here, right now."

Easy now warned the voice in his head, it's the first date and you're telling her you don't want to leave her, cool the beans for fuck's sake.

"Would you like company at the football this afternoon, Gus?" asked Sara. "Some of us girls quite like watchin' the footie."

Thoroughgood made no effort to keep the smile off his face and, swept away by the spontaneity of the moment, he leant across the table and kissed those beautiful full red lips.

They made their way, this time hand in hand, up Byres Road, crossing into Queen Margaret Drive. Thoroughgood provided a running commentary as he told Sara about the Botanic Gardens on the left and the Sally—short for salmonella—fast food wagon where he used to get the "best chilli burgers in Glasgow" after a student night out, way back in the eighties.

Leaving the grimy tenements midway up Queen Margaret Drive, which were still, naturally, quoted as des res West End locations by the local estate agents, they turned right along Maryhill Road.

"Two-thirty and still time for a quickie," suggested Thoroughgood.

Sara nodded a yes to that, and he added:

"I hope you aren't too fussy, I usually have a pre-match pint in Munn's Vaults, just round the corner from the ground. It has plenty of characters inside, as opposed to just plenty of character!"

A pint of lager and a Bacardi and coke later, they were taking their seats in the Jackie Husband stand, Thoroughgood still pinching himself to confirm he wasn't dreaming. Sara proved to be amazingly knowledgeable about football. Born in Nottingham, she had been raised on the legendary tales of Brian Clough and had a preference for the underdog, parallelled by Thoroughgood's support of Scottish football's greatest underdogs, the Harry Wrags, as Partick Thistle were called (amongst other nicknames).

As it turned out the game was a cracker, Thistle triumphing four-two over an Airdrie side with two men sent off. Afterwards they set a blistering pace down from Firhill back into Byres Road. The twenty minute walk in the driving rain and icy wind left them chilled to the bone and Thoroughgood suggested the best place to remedy that would be a seat in Cottiers Bar at the top of Hyndland Road.

The voice said, Just round the corner from your place, dirty dog.

The warmth from the glowing brazier filled with coals inside the converted church, which was now a bar, restaurant and theatre complex was, Sara had to admit,

"Just what the doctor ordered."

The conversation, as befitted the mellowness of the early evening atmosphere inside, soon became deeper. Not for the first time it was Sara who took the lead and asked Thoroughgood why he was still single in his late thirties.

"Nice of you to remind me," he'd groaned.

And so he let it all hang out: Celine, Meechan, the hit and run that had almost cost him his life, his suspicions. How he desperately wanted a family but found his own insecurities and the demanding nature of his job getting in the way of even making a start to a meaningful relationship.

After he'd emptied it all out the look on his face betrayed his thoughts: he'd said far too much on a first date, and his eyes sought sanctuary in the flames of the brazier. Again Sara surprised him.

"You know I guess we aren't too different in that respect."

And she unburdened herself of the reasons behind her own single status. She'd fallen in love at Cambridge with another student and found herself pregnant in her final year. The pregnancy had signalled the end of the relationship after the father demanded an abortion. Sadly, a miscarriage had followed, and although she had managed to graduate with a first class degree in English Lit., the scars had run deep.

Her trust in the opposite sex had been shattered and she threw herself into her career. The Civil Service had afforded her the chance to travel and meet and mix with people of power and diversity, and she readily admitted she loved the job. Indeed, although she was looking for a property in Glasgow, she had only planned to see out the duration of her two-year posting. Thoroughgood, hanging on her every word, interrupted:

"If you don't mind, can I ask why you are telling me all of this, Sara?"

A sigh and then the full gaze of those brown eyes turned on him, dancing with the light of the fire's flames, and he felt like he was melting.

"Because I think you have been honest with me, Gus, and I can see that must have been painful for you. I feel like I can trust you, Detective Sergeant."

143

She added playfully, "Please don't let me down!"

"I think that deserves a toast," saluted Thoroughgood, drawing his chair back and jumping to his feet, oblivious to the confused faces of the other early evening drinkers.

"To lonely hearts, then," and they clinked two glasses of Pinotage together.

It was seven-thirty, and Thoroughgood, full of Dutch courage, chanced his arm.

"Listen, I know a great Chinese that does delivery, would you like to come back to mine? It's just round the corner."

She looked at him with an appraising gaze and to his amazement said,

"Yeah, I'd love that, Gus."

And for once, police work was the furthest thing from Gus Thoroughgood's mind.

19

THE HARSH Northern Irish voice at the other end of the phone meant the caller didn't need to bother identifying himself to Meechan.

"Morning Mr Meechan, Frankie Brennan here."

"Frankie, to what do I owe this unexpected pleasure?" queried the crime boss.

"Well boss, it's about last night. We had some trouble at the steading. I don't think you are going to like this, but …" In his slow and clumsy English, Brennan spared his boss no details of the events from the previous evening, taking time to include the business at the end when the mystery visitor had been taunting him about a net.

When Brennan suggested that maybe it had been one of the residents who thought they were poachers, Meechan's irritation boiled over.

"Poachers! For fuck's sake, Frankie, I hardly think so. Are you sure you didn't get a look at him? And, more to the point, you said there was a car waiting on him. Was it a CID motor or could it have been one of the squads?"

"I cannae see it boss, it was one of those coupés, maybees an RX-8? Boss, I know you're a bit dodgy about the poachin' shot but just hear me out on that one. Four guys from Glasgow comin and goin' at strange hours and, on top of that, we made sure we were seen with the fishing tackle and such.

"Okay, you only get trout and perch on Loch Ard, but half a dozen miles away there's the Endrick and that's teeming with salmon. Out here, those white settlers who have paid big money for their holiday home and salmon permits would get pretty pissed off at any Glasgow wide boys they saw had turned up on their doorstep and were cleaning them oot."

Meechan sounded doubtful.

"That's very interesting, Frankie, but I'm not convinced. Still, as long as you and the boys have cleaned out anything that could give any pointers to the Springburn jobs that's fine. I want you back in Glasgow. Hole up for a while until we see how this all pans out. The safe house has been blown and you won't be heading back out to Loch Ard in a hurry. Just make sure you aren't followed by anyone, Frankie."

"Will do, boss," said Brennan, and the call ended.

It was now nearly eleven a.m., and after showering and dressing Meechan still couldn't get rid of the nagging doubt there was something not quite right about the events out at the cottage. What if it had been the cops who had been behind it? What exactly would they have got from any surveillance operation, other than the location of the safe house and the gang captured on camera? There was nothing else to connect his boys with the killings in the north of the city. Perhaps it was worth giving a call to Charlie Coyle in Paris. It never did any harm to get a bit of advice from your brief, even if Meechan admitted to himself, he was probably being slightly paranoid.

"Good morning Declan," said Charles Coyle's insincere voice. "How can I help?"

Meechan quickly put his brief in the picture, and Coyle supplied the calm reasoned answers that made him so

146

valuable to the crime boss. The lawyer acknowledged it could well have been some kind of surveillance operation by the cops or one of the squads, but a pretty amateurish one if that was indeed the case. Equally so, argued Coyle, it could well be that Frankie Brennan was right and the locals were getting restless over the arrival of a group of Glaswegians who'd never been seen before, and were now coming and going at all kinds of unnatural hours in the middle of the salmon season.

As Coyle got down to the nitty gritty and, as always, outlined the worst case scenario, he had Meechan's total concentration.

"Let's say it was the police, Declan, what do they have? There was no sign of any unauthorised entry that the boys noticed? So that would rule out any bugging of the cottage. Yes, they could have filmed the four boys, but what does that add up to? As we both know there will be no identities based on what happened in Springburn on Friday night. The boys were all stocking-masked, I take it?"

"Naturally," confirmed Meechan.

"So all the cops have at this stage, if it was them, are four faces. There is every chance Frankie Brennan and Gary Reid will already be known to them, so they aren't getting anything they don't already have. Jarvis and Simms are probably on record as well, although maybe as juveniles. So what they have at the end of the day is the identity of four males, but for what? I think that they would struggle to even haul the boys in on a Section Fourteen detention."

Coyle paused for a minute, and then added:

"Of course, if they have Brennan on film with a sawn-off shotgun then he will have some explaining to do,

147

but that will depend on the quality of the pictures and their legitimacy. Personally speaking, this just doesn't sound like any authorised and coordinated surveillance operation. In fact, it sounds like an amateur night out."

Something was still gnawing away at Meechan.

"What if it was the cops and they had some kind of inside information, Charlie? I just don't like the way we've had visitors right out of the blue."

The lawyer cleared his throat at the other end of the mobile, composing himself and buying time before he offered an answer.

"In any kind of organisation, and if you don't mind me saying so, Declan, particularly in your type of business, there is always going to be a risk of informants. That would explain the unexpected nature of the visit, but you trust every member of the gang, don't you? Plus any information being fed to the police would, obviously, have to have come from outside of the four of them. Certainly you can never be too careful, but I think that is unlikely."

"All right Charlie, we'll leave it there. If I need you, I assume you're on the mobile and you'll be back in Scotland tomorrow night?"

"Without fail, Declan."

Meechan told himself to not be so paranoid, and calm down. What was there to worry about? He had a dinner date with Celine lined up tonight, and a proposal he hoped she couldn't turn down.

20

"SEVEN P.M. bang on. Pretty punctual even for you, Tommy," admitted Meechan. "So tell me the good news."

"Ah boss, it really is beautiful up here on Barra but what a fuckin' headache I've got! I can't remember the last time I've put away so much whisky, but the locals know how to throw a shindig all right. Must be near ten years since I danced as much as I did at the ceilidh last night, by Christ, my feet are near as loupin' as my heid."

Meechan laughed. "You have my sympathies, Thomas! Now, is there anything else you would like to tell me?"

"Aye boss, there is indeed. I'd say we are now officially watertight up here in the Western Isles, and I would also say there is pretty significant room for expansion. I liked Morriston the minute I met him, and I now have an open invite to his house! If we can be ready for him, he's promised to have the next delivery down with us in Glasgow on Thursday, this week coming. How does that sound to you, Declan?"

"Bloody good," admitted Meechan. "So you're more than happy to leave Morriston holding the fort up in Barra for us? And what will be the split for the next delivery Tommy, did Morriston let you know?"

"Forty kilos of coke, with a street value of around nine hundred grand, and half a ton in smack, worth nearly three hundred and fifty grand. Morriston has guaranteed us one delivery every two months. That put a smile on your face, Declan?" asked Rankin.

"That's good, very good, but what about the refrigeration plant? Did you get a good look round?" asked Meechan.

"I did, Morriston showed me how they used to work things under the Johnsons and a couple of wee ideas he has for tightening things up. I like where he's coming from.

"The drugs go in the freezer units and are concealed within some of the frozen fish produce packages, in the back of the artics. Morriston wants that part of the operation kept to the eyes of as few as possible. It seems Johnson was a bit lax, and rumours were starting to float around Barra that frozen fish wasn't all the trucks were being packed with. Morriston is going to have a couple of guys he trusts from the mainland installed as uniformed security to make sure the final check, when the drugs are loaded, is done with no prying eyes."

"If you're happy with that, it suits me, Tommy. And you're back around when tomorrow?" asked Meechan.

"I should be in Glasgow by four p.m., Declan."

"Good. I want you to make your way straight to the office; I'm not sure, but we may have some trouble brewing up. I don't want to go into it on the phone, but the aftermath of the Brown turn didn't go according to plan and we had some uninvited guests out at the safe house. There are a couple of other business deals that have been put my way though, Tommy, and they are certainly interesting. But it could be time for a wee bit of diversification that may well make the Barra operation a little safer when it gets on the mainland."

"Okay boss, if you're happy with things up here, that's all. I think we might just have one to watch with the boy Morriston. It may well be worth inviting him down the road, butter him up and make him feel important 'cos he certainly pulled the stops out for us over the weekend."

Then Meechan turned his attention to other matters. His desire to add to his club and pub empire had been partially sated with the granting of the planning permission allowing the creation of the complex, which he decided there and then, in a moment of spontaneity rare to a nature that by definition only followed a meticulously planned route, would be called the West End.

Now the prospect of taking over a firm of undertakers out in Hardgate was more than a little interesting to him. The business had been a family one, handed down through three generations after being started by an Irish immigrant at the turn of the last century. With the death of the final son at the end of last year, the business was at the point of going to the wall. It was then that one of the cousins who also turned out to be a distant relation of Meechan's, Peter Malone, had approached him through Frankie Brennan to help get the business back up and running with some financial support in return for, well, whatever he wanted. As Meechan mulled it over he had to admit an undertaker's business would yield endless "business" possibilities for an inventive criminal mind.

Gary Reid's head was still aching from his accident in the woods when he finally made it into his flat at two-thirty p.m. that Saturday. Reid's childhood had been a war zone, beaten and bullied by an alcoholic father who hit the bottle when his machinist's job in the Clydeside dockyards was no more. The old man's increasing violence had hospitalised his mother and eventually led to the ten-year-old and his mum staying in one of the Women's Refuges over in the Red Road flats up in Balornock.

The move hadn't stopped the constant fear that Jimmy Reid would come through the door, taking it off its hinges with one almighty boot, then unsheath his belt before lashing mother and child with the buckle in another act of barbarous brutality. But old Jimmy was found battered to death, left in a gutter after being knifed for a gold wristwatch he'd been presented with by Yarrows dockyard for long service, the only thing of value that he had left.

An only child, Gaz Reid had been left indelibly scarred by the unhappiness of his formative years, and he often wondered if that was the root cause of why he was, in his own words, "a poofter." But all the pain seemed to go away when the small bald nurse was in his company. He could unburden himself and the pain of his childhood memories; there was no one else left now his maw, Betty, had passed away last July.

The violence which underlined everything Reid's life now stood for at times disgusted the gangster. A voice in his head would sometimes scream stop when he was beating the crap out of some rival Declan Meechan had ordered silenced or roughed up. But now he could unburden all the pain of his childhood, and the guilt that he was becoming the monster that had been his father, all thanks to Gerry.

At 4:05 p.m. Reid's buzzer sounded and a voice said: "And how is the patient?'

"Gerry, come away up before I turn into a fuckin' paracetamol tablet!" said Reid.

Opening the door, the two exchanged smiles and

McIlroy followed Reid into his living room, noticing the open bottles of paracetamol and Jack Daniels before raising his eyebrows at Reid.

Sitting down on the settee, McIlroy said: "I think you'd better let me take a look at that, Gary."

"I was hopin' you'd say that, nurse," replied Reid.

21

EIGHT P.M. Sunday night, and Thoroughgood's train of thought was broken as his mobile went off.

"That you, Thoroughgood? Hope I'm not interrupting anything," enquired Detective Superintendent Tomachek.

"Nothing at all, boss, just trying to read the Sunday papers. Any news on the Loch Ard film? Have we got all the idents from it?"

"Indeed we do, my boy, indeed we do. Frankie Brennan was there, larger than life just as you said, so no surprise there. It would appear his number two was Gary Reid. He's also well known to us. PC's for drugs, violence and robbery, much the same as Brennan. As for the other two, well, this appears to be a big step up the criminal ladder for them. They're really no more than kids.

"Charles 'Chico' Jarvis and Ricky Simms, both aged twenty and both former car thieves from Partick, who have caused us a helluva lot of inconvenience and the tax-paying punter a fair bit of expense. They grew up in the same street in Yoker and are listed as currently staying at the same addresses to this day. Very handy, I'm sure you'll agree."

"That's a fair step up for them all right boss, to be getting in tow with two nasty bastards like Brennan and Reid. This has got Meechan's dabs on it all over; they've obviously come to his attention, probably been used as drugs runners and then been offered a chance to cut their teeth on something a bit more serious. It doesn't get more serious than murder, though."

"Aye, you're right there, Gus my boy. But the question is what do we do with them next? I've held off calling Henry Farrell over at the East, as I thought you'd prefer to speak to me before we go giving him a lead he scarce deserves. That said, Gus, he is the enquiry officer for the Browns' shooting and with the HOLMES unit now in full flow, the lead is going to have to be handed over to him, and by that I mean when I come off the blower to you."

Thoroughgood had been waiting on tenterhooks all weekend for his superior's call, not sure whether he would go straight to Farrell with the identities of the gang, or whether he would come to him first.

Possibly Tomachek's intense dislike of Farrell had made his decision for him; nevertheless, Thoroughgood was not about to look a gift horse in the mouth.

"Thanks for belling me, boss. Can I offer my opinion?"

"That's why I'm calling you, Thoroughgood. Get on with it, dear boy," ordered Tomachek.

"I think you've got to get the boys out and bring them all in on Section Fourteen detention, boss. Apart from anything else, you've got Brennan stoating about with a sawn-off shotgun and at least one of the three others was carrying a sawn-off, if memory serves. But first, you bring the two kids in and leave enough time for the jungle drums to beat so that the wind gets well and truly up Brennan and Reid.

"Obviously we've got to exploit the kids' naivety and inexperience. Okay, we've got fuck all in the way of evidence and witnesses, but you know yourself that Morse's info was spot on. As far as the two kids are concerned, hopefully even a twat like Farrell will be able to break them and get something incriminating from their detention."

"I'm with you on all of that Gus," said Tomachek, "keep going."

"The other thing here, as I'm sure you are aware, is that we, the police, have to be seen to be doing something. 'Police make four midnight swoops on murder suspects' is the type of front page headline the Chief Constable will want to wake up to tomorrow, not 'Police fail to make any moves on triple slaying,' wouldn't you agree, boss?"

"I would indeed, dear boy. Pray continue," quipped Tomachek.

"As for Brennan and Reid, well, you know you're going to get fuck all out of them, and so will Henry Farrell. That would give you a lever, boss, if you were so inclined, to suggest to Farrell that he leaves Brennan and Reid to Hardie and me.

"I'm sure if you were to stress the part my informant played in bringing the four suspects to our attention and underlined the fact that the detention of Brennan and Reid is a thankless task that will yield fuck all, then that weasel would be quite happy to sit back and twiddle his thumbs, especially if he has burst either Jarvis or Simms."

"All right, Thoroughgood, you've put together a compelling case. I'm going to call Farrell; poor bastard will be on his third twelve-hour shift on the bounce at London Road, good enough for him I say. I'll tell him what the plan is: he can liaise with West End CID at Partick. I'll be demanding that he has Jarvis and Simms detained before midnight tonight; knowing that bastard, he'll try and drag things out so he can make maximum ovvies.

"I'll also be ordering him to keep me personally up to date, as I will probably have to do likewise with the ACC Crime and the Chief Constable. Rest assured, Gus my boy, your name will be mentioned in despatches. Right, I suggest that you call that sidekick of yours, Hardie, and make sure he's on his toes for once. Keep your mobile at your side, Gus, I will be in touch presently," Tomachek concluded.

Nine p.m. and Thoroughgood's mobile went off again.

"Right, Thoroughgood, I've filled in Farrell and it's all systems go. I'm afraid you and Hardie are going to have to get your fingers dirty right now. West End are men down in CID and so are Anderston. Apparently they were all out for a curry last night, and the whole bloody lot of them have the trots bad. You and Hardie are going to need to get your arses into Partick and link up with the uniform that will be accompanying you. You'll be delighted to know Farrell is already there coordinating things.

"One last word, Gus: just be bloody careful. I don't want you and Hardie involved in your second shootout of the weekend, understand? I had a look at Brennan's PC's and he is one nasty dangerous big bastard. That said, dear boy, I expect him in the Stewart Street office or City Centre as they call it now, on a Section Fourteen before midnight. I've agreed with Farrell that he can take Jarvis and Simms back to London Road while you keep your bodies in the Central at Stewart Street nick. That way you can stay out of each other's way."

"Suits me, gaffer. I assume you'll be wanting a call when we have the bodies in place?"

"You assume correctly, Detective Sergeant Thoroughgood, so until then, toodle pip."

At nine-thirty p.m. Thoroughgood and Hardie rendezvoused in the shiny new CID office at Partick Police station in Dumbarton Road.

"I liked the old Marine," moaned Hardie. "It must be like working in a bloody toilet, it's that bright and shiny in here. Christ, there must be enough disinfectant splashed all over this place to keep an army of pensioners smelling fresh as daisies."

"You'll be a pensioner yourself soon enough, faither!" responded Thoroughgood. "Try and remember we're just passing through. Anyway, did I tell you old Tomachek has wangled it for us to take Brennan and Reid back to Stewart Street?"

"That was nice of him. So tell me, gaffer, what happens if your new best mate, Frankie Brennan, recognises you from your midnight parley the other night? That should make spending six hours with him a real treat, eh!"

"That is precisely why, faither, you will be taking two uniform officers to his home address and, just to be on the safe side, you will have Tactical Firearms Unit backup into the bargain. I'll be taking the same with me to Reid's in Earl Street."

"Cute," admitted Hardie. "So Reid stays in Earl Street, do you think we could pin the Bible Johnny murders on him while we're at it?"

Thoroughgood, used to his partner's flippancy, ignored the quip and continued:

"Just snaffle Brennan, don't wind him up and get yourself back to Stewart Street."

"Message received loud and clear."

With that the two detectives split up, accompanied by their uniform back-up in two unmarked CID vehicles, both vehicles followed at a discreet distance by TFU vehicles. Any attempt at subterfuge was pointless, as the locals almost knew the unmarked polis vehicles better than the CID themselves.

Earl Street was less than a mile away from the Partick nick. Thoroughgood and PC's Flynn and Grant arrived outside number fifteen just before ten p.m. The street was empty, cleared by the torrential rain. After a nod to the TFU officers when they had taken up suitably unobtrusive positions, Thoroughgood tried Reid's buzzer without success, but Mrs Ritchie in the ground flat right was happy to oblige him with entry to the close. No reply to repeated knocking at Reid's first floor flat, and no signs of life through the letterbox. Thoroughgood popped a calling card asking Reid to contact PC Flynn at Partick office regarding a routine matter. No doubt Reid would get the word he'd had visitors when he did elect to return home.

Thoroughgood and his two new uniform mates split up to do door-to-door round the three-storey tenement. Only Mrs Ritchie on the ground floor appeared, although Thoroughgood would put good money on there being at least one other resident home but reluctant to speak to the polis.

Admitting defeat, Thoroughgood waved the TFU officers off, jumped into the back of the unmarked Astra and radioed Hardie. "No luck at Reid's, you in position at Brennan's?"

"Eh, no," was the embarrassed reply from Hardie.

"What do you mean no?"

"We haven't managed to get out of the backyard at Partick nick, cos we've got a tank full of diesel in an unleaded Focus," Hardie admitted reluctantly.

"No one ever tell you that not all Strathclyde Police Fords are diesel?"

"I know that now, gaffer."

"Forget about it, faither, I'll be right back with you. Reid was out for the night and there is no info from any of his neighbours, so we might as well join up and go get Brennan together. In any case I'm sure he'll be delighted to see me."

After Thoroughgood had returned to West End Office at Partick, they checked the address they had for Frankie Brennan. It was a flat twenty floors up, in the high rise at Lincoln Avenue, Knightswood.

When he heard this Hardie was decidedly upbeat.

"Well, there's only going to be one escape route there, Gus—oot the windae! If he's in we've got him. Especially as we are goin' team-handed and with TFU back-up, I think even Brennan is gonnae think twice about having a go."

"Never mind that; my guess is Brennan won't be home so I think we can dispense with the TFU boys. It's odds on him and Reid will be laying low somewhere safe until they see how the wind blows. Anyway, forget about that, faither; after your cock-up with the diesel it's your turn to read him the Section Fourteen caution. Have you got your aide-memoir card or do you have it off by heart?" asked Thoroughgood with a wink.

"Eh, well, as it happens that's a no to both, but I'm sure either Constable Flynn or Grant here will be able to help me with that one," said Hardie, turning to their two uniform colleagues.

"I've got one here down the inside of my notebook cover, DC Hardie," said Flynn. "There you go," and he handed it over to the grateful Hardie.

The giant shadow cast by the multi-storey towerblock was now looming large, and Thoroughgood wanted to make sure everyone knew what they were doing. When the CID vehicle pulled into the side of the road just outside the flats, he decided upon a last-minute briefing. Turning round from the passenger seat, he let his eyes sweep over Hardie, Flynn and Grant.

"Okay, all bullshit aside, we just don't know what we are going to get with Brennan. Just two nights back DC Hardie and I observed him in possession of a sawn-off shotgun, and although I don't think for one minute he is silly enough to be tooled up inside his own flat, his record is extremely violent. So remember, you get no medals for bravery. We have a job to do, which is to get him, willing or not, to Stewart Street nick under Section Fourteen detention.

"I would prefer it if we could manage that without any trouble. He is not the type of boy we want to be rolling about the bottom of a lift with. Let's make sure we don't go saying anything that could upset Brennan and turn this whole business into something out of a Frankenstein film. Do you understand me?" asked Thoroughgood, but his eyes were resting solely on Hardie.

A moment later they were in one lift, heading up to the twentieth floor and a date with Frankie Brennan. When the lift light flashed at floor twenty the two uniform officers and Hardie made their way out. Thoroughgood remained in the lift, holding it ready for the anticipated return of his colleagues and one Francis Patrick Brennan. There were four flats per floor, and the lift was diagonally opposite Brennan's door. Hardie looked round and gave Thoroughgood a wink, then pressed the doorbell.

After what seemed like an eternity but was in fact less than thirty seconds, the sound of footsteps could be heard coming to the door, and the scraping of a key being turned, and the door was open. There, stooping to avoid knocking his head on the top of the door frame stood Frankie Brennan, an insincere look of surprise written over his face.

If he could have, Hardie would have turned round and let Thoroughgood know just what he thought of his judgement call right there and then, but the last thing he wanted to do was to alert the giant to his gaffer's presence.

"Officers, to what do I owe this unexpected pleasure? Have you got the right flat, aye that's it ye'll be on the wrong floor surely?" Brennan grinned with malice.

Hardie soon made it clear to Brennan that the mistake was his.

"Francis Patrick Brennan?" he asked.

"To be sure," came the reply.

"We are here to detain you under Section Fourteen of the Criminal Procedure (Scotland) act 1995. If you will listen to me it's my duty to caution you to that effect ..." and Hardie, with the help of PC Flynn's aide-memoir card was off and running.

Brennan was all smiles:

"Listen officer," he said with dripping sarcasm, "I can tell you now that on the night in question, at the time you have detailed, I was fishing for salmon on the River Forth near Kinlochard, and I have witnesses to that effect. But if you want me to come into the station to help you with your enquiries, it's no skin off my nose to be sure. After all the telly is crap this time on a Sunday night. But surely you have something better to do with your time?"

Hardie was all business. "I'm afraid not, and according to our information, Frankie boy, you have been a very busy big sod this weekend, you and your fishing buddies."

162

For the first time recognition almost broke out on Brennan's face, but the big man persisted with his act of innocence.

"I'm sure this all some kind of misunderstanding, detective but hey, let's get on with it," he said, spreading his palms out.

PC Flynn, a probationer "not long out his wrapper," as the phrase goes, showed his lack of experience with an ill-considered lunge for Brennan's wrists with his handcuffs. Grabbing the officer's cuffs by the rigid central section, Brennan kept a hold of them for a few seconds to make the point that he wouldn't be putting any cuffs on if he didn't want to.

Unfortunately PC Grant, another rookie, sensed the threat of violence: he immediately unholstered his CS gas spray and pointed it in the direction of the giant Irishman. Brennan just smiled.

"Now listen, sonny, there is no need for any of the hard stuff. I'm gonnae be comin' all peaceable like, it's just that yer mate here gave me a fright with the way he whipped out his cuffs here."

Nodding to PC Flynn, Brennan said,

"On you go, sonny, but please not too tight, I bruise easy," and he winked in a way that suggested any discomfort to his wrists would be redressed at a date to be determined in the future.

Hardie reasserted himself.

"Listen big fella, let's just all stay calm. The boys here are a bit green and they are just trying to do their job. The sooner we get you down Stewart Street nick, the sooner we can get this whole misunderstanding sorted out and your alibis established. So if you don't mind letting PC Flynn put the cuffs on,"

Hardie gestured to Flynn to try again, "we can be moving on quite nicely."

Brennan smiled and held his hands out again. PC Grant reholstered his CS spray canister, and the mounting tension seemed to drain from the twentieth floor landing. Flanked by Grant and Flynn, Brennan headed towards the open door of the lift, and it was then he clapped eyes on Thoroughgood.

22

IF FRANKIE Brennan recognised Thoroughgood, he showed no sign that was the case. The combined weight of four police officers and one six-foot-five-inch male suspect was way too much for the council lift to contend with, so it was decided that PC's Grant and Flynn would make their way down the stairwell to the ground floor.

Brennan remained motionless, like a giant statue of some cruel ancient Roman god, in the corner of the lift, nothing but a slight sneer playing across his features. The lift started off on its twenty-floor journey to the ground floor, and Thoroughgood saw the giant move his eyes in an upward direction. The DS followed the giant's gaze and noted the camera situated in the ceiling of the lift. Brennan's gaze dropped, this time resting on Thoroughgood:

"Convenient, isn't it, that the camera never works in this lift?"

Then he smashed his head into the bridge of Thoroughgood's nose and everything went dark. Hardie hadn't seen the attack coming either, and as Brennan's forehead impacted on Thoroughgood, he watched in stunned disbelief as his mate immediately crumpled onto the lift floor, knocked cold by the power of the blow, his nose spewing blood.

"Now why did you have to go and do that, Frankie?

That's a nice little charge of Police Assault you've just earned."

Brennan turned and looked at Hardie.

"Ye see detective, Frankie Brennan never forgets a face and yer man there would be well advised to remember that. I would say that would be us equal for the dunt he gave Gazza Reid on the head back in them woods at Loch Ard."

With that the giant smiled benignly, quite happy that revenge of some sorts had been meted out. But Hardie was equally good at pulling off a surprise: as Brennan stood staring straight ahead, his piece said, Hardie played his joker and smashed his right knee up into the giant's privates. Brennan let out a slow groan as his knees began to give way but slowly, with great effort, he straightened himself up.

"Likewise, Mr Brennan," said Hardie.

Thoroughgood remained slumped against the wall of the lift like a ragdoll, opposite Brennan's towering frame. Hardie kept his eyes trained on the criminal, acutely aware he was vulnerable enough without dropping down to check on his mate. Judging by the rasping sound coming from the giant, he was still in some pain and more occupied with his own discomfort than any thoughts of exacting retribution on Hardie.

The ping of the lift bell announced its arrival on the ground floor, and to Hardie's relief and delight, PC's Flynn and Grant were both waiting, albeit puffing, in the foyer.

Hardie beckoned to the cops. "Here, take our man out and put him in the back seat of the motor between you, DS Thoroughgood needs a wee bit of a hand here."

Brennan, making a point, marched out under his own

steam but was happy enough to allow the two uniform PCs to lay hands on him and guide him out of the foyer and over to the Astra.

Hardie hunkered down opposite his mate.

"You okay, Gus?"

Thoroughgood groaned but managed a "Think so."

Putting his hand up to his nose, he pulled it away covered in blood and Hardie quickly offered him a dog-eared greying handkerchief to help stem the flow of red streaming from the DS's smashed snout.

"So he recognised me after all," said Thoroughgood.

"Aye, he did that Gus. He said as much after he'd stuck his nut into your face. Still, we can slap charges of Resisting Arrest and Police Assault on him and that will be enough to keep him inside overnight, plus we have the pics of him parading about Loch Ard with a sawn-off shotgun. It all helps, Gus!"

Before setting off for Stewart Street, Thoroughgood and Hardie left their uniform colleagues with Brennan in the back of the CID motor and took a quick look round the street. There was no sign of the dark blue F-plate Cavalier that had been parked outside the farm steading on the banks of Loch Ard.

"Damn," said Hardie, "that's another line of enquiry down a dead end. If we'd turned the Cavvy over I'd bet Scenes of Crime would've picked something up from it, linking that big ugly bastard to the shootings."

"I expect it'll turn up torched somewhere," replied a distinctly downbeat Thoroughgood from behind the blood-splattered handkerchief with which he was dabbing his shattered nose.

The ten-minute journey back to Stewart Street was completed in silence. However, when the four officers and their giant captive ground to a stop in the backyard at the City Centre station, Brennan made sure he gave Thoroughgood the type of stare that let him know their score was far from settled.

The Duty Officer, a uniform inspector, had been primed via radio that the CID motor was on its way in with Brennan. After the reason for his detention and the charges Resisting Arrest and Police Assault had been established, Brennan's rights were read to him and he was escorted to an interview room by PC's Flynn and Grant. Hardie and Thoroughgood headed through to the CID room, caffeine badly needed ahead of their interview with Brennan. Walking through the door, the last person that Thoroughgood wanted to see was the gloating face of DCI Henry Farrell.

"Walked into a door, did we Thoroughgood? Or has that smart mouth of yours got you into trouble again?"

Thoroughgood kept his composure.

"Nice to see you too, Detective Chief Inspector. I thought you were taking your suspects back to London Road office, or have you come up empty-handed again?"

Farrell fiddled with the shiny metallic rims of his trendy square glasses.

"On the contrary, both Simms and Jarvis are undergoing interview at East HQ as we speak. I just thought it would be useful to catch a word with you and Detective Hardie here before you went into interview with your body. But I have to say I am now a bit concerned you will need some medical attention before you're up to that."

"I appreciate your concern, DCI Farrell, but a couple of paracetamol and a mug of coffee and I'll be right as rain. So how can I help you?" Thoroughgood tried, without much success, to keep the contempt out of his voice.

"This source of yours, Thoroughgood, I just wanted to establish how much trust you put in him? Anyone I know?"

Farrell may have been the officer in charge of the Brown murder enquiry but for him to come straight out and ask who his man was was plain bang out of order. Thoroughgood refused to rise to the bait.

"He's tried and tested, sir, and I believe there will be more information of a similar quality to come, but he is a registered informant and you know the rules about divulging the identities of touts."

"Very good Thoroughgood, I just hope you have him registered with the CHIS Unit and they are aware of all this activity."

Thoroughgood turned his back on Farrell and headed for the kettle. Sometimes it was best to hold your fire.

At that point Kenny Hardie conveniently handed Thoroughgood a mug of coffee and two white tablets. Accepting it gratefully, the DS cradled the paracetamol in his hand before throwing them into his mouth and washing them down with a mouthful of the brown liquid. The implied contempt was obvious.

"Is there anything else, sir?"

"Just make sure you email me with a full report on completion of your Section Fourteen interview and update HOLMES before you go off in the morning."

Farrell got up off the desk he had been perched on and drew himself up to his full five-foot-something. He made his way to the office door before turning to Thoroughgood.

"I'd get that nose of yours seen to, Detective Sergeant, otherwise it's likely to play havoc with your love life!"

Thoroughgood turned to Hardie as if he'd never heard the remark.

"Come on, Kenny, we have a murder suspect to interview."

Brennan sat impassively on the other side of the desk inside interview room one. His huge frame looked anything but comfortable in the cheap red plastic moulded chair, which was as good as it got in terms of the comforts of Stewart Street nick. The desk, a wobbly affair with the fake enamel surface peeling back, looked as if it would break under the weight of his huge forearms at any time.

Hardie flicked on the switch that put the bulb outside the interview room to red to signal it was in use. Thoroughgood made straight for the desk and sat down, resting his mug of coffee on the scarred surface. Hardie pulled up another of the plastic chairs and nodded to PC Flynn that he could leave the interview room. He made a play of opening a folder he'd brought in with him on the desk and then began to place the photographs out one by one, as if he was playing a game of solitaire, in front of Brennan. Eventually he looked up at the giant and held his gaze for a second's silence.

"Frankie Brennan, you know why you have been brought here? We are about to start the tape in accordance with Section Fourteen of the Criminal Procedure Scotland (Act) 1995. Before we do, you want anything in, a cup of tea, coffee or such like?"

"That's very kind of you, Detective Sergeant Thoroughgood. I can't remember the last time I bust someone's nose wide open and then they offered me a cuppa." Brennan flashed a malevolent grin across the table.

"Okay, Frankie Brennan, in accordance with Section Fourteen I am starting the tape. Present are myself, Detective Sergeant Gus Thoroughgood, Detective

Constable Kenny Hardie and Francis Patrick Brennan. It is incumbent on me to check that you are both physically and mentally well, and in need of no medical help or suffering from any conditions that would or will impair your ability to comply with the grounds of your detention."

"I'm just fine to be sure, detective," replied Brennan.

"Frankie, we have received information you are responsible for the murder of Walter Brown in the premises of his bookie's shop in 237 Springburn Way, at six p.m. on the night of Friday 11th April. We also have photographs here which show you in possession of a sawn-off shotgun we believe was used in the murder of Walter Brown."

Thoroughgood turned the first of six snaps of the Irishman outside the farm steading in Loch Ard, his hands grasping what appeared to be a sawn-off shotgun.

Brennan picked the photos up one by one and examined them. "And?" was all he said,

"What have you got to say with regard to what I have just put to you?"

"Nothing without my brief and then nothing again, and if that is all you've got, Detective Sergeant, then you're wasting both your time and mine."

"Do you have anyone who can verify your whereabouts on the night in question?" asked Thoroughgood.

"Of course I do. I was on a fishing trip with three friends and they will all be able to back me up on that. In fact, at six p.m. on Friday night we would have been in the process of gutting our catch. Didn't you know the salmon season started only a fortnight back?"

Thoroughgood and Hardie exchanged glances before Hardie took up the baton.

"Well Frankie, I suggest you furnish us with the names of your three friends because we'll need to speak to them as soon as."

"Not a problem, Detective. Gary Reid, Charlie Jarvis, and Ricky Simms will, I'm sure, all be delighted to help you with your enquiries."

"That's damn decent of you, Frankie. Now what about the sawn-off shotgun that you seem to be in possession of in our pictures here: can you explain your possession of it?" asked Hardie.

"But of course, officer," Brennan flashed his feral grin once again.

The giant leaned back in his chair and stretched his arms and hands out behind his neck as if to emphasise his enormous size.

"Well detective, it's like this. We're stayin' in an old farmhoose for a bit o' fishin' and someone has left this old shotgun inside the door. In the middle of the night we heard a noise on the roof and then smoke comes billowing down the chimney and I thinks to meself, there's someone out there up to no good. So I heads out the door and on me way oot I grabbed the first thing I saw, which was the old shotgun, and made me way outside.

"But I just want to make sure we are clear on one thing here, detective. It was a shotgun, a broken shotgun that you see me handling in those pictures, not a sawn-off shotgun. And to be fair, I'm wonderin' what a Detective Sergeant from Strathclyde Polis is doing takin' pictures of me and my mates out in the Trossachs, in the middle of the night. But that's all I have to say, I'm not guilty of any of the charges you are trying to lay on me. I have alibis to that effect, and now I would like to speak to my lawyer, Gerry Shaw, of Coyle, Shaw and Partners."

"But Frankie, you know yourself you aren't entitled to a lawyer when you're being detained under Section Fourteen of the Criminal Procedure Act. We could make sure you have one reasonably named person informed if you like," admitted Thoroughgood.

"Gerry Shaw would be that man," said Brennan agreeably.

"Okay, Francis Brennan, I am suspending the interview in accordance with Section Fourteen procedure to allow myself and Detective Constable Hardie to make further enquiry into the allegations that have been laid before you. I time that at 11:35 p.m."

Hardie scraped back the plastic chair and headed for the door in order to get uniform in to escort Brennan back to his detention cell. Thoroughgood remained seated, his eyes locked on Brennan's.

"You ready for a long night, Frankie? That's us just over one hour into your detention, nearly five more to go. Oh, and I think you should know, your two mates Jarvis and Simms, they're helping us with our enquiries over at London Road." It was Thoroughgood's turn to fix Brennan with a sickly sweet smile.

"Young boys those two, inexperienced; I'm sure that with enough pressure, we can get something out of them. So just head back to your cell and think that one over. When we come back here in a couple of hours, then we'll see what fresh evidence has turned up."

Thoroughgood turned round as he heard the sound of the interview room door open. Hardie walked in.

"Everything okay, boss? Now Frankie, I hope you ain't thinking' about round two?"

Brennan smiled but his attention was still very much on Thoroughgood:

"Never crossed me mind, detective."

"That's good, because you'll already have the Police Assault added to your other charges when we are finished with you here, sometime tomorrow morning."

"Come come, detective, we both know there'll be no other charges. This is just a game of cat and mouse and you've got nothing that's going to stick."

PC Flynn had now entered the room and beckoned to Brennan to follow him. As he passed, Thoroughgood added:

"I just wouldn't be too sure on that, Frankie."

Thoroughgood and Hardie reconvened in the DS's room, the latter slamming the door shut behind him to emphasise the need for privacy. Thoroughgood paced over to his desk and sat down.

"I guess it's not as though it's a surprise: getting something out of Brennan was always going to be like getting blood out of a stone. What really sticks in my throat is that we're going to have to call over to London Road and see if that bastard Farrell has managed to burst either of the kids. If he's got fuck all then we're pissin' against the wind and that big bog trottin' bastard will be walking out of here laughing at us."

"Well, we knew that was the likelihood, gaffer. You know Brennan, it's not as if he's going to be heading for the Costa Del Crime the minute he leaves us. His life is here; his whole identity is about working for Meechan. He's a fuckin' caveman, gaffer. Do you expect him to give that all up?

"No way, when he figures we've got fuck all to pin against him. The other thing we've got a problem with is that our little op wasn't cleared with Surveillance and is basically non-permissible. No, anything we're going to get will come from the two pups at London Road and their interrogation masterminded by Strathclyde Polis's version of Sherlock bloody Holmes. If you want gaffer, I'll make the call: after all, you've got the perfect excuse with your bust snout!" Thoroughgood involuntarily touched his smashed nose and winced.

"Thanks for that, faither. Aye, that's all very fine and dandy, but it'll still be fuckin' painful when Brennan gives us the victory V's on the way out."

"Let me make the call, gaffer, and see what's happenin' up the road. You never know."

Hardie was already punching in London Road CID's number when Thoroughgood nodded in the affirmative.

"Hi there, DC Kenny Hardie here, I wonder if I could speak with any of the officers involved in the detention of Charles Jarvis or Ricky Simms?"

"All right Kenny, me old mucker? It's Ross McNab here, how can I be of assistance? By the way, how's yer gaffer? I heard about his mishap with that big bastard Brennan. Has he gone to hospital to have his busted beak checked out yet?"

Thoroughgood heard McNab's voice from the other side of his desk and signalled to Hardie to give him the phone.

"Appreciate your concern but I'm still here. Just wonderin' if you've had any luck with either Jarvis or Simms? Brennan is laughin' up his sleeve at us here."

"Well for starters, they're both going custody for the Sheriff Court tomorrow morning on outstanding warrants for car theft and drugs. So we don't have to worry about them walking anywhere in the not too-distant future. As far as the rest goes we're struggling. I'd say that big brute has put the fear of God up them. They're not going to say anything other than that crock of crap about a fishing trip."

"Bastard," groaned Thoroughgood.

"You can't be surprised at that Gus; after all, if you're a twenty-year-old kid would you cross Brennan or Meechan? It's literally more than your life would be worth."

"What's that tosser Farrell saying to it?" asked Thoroughgood.

"It's a strange one, he doesn't seem to be too bothered. Maybe you getting your nose splattered by Brennan has made his day! I think he's happy that at least he's been able to pull a couple of suspects in and has something to enter in the HOLMES enquiry."

"Cheers mate, you could do me a favour and tell Farrell I called and that a full update will be with him via email ASAP. The less I have to speak to that bastard the better."

Feet up on opposite sides of Thoroughgood's desk, the two detectives knew they had reached a stalemate. They had nothing that would stick on Brennan, and when his lawyer got involved he would have a field day.

Where the fuck was Morse when you needed him? thought the DS.

23

THOROUGHGOOD'S SMASHED nose was duly examined in the GRI casualty and after the damage had been assessed, the wound cleaned of congealed blood, he was assured by a floppy-haired SHO that the break would heal by itself, given time.

Armed with a bottle of painkillers and accompanied by Hardie, he returned to Stewart Street office. The rain had stopped and the absence of its impact on the Focus' windscreen seemed to emphasise the silence that engulfed the two detectives.

"So what happens after we release Brennan?" asked Hardie.

"All we can do is see what Morse comes up with in the morning. It doesn't look like we're going to get anything from either crime scene. I checked the latest updates from Scenes of Crime and it's not promising. After Brennan is released and the two kids are processed on their warrants we're back to square one, but this time Brennan and Meechan are warned that we are onto them. Maybe not enough to make them leave the country, but it'll certainly make them a good deal more careful."

"That means we're pinning an awful lot of hope on Morse's shoulders," admitted Hardie.

"You gotta better idea?" said Thoroughgood, popping a painkiller and shutting his eyes temporarily in the passenger seat.

Three-fifteen a.m., and Thoroughgood and Hardie sat down opposite Brennan for round two. The smile on the Irishman's face was familiar to the two detectives by now.

"Time for you to put up or shut up, detectives. My alibis checked out? So what charges dae ye have to prefer against me?" asked Brennan.

"Before we put the tape on and get all formal again, Frankie, I'd just like to say one thing to you. Just because you are going to walk out of here in fifteen minutes doesn't mean this is over. We know you and your three mates are responsible for the murders of the Brown family and we'll make it stick, believe me. Everywhere you go, you'd better be looking over your shoulder because we'll be watching you, waiting for you to slip up."

Thoroughgood leaned over the table until his face was barely an inch away from Brennan's features:

"You might think you can intimidate people with your size and your brutality but I'll wait for my chance to pay you back for this." Thoroughgood pointed at his nose. "Until then, I look forward to that moment."

"Developing an obsession like that isn't good for your health, Detective," grinned Brennan.

"When you go running back to your boss, just make sure you tell Meechan that the net is closing."

A baffled look of recollection crossed Brennan's face.

"Sure enough, isn't that just your problem Mr Thoroughgood? You've cast your nets far and wide," Brennan spread his arms out before him and turned his palms upwards, "and lo and behold, just like in the Good Book, ye have caught nothing."

Within fifteen minutes Brennan walked free, a charge of Police Assault the only one preferred against him.

"Time to start all over again," said Hardie.

178

"Aye, I think it's time we called it a night, old friend."

The truth was they were no nearer to laying a finger, never mind a glove, on Declan Aloysius Meechan. Thoroughgood spent the night, or the four hours remaining, sleeplessly tossing and turning. At eight a.m. the phone rang.

"Good morning, Mr Thoroughgood, and how are we today?" said Morse.

"Shit," was all Thoroughgood could come up with.

"Well in that case, if you can meet me at ten a.m. in Tinderbox, we can have a coffee and a chat that might well cheer you up quite a bit. How does that sound?" asked Morse.

"Why, have you learned to turn water into wine, Morse?"

"No, but I might finally be able to provide you with the information that will put away Meechan's gang and maybe a bit more besides. Oh, and how is your nose Detective Sergeant?"

"Morse, you never cease to amaze me," said Thoroughgood and put the phone down.

Thoroughgood could see Morse had his medical uniform on under his bubble jacket, and assumed the informant would be starting a backshift sometime soon. Morse had selected a table right at the back of the coffee shop, nice and discreet, and Thoroughgood hoped this boded well for the importance of the information he was going to be parting with.

"Frankie Brennan certainly made a mess of your nose, nice black panda eyes! You should have called me and I would have put a far better dressing on it than that sad excuse. I'll bet you went to the Royal."

Thoroughgood nodded his head in agreement.

"Typical, they don't take the time of day in that hovel."

"I'm touched by your concern. Before I forget, you should make a phone call to the Glasgow Housing Association this afternoon, and your mum will be sorted for her house."

"Why thank you, Mr Thoroughgood."

The DS took a long slug of his coffee, and then a second gulp to wash down the painkillers he'd forgotten to take when he got up.

"Well Morse, I'm all ears."

"Last night you hit four different houses looking for the gang members and only managed three out of four. Gary Reid was missing?"

"That's correct," admitted Thoroughgood.

"That's because Gary was with me." Morse paused for effect.

Thoroughgood's eyebrows shot up involuntarily but the movement jarred his broken nose, causing him to wince in pain. His right hand cupping his smashed snout, he groaned before adding: "Go on."

"I've been seeing Gary since just before Christmas, and he has become more and more disillusioned with his life and has started to confide in me to quite an extent. As you might well guess now, it was from talking to Gary that I was able to provide the information relating to the safe house."

"That explains a helluva lot all right wee man. But what exactly are you saying here?" asked Thoroughgood.

"Gary was badly beaten as a kid by his alcoholic father, and I think he's beginning to get worried there are parallels between his father's violence and his own. He's struggling to reconcile his life with what happened to him as a kid. The more we've talked about it, the more he has unburdened himself to me. It was Gary who shot Jimmy Brown, and while there was an element of revenge in that, I think Gary has reached the stage in his life where he is becoming sick with all the violence."

"That's all very nice and cosy, Morse, but there's got to be more."

"There is. He lives in fear of being outed as a gay. He's admitted to me he's let slip a couple of times to Frankie Brennan about being in a gay bar or club and just about managed to get away with it, but he's paranoid he's going to bump into someone or be spotted and then that will be it in his line of work. He thinks he's managed to pull the wool over Brennan's eyes but he's not so sure about Declan Meechan.

"Meechan has eyes and ears everywhere, especially in the club scene, and I think Gary's come to a point where the worry and stress of keeping it all quiet and playing the tough guy is proving too much. If he's caught out he'll be humiliated and no longer any use to Meechan: we both know how that will end."

"Okay, that's a bit more like it, but what does it all mean in real terms? Is Reid going to grass Brennan and the boys in turn for immunity and a new life? And what is he going to be able to give us on Meechan?"

"To be honest, I can't say for certain, but he wants out and can't see any way of getting clear of the life he feels he has become trapped in. Brennan called him at the back of three this morning to tell him about his little run-in with you, and I could tell by the look on his face that he is pretty close to breaking point. He hates Brennan's guts, but like everyone else he's shit scared of what Brennan would do, first of all if he found out Gaz is gay and second, was wanting out.

"I'm not at the stage where I can suggest to him it might be time to talk to the polis because he's going to smell a rat. That could just send him the opposite way, but if I can help him arrive at that conclusion by himself then you could be in there."

Thoroughgood took his time, his mind twisting and turning the pros and cons of this unfolding situation that could yet provide the chink of daylight he and the Murder Inquiry team so desperately needed.

"If Brennan called him after he walked out Stewart Street, City Centre nick, then your friend will know we want him in on a Section Fourteen detention for the same reason we pulled Brennan, Jarvis and Simms. Before we do that, we need Reid to take the step forward from having serious doubts about his life and the crimes he has been committing, and wanting to come right over and blow the whistle.

"Realistically I'm duty bound to try and get a hold of Reid as soon as possible; and if we just don't bother, what kind of message is that going to send out to Brennan? I don't know how you're going to do it, but what we need is for Reid to be ready to burst like an over-ripe melon by the time I pull him in. So when are you seeing him next, Morse?"

"Well, I'm backshift today, but I'll see him when I'm finished because he's staying at my flat up in Springburn."

"For fuck's sake, you're taking a chance there. That's just a wee bit close to home when you have bastards like Brennan running about armed to the teeth and looking for any excuse to pull the trigger!

"I take it you'll be speaking to your man over the course of the day? The best-case scenario for this whole thing would be if he was to give himself up on a voluntary attendance. He could come in lawyered up if he wanted, but you would need to make sure his lawyer was neither Charles Coyle or Gerry Shaw or anyone from their firm. Word would get straight back to Meechan, and then Reid would be right in the shit up to his neck."

Eventually, his eyes staring into the bottom of his latte glass, Morse said,

"If I was you, Mr Thoroughgood, not that I'm telling you how to do your job, I would have uniform make a couple of visits to Reid's flat on the grounds that you're still after him and want to pull him in. Word will get back to Brennan and Meechan from the street, and that will buy me the time to work on him over the course of the day. But the final decision will be Gary's, and you will need to be able to make assurances regarding his future and what is going to happen in court. If he's going to stick his head on the line here, even if it is for a way out and a new life, he's still going to give you your only chance at the gang."

"Yeah, I hear all that. Just clear one thing up for me: I take it Reid hasn't been silly enough to give your address out to Brennan or any of the other likely lads?"

"No way."

"And where the hell is this going to leave you if Reid goes for it?"

"One step at a time, Detective Sergeant; by the end of the day you'll need to be in a position to make cast-iron assurances about the rewards for Gary to do just that."

Thoroughgood drained his coffee and pushed his chair back, about to leave.

"Aren't you forgetting something Detective Sergeant? Like the small matter of my payment?" said Morse.

"I'm afraid I can't do anything about that until I sit

down with my Detective Superintendent later today. But you know the way it works Morse, you won't get it all in a oner; with this business with Reid I don't know how that is going to affect the payment procedure. I also need to be careful about notifying the Central Handling unit. They're gonna be a bit funny that we have come this far down the line and I haven't briefed them. But I promise you, Morse, I'll bring it up with my Super and you'll get something the next time we meet. Is that good enough?"

"I suppose it'll have to be," said Morse, distinctly unimpressed.

"Just how sure are you this CID can be trusted? This is the only shot I'm gonnae get at an out and to make a life elsewhere: it's gonnae be all or nothing, Gerry," said Reid, his agitation close to boiling over.

Morse was not about to reveal he had already met Thoroughgood that morning for a coffee, but was keen to coax the gangster further down the road of turning in his fellow gang members.

"Why don't you let me give him a call, you could go in and see him tonight and take it from there? Listen Gary, we both know your problems aren't going to go away: they're only going to get worse. Don't you think this is your best chance of getting out and making a clean break on your terms?"

"Aye, I guess you're right Gerry. Okay: make the call and if yer man is up for it we go in tonight after you've done your shift."

"I think that would be the right move, Gary. Now what you will need to do is get your head straight over what you are going to say when we head into the cop shop." Morse got up and then added:

"Now if you'll excuse me, I'll make that call."

Morse made for his bedroom and punched in Thoroughgood's mobile number.

"It's Morse. Gary has decided it would be a good move to come in and speak to you tonight. So I'm going to come in with him after my shift finishes. How would nine-thirty p.m. suit?"

"That's brilliant, wee man. Nine-thirty would be spot on. Now are you quite happy he will be safe at yours for the rest of the day?"

"I told you, not another soul knows he is here. We'll see you in the front foyer of Stewart Street nick at nine-thirty p.m. then."

"Done," said Thoroughgood, and cut the call.

The news brought a huge smile to a delighted Detective Superintendent Tomachek, who bestowed a benign slap on Thoroughgood's back, his relief all too evident.

"That's first class, Gus. We really can't ask for much more than that, can we now? Okay, I'd better get on the blower to Henry Farrell over at London Road: I'd never hear the end of it if I failed to inform him, miserable wee sod that he is. Obviously he may want to have some kind of input with regard to the interview of Reid, but given your tout is going to be bringing him in, I'm sure he can be made to see sense whether it's Farrell's Murder Inquiry or not.

"And of course the Chief will be delighted. Yes, pull this one off, Thoroughgood, and I can see the chip on that shoulder of yours being replaced by a couple of pips. Let's just cross our fingers we can get Reid in without anything going wrong. We're so close I can almost see the headlines on the front of the Evening Times!"

24

MEECHAN WAS angry. Frankie Brennan called him after his release from City Centre Police Office and he got a whole lot angrier. Angry that his subordinates had been sloppy enough to be trailed back to the safe house, angrier that two of his gang had now been retained in custody thanks to outstanding warrants, and incandescent that "that bastard Thoroughgood" appeared to be taking a personal interest in putting a spoke in his plans. The information which had helped Thoroughgood locate his gang must be coming from somewhere close to home and that, Meechan realised, was the most worrying aspect of this whole little affair, even if in real terms there had been no setback suffered.

At three p.m. Rankin duly arrived, and after Jenny had brought two steaming lattes into the office, it was Meechan's turn to bring his right-hand man up to speed with the overnight developments. Rankin was less than impressed.

"Brennan's a clumsy big bastard and he can be a bit sloppy. But if the cops have got nothing from either the bookies or the car showroom, then he's done his job well enough. What worries me is, if he wasn't tailed out of Springburn, then where the fuck has Thoroughgood got the location of the safe house from? Something isn't right on this one, Declan."

Meechan nodded in agreement. "I think I know where our problem is coming from."

Rankin ran the fingers of his left hand up and down the Mars Bar that ran four inches down the right hand-side of his face and then flicked at the diamond earring in his right lobe.

"I'm all ears, boss."

"I think we may have a problem with Gaz Reid. I've been hearing stories about him hanging around a couple of gay bars in the town. Now, there's been nothing that's caused me concern when it comes to him doing the business for me, but it's something I've been keeping tabs on. We both know that at times he's had his problems with the booze but he's the type of evil bastard you need in your team and according to Brennan, he did a very nice job on Jimmy Brown with a machete. Apparently half the poor bastard's insides were spilt all over the showroom floor before Reid blew his brains out.

"But he's gone walkabout and, although Brennan spoke to him on Monday morning after he got out of City Centre cop shop, it's beginning to worry me that we don't know where the fuck he is, and more importantly, who the little arse bandit is with."

"I see where you're coming from, boss. Wee Reid a poof, well fuck me, I would never have guessed! Aye, that could cause problems for us further down the line, even if everything is okay with him right now and he's just lying low. Can I ask, Declan, does big Brennan know his number two is a fag?"

Meechan smiled the hooded malevolent grin that could bring a chill to even the hardest ned:

"Nope, Brennan is blissfully unaware. I've kept him that way because if we need Reid silenced, then the news he's been keeping from his big buddy is likely to make Brennan angry enough to do whatever I require him to. See where I'm coming from, Tommy?"

"Very nice, Declan, and I'm sure the big giant would thank you for the opportunity to right that wrong. So what exactly are you saying about Reid, do ya' think he's been squealing to Thoroughgood?"

"Thoroughgood has too many contacts in Partick and there's every chance he's crossed paths with Reid sometime in the past. We need to find Reid and make sure there isn't a problem with him and if there is, that Brennan sorts it quick. I think the best way to get to the bottom of this one is to activate a little insurance policy I have tucked away."

At precisely three-thirty p.m. Meechan's buzzer went off and Jenny's sultry voice advised him "Lazarus" was on the other end. Meechan winked at Rankin and put the call on speaker phone.

"Ah Lazarus, I have been expecting your call. You know my concerns regarding our mutual friend Gary Reid. Would I be right to be concerned in that regard, my friend?"

"You would indeed, Declan. I'm afraid you were right, the information that took Thoroughgood and Hardie to the safe house came from Reid via a tout but there's a lot worse to come Declan, a lot worse."

"I'm sitting comfortably," said Meechan, shooting Rankin a here-we-go look.

"Reid is holed up in Springburn with the tout and he's planning to sign himself in at Stewart Street nick tonight. He's looking for a new identity, new life, the lot, in return for the full Monty."

At five p.m. Frankie Brennan arrived at Meechan's office.

"Sit down, Frankie," said Meechan as Tommy Rankin shot the Irishman a quick smile.

"All right big fella, keepin' busy?"

"Tommy boy, how wis the Western Isles? You dried oot yet?"

"Aw, it'll probably be the end of the week before my liver is right again," admitted Rankin.

Meechan quickly brought the small talk to an end.

"Frankie, there is no other way to tell you this other than straight out. Gary Reid is intending to turn us all in to the cops tonight. I'm afraid I've only come by the information in the last hour or so, and to be quite frank, big man, I didn't really know how to tell you."

Meechan's gaze settled on Tommy Rankin, a silent request for his number two to carry on softening the blow.

"Frankie, the boss and me both know that yous two were close and have been working together for a long time now. But there's a bit more to this than just Gaz wantin' to grass us all up, I'm afraid, big man."

Brennan sat motionless; his giant hands, palm down on the thighs of his denims, had begun to grip the material with increasing force while the colour drained out of his face. But he said nothing.

Rankin continued: "I'm afraid the wee man is a fairy. And me and the boss both think that's what is behind all this. It turns out he's been seein' some queen for a while now and this geezer is a tout for the polis. We think he's persuaded Gaz to turn himself in and squeal in order for a fresh start somewhere over the fuckin' rainbow. Obviously we can't allow that to happen, Frankie."

Meechan now took up the baton, noticing as he did so that Brennan's usually slack mouth was pulled tight and his huge jaw set, but still the giant remained silent.

"Look Frankie, I discussed this with Tommy and we thought maybe you would want the chance to shut Reid up. After all, he's made a fool of you for all of these years. He had plenty of time to tell you if things weren't going right but he never said a dicky bird, did he? Now it turns out that all the time he was lookin' for a chance to squeal to the mob. And by that, I don't mean any dumb fuckin' half-assed copper, I mean that bastard Thoroughgood.

"We have until nine thirty tonight and if we don't get Reid before then, we're all gonnae be going down and you more than most, big man. By six p.m. I should have an address for Reid and then it's a simple question of getting up there and shuttin' him up once and for all. What do you say, big man? You up for it?"

Brennan nodded his head; speech, it seemed, was still a problem. The giant cleared his throat.

"Ten years me and Gaz been doin' jobs for you, and Mr Gray before ye boss, and he's never said a word. We've been in some tight corners together and he's said fuck all. Now the little poof wants out does he and he's gonnae turn us all in? Not on ma dear mammy's grave he ain't. I'll do him for ye, boss, and it will be a perfect joy. You just let me know where he is and I'll fuckin' carve him up and hing him out tae dry."

"That's good Frankie. Once it's done you'll need to go to ground for a while, but Tommy here has some new found friends up in the Western Isles and you'll be hitchin' a lift on the truck bound for Barra on Thursday. That sound okay?"

"No worries, boss. I'm gonnae enjoy making that wee bastard squeal."

25

THOROUGHGOOD WAS struggling to keep his mind on the job. Paperwork had never been his strong point but now, with the introduction of the Professional Standards Unit that sat in the same corridor as Complaints and Discipline at Force HQ, everything had to be watertight. Still, he couldn't help his mind wandering to nine-thirty and the arrival of Gary Reid at Stewart Street. Reid refused to come in alone before then or without the accompaniment of Morse. It was now five-thirty p.m. and time for grub, but that also meant there were still some four hours in which things could go drastically wrong, four hours in which Meechan could get to Reid and silence him.

Thoroughgood made his way over to Hardie's desk in the CID room and plonked himself down. The veteran detective was busy checking through his notebook. With Professional Standards there to make your life a misery, it paid to make sure all entries in your official police notebook were properly dated and no dodgy-looking spaces were left open, inviting additions at a later date. Hardie took another slug of his tepid coffee and as he looked up, saw his gaffer parked in the chair opposite.

"Okay Gus, what's wrong? You Hank Marvin?"

"You know me so well, faither!" was the initial reply, but Hardie could tell there was more worrying his DS than hunger pangs.

"You sure it's nothin' else, like whether we should be up in Springburn babysittin' Reid?"

"That's exactly it. I know it's all down to him but he shouldn't be anywhere on his own outside of a cop shop. I figure at the very least we should have a couple of East cops parked outside the flat or somewhere nearby. I'd certainly be a lot happier if we did get something in situ'."

"Aye, I tend to agree with you on that Gus, but it's not our division so what can we do? Morse is adamant that no one knows where Reid is, so I think we've just got to trust him on this to get his man in."

The sound of a phone ringing from the adjacent Detective Sergeant's room punctured Thoroughgood's thoughts and he headed into his room:

"Stewart Street CID, DS Thoroughgood speaking, how can I help you?"

"Very impressive," said DCI Henry Farrell. "Good to see you haven't sloped off for your refreshment break already, Thoroughgood."

Thoroughgood failed to see the need for small talk and cut right to the chase.

"Detective Chief Inspector Farrell, what a pleasant surprise, how can I help?"

"That's just the point, Thoroughgood, it's how I can help you. I've just spoken to Detective Superintendent Tomachek: I have concerns about your man Reid staying in some flat in Springburn with no one to watch over him. When you've a witness who is getting ready to grass up someone like Declan Meechan it pays to cover all options. I don't know about you, Detective Sergeant, but I'd feel a lot more comfortable with two plainclothes officers parked discreetly nearby. The trouble is I don't know where to send them."

For once Thoroughgood had to admit he was in complete agreement with his despised superior.

"I agree completely, sir. It's my intention, along with DC Hardie, to head up to the flat at nine-fifteen to bring Morse and Reid down to Stewart Street, but that still leaves nearly three-and-a-half hours when Reid is going to be like a sitting duck. It would be great if you could get a couple of officers up there: the house number is thirteen Carron Street and the flat is middle right. How soon can you get someone up there?" asked Thoroughgood.

"Well, you know what its like over piece-breaks but I would certainly think by the back of seven we'd have someone in place, before, if I can swing it. The problem is all of our CID are carrying out actions driven by the HOLMES Major Inquiry Unit for the Browns' murder. We've also seconded quite a few off the basic shift strength, so it's not going to be as easy as I'd like to get two cops up. But I'll do my best to make sure Gary Reid is well taken care of."

The DS couldn't grumble at Farrell's offer. No one else had seemed to place any importance on babysitting Reid till he sang and, given that the DCI was heading the MI into the triple-slaying of the Browns, he would be the busiest officer in the East right now. Taking all of that into account, Thoroughgood thought an attempt at extending the olive branch would be no bad thing:

"Listen, DCI Farrell, I really appreciate this. I know how busy you must be but it goes without saying that if Reid squeals, then you will have your MI cleared up and a nice big pat on the back from the Chief."

"Good man, I hope you're happy with what you get," rounded off Farrell.

Hardie had been standing in the doorway to the DS's

room since he'd heard Thoroughgood mention Farrell by name.

"Wonders never cease! Fancy a Chinky?"

"Let's go," was the reply from his gaffer.

Gary Reid checked his wristwatch for the umpteenth time that day. He saw he had less than three hours until he could bargain his way to redemption and a new life. He needed a fag, opened the veranda door and took a step out onto the small cement balcony at the front of the flat. The weather was mild for April, further proof that global warming was doing its damage. In fact, Reid reflected there hadn't even been a single snowfall in Glasgow that winter. He started to think about just where his life would be played out after his chat with the CID and the resulting court case that would probably blow the Meechan crime gang to pieces. Maybe there hadn't been any snow, but Glasgow could still be pretty damn chilly and all that rain did his nut in; it was so depressing to wake up and hear the rain pissing down day after day. Aye, he'd ask for somewhere hot, fuck's sake if he gave them the whole shooting match then why couldn't the polis put him up in Marbella, somewhere nice, with the sun shining down for 365 days a year.

Brennan had parked the dark blue Cavalier at the top end of Carron Street just before six-thirty p.m. There was only one way into the side street off Hawthorn Street which ran right past the front door of Springburn polis office. Running parallel with Carron Street were three high-rise flats and at the top end of the roadway Carbisdale Street. Brennan found a place where he could park the Cavvy and get a perfect view of number thirteen.

One of those high-rise flats was Eccles Street, where

he had taken care of a troublesome small-time drug dealer and bouncer called Franny Hillkirk. It had been a piece of cake, Brennan recalled.

Brennan knew that in their line of business a weakness like the one Gaz Reid had been nurturing in secret made you vulnerable, made those you worked with vulnerable too.

No, thought Brennan, one way or another there's only one way this ends and it's probably for the best, Gazza.

Looking up through the Cavvy window, he saw Reid appear on the balcony of the middle flat right, number thirteen Carron Street.

Jesus, Gazza, I could take you out with a shot from the roadway and you wouldn't even know who had done ye.

But Brennan had other plans for Gary Reid's end. He was determined to make sure Reid knew exactly who his killer was, and that he would be able to savour the final agonised moments of his former sidekick. Brennan continued to watch as Reid puffed on his fag.

No doubt a Camel, thought Brennan. Ach well Gazza, at least you enjoyed yer last fag.

Flicking the butt over the balcony railing, Reid turned and headed back into the warmth of the flat. Down in the car park opposite, Brennan climbed out the Cavvy and ambled along Carron Street.

Thoroughgood spooned in a last mouthful of his chow mein and looked up to see Hardie had already finished his chicken curry.

"Fuck's sake, faither, I don't know how you manage to hoover it down like that. Don't you ever get heartburn?"

Hardie rubbed his belly, which protruded in unruly fashion over his belt and then some.

"You know what it's like in this job, Gus, when you get a chance to eat, you don't hang about or else something will come along and that's your belly rumblin' until after yer shift. What's wrong with enjoying your food anyway? It's not as if you turn your nose up at a decent plate of grub now, is it? Especially when I'm payin'—again."

The two detectives were seated in the Full Moon Chinese express restaurant in Sauchiehall Street. Cheap and convenient, the Full Moon was so bright it resembled a toilet, but invariably you were eating almost before you were seated, such was the speed with which the restaurant dished out a limited menu of traditional Chinese favourites.

Thoroughgood had been watching the clock on one of the restaurant's whitewashed walls since he sat down. Hardie had no need to ask why. Although the DS had been pleased with DCI Farrell's offer to have two cops parked outside Morse's flat after piece-break, it still left a gap that had an hour to run before Reid had any protection.

Reading his gaffer's mind, Hardie said:

"Listen Gus, it's naw exactly jumpin' in the Central right now. So if it makes you feel any better, why don't we take a run up to Carron Street and make sure our man is tucked up okay? Farrell's no gonnae know we've been up and if it makes you feel any better, let's do it. At this rate, the only punter round here with indigestion will be you!"

"Would you mind, Kenny? It's just if anything happened to Reid and we missed our boat, I don't think I'd ever forgive myself."

Hardie was already on his feet.

"Listen, if Meechan finds out Reid is about to grass him up he will do everything he can to shut him up for good. If Reid had half a brain he would have got himself into Stewart Street at the earliest. Waiting about for Morse to hold his hand could be one costly mistake. Come on then, we can be there in ten minutes."

As Brennan had thought, the door at number thirteen was a security entry. He had two options: take a chance at buzzing the other five flats or prise open the door with the jemmy. Looking at the name plates he was frustrated to notice the middle flat was missing a name tag, which meant a great opportunity to find out the name of the polis' tout was lost.

He pushed the button for flat three-one and after a short pause an old croaky voice said:

"Yeees?"

"Evening, Cooperative Insurance here."

"Come away in son," the voice crackled over the buzzer entry system and Brennan pulled the front door open.

Two steps at a time, he made his way up to the first floor landing, holding back just before he reached the middle flat's door, which he noted had a spyhole. Should he use brute force or try a ruse once more? The hideous lime-green wooden door wouldn't offer much in the way of resistance, thought Brennan. One boot, maybe two at most, of his size twelves, Aye, fuck it, and he aimed the kick.

The impact left the door hanging on its security chain, and when Brennan fired in a second kick there was no resistance left as it flew back against the wall behind it. Gazza Reid had been lying dozing on the couch in the front room after his fag when he heard the first bang. In his semi-conscious state he'd thought it had come from the close or the street outside, but when he heard the second bang, he knew he had company.

26

STALKING HIS way across the hall, Brennan followed the noise of the television. He pulled out the Colt Python before he reached the door and levelled it before kicking the door open. Opposite he could see the television where Reporting Scotland was busy blaring away, and the balcony on which Reid had been taking his cigarette break only five minutes earlier was behind it to the left. A couple of yards further over was a settee but there was no one sitting on it, just a white baseball cap lying upside down. The coffee table in the middle of the room had an ashtray, a packet of Camel cigarettes and a Zippo lighter, but from this angle Brennan could see nothing else.

Reid had to be to the right of the open door but Brennan, ignorant of the layout of the flat, didn't know just how much room space was to the right. If Reid was waiting for him in that area then he could expect an attack of some sort. Anticipating close-quarter contact, the giant put away the Colt, caressing the custom-made walnut grooved grips as he placed it inside his overcoat. There were few men the giant had ever come across who made him feel wary about his prospects of success in head to head, known in Glasgow as "the square go," and Gary Reid did not fall into that category.

Gritting his teeth, Brennan walked through the doorway and as he emerged, Reid brought the dining table chair down with all his might. The power and swiftness of the blow would have been enough to fell unconscious any normal adversary, but Brennan had been waiting and was already half-turning with his hands outstretched to fend off the blow. Taking some of the impact on his huge paws, Brennan managed to hold the chair up before it struck his skull and gradually he began to wrest control of it from the desperate Reid.

"Ye treacherous little faggot, I was expecting that," growled the giant through gritted teeth, and smashed his knee into Reid's guts.

The power of the blow sent Reid staggering back against the wall, where he crashed into the fireplace. Frantically Reid struggled to stay upright, his eyes all the time trained on Brennan. The Irishman shot his former sidekick a feral grin as he placed the dining chair back at the small oval table which sat in an alcove.

"So, Gary, thinkin' of singing to the polis? Naw, I cannae be havin' that. Ten years we've been together and that's all they matter." Brennan clicked his fingers.

"And you a gay blade into the bargain. What's wrong, didn't you think you couldn't tell me after all we've been through?"

Reid knew he had to stall, play for time, God knows what for, but just to keep Brennan talking.

"It wisnae like that, Frankie. I know what you think of gays and if I had told you, what would your reaction have been? We would have been through as mates and then how could I have worked for Meechan again? I would have been ruined, a laughing stock. That's why I kept quiet."

Brennan was unsympathetic.

"It may seem hard for you to believe, Gazza, but I think I could have got ma heid round that. So you've been a faggot all these years I've known you or is this just a recent thing?"

Reid saw a glimmer of hope in his desperate situation; maybe he could talk Brennan round. After all, the giant had always had a soft spot, even if few knew it was there.

"I've always had my doubts that I was different in that type of thing, Frankie, but of late it just seemed to get stronger in me and I knew I needed out."

"Aye, oot ya wee bastard, but oot at who's expense?" demanded Brennan as he smashed his right hand into Reid's guts.

Gasping for air, Reid writhed on the floor but only for a moment. Brennan lifted him up with one hand while he threw the glass coffee table out of his way with the other like it was a piece of balsa wood and then threw Reid across the room back onto the sofa.

"That's the bottom line, ya wee miserable snake though, isn't it? You're going to go squealin' to the pigs to save your own skin. After all we've been through and all Mr Meechan has done for ye, you'd fire us in the first chance ye get. That cannae be happenin' now, can it Gaz?"

Brennan towered over him and started to reach into his overcoat. Gaz Reid knew he had to do something now or the end was indeed going to be nigh. He smashed his head into the giant's privates and this time it was the huge Irishman who staggered back, doubling up in agony.

Reid knew he wouldn't have the upperhand for long. Immediately his eyes scanned the flat for some sort of weapon with which to press home his advantage. Lying next to the upturned coffee table was the marble ashtray he'd been using only moments earlier for far more recreational pursuits. His breath still coming in shallow rasps, Reid forced himself to his feet, grabbed the ashtray and advanced on the giant who was just starting to unwind from the doubled-up position to which Reid's headbutt had reduced him.

Once again Brennan found himself trying to ward off a blow, as his one-time mate rammed the ashtray down on his head with all his power. This time there was impact and the splintering of bone but it was Brennan's left hand that had absorbed the assault; as it did so his right cracked off Reid's jaw and sent him flying onto the dining table.

Brennan was in no mood to make further mistakes and he quickly removed the flick-knife from his pocket, pressed the button and took satisfaction from the sight of four shiny inches of cold steel shooting out before him. The terror in Reid's eyes was obvious as he lay sprawled on his back on top of the dining table: he knew there would be no reprieve. The giant closed to within a couple of feet when Reid managed to get both his feet up and punch them into Brennan's guts and then, in almost the same motion, he vaulted off the dining table and grabbed the discarded glass coffee table.

Faced with having to smash his way through the coffee table to get to Reid, Brennan's temper finally snapped, and he let out an enraged roar as he booted it to one side. Reid recognised the hopelessness of his situation as Brennan grabbed him by the throat with his right hand and sliced the flick-knife down the right hand-side of his face. A flap of skin fell away. Standing back to admire his handiwork, as the wound began to sob blood, Brennan said:

"Well now, what a pity, none of your faggot friends is going to fancy you now, are they? But I haven't finished, have I?"

"For pity's sake, Frankie, give me a break. I swear on my …"

Reid got no further as the giant rammed the flick-knife up into his guts and administered the career criminal's trademark, twisting the blade in a clockwise direction to inflict maximum damage to vital internal organs.

Reid slumped onto the blade, his eyes wide in the knowledge that the wound was surely fatal. Brennan looked down at his skewered ex-colleague, his face a mask of hatred. He jerked the blade free violently as a sucking sound emanated from the wound. Reid placed both his hands to his guts as if trying to stem the flow of his vital liquids; he turned his head down and looked at the red juices spilling over his hands, gasping,

"You've done me Frankie, you've fuckin' done me all right."

Cleaning the four inches of steel with the rag he always kept on his person for such work, Brennan's smile was full of satisfaction:

"Aye Gazza, you've squealed all right but naw like ye planned wee man."

The sound of police sirens punctured the night air and Brennan heard the outside door being booted in. Reid was now on his knees, the trail of blood quickly turning the fake sheepskin rug in front of the fake black ash fireplace ruby red. Brennan looked down on Reid without a shred of pity.

"Well Gaz, it looks like I'm gonnae have to leave ye to die in peace. A pity that."

Quickly the giant crossed the living room to the balcony and pulled back the net curtain. He could still hear the siren but there were no marked polis cars in sight; then he clocked the red Focus which meant the footsteps coming from the close were CID. He opened the door and took a step onto the balcony, a fifteen-foot drop.

Nae bother, he thought, and swung his burly frame over the balcony rail, wincing at the shooting pain from the blow to his left hand he'd forgotten about.

He dropped onto a postage stamp of grass immediately below, swung himself over the pitiful excuse for a hedge boxing it in, then walked briskly away to his left, cutting through the high-rise car park and disappearing into the darkness under the railway bridge at the bottom of Hawthorn Street.

Ah, sweet revenge, he thought.

Thoroughgood and Hardie came racing up the stairs to the sound of raised voices and the crash and bang of a disturbance coming from the middle landing. When they reached the first floor they saw that the door of the middle flat was hanging loosely from a hinge. All had gone quiet apart from the blare of the television.

Thoroughgood shot Hardie a warning glance and both extended their telescopic batons. The DS took a couple of steps through the doorway:

"Police, anyone home?" he called.

No reply. Straining his ears, Thoroughgood could hear a low groaning noise coming from what he took to be the living room at the front of the flat. Hardie directly behind him, he eased into the room, baton in hand and eyes scanning for movement. He needn't have worried. On the floor, his hands clasped over a gaping stomach wound, lay Gazza Reid, groaning in agony. The billowing curtains from the balcony indicated whoever had attacked Reid had gone.

Hardie, nonetheless, advanced to the balcony and

took a look out, peering down below to the grass bank bordered by the ludicrously small hedge.

"Aye, whoever did it has gone over the veranda railing, it's a fifteen- foot drop with a nice cushy grass landing pad below. Hopefully Scenes of Crime will get a footprint lift from that though." Hardie realised he had been talking to himself and drifted back through the net curtain and into the living room.

Thoroughgood had already called for an ambulance and was trying to offer Reid some words of comfort:

"Come on Gary, the ambulance is on the way, just keep your hands on the wound. Do you know who your attacker was?"

Reid trembled with the effort it took to open his mouth, his whole body quivering as he tried to draw himself up but eventually he managed a croak:

"It was Brennan, Frankie Brennan, who stuck me."

The DS was worried about Reid's obvious agitation and tried to calm him down:

"That's brilliant, Gary. You just take it easy, the ambulance will soon be here and we'll get you patched up in no time. But we don't want you overdoing it in the meantime. Just take it easy."

Hardie continued to check the living room for evidence.

"If Brennan's not been wearing gloves we'll definitely get a lift. That means we need you to hang about, Gary. I don't suppose you want the big bastard who did this to you to walk away."

Reid nodded his head unconvincingly and winced with the effort. It didn't take the ambulance crew long to arrive at Carron Street and the paramedics admitted that, although it was far too early to say, the chances were that Reid had suffered a puncture wound to the spleen. The likely outcome would not be known until they had reached the GRI.

"We don't seem to have much luck up in Springburn, do we gaffer?" asked Hardie. "That's twice we've been up here in the last month and what do we have to show for it, one dead and one dying. Some success rate!"

"Aye, but this is just all too typical of Strathclyde Polis. You give them a key witness in a triple gangland murder case and what do they do? Leave him to babysit for him-fuckin'-self! What chance do you have? Reid should have been looked after the minute we knew he wanted to come into us. The whole thing is a joke. Can you imagine the press we'll get if they get hold of this one? We'd be a complete laughing stock. Still, it's not my problem, thank God, but I'm sure Tomachek will want to know."

Tomachek's rage was palpable. He spared Henry Farrell nothing, but both the Detective Super and his DS knew full well that with the triple murder inquiry taking up so much manpower and the officers' rights to a refreshment break, sacrosanct, Farrell was not completely to blame. Particularly so when he had confirmed he would send men up to Carron Street to look after Reid. However, while Reid's life may now be hanging in the balance, both Thoroughgood and Hardie had quite clearly heard the wounded witness mention Brennan's name as the man responsible for his injuries.

The living room of the flat looked like a scene from a Wild West saloon fight, and the footprints from the grass below the balcony would provide SOCO with a feast of forensic evidence. For the second time in a fortnight, Thoroughgood and Hardie found themselves waiting for the Senior Detective officer on duty in the East to come and take control of the locus. For the second time, that man was DCI Henry Farrell.

The full circus had sprung into life at number thirteen Carron Street and Thoroughgood and Hardie quickly removed themselves from the locus of the attempted murder, as it was at this stage. At the bottom of the close they debated the need to remain at the scene of the crime until Farrell finally showed up.

Thoroughgood, his anger scarcely abated, was for heading to the Western Infirmary to inform Morse that his flat had become the scene of what could turn out to be a fatal attack on his lover. Although Hardie knew exactly where his gaffer was coming from, he still believed in giving Farrell his place, however little he actually respected him. The point of their conversation soon became redundant when DCI Farrell arrived a little before seven-thirty p.m.

"Thoroughgood and Hardie, we've got to stop meeting like this!" Farrell's attempt at humour was the last thing either of the detectives expected.

"I hear our witness is still hanging onto his life. I spoke to the ambulance boys on the way out and they're saying he'll undergo emergency surgery later tonight. They reckon the knife wound may have punctured the spleen. Apparently Reid only survived because the blade was so thin, possibly a flick-knife."

Thoroughgood's eyes met Hardie's as the two shared a curious look at Farrell's new approach.

"Listen chaps, I want you both to know I appreciate your efforts in getting up here as swiftly as you did. There is no doubt whatsoever that if you hadn't appeared on the scene when you did, then we'd be talking murder here.

Any evidence Reid had ready to put our way would be gone forever. As far as I'm concerned, if he pulls through, then all the credit is due to you two. I will make certain that is known in the places that matter."

Thoroughgood managed a weak: "Thank you sir." Hardie's mouth dropped open before he quickly attempted to regain his composure with an unconvincing smile.

But Farrell had not finished.

"I have to stress that I did everything in my power to get officers stationed outside the flat door as soon as I was aware of Reid's whereabouts. You know the shifts aren't running at anything like full strength, and with this murder inquiry ongoing and HOLMES actions deploying the CID strength and plainclothes units on this, that and everything, we just weren't able to rustle up anybody until seven-thirty p.m. But I tried, believe me, I really did."

So there it was, thought Thoroughgood, the trade off: I'll make sure you get a suitable pat on the back if you don't make things difficult for me regarding the absence of uniform outside thirteen Carron Street.

"I take it you won't mind if we email our statements over later tonight? I feel it's down to me to go and let Morse know what has happened to his ... contact," Thoroughgood confirmed.

"By all means, Detective Sergeant, and once again, my sincere thanks for your night's work," with that Farrell headed up the stairs.

The two detectives walked out to the Focus in silence but once they had taken their seats Hardie exploded:

"What a fuckin' wanker. Can you believe the cheek of that bastard? If he thinks all that smarming is going to stop me complaining about the lack of plod outside the flat then he's barking friggin' mad, never mind barkin' up the wrong tree."

"Listen faither, that can all wait. Right now we need to tell Morse his lover might not make it through the night. His house is in a state of complete wreckage, and guess what? It's all down to Strathclyde Polis. How do you think the wee man is gonnae take that then?"

Hardie shrugged his shoulders.

"All you can do is tell him the truth, gaffer. His man is still alive with a fighting chance, and that's down to us. Plus I wouldnae be losing sight of the fact that we have him clearly naming his attacker, and hopefully a whole lot of forensic evidence into the bargain."

Thoroughgood remained unconvinced, but Hardie was determined to put a positive spin on the situation.

"Aye, it's bad, gaffer, but it could be a whole lot bleedin' worse."

27

BY THE time Thoroughgood and Hardie arrived at the Western Infirmary it was eight p.m. Morse was due off his twelve-hour shift any minute.

Thoroughgood, acutely aware of the sensitive nature of the news he was about to break, elected to text the nurse and let him know he was waiting for him in the CID Focus parked in Church Street, at the side of the Western. Soon he spotted a familiar figure walking up the slight incline towards them. Jumping out of the passenger seat he immediately opened the back door of the Focus behind him, offered Morse a weak smile and gestured to him to take a seat. Morse was no one's fool, and Thoroughgood could tell by the taut look on his face that he had a good idea of what was coming next.

"Good evening detectives, this is all very considerate of you offering to take me home, or is there another reason behind your presence here?"

"I'm afraid there was an attempt on Gary Reid's life tonight at your flat."

There was never an easy way to deliver bad news but Thoroughgood knew, after years of experience, trying to soften the blow only prolonged the painful impact.

"Gary was beaten up and stabbed in the stomach, and the wound has punctured his spleen. At this moment he is on the operating table in Stobhill and they reckon his chances are around fifty/fifty, depending on what they find when they go in. It looks like the blade that was used to do the damage was a thin one, possibly a flick-knife; that has saved him for the time being as the knife missed the vital organs."

Morse's face was ashen and his eyes seemed to shrink into their sockets:

"Can I ask if we know who did it?"

"Yeah, it was myself and Kenny who were first on the scene, we just missed him by a minute or two. It was Brennan. Gary managed to tell me it was him before he lost consciousness."

Morse was frantically playing with the earring dangling from his right ear, but said nothing as he digested the news.

"Unfortunately, Morse, there's more. Brennan slashed down the right hand-side of Gary's face with the blade and he'll be scarred for life."

Again silence, and then Thoroughgood noticed the tears streaming from the informant's eyes. To his surprise, it was Kenny Hardie who quickly offered the tout a hankie. Clearly in shock, Morse didn't know where to start. Thoroughgood had seen people react in a variety of ways to bad news over the years. Anger and the need to hit out were quite common, usually aimed at the messenger. Shock was also more than understandable, but somehow he had expected Morse to be different. Possibly because the wee man had been surprising him ever since he had first met him outside the People's Palace, but he had never expected to see Morse at a loss for words. Eventually the informant found the composure to speak.

"So when will we know if Gary is going to make it?"

"It's a case of waiting to see if he comes through surgery. He's lost a lot of blood from his wounds, but I'm told they are hopeful."

"So what does this all mean for me, Mr Thoroughgood? If they know where my house is, how can I stay there, where can I go to be safe if they're going to come after me next?"

"You've no need to worry there, Morse. You can kip at mine until we can get you a safe house, but you might want to come round with us to your flat to get some clothes and stuff together. Obviously, though, it's not going to be a good idea for you to be going back to work and in any case, you'll hopefully be able to see Gary tomorrow."

Morse continued to sob but eventually blurted out:

"All I wanted was a chance to get away from Glasgow and it's all gone wrong, Gary could pay with his life and it's all down to me. It's such a mess."

It was late before Thoroughgood and Morse returned to the Detective Sergeant's flat. Brennan's description was circulated; a search of his home address had proved negative but the city was being scoured by all available police resources for the giant Irishman who seemed somehow to have melted into the shadows under the noses of Strathclyde Police.

The whereabouts of Brennan was also causing Meechan more than a passing concern, and he had instructed Tommy Rankin to get a couple of "the boys out" to look for the Irishman. The last thing Meechan wanted was a loose cannon on the streets in the form of the giant wrecking ball that was Frankie Brennan, and he now had concerns that was exactly what was about to happen.

The fact that Meechan's immediate plans were in

suspension until it became clear whether Reid was going to pull through did not help the crimelord's mood. His mind was soon working on a plan to deal with Brennan if the giant had gone off the rails. Meechan reached for his mobile.

"Is it convenient to chat, Lazarus?" Meechan asked.

"Yes," was the one-word reply.

Brennan needed time to sort the mess in his mind. He guessed the cops would put two and two together, and his home address would be one of the first places on their list. There was no point speaking to Meechan; he had nothing more to say after his original call. No, what he needed was time alone, somewhere he could put everything in perspective and try and make peace with his maker.

Strangely enough for a cold-blooded killer, Frankie Brennan had always been deeply religious. He headed out of Springburn on foot, using the side streets and staying in the shadows; by the time he reached Charing Cross he felt confident enough to hail a black hack. He instructed the driver that he wanted to be dropped at Dumbarton Road, turning up into Hyndland Street before arriving at the massive red sandstone building that was St Peter's chapel.

All through his life the chapel had provided him with a listening ear and a promise that by repenting for the sins that haunted him, from time to time, he would be forgiven. Brennan knew his mates laughed at his need to turn to religion, but ever since he could remember he had gone to chapel. It had always helped and all he knew was that, right now, he needed help.

When he reached the front door, there was a light

on inside. Carefully, he turned the handle and entered. Genuflecting, as he had been taught as a small boy all those years back, he made his way down to the front of the chapel and knelt, and there Frankie Brennan prayed for forgiveness.

Rankin had guessed the giant might need divine intervention to come to terms with the crumbling of his world and the betrayal of his best friend. For a small donation he had persuaded the priest to open St Peter's, then waited patiently, screening the main body of the chapel through the slats of the confession booth. As he knew he would, eventually Brennan had showed.

He allowed the giant a couple of moments to come to terms with his demons and make peace with his God; Rankin viewed religion as a weakness. He walked up the aisle and eased himself into the pew behind Brennan, taking in every little movement in the Irishman's back. Every little tensing of muscle and sinew indicated Brennan was aware he had company.

"Hullo Frankie. Is this helping dull the pain?" asked Rankin.

Brennan turned stiffly. Even in the half-light of the dimmed chapel, Rankin could see the tears in his eyes and the trails of moisture lining his cheeks. Brennan showed no interest in concealing his torment.

"Ever since I was a little lad, when things, they'd go wrong, I came to chapel to make them right. First with me ma' and da' and now they're gone, on me own. Things have gone wrong badly this time, Tommy. I don't know that they can ever be right again with me." The giant hung his head in his hands.

Rankin had never seen Frankie Brennan so low, so vulnerable and so utterly desolate. He liked it, for in his calculating mind it showed there was plenty of weakness for him to work with.

"Listen Frankie, I know this whole thing has been real tough for you but me and Declan, we're your friends; we're not going to abandon you the way Gazza did. It's bad enough you find out the guy who's been watchin' your back, and you his, has been lying to you all these years. Pretending he's something he ain't but then to find he's gonnae be grassin' you up to the rossers, man, it would blow anyone's world to bits. But we need to get you thinkin' straight again, and quick, because Reid isn't dead and he managed to give the filth your name. But worst of the lot, the word is he's gonnae pull through."

Brennan's head rose, and the old feral fire burned in his emerald green eyes momentarily, only to be doused almost immediately by the despair he seemed determined to wallow in:

"So I've let Mr Meechan and yourself down, Tommy. I didn't do the job and that grassin' little Judas lives and will end up putting us behind bars, all because I made an arse of things."

Rankin held his hand up to stem the torrent.

"That may be the case, Frankie, but Declan wants you to know you're part of our family and we're not going to see you go down. We aren't planning on goin' down ourselves. First we need to get you out of here, cleaned up and calmed down and then far, far, away, and I know just the place."

"You'd do that for me after the mess I've made of things?"

Rankin held his hand out and grasped Brennan's massive paw, palm to palm:

"Of course we would, Frankie, now let's get going."

Rankin ushered his shell-shocked mate into the back seat of the shiny grey BMW.

"Okay Tam, take us out to Mr Meechan's up by Mugdock."

The huge black wrought-iron gates of Meechan's mansion opened as if they had been expected. Rankin ushered the Irishman into an oak-panelled anteroom just off to the right of the hallway. There, staring into the dancing shadows of the log fire, sat Meechan. Turning his head slightly, he looked up at Brennan and pointed to the cream leather armchair opposite him. The giant, who suddenly resembled a naughty schoolboy, wandered over and sat down obediently.

"Tommy, there's a bottle of Jamieson's in the cabinet. I think we all need a drink," said Meechan. His icy gaze fell on Brennan.

"Well, Frankie, this is all looking a bit of a mess and it's only going to get worse if Reid pulls through. I expect Tommy has put you in the picture with everything?"

"He has, Mr Meechan, to be sure."

"I think it would be best if you were to lay low here until we can get you away on Thursday."

Meechan stopped to enjoy the Jamieson's Rankin had poured for him, and charged his glass with his two associates, one of whom didn't know he had a death sentence hanging over his head.

Brennan broke out of his despair. "Boss, can I ask what yer gonnae do if Reid looks likely to pull through?"

"The matter is all in hand, Frankie. Suffice to say his life expectancy is short in the extreme. The good Lord maketh and He taketh away, so to speak."

28

HEAVILY SEDATED, Reid had made it through the night and awoke to the usual noises which accompanied life in a hospital ward. Attached to a drip and aware of the burning ache caused by his surgery the previous night, even a shift of weight in his bed was almost too painful to contemplate.

He was nil-by-mouth for the foreseeable and although that was the case for nearly everyone in intensive care, when he saw what fell under the description of "breakfast" he felt relieved. Reid had never been in hospital in his life, something he guessed was pretty lucky considering his line of work. As he surveyed the surrounding ward and out into the corridor beyond the doors where the two polis stood guard, he began to realise what they meant by crisis in the NHS.

Stobhill Hospital was simultaneously grimy and gruesome, even though it compared favourably with the GRI. The latter had a record for hygiene problems, and the Royal's dark grimy Victorian exterior appeared more like something out a Bram Stoker novel than Glasgow's biggest and best infirmary. Perhaps it was just as well his little accident had happened in Springburn and consigned him to a Stobhill berth. And of course he was alive and his path was now mapped out for him, all need for doubt and debate removed by Frankie Brennan.

Ironic that, thought Reid, by trying to use me as a pin cushion the big fucker has pushed me straight down the throats of the polis.

By the end of the afternoon he would have unburdened himself of all his guilt, all the anger and confusion that had been building up inside him these long years. He would have the last laugh on Brennan, Rankin, Meechan, the lot of them: the thought brought a smile of satisfaction to Reid's face.

His mind wandered to Gerry McIlroy and what would become of the two of them. He held his hand to the right side of his face and felt the four-inch scar that ran its length. The scar that meant Brennan had left his mark on him, even if he had failed to send him to his grave. Reid had always found it hard to reconcile Brennan's cruelty and the pleasure he took from his work with the contrition he showed as he repeatedly sought to make good for the horrific sins he had perpetrated, through his belief in Christ.

Reid was a believer himself, but the broken nature of his childhood had meant his faith in Christ and Roman Catholicism was not underpinned by the same zeal as Brennan's. Yet at that moment, he realised the need to unburden his soul was something he desperately wanted to do, a sort of spiritual starting afresh for his new life.

He'd never thought he would have been so pleased at the sight of two coppers in uniform, but that was the case now. For all these years he had treated anyone wearing a polis uniform with contempt and hate, viewing them as having sold out to authority and trading in their individuality for the sake of the power that went with a uniform, and in this case, a couple of Heckler and Kochs.

But after speaking to the two cops babysitting him, he'd discovered that if you gave them a chance they were just normal geezers like him. Family, kids and concerns, they had it all. Having said that, Mikey seemed more interested in chatting up the nurses at their station along the corridor, while Bob buried his head in a Sun.

The priest wandered along the corridor toward the intensive care ward, smiling graciously and benignly as he held his prayer book in one hand and a plastic bag containing holy water in the other. His rosary beads were wrapped around his fingers.

Stopping at the nursing station, he politely said,

"Good morning" to the duty sister.

Flustered by a constantly ringing phone and a depleted shift, and hit harder by a viral outbreak, she nodded a brief "Hullo, Father."

Engrossed in her staffing problems, the sister took almost no notice of the tall black-haired priest with the harsh Northern Irish accent. The priest continued along the corridor heading for the two police officers sitting outside the ward.

"Good morning, my sons, Father Gerry O'Hare, Roman Catholic chaplain for Stobhill, just along to provide some spiritual comfort and encouragement to my flock."

PC Bob nodded and then reburied his head in the Sun. PC Mikey stood up and offered his hand in greeting:

"Good morning Father, they're all yours."

"Thank you my son," Father Gerry said, making the sign of the cross and strolling into the ward to tend to his flock.

The good Father made his way to a bed containing an elderly male who was barely conscious, opened the plastic bag containing the holy water and sprinkled it on the old man's head. Holding his beads in one hand, he opened the prayer book and muttered a prayer over the apparently comatose patient. It was hard to tell if the old man had heard a word, or was even aware of the priest's presence, but Constable Mikey certainly was and gave a good-hearted thumbs-up from the doorway.

Smiling down at the old man Father Gerry walked across the ward to Gary Reid:

"Good morning my son, how are you today?" he asked in a concerned fashion.

Gazza Reid couldn't believe his good fortune.

"Ah Father, I'm a bit sore to be honest, had surgery last night and it's painful to even move in the bed. But I'm so glad to see you."

"That is always nice to hear, my son, it's not always the case you know. I take it you would like me to administer a blessing? I will anoint you with the holy water then if you wish, I will say a prayer."

Reid continued to smile.

"That would be great, Father, but I'd also like to receive confession and unburden my soul of the sins that are blighting my life. You see, Father, I have the chance to make a fresh start and to make a new life but before I do, I need to confess."

Father Gerry stroked Reid's arm: "That is good, my son, for the Lord holds those dear who wish to make good their soul and repent their mortal sins."

"To tell you the truth Father, I'm just so pleased to have this opportunity. Last night I was stabbed. I thought my time had come and I would never have the opportunity to repent, never mind receive my Last Rites. Father, you must be the answer to my prayers."

"Ah, Gary is it?" Father Gerry pointed up at the name board above Reid.

"You make my heart sing with joy; it is my good fortune to meet you upon the Lord's work this morning.

Do you want me to draw the curtains so you may confess in privacy?"

"That would probably be best, Father, as the sins I have to unburden myself of are for your ears and those of the Almighty only."

"Very good, Gary, let me just check with the officers that's going to be all right. I take it they are in here for your benefit?"

Reid nodded and watched as Father Gerry strolled lithely back to the doorway for a brief chat with PC Bob who, after a brief shake of the head, resumed devouring his Sun avidly.

Father Gerry returned to Reid's bedside and, smiling, set about pulling the plastic curtain around the bed. He opened the plastic bag with the holy water and sprinkled it in the shape of the cross over Reid's forehead. The priest opened the prayer book and Reid noticed something glint inside the unfolding pages. Father Gerry smiled once more, then stood up and, removing the blade from his book, he quickly placed his left hand over Reid's mouth. Leaning over the patient he spoke:

"In the name of the Father and the Son and Declan Meechan, may you rot in hell forever more, you grassing bastard."

Father Gerry ran the knife across Reid's throat, holding him down in an iron grip as he watched the blood gurgle out of the wound.

Reid twitched desperately and tried to break free but did not have the strength in his weakened state. His writhing soon subsided and his eyes rolled to the heavens above. Father Gerry bent over and closed the staring eyes. He emptied some of the holy water from the plastic bag onto a towel at the side of the bed and cleaned the blade before returning it to the centre of the prayer book. Without haste he turned Reid's head towards the nearby window, taking care to clean up some of the blood streaming from the wound before placing the towel in the bedside bin. Quickly he checked the mirror on the side of the wall, making sure there was no evidence of his morning's work on his dark suit and satisfied, he parted the curtain and walked towards the door. Smiling at PC Bob, he said:

"Thank you, my son, I think Gary will sleep the better for confession. I took the liberty of leaving the curtains shut in that regard."

"Nae bother, Father, all the best."

"You too, my son."

Father Gerry walked serenely along the corridor, smiling as he passed PC Mikey, who waved back cheerfully, and made his way out of the exit doors and down the stairwell.

It was close to midday when Thoroughgood's mobile rang. The DS had just been running over with Morse how he planned to take the interview with Reid, which would result in his whistle-blowing statement. Morse knew immediately there was something wrong from the look on Thoroughgood's face and the raised voice at the other end of the mobile. The DS walked through to his bedroom and shut the door.

Five minutes later he returned to the kitchen where he saw Morse seated at the table, the colour drained from his face. A feeling of déjà vu swept over Thoroughgood as he related the events that had unfolded in the intensive care unit up at Stobhill Hospital that morning. The overwhelming feeling was that he had failed the wee man once again. There would be no fresh start for Morse, no new life with Gary Reid: the outlook for the informant was utterly bleak.

29

THE FALLOUT from this latest fiasco was quick and ACC Crime, Graeme Cousins, had almost immediately summoned Superintendent Tomachek and DCI Farrell to a meeting at Force HQ, Pitt Street at two p.m. on Tuesday afternoon.

Cousins—or "kissin'" as the rank and file liked to call him—made it perfectly clear the force's reputation was now on the line, as well as the Chief Constable's ever-diminishing hopes of a knighthood. He had ordered that every informant's palm must be greased in order to get the information that would allow the current spate of killings, which now stood at seven, to be brought to an end.

Before he'd even returned to Stewart Street City Centre office, Tomachek had been on the blower telling Thoroughgood he expected both him and Hardie in his office within the hour, and they had better have their thinking hats on.

Having made sure Morse was happy staying in his flat on his own, emphasising that the tout was to call him the minute he thought something wasn't right, Thoroughgood was actually relieved, guilty though he felt, to be leaving the grief-stricken Morse home alone. Leaving the flat, he was immediately forced to turn the collar of his Barbour up to shut out the stinging rain funnelling into the close.

He jumped into the waiting CID motor to find Hardie

strangely subdued. His only contribution for the duration of their ten-minute journey was summed up in the terse one-liner:

"What a fucking mess, and not a bleedin' thing we can do about it."

Detective Superintendent Tomachek was not so reticent in his summary of events:

"I'll tell you exactly where we are right now. We have an incompetent little jobsworth leading a multiple murder inquiry without a fuckin' clue. His only lines of enquiry are those generated by the HOLMES Unit, and we all know how fuckin' pedestrian they are. Our only witness is lying in the morgue after having his throat slit by a priest in the middle of intensive care up at Stobhill while two uniform coppers sat outside chatting up nurses and reading newspapers.

"Balls and buggery, I say. I can see the headlines about killer priests right now. On top of that we have Declan Meechan's most brutal enforcer, identified for an attempted murder on the deceased and fingered for the Brown triple killing, gone to ground, and we don't have a fuckin' clue where. I'll tell you what it is, it's a fuckin' disgrace, a disgrace do you hear?"

Tomachek finally took time to come up for air but it was an impressive rant, even by his standards.

"Now, I know the only information we have come up with has come from your tout. I know if it hadn't been for the pair of you Reid would have been dead twenty four hours earlier than he was, but boys, we need to get our heads together and come up with something. It's bleedin' obvious Henry Farrell is way out of his depth, and the good name of Strathclyde Police is going to go down the pan because of it. Gentlemen, your thoughts please."

223

Thoroughgood looked at Hardie as if to say "on you go" but the veteran detective knew better than to become the filling in a sandwich between two superiors.

Eventually the DS opened his mouth, albeit still uncertain what would come out.

"We know Frankie Brennan was behind the attempted murder on Reid and that he also took part in the killing of the Browns. That's a start."

All of which led to a slightly nonplussed raising of over-substantial eyebrows by Detective Superintendent Tomachek:

"Bally marvellous. Tell me something I don't know."

Thoroughgood persisted:

"We also have two kids in the Bar-L on warrants who were part and parcel of the Brown triple murder. I think Hardie and I should pay Simms and Jarvis a visit inside Barlinnie and see if we can't entice them with the same deal we were going to put to Reid. As for Brennan, my guess is that Meechan has him holed up somewhere or he'll be murder victim number eight within the next twenty-four hours. Either way, we're really going to struggle to pin him down. Nope, for me gaffer, I'd say go after the kids."

"What about this fuckin' priest? Who the fuck might he be?" asked Tomachek, running his smokestained hands through his greying hair. Hardie spoke up.

"He's got to be a contract killer brought in to do a one-off job. We all know about Meechan's links to Belfast and the Provos. A priest with an Irish accent? I think we have our answer there. We're going to be struggling on that one boss. Okay, the CCTV up at Stobhill Hospital will give us a decent visual, but there's about as much chance of our Father being a genuine priest as there is of Partick Thistle ever playing in the SPL again," Hardie continued:

"We'll get an all ports and airports warning out to try and nab him before he gets out the country but you know as well as I do, professionals have so many tricks up their sleeves when it comes to changing their appearance, we're probably going to be onto plums. We need to fax a copy of the file to both the Garda and the Police Service of Northern Ireland. It's not beyond the realms of possibility that our man has PC's for this kind of MO, i.e., dressing up as a priest to send someone to meet their maker."

"Very poetic, Hardie. I suppose I should have expected no less from a man with a name like yours, but fair enough nevertheless. Now, what about Morse? Does he have anyone else in there who could help us out?"

Thoroughgood stayed silent. He knew full well the wee man was still in contact with Celine, but could he really bring himself to ask Morse to stick his neck out once again and set up a meet with her? For personal reasons, he was not sure he could carry one through after the old sores his last meeting with her had re-opened.

Thoroughgood cleared his throat:

"There's maybe another avenue, boss, but one I don't want to elaborate right now. All I can say is that I will make enquiries and see if we can get anywhere with it, and let you know as soon as I can. But it is a long shot."

Tomachek raised those eyebrows again and looked down at his desk, apparently suffering a panic attack after realising he was without his beloved pipe. After a moment's scrambling through his drawers, he located pipe and tobacco but no light.

"Where's that bastardin' lighter? Fucked if I know why I ever gave up using the Swan Vestas."

"This do, boss?'" Hardie said, leaning across Tomachek's desk with a ready light.

"You're a good man in a storm, Hardie." Tomachek luxuriated in a huge inhalation of his favourite Condor tobacco.

"Now where the fuck, gentlemen, were we? Ah yes, a long shot, you say, Detective Sergeant? Well, at this stage a long shot is about the only shot we've got. We had bugger all luck with the all stations warning that was issued after Reid had his throat slit.

"I assured ACC Cousins I would get the lookouts and descriptions out for him as soon as. So I want you two to concentrate on getting the all ports and airports warning out, and the description over to the PSNI and Garda. Tomorrow your top priority is to speak to Jarvis and Simms in Barlinnie. I don't care what you have to offer them to loosen their tongues, just do it, so I can shit on that bastard Farrell from as great a height as possible!"

Declan Meechan had had a busy day; one that was now yielding some very satisfying results. Brendan O'Driscoll, or Father Gerry O'Hare, had texted him as agreed, to confirm that Gazza Reid was no longer an issue. Approximately ninety minutes after the first text, O'Driscoll texted again to confirm he had touched down at Belfast Airport safe, sound and in the guise of an American tourist. Father Gerry was no more, for the time being at least.

By mid-afternoon Meechan was once again closeted with Tommy Rankin discussing what to do with the second of his "major headaches," Frankie Brennan, who remained secure within the confines of Tara.

For Rankin there were two ways to deal with the issue.

"The bottom line, Declan, is: has big Frankie become

too much of a liability? I think he has. You could send him up to Barra, but so what? That isn't going to change the fact that Reid ID'd him to the cops anyway. Okay, Frankie would never burst to the mob about the Browns or any of the other business he has done for you with the likes of the Johnsons, but you'd almost be doing him a favour setting him up instead of banged up for life. We both know it would drive the giant mad."

"So what you're saying, Tommy, is that it's not a question of whether we set Brennan up, it's how?" quizzed Meechan.

"Look, what about trying this one out for size, Dec? We take care of Brennan ourselves up at Tara. Make it look like he'd broken in and was trying to take you out: add a nice bit of damage to make it look like there'd been a struggle and you had to take him out in self defence. If all the evidence at the scene of the crime points to it, then the cops will just have to swallow it. Or alternatively, what if you have a word with your friend Lazarus and we set Brennan up outside the office and let someone else pull the trigger?"

"What happens if Brennan lives? Then he's going to smell a rat and we have major problems 'cos if he thinks we've framed him, the big fella is gonnae squeal."

Meechan steepled the fingers of either hand together, a sure sign that he was deep in thought

"It's a shite of a situation all right, but one I'm not going be rushing into. I have a bit of a soft spot for old Frankie, he's been with us from way back, Tommy, and the whole business with Reid has been a real boot in the balls for him. No, it can wait till the morning after all the pressure is off. Reid has gone to the great white hospital in the sky and will be talking to no one, and we have Frankie under lock and key at my place."

By six p.m. Hardie had dropped Thoroughgood back at Partickhill Road and the DS steeled himself for his meeting with Morse. Unlocking the front door, he was immediately assailed by the smell of fresh polish. Keeping the large ground-floor tenement flat clean was never easy given the non-stop hours demanded of any member of Glasgow's CID. He could hear the sound of the washing machine from the kitchen, and automatically made his way in to find Morse sipping a coffee and scanning the pages of the late edition the Evening Times.

"It's some headline, Mr Thoroughgood: 'Police let killer priest slip through their hands: Only triple murder witness has throat slit in Stobhill.' As far as bad publicity goes, that's about as bad as it gets."

"Aye, you're right there, my boss has just had his goolies booted by the ACC Crime, and Hardie and I spent an hour with him trying to rack our brains about any new leads that we could come up with."

"And did you?" asked Morse.

"Yeah, I think so, and I'm wonderin' if you might be able to help out with one of them. But first, how are you, Morse? Have you had time to take stock and get it all in perspective? I don't know what you and Gary had planned, but I would imagine you want to do everything in your power to help put the man who ordered his killing behind bars."

"It was one of those rollercoaster affairs and I've spent most of the afternoon going over how we managed to become so close in such a short time, but I guess you never know what is around the corner. If we did, life would be a lot easier, wouldn't you agree?"

No prizes for what he means by that, thought Thoroughgood; if we'd done our job properly then Gary

228

Reid would still be here and tucked up in some safe house instead of laid out on the slab down at the morgue with his throat cut from ear to ear.

"I dunno, Morse, if you knew what was around the corner what would that mean? That you'd never get out of bed in the morning?"

"I guess you could be right. Anyway I thought your flat could do with a bit of polish, I hope you don't mind. You said something earlier about the man who ordered Gary's killing? Do you mean it was a contract killing? And I take it by that you mean Declan Meechan?" asked Morse, his eyes burning with interest.

"Who else? It's looking like Father Gerry O'Hare, as the priest called himself, was a contract killer brought in from across the water. He had a Northern Irish accent, we think. We've put out an all ports and airports lookout for him but this whole thing is such a bloody mess, it wasn't done until nearly four hours after Gary was murdered. If Father Murphy was heading back to the Emerald Isle via Glasgow Airport, he had more than enough time to be back in Belfast or Dublin, sitting at his favourite bar with a pint of Guinness and a copy of the Irish Times and a whacking big wedge burning a hole in his back pocket by then."

Thoroughgood flicked the kettle back on and prepared a coffee before continuing with his resumé.

"I've got Hardie sniffing about a couple of leads with the PSNI and the Garda and we'll see what happens there, plus we've emailed and faxed descriptions of Father O'Hare over to see if we can jog a few memories. There's always the slight chance our man has done this kind of thing before; whether he has any previous convictions, though, is another matter."

He poured the boiling water into his favourite Partick Thistle mug, stirred, and took a large sip.

"Well, that's better than nothing Mr Thoroughgood …"

Morse found himself interrupted in mid-flow by the DS:

"For Pete's sake, will you stop calling me that? If you're staying under my roof you'll call me Gus, all right?"

"Sorry Gus," said Morse, shaken by the momentary aggression in Thoroughgood's voice. "Does that mean I'll be staying here for a while yet then?"

"I'm afraid it does but it's not a problem, and you seem to be making yourself at home all right!" said Thoroughgood with a grin.

Morse raised his mug in salute:

"So just what is it that you think I might be able to help you with, Gus?"

"We both know you're still friendly with Celine, although obviously I don't know just how friendly. As you know, I spoke to her after the attempt on Meechan's life, in George Square: she seemed very cosy with Meechan over the lunch table. But Celine is very good at playing the odds to look after herself. I haven't a Scooby what she might or might not know, but right now we have so little it's got to be worth seeing if she'll meet me for a chat. The only way I am going to be able to make that happen is through you, wee man. So has she, by any chance, been in touch with you over the last couple of days?"

"Yes, I'm still in touch with Celine and I daresay she would meet you, Gus. Just how much she knows about what has happened, or what has been going on behind the scenes to make these things happen, I don't know. Of course she doesn't know where I am. After what happened to poor Gary there's no way I would let anything like that slip, but I could text her and see if she'd meet me for a coffee and then ask. I reckon she would meet you somewhere discreet."

Thoroughgood could not stop a smile betraying his inner emotions.

"So I take it she knew all about your relationship with Gary? Did she know about Gary's intentions to grass up the gang, though?"

Morse shook his head.

"No, she didn't, and that may be a sticking point but I won't know until I ask her if she'll meet me. All I know is she sent me a text at two-thirty p.m. this afternoon saying she was sorry to hear about Gary and to take care. Can I ask one thing, Gus?"

Thoroughgood smiled in the affirmative.

"Just how much of this is personal and how much is business? Correct me if I'm wrong, but aren't you seeing someone now? I thought I heard Hardie taking the mickey about you having met her at speed-dating?"

"That's right, and you're beginning to sound like bloody Hardie into the bargain!" said Thoroughgood, laughing.

Morse remained serious.

"Declan Meechan asked Celine to marry him at the weekend. She said yes."

Thoroughgood looked like he'd been hit by a sledgehammer, put his mug down on the table with a bang, got up, and walked out.

30

SELF-ANALYSIS had never been Thoroughgood's strong point, he remembered as soon as he had slammed his mug down and stormed off, a reaction he immediately regretted. However, there was no getting away from the fact Celine had information that could greatly benefit the faltering murder inquiry. This might now prove an irrelevance if she had agreed to become engaged to Meechan. It could only mean one thing: she had decided her life was with him. Yet some part of Thoroughgood still hoped that if he could meet her it would serve both his professional need for information and might yet make her see what an act of folly it had been to pledge herself to Glasgow's most ruthless gangster.

He could not deny, as hard as he tried to do so, that a fire still burned brightly within him for her. So where did that leave Sara Spencer?

Would it be fooling himself to think that, should Celine agree to meet him, he could keep his composure and concentrate solely on gaining her help to bring down the man on whom she had just banked her future? An exercise in futility it may turn out to be, but the fact she had stayed in touch with Morse and knew all about his relationship with Gary Reid did give him hope that while she had decided to commit herself to Meechan, she did not necessarily agree with everything he stood for.

Okay, said the voice in his head, but what if you can't keep it together and it all comes pouring out? So what about Sara, is there any point?

Thoroughgood, deep in thought for the previous five minutes, stared out of his flat window while the melancholic strains of Fish and Marillion bewailed the agonies and inner torture of being Fugazi. Thoroughgood had to admit that when it came to women and his love life, he was indeed most probably fucked up, or "Fugazi" as it was termed by the veterans of the Vietnam War. If he was screwed up, did that make Sara some sort of Second Division emotional Cinderella to him? If it did, then he should show her some respect and make it clear tonight before wasting any more of her time. Time was something he didn't have much to spare, given that it was now six forty-five p.m. and he needed to shower and change out of his black suit before she arrived at seven-thirty.

First he had to get things straight in his head. He had enjoyed himself so much with Sara it had opened up many possibilities, even if she had hinted she would be moving on when her Civil Service secondment to Glasgow finished in a year's time. But then, as Thoroughgood had discovered to his cost, so much could change in twelve months, and he had the scars both emotionally and physically to prove it, thanks to that bastard Meechan.

The tracks on his Marantz CD player which, although fourteen years old, he still cherished like the memories of a schoolboy's first romance, only added to his torment. Emerald Lies, She Chameleon, the complexity of Fish's lyrics framed his every agony. Thoroughgood realised that what was hurting him so much right now was his inclination for an emotive machismo reaction to the unavoidable fact that he had lost the one girl he had ever loved to the man he hated and despised most on the planet.

He had to move on, and what offered him the best chance to do so? The answer he couldn't see past was Sara Spencer. The lounge door creaked open.

"Are you all right, Gus?" asked Morse, almost in a whisper. "You know I'm a good listener, so Gary always said, if you want to talk about things. It is not a sign of weakness to admit you're still in love with a ghost from the past, even if she has been haunting you for so long."

"Look Morse, I really don't have time for this."

The words were out of his mouth almost before he could regret them, and as Morse turned to leave he grabbed the informant's arm.

"Listen, I'm sorry, I didn't mean it. It's just that Sara is due round at seven-thirty and to be perfectly honest, my head is up my arse over this whole business."

"I can see that," said Morse. "It's obvious how much Celine meant to you and maybe still does, but you have to accept she has decided to move on. Maybe that's what her engagement to Meechan is about, rather than any rejection of the love you once had between you, and your feelings for her now. Everybody has to move on, Gus, and that includes you."

Thoroughgood was consumed by guilt: it wasn't as if someone close to him had died, unlike Morse.

"I'm sorry, Morse. I can't believe I've been so selfish, considering what you're going through."

Morse was determined to sidestep any conversation concerning his emotions, and the best way to do that was to focus on Thoroughgood's vulnerability. Too quickly he blurted out:

"I mean, listen to the music you're playing. Fish? How

old is that? Twenty years plus and as depressing as an empty funeral. It's like you've become frozen inside an emotional bubble. Maybe that's the problem: Celine has finally done something to burst it and you are struggling to cope, because the memories you've been clinging to are now irrelevant. If you don't move on, then irrelevant is what you're in danger of becoming when it comes to the female of the species."

"And you would be an expert?" snapped Thoroughgood.

"As it happens I would, because so many of my friends are females and I—unlike you, Gus—was in a stable relationship."

Thoroughgood moved over to his other prized possession, the 1875 Chiffonier which doubled up as his drinks cabinet.

"Fancy a bevvy?"

"Bacardi and Coke, thanks," said Morse.

After he had poured himself a gin and tonic, Thoroughgood sat down in his Chesterfield armchair, appreciative that Morse had opted for the sofa; a large gulp and Thoroughgood leaned back and shut his eyes, as if that would make it all go away.

"Do you want some advice? Even if you don't, I'm going to give it to you, because that's what friends do. How many girls do you know are prepared to spend their first date watching Partick Thistle and then want to come back for more? I think you've got to give her a chance; after all, what have you got to lose?

"As for Celine, I understand where you're coming from wanting to meet her, and I'll do my best, but to be honest, I think you'll be wasting your time both professionally and personally. Possibly this is the best thing that could happen to you, Gus. Maybe it's the only thing that will finally allow you to move on. But for tonight, forget about Celine and concentrate on Sara and having a great night out."

Thoroughgood raised his drink.

"Aye, you're probably right, wee man. Ironic, isn't it? I thought I was coming home to provide you with company, a sounding board, cheer you up or whatever and before I know it you've been in and out of my head like Sigmund bloody Freud. I think it's time for a shower!"

"Sounds like a good idea," said Morse.

Fifteen minutes later Thoroughgood was back in his favourite window-staring pose but refreshed and resplendent in faded jeans, his favourite blue-and-white striped Aquascutum shirt and brown suede jacket. His G&T refilled, he had entered the lounge to find Morse had removed his treasured Marillion CD and replaced it with the cool and mellow tones of Massive Attack.

"Oh I get it, this is part of dragging me and my image into the twenty-first century?"

"It's far more likely Sara is going to be impressed listening to this than that excuse for a suicide note, and it wasn't helping me out much either after what has happened this week."

Thoroughgood immediately felt guilty. "I'm sorry, I just got caught up in the whole self-analysis thing. Anyway, I don't want you scuttling off when Sara comes in. I'd like you to meet her while we have a quick drink before we go out, and then you can give me your opinion later on."

The doorbell rang. Thoroughgood had to admit Sara suited black, as he drank in her appearance framed in the dim glow of the lightbulb.

236

Tight black trousers with a sort of shiny stripe splitting the fabric, and a black leather jacket. She wore her hair loose, and he immediately missed the hat she'd had on at Firhill. Acutely aware that she was under the gaze of the most candid of assessments, she spoke, smiling:

"Well, are you going to ask me in or let me freeze to death out here?"

"Freeze to death out there of course!" he replied leaning forward to kiss her on the lips and enjoy a lungful of her perfume—what was it anyway?

Thoroughgood led her through to the flat lounge and introduced her to Morse:

"Sara I'd like you to meet a friend of mine from work, Gerry. He's staying here for a short time while he's having some work done on his house." A white lie never hurt anyone.

"Pleased to meet you, Gerry; are you one of Gus' copper chums then?" An innocent question, but a bloody awkward one for the wee man to field.

"Eh, well, you could say that, Sara. How do you do?"

The chat was superficial and pleasant and when Sara complimented Thoroughgood on his choice of music, Morse nearly choked on his Bacardi and Coke. By eight p.m. they were saying their cheerios and heading down Hyndland Road.

"So where are you taking me tonight, Gus? Chinese again is it?"

"No, I thought you enjoyed our Italian lunch so much the last time, we'd try a little place I've been going to for years, just off Partick Cross, called La Riviera."

"Very nice. I've heard a lot of good things about it," admitted Sara.

Fifteen minutes later they were pulling up seats

inside La Riviera and enjoying the view out across its red terracotta roofs and blue skies; at least, those of the painted backdrops providing the restaurant's famous colourful interior design.

Starting to feel good about himself, not least the prospect of spending a pleasant evening in Sara's company, Thoroughgood ordered a bottle of Barolo. The arch in Sara's eyebrows he took for a seal of approval. She looked lovely all right, in a jewel-encrusted black top which accentuated her curves; she playfully tapped the inside of his ankle with her foot in a cute little manoeuvre that boded well for later on in the evening.

They were just about to begin with the bruschetta when Thoroughgood was transfixed by the couple coming through the restaurant door. Declan Meechan and Celine Lynott had just entered La Riviera. It didn't take a genius to work out something was wrong, as Thoroughgood's small talk all but dried up. Sara leaned across the table and spoke:

"Look Gus, I know something is the matter and I don't know whether I've done anything to upset you. Has it anything to do with that couple who have just come in and are sitting down to our right?"

Thoroughgood finished his bite of bruschetta and washed it down with a generous mouthful of Barolo.

"I guess you could say it does, Sara. It just makes me sick that I can't seem to go anywhere in this city where my work doesn't get in the way."

"What do you mean, Gus? I don't understand."

After his discussion with Morse earlier in the evening, Thoroughgood knew that if his relationship with Sara was to stand any chance of success, then honesty was not only the best policy but the only one.

238

"I'm afraid, Sara, that the man is almost certainly the person behind the seven killings which have happened in the city in the last week. The female is his fiancée. Less than a week ago I had to interview them after there was an attempt on their lives in George Square.

"He is probably the most powerful criminal in Glasgow right now, although he does his best to cover it up with a string of legitimate fronts. Underneath it all he is absolutely without scruples; he will, and does, have anyone who gets in his way removed. Ten years ago he very nearly managed to do that to me." Thoroughgood required another deep draught of Barolo.

"So that's Declan Meechan? I've seen his picture in the Evening Times but he looks a lot bigger in person. I don't like these eyes of his, though. They're cruel," said Sara.

"Oh, Meechan is cruel all right, cruel and brutal and his ambition knows no bounds. It stretches from bribing council officials into allowing planning permission for his huge West End multiplex project. It includes hiring a hitman dressed as a priest to cut the throat of one of his gang members who wanted out and was ready to squeal on him …" Thoroughgood's tirade was interrupted by the approaching sound of footsteps.

"Detective Sergeant Thoroughgood, we meet again for the second time inside of a week. We really must stop bumping into each other or people will start to talk, especially in the present climate," spoke Declan Meechan, towering over the couple.

Thoroughgood said nothing, his set jaw made words redundant. Sara looked up at Meechan nervously and for the second time that evening she could feel eyes, callous and spiteful orbs, coolly appraising her.

"Well, Detective Sergeant, you are a lucky man tonight. Please introduce me to your lovely lady here."

"Why would I want to introduce any friend of mine to a murdering piece of sewage like you, Meechan? No, I think you've said enough, and now it's time for you to toddle back off to your fiancée and stop polluting the air around our table." Thoroughgood was barely able to keep his mounting anger in check.

Meechan's smile was sweetness and light:

"Ah, typical policeman, no manners, no class but interesting to hear you know Celine and I got engaged. How does it feel to know the woman you did," Meechan turned his smile on Sara as he spoke, "or is it still, love, has agreed to be my wife, Detective Sergeant Thoroughgood? The bottom line is you're a loser at work and a loser in play and Celine would never choose a loser. I hope you manage to enjoy your evening, young lady, despite the company you keep."

With that Meechan turned round and made his way back to Celine; sitting down at his table he turned back to look at Thoroughgood and Sara, flashing a quick wave of his hand before taking Celine's in his and allowing the giant diamond to sparkle on her finger.

This time it was Sara who took a giant slurp of her wine.

"I think you have some explaining to do," she said.

Thoroughgood shrugged his shoulders at the hopelessness of it all.

"Where do I start, Sara?"

"The beginning is the best place," she said without the slightest hint of humour.

"Roughly ten years ago I was a young beat cop in Partick who was desperate to get my CID Aide. To

240

do that I had to impress my superiors by clearing up housebreakings, get information that would allow me to pull in neds for robbery and other stuff. I managed, with the help of a tout, to talk a prisoner from Peterhead high security prison who was on the run, to give himself up. At the time the criminal underworld in Partick and the West End was run by a man called Jimmy Gray. By the time I got into the CID on my aide, I tried to cultivate a ring of informants that would allow me to cause Gray as many problems as possible. One of these informants, or touts as they were called, was Celine Lynott."

Thoroughgood reached forward and picked up the bottle of Barolo, refilling both of their glasses with the last drops of the rich red. Signalling over to the waiter, he ordered a second.

"That may be a bit presumptuous, considering the conversation we have just had with Meechan, Gus," said Sara.

"I'm taking a chance on you staying for the steak au poivre. If my company is no longer required, at least don't rob yourself of experiencing the best sirloin in the West End." Thoroughgood did his best to bring some levity to the conversation and detected a slight rise in the temperature from the other side of the table, but still no smile.

"You were just about to tell me about you and Celine, Detective Sergeant, or at least I hope you were or I'll be missing the best sirloin in Glasgow, won't I?"

Thoroughgood cleared his throat nervously.

"At the time Celine was a croupier on the Riverboat Casino and I fell for her, plain and simple. That also coincided with the arrival of Declan Meechan, fresh on the scene from Belfast and full of brash ambition. From nowhere he started to climb the ranks of Gray's empire, and of course he met Celine and decided he wanted her for himself.

"When he found out that she had been seeing me, he arranged a little accident for me by way of a hit and run. It took twelve hours of reconstructive surgery and a mechanic's box of nuts and bolts to put me back together. Meechan had also been filling Celine's head full of lies about me using her for information and sex and treating her little better than a cheap whore. She never came to visit me in hospital and it took a year of rehab and physio up at Castlebrae, the police rehab place, to get me back to work."

"So that explains why you and Celine split up, but if that was ten years back, why has it taken her so long to agree to become engaged to Meechan?" asked Sara.

"You don't miss much, do you? Although the damage was done in terms of our relationship, a mutual friend made sure she knew Meechan was poisoning her against me, and it was all a pack of lies, so he could make her his own. When this friend ended up bobbing up and down in the Clyde she decided it was over with Meechan as well. I don't know what's brought them back together, you'd have to ask her."

"But I'm not interested in her, am I, Gus? What I want to know is, is it over between you and her, never mind him, right now in the here and present?"

At that point the steak arrived.

"I don't suppose I could wait until after the main course?"

Sara's face said it all.

"To be honest with you, Sara, because that's what you deserve, until I met you on Saturday, I didn't know. I

242

think I've been living in a bit of a timewarp and perhaps I haven't moved on from what happened ten years back. Bearing in mind this is only our second date, I don't want to go scaring you but I think maybe you are helping me to see, if I may quote, that 'The past is a foreign country, they do things differently there.'"

At last Sara smiled and Thoroughgood could feel himself breathing again, even as he was fighting against the overwhelming desire to glance at Celine.

31

BY NINE-THIRTY a.m. Thoroughgood had already finished his first round of toast when Morse slipped into the kitchen, putting on the kettle before informing the DS he'd sent a text inviting Celine for coffee. When a reply came in, Thoroughgood knew instantly from the smile on Morse's face that the news was good.

Morse took the tube into the city centre and as the underground bustled along, he found himself wondering if he had any right to insert the type of doubt in Celine's mind that may come between her and happiness. He'd realised when Thoroughgood had come in the previous night that however much the DS enjoyed Sara's company, there was still something he carried deep inside his soul for Celine.

For everything Thoroughgood was doing for him, he had to do the best he could in return with Celine. The fact she was engaged to the man who had ordered the contract killing of his lover meant he would take deep satisfaction in driving a wedge between Celine and Meechan, much though he tried not to admit it to himself.

Soon he found himself walking down Buchanan Street, the rain pouring down on top of him and bouncing off in hundreds of tiny explosions of liquid. He pulled his Berghaus up to his chin, but the combination of the slashing diagonal rain and the chill April breeze made for a wholly unpleasant experience. Shoppers scuttled for the cover of shops while the usual street canvassers, ready with the most inane questions to ask the Glasgow public, did their very best to attract attention and stall the soaking pedestrians. The weather ensured that even with huge golf umbrellas held invitingly, they were not having much luck.

Morse continued down the pedestrianised street, one of the busiest shopping thoroughfares in the city, then turned into the teeth of the stinging rain, and Royal Exchange Square where, opposite the Modern Art Gallery, was situated Costa Coffee's city centre shop. Quickly, he made his way inside and saw one of the window booths was vacant.

He stared out of the window, smiling at the obvious irritation of the dripping punters passing by. Scrutinising the Modern Art Gallery, a huge granite grey building which reminded Morse of some huge eighteenth-century church, he spotted Celine. Dressed in black leather boots and a cream raincoat; shuddering under a huge umbrella as she did her best to remain poised and elegant despite her obvious discomfort. She saw him in the window seat and gave a wave.

Five minutes later the two of them were enjoying a warming sip of the massive "regular" lattes, a house speciality. Morse reckoned it took another quarter of an hour to get the small talk out of the way and allow him to become comfortable enough to get to the bottom line. It was Celine who forced the issue.

"So Gerry, it's been nice catching up with you and now I've shown you my engagement ring, I guess we can get down to the real reason you were in such a hurry to see me today."

"You're right, Celine, but it's hard to know where to start."

"Would it have anything to do with our chance meeting with Gus Thoroughgood and his new lady friend last night?" asked Celine in forthright fashion.

Morse knew then that honesty was the only worthwhile policy: "That's part of it but there's an awful lot more and it concerns your fiancé, Celine. If you forgive me for being nosy, why have you suddenly decided to agree to become engaged to Declan after all these years spent rejecting his advances?"

"That's just it, Gerry, a lot of water has gone under the bridge and Declan has always been there, waited for me and let me know how much he wanted me. I guess when the stuff between him and Gus happened all those years back it freaked me out, but then you know that. When you're a kid you think you have forever to find the right person, that there's always someone better round the corner. I began to think that, despite rejecting his advances, Declan had shown me respect professionally by putting me in charge of his city business and letting me make my own decisions. What kind of man does that for a woman who is constantly denting his pride and telling him she doesn't want him?"

Morse looked out the window thoughtfully, then shrugged his shoulders but said nothing.

"Well, it's ten years on and no one better was round the corner, but Declan was still there and still letting me know how much he wanted me. Maybe he just wore me down, but there has always been something between us and eventually I just thought the time was right to say yes."

Morse grimaced. "So, what about Gus Thoroughgood? Do you still feel something for him?"

Celine smiled. "Yes, to be honest I do, but I don't want to be torn in two again like I was back then. I've been there and done that, and now I've made my choice I'm sticking to it, or haven't you noticed this?" She flashed the diamond under Morse's nose. "Do you think I would be wearing it if I hadn't made my decision?"

Morse decided it was now time for shock tactics.

"What if I told you that two days ago your fiancé had the man I love murdered, his throat slit while he lay helplessly in a hospital bed? What if I told you your fiancé is behind the gangland killing of seven persons including my lover? What if I told you Declan has not finished his killing spree yet, and that he is importing massive quantities of coke and heroin into the city?"

Celine's face clouded over with a mixture of hurt and anger. "And just what do you want me to do about that?"

Morse struggled to stop the surprise at her reaction showing on his normally unreadable features. It had been a response he had not expected.

"But surely you don't want to promise yourself to the most vicious gangster in the city? You must know it will all end in tears one day and if you go through with this, Celine, it will be you who is left to pick up the pieces, even if you are a very rich widow."

"I don't know about what you have just said, but I'm not going to say it would be a surprise if some of it was true. But I know Declan Meechan loves me and has spent so long proving just how much he does. Do you think the people you're saying he is responsible for killing wouldn't have killed Declan if they had got there first? You have a short memory if you've forgotten that I was with Declan when a taxi pulled up, someone leant out the window and fired three or four shots at us. What does that tell you about the type of people Declan is up against? I'm sorry to hear what happened to Gary and no one deserves to have their life ended the way he did, but can you say to me with any honesty that he wasn't a player himself?"

Morse opened his mouth to say something but thought better of it when Celine put her hand up to warn him there was more. She lowered her voice before carrying on.

"I know there are some things I'm better off not knowing, but I am prepared to put up with that. In this life, Gerry, you only get one chance at happiness, and I thought mine had gone, so forgive me if I put myself first."

Morse knew then he had probably overstepped the mark, but he had still failed to ask Celine if she would meet up with Thoroughgood. Before he cut to the chase he felt he had to have one last go at making Celine realise she'd chosen the road to ruin.

"Listen, Celine, we've known each other for the best part of fifteen years, since you were a teenager; when have I ever lied to you? Don't you think I want you to be happy? Of course I do, but you've got to weigh up all the facts and not be selective in what you chose to see or hear. You and I both know what happened the last time someone got too close to you, and they ended up the victim of a hit and run. It took Thoroughgood over a year to make it back to work and he was bloody lucky he lived, never mind worked again.

"Now maybe Declan Meechan doesn't actually pull the trigger or draw the knife but he's the man who's behind it, just like he's the man flooding the city's streets with gear and the clubs with coke. Is this the man you want to settle down with when there's still at least one decent man out there who loves you, who you seem to have completely forgotten about?"

Morse could see some of the anger draining from Celine's face; she knew what was coming next but the informant couldn't make up his mind whether she would like what he had to say. He paused briefly to drain his latte.

"You and I both know Gus Thoroughgood is still in love with you. How can I be so sure? Well, I'm staying with him at the moment because the cops say it's not safe for me to return to my flat in Springburn, the same flat Gary was knifed in by one of your fiancé's henchmen. I've been staying at Thoroughgood's place ever since, and you know what? The man is living in a timewarp because he hasn't been able to put behind him what happened all these years back when Declan Meechan had him hospitalised with so many fractures they thought he'd be crippled for life. He can't get over the fact that, through no fault of his own, the one woman he ever loved—and thought loved him in equal measure—was taken from him by a cold-blooded killer.

"Now he finds she has decided to forgive the killer and agree to be his wife. Do you know what that can do to a man inside? I'll tell you, it's taken Thoroughgood right up until now to start to move on and just as he is making the first steps to kickstart his life, up you pop with Meechan, the man who ruined him, stole the woman he loved and nearly had him killed."

Morse came up for air and as he did Celine seized her chance:

"Well, for a man nursing a broken heart for ten years, he looked pretty happy with his new girlfriend in La Riviera last night."

"And hasn't he got a right to some happiness, Celine? You've just said you owe it to yourself look out for number one because you only get one shot at happiness in this life. In any case, I'd hardly compare a second date to an engagement, would you?"

Celine pinched her forehead between two fingers and massaged.

"So what's the point behind all this, apart from ruining any happiness I might have found at last?"

The time for bullshit was gone and Morse knew it.

"Gus wants to meet you."

"What?"

"Look, what harm will one last meeting do either of you? I'd say you still have some doubts in the back of your mind about whether you are doing the right thing, whatever you say. As for Gus, I think he needs closure and if you were to meet him then maybe you would both come away with exactly that. As long as Meechan doesn't know, what harm can it do? But it's up to you. I'm only the messenger and Gus said it's your call on the time and the place."

Celine shook her head unconvinced anything good would come from going over old ground that would in all likelihood cause them both a lot of pain. She stared out of the window and watched the rain bounce off the concrete. Eventually she spoke:

"All right, Declan is going to be out of town tomorrow. Tell Gus I'll be up at the reservoir in Milngavie at four p.m. He'll know where to find me."

Morse smiled again, the relief sweeping over him like a tidal wave.

"For what it's worth, I think you're making the right call, Celine. Just do me one favour."

"And that is?"

"Go with an open mind."

"I'll do my best. Cheerio, Gerry."

With that she stood up and walked out, and something about her manner made Morse feel that was the last conversation he would ever have with Celine Lynott in this world and maybe even the next.

32

THOROUGHGOOD AND Hardie's first port of call was Stewart Street Office, where they checked for any results from their dispatches across the sea. As they had predicted, at close of play on Tuesday, "Father O'Hare" had slipped through the all ports lookout broadcast shortly after he'd slit Gary Reid's throat to the bone.

So far there was no official response from the description they had faxed to Dublin but after checking his office line Hardie had discovered a message from Belfast CID, and a DS Sean Devlin, to give him a bell back.

"Sounds good," said Thoroughgood. "Well, what are you waiting for, faither?"

Hardie quickly made the call and was met by the unique sound of a strong Northern Irish accent on the other end of the line:

"Aye, Sean Devlin here, who's askin'?"

"It's Kenny Hardie from Central CID, Strathclyde Police, Sean, thanks for returning my call about Father Gerry O'Hare. How're you keepin'?"

"Not so bad Kenny, yersel?"

"A lot fuckin' better if we weren't in the middle of a gangland war that's left us with seven unsolved murders and more on the way. The shit has really hit the fan over here; in fact, I can't remember anything like it in my twenty years service."

"Fuck me Kenny, is that all it is, just the twenty now?" and there was a barking laugh that seemed to boom out all the way across the Irish Sea. "Aye, but you'll be wantin' anything I've got in double time."

"That would be a help, Sean. Me and my DS are headin' out to Barlinnie to try and get something out of a couple of neds banged up there and we have the Detective Superintendent jumpin' up and doon like a kangaroo on fire. So if you wouldnae mind …"

"Yer man is Brendan O'Driscoll and he's a hired gun, all right. He was a shooter for the IRA back in the early Nineties; yer man Declan Meechan and our Brendan here have history together for sure. Since the Troubles have cooled he's disappeared onto the continent and has been doing some work for the Russian Mafia. Aye, our Brendan has ice water runnin' through his veins and that would be just his style, turnin' up as a priest to administer the Last Rites on some poor sod. Anyways we've put a lookout out for him but he's a clever sod, you cannae be expecting him to stay lookin' like a priest for too long. In fact, I'd suggest Father O'Hare was no more within five minutes of the hit. O'Driscoll is top quality, in fact you wouldnae be needin' any better."

"Well that's great, Sean, but what you're telling me is that although we now know who he is, catching him is a totally different ball game," groaned Hardie.

"Put it this way, Kenny, he hasnae had the jail over here since he was a kid, but what I'd suggest you do is check Interpol intelligence on him and see what ye can come up with. I'm pretty sure he'll make for the continent, even if he did come back into Belfast after the hit; when he gets there he might just be lettin' his guard down, son. Anyways, if I get anything at this end, I'll be straight on the blower."

"Thanks, Gerry. By the way, when did you get the promotion?"

"That's been eighteen months now, what about ye? Any chance of a leg up?"

"Fuck all," was the terse two-word reply.

"Well, you keep yer pecker up, Kenny son. God save Ireland!" and with that bizarre send-off Devlin was gone.

Hardie provided a blow-by-blow recount of his call with Devlin to Thoroughgood and after checking the Police National Computer reference numbers for him, they were able to bring up a grainy black and white photo of O'Driscoll that must have been fifteen years old.

"Okay faither, at least we have something to go on. Now get someone from the uniform bar to get onto Interpol and see what we can turn up on O'Driscoll. You just never know. If he's been working for the Russian Mafia then someone might have something for him from there, or maybe in Germany. Just make sure uniform cover all bases."

Hardie nodded his head. After five minutes he met Thoroughgood at the back of City Centre nick and they dived into the restored red Focus and headed for the Bar-L.

They turned off the M8 and down into Riddrie, with the forbidding shape of Barlinnie looming large like some eighteenth-century army barracks holding a dark grisly secret within its huge walls. The Focus ground to a halt at the solid steel gateway, and the challenge to identify themselves came from a speaker situated at the driver's side of the vehicle. The formalities of identification had to be observed rigidly in the highly regimented world that was HMP Barlinnie. Eventually the twelve-inch-thick steel doors lifted and they drove through, winding round a tight roadway behind the massive curtain walls.

254

Thoroughgood had faxed a request the previous afternoon, countersigned by Tomachek, for their visit to the Governor's office, explaining the identities of the residents they wanted to speak to and of course the reason for it. Eventually, following the routine body search administered to anyone who entered the Bar-L, they were ushered to the prison interview rooms well away from Hall C where Simms and Jarvis were housed, by a prison officer who had obviously had a sense of humour bypass.

Any attempts at conversation were completely ignored, and soon Hardie and Thoroughgood fell into a sullen silence as the morose warden led them to an interview room.

Eventually the silence was broken when Prison Officer Grey—how apt, thought Hardie—enquired if they'd like a coffee. Both nodded in the affirmative and were treated to a view of Warder Grey's back in double quicktime. But to be fair to the dour prison officer, he soon returned with a tray, two coffees, a jug of milk, a bowl of sugar and two Tunnock's Caramel Wafers.

Hardie could not hide his glee. "Man, this is better than I get at hame."

Thoroughgood thought he saw the twitch of a smile at the corner of Grey's mouth, but it was soon gone.

"So who are we getting the privilege of our first interview with, Officer Grey?" he asked.

"It'll be Ricky Simms and I'll have the wee scroat along for you in five minutes."

The two detectives exchanged glances. Both had made themselves familiar with the Section Fourteen detention interviews of Jarvis and Simms the previous day. Simms was undoubtedly the more naive of the two young would-be gangsters.

"That's a bonus, gaffer," said Hardie. "If we can burst him or at least convince him to come across then we have much more chance with Jarvis, the hard nut of the two. What's the angle then, boss?"

"I would think word has percolated through the walls of the Bar-L that one of their mates has had his throat slit by a priest, and the other has gone missing. What concerns me is if Meechan has had anyone give them a warning from the inside. If they've been got at then we may have a problem. We have to convince them that, either way, Meechan will have a sticky end lined up for both of them, whatever happens. Our main problem may be just how much they know and whether it goes high enough up the tree to allow us to finger Meechan. Either way, faither, we need a result."

Thoroughgood took a gulp of coffee and removed his Barbour jacket, placing it over his chair and turning the cuffs of his immaculately- pressed white shirt—Morse had done his ironing as well as his homework—making ready for the interview.

Hardie's eyebrows shot up and then he laughed.

"Nice creases down the arms. You got that wee bird doin' yer ironin' already gaffer?"

The door was thrown open and Warder Grey pushed in the reluctant, petulant form of Ricky Simms.

"Sit doon, son," said Hardie, pointing to the chair at the other side of the table,

"Can Warder Grey get you a cup of coffee or tea?" Hardie winked at Grey but got no response.

"Naw, ah'm fine. Whit's this all aboot? Ah've already spoke to the mob about the Broons."

"Now, now, let's just take our time and make sure we observe all the formalities for the benefit of the tape here,"

256

said Hardie as he quickly went through the usual list of required caution and checks. Hardie looked to his DS to take the lead but was met with a smile which invited him to continue instead.

"A lot has changed on the outside since then, and for your safety's sake you need to listen to what we've got to say and have a long hard think."

Simms stuck his right index finger up his left nostril and had a rummage in a barely concealed gesture of contempt.

"You've got nuttin' I'm gonnae want to hear, CID."

Hardie was far from discouraged and leaned across the table giving the sleeves of Simms' prison shirt a little tug in the process:

"Oh, but I think I have, wee man, and you aren't going to like it one bit. Do you know what's happened to Gary Reid and Frankie Brennan?"

"We get the fuckin' papers in Bar-L."

"First class, but did you know that the man who slit Gazza Reid's throat was bought and paid for by Declan Meechan? That he's a contract killer who has been workin' for the Russian Mafia but is also an old Belfast mate of Meechan's?"

Warming to the task, Hardie leaned back in his chair before continuing with some relish:

"Did you also know that big cuddly Frankie Brennan has gone missing and there's every chance he'll go the same way as Reid? Now when that happens, wee man, the only two who can fire Meechan in will be you and your wee playmate Chico. You're a smart wee boy, allegedly: I'll let you work out the rest."

Simms' pale features stretched taut across his skeletal face. He knew exactly what was implied. Hardie, seizing the moment, attempted to press home the advantage:

"Now, wee man, if you're thinking, and I'd wager ma last tenner you are, that Declan Meechan always takes care of his own, then you are obviously needin' a padded cell instead of a jail cell. Sooner or later you and Chico are gonnae have a nice wee accident inside Bar-L, and how easy do you think that would be to arrange?" Hardie clicked his fingers in illustration.

"Easy as ABC I'd say, matey. Yer throat cut with a razor in the bogs, something sharp in the back when you're in the laundry, or a hypodermic full of something nasty pumped into you while you sleep. Take your pick, wee man, cos it's only a matter of time before you and Chico buy it, and then there was none." Hardie finished with some satisfaction. The silence reverberated around the interview room's stone walls. Simms opened his mouth:

"Whit you sayin' CID?"

Hardie stretched, arching his back over the rear of the chair which groaned its resentment as he displayed his ample beer belly, then bounced forward, elbows thumping onto the table. It shook and so did Simms.

"What I'm saying, wee man, is that you need to get yourself somewhere safe, somewhere Meechan or whoever he pays for cannae lay a glove on you and there is only one way that is going to happen, capiche?"

Simms looked unhappy as recognition of what the DC was saying finally dawned on him.

"I'm no a grass, CID."

"No one is saying they want you to grass … in as many words. But don't you owe it to Gazza and big Frankie? Fuck me, I'm sure they'd do the same for you if the boot was on the other foot. Hey, if you want tae go the same way as them then that's fine, but how old are you, Ricky?"

258

"Twenty," whispered Simms.

"Don't you want to see bit more of life? We put you up somewhere safe and then make sure you have a fresh start, miles away from Glasgow, and with Meechan all tucked up behind bars somewhere far cosier than Bar-L. All you have to do is tell us what happened the night the Browns bought it and anything else you know, and you can look forward to collecting your pension and seeing the grandweans grow up. If you don't, all you've got to look forward to is a nasty end that you know is coming but you don't know just when, or how it's gonnae hit you. Either way, you wind up on the slab with the pathologist slitting your guts wide open and poking about trying to tell us what happened."

Thoroughgood thought he'd back up the pleasant little picture Hardie had been so busy painting.

"Come on Ricky, it's not rocket science. We can have you out of here straightaway if you agree to help and somewhere you don't have to look over your shoulder. You give us the whole script and we sort you for life. Make the wrong choice right now and I can promise you your life is over, just like DC Hardie says."

Simms shook his head but it was hard to say whether this was a mixture of desperation or recognition that it was time to save his own skin.

"What about Chico?"

Thoroughgood smiled reassuringly.

"We're going to be speaking to Chico right after we've finished with you and we're gonnae offer him the same deal. If he agrees to speak to us then it makes our case against Meechan so much stronger. Two of you firing him in and he is certain to go down."

Another silence as Simms weighed up his options but reality had already dawned: there was no choice.

"Okay, I'll cough."

"You're not gonnae regret it, wee man, not on your life,' smiled Hardie with dripping sarcasm, and clicked off the tape.

"Warder Grey, would you escort the young man to our little holding room and then we'll take Jarvis when you're ready. Oh and another coffee would be nice!"

"Up yer arse," shouted Grey from over his shoulder.

"Result," said Thoroughgood, "it would almost be game, set and match if we can persuade Chico to sing as well, but I don't know from what I've heard about him if that's going to be so easy."

"Damn sight easier now his wee play-matey has decided to turn though," observed Hardie.

"Aye, we could have this all wrapped up by the weekend."

Thoroughgood, a man who habitually saw his glass as half-empty rather than half-full, urged caution.

"You'll be lucky. Getting Simms and Jarvis to sing is one thing but there'll always be something more. We've still got to try and find Brennan, because whatever the two baby-faced assassins know, you can bet it's nothing compared with the notes Frankie the choir boy would be able to hit. Nope, let's take it one step at a time and see what Chico has got to say for himself before we get carried away, faither."

"Sometimes this job would burst yer arse," was all Hardie had to say on the matter.

Moments later Grey entered the interview room with Chico Jarvis but minus the two extra cups of coffee. Hardie couldn't help himself:

"Not even a caramel wafer to spare, Mr Grey?"

Grey failed to bite:

"Charles Jarvis as requested."

Jarvis immediately walked round to the other side of the chair and plonked himself down, sprawling his arms and dangling his denim-clad legs over the edges of the moulded seat. It was a statement of intent:

You don't fuckin' scare me, CID.

"Make yourself comfortable Chico," said Thoroughgood, still not sure quite how he was going to play this one.

"You know we've just had a nice wee chat with your mate Ricky?"

"What's that gotta do with me, copper?" he spat out.

"Ricky has seen sense, Chico; he's going to be helping us with our enquiries in the interests of his health. I hope we can convince you that would be the smart move for you as well," said the DS.

"That little grassin' shite. I told him to keep his friggin' trap shut."

"How nice of you to put it like that, but given what has happened to your mates Gazza and Frankie, it's not exactly the smartest piece of advice you could have given your best mate, is it?" sneered Hardie.

"What do you know, pig?" rapped Jarvis.

"I'll tell you what I know, Chico. I know that Gazza Reid has had his throat slit and Frankie Brennan has gone missing and I know that's because someone is making sure there are no loose ends tying him to the killing of the Browns. But that's just the fuckin' problem for you and your little chum Ricky. The pair of you are the only loose ends left and you aren't going to be allowed to dangle for much longer."

"Ah heard that Reid was squealin' to yous and he got what he deserved. It's fuckin' obvious the reason big

Frankie is missing is because you lot are lookin' to catch him and pin any bit of shit yous can tae him. So, like I say, you can fuck off."

Hardie snatched a quick glance at his gaffer:

So someone has managed to brief the little shit and he's bought it all, hook, line and sinker, he thought.

"Is that right, Chico?" asked Thoroughgood.

"Yous know it is," Jarvis said, running his fingers through his short spiky hair.

"The problem for you, Chico, is it's only fifty per cent right. Reid was going to help us with our enquiries, but I'm afraid big Frankie was sent out to shut him up and cocked up. That's why your boss had to put a contract out on Reid to get the job done properly. Now big Frankie has become a liability to Meechan and no one knows where he's gone. Don't you think that Meechan will have you and Simms sussed out? Don't you think he'll know that if we lean on Ricky he would be likely to burst? And if Simms bursts then you're fucked either way, aren't you Chico?

"We've got enough circumstantial evidence to back up anything we get from Ricky to put you away for a long stretch, and that's only if Meechan decides he can take the chance and let you live. But do you think he is going to do that, knowing you have enough knowledge to put him away if you follow suit with Ricky? The answer to that, pal, is a big fat no fuckin' chance. If you can't see that then we won't be wasting any more time with you, cos frankly my dear, I don't give a damn what happens to a miserable little piece of shit like you. Do we really need you anyway? As the man once said, maybees aye maybees naw."

Thoroughgood stopped for effect, raised his shoulders and frowned.

"Not really is the answer."

Getting up from his chair he stood and beckoned to Hardie to do the same.

"I look forward to hearing how it happens, Chico: just remember what I said when the blade goes biting through your flesh and the blood starts pouring out over your hands, 'cos it'll be all too late by then."

"Adios Chico," said Hardie, then turning to his gaffer, "I'll give you a ten spot he's deid by the end of the week, toes sticking out a laundry basket."

"I'll take it," said the DS and they both turned to leave.

"Hawd on," said a voice from behind them. "Awright, I'll talk," croaked Jarvis.

Thoroughgood glanced sideways at Hardie.

"Did I hear something, Detective Constable?"

Hardie smiled at his gaffer and nodded his head as they both turned to stare at Jarvis, who seemed suddenly to have shrunk at least three sizes in his denim prison uniform.

"Smart boy," he said.

33

WITHIN HALF an hour of persuading Simms and Jarvis to turn Queen's evidence, the two fledgling criminals and their CID minders were back at City Centre, Stewart Street. Simms and Jarvis were deposited in separate detention rooms to make sure the latter didn't exercise an unhealthy influence over his buddy, pending further and full detailed interviews, while Thoroughgood and Hardie headed for Detective Superintendent Tomachek's office with almost identical smiles on their faces.

Thoroughgood knocked on the door and a booming "Come in" sounded from the office behind it. When they entered, Tomachek was immediately up and out of his chair offering a congratulatory handshake.

"Well done, my boys, now spare me no details." Thoroughgood, ably assisted by Hardie, soon filled in the blanks for his commanding officer. While Tomachek's glee was almost unbridled, his DS was keen to apply a reality check, like the emergency brake to a runaway train.

"Boss, we know we're going to get everything the boys can give us because even the hard nut Jarvis was bricking it by the end, but the problem might be just how much they can give us.

"There's no doubt we're going to have enough to put Frankie Brennan behind bars for life, but the big problem is getting ahold of Brennan while he's still breathing. We've had our touts keeping their eyes and ears open, and so far there has been nothing. That isn't easy considering who he is and his size. What if they can't give us much more than hearsay evidence as far as Meechan goes? If that's the case, we have a real headache ahead and the prospect that he will wriggle off scot free again."

"How's it going to look having one gang member dead, one missing and two turned evidence? It's all a bit, well, messy for the want of a better word."

Tomachek refused to have his high spirits lowered.

"For God's sake, Gus, you aren't telling me they won't have something we can't lay at Meechan's door? After all, who the bloody hell did they take orders from?"

Hardie answered that one:

"That's just it, boss. They're both a long way down the food chain and it's more than likely it was Frankie Brennan who gave out the orders and took them from Meechan. That's why we really could do with getting our mitts on big Frankie."

"Aye, I see what you mean, but let's wait and see what the boys have got to say. Now they're witnesses for the Crown we have made sure, you will be glad to hear considering what happened with Reid, that we have safe houses already taken care of. What you two need to do is convince them both that the offer is very much within a limited window of time and that we won't be dicked about; I want them left in no doubt they will find themselves back at the Hotel Bar-L in double quick time if we don't have something to pin on Meechan."

Through the screen of smoke Thoroughgood saw Tomachek's lips move once more:

"We also need to get out of these two where Brennan

is likely to be; they must be able to make an educated guess, at the very bloody least, where he's holed up."

"You'd like to think so, boss," agreed Thoroughgood.

"Anyway, I'm going to take almost as much satisfaction from telling DCI Farrell you've burst Jarvis and Simms as I have from the news that you'd finally got them to turn Queen's evidence. Needless to say, that's going to mean questions being asked in the Ivory Tower as to why his boys failed to get a result under Section Fourteen at the start of this whole sorry mess.

"All right, you may have had some advantages with which to apply the pressure, but I certainly won't be volunteering any of them to ACC Cousins when I phone him immediately after you've left my office!" Tomachek's raised eyebrows made it clear their chat was finished.

They headed back down the stairs to the DS's room and, switching his mobile back on, Thoroughgood found a text message from Morse revealing that Celine was prepared to meet him up by Milngavie Reservoir at four p.m. tomorrow. It meant more to him than any of the other developments that day.

"Look Ricky, as DC Hardie has explained to you, we are already aware of both Gary Reid and Frankie Brennan's roles in all of this, much though we value your confirmation of that. I want you to take your time and try and recall any occasion when you were in the company of Declan Meechan and he said anything that would tie him in with the murder of the Walter, Jimmy and Davie Brown," said Thoroughgood.

Simms' face seemed to glaze over and the DS saw Hardie loosening his tie frantically, his temper ready to blow.

"Come on, son, there must have been something that would help us out here."

Simms' face was glum but then a glimmer of recognition sparked across it:

"Aye, there was. When we got back fae Aberfoyle and Brennan was dropping us off, we went by Mr Meechan's office and he thanked us both for, what was it he said, aye, 'Doing a good joab on the Browns.' After he paid us a grand each, he told us if we kept our noses clean there would be plenty more where that came from."

"What do you mean a job well done, son? Was that it?" demanded Hardie.

"Aye, it wiz. Like I say, we nearly always dealt with someone else, either Reid or Brennan. Sure, if he saw you at one of his clubs, like the Volcano, Mr Meechan would ask how business was goin' and slip you a wedge, but that was it."

It was much the same story with Jarvis. It was almost always Brennan who gave them their orders, Meechan a distant figure, apart from that one small slip-up in his office after the Brown job.

"Aye, he was well chuffed wi' the number we did on the Broons. He slipped me another fifty on the way out and said to me it was one of the happiest days of his life."

There was just enough information gleaned to arrest Meechan and charge him with murder, in that he was art and part, but Charlie Coyle would have a field day tearing their evidence to pieces in the resulting High Court case. A very public embarrassment for Strathclyde Police, and Meechan's grinning face would be slapped all over the front pages claiming he had been stitched up but that justice had prevailed.

To which Hardie's "Fuck that" echoed precisely Thoroughgood's own thoughts on the matter.

One little ray of hope shone out in the cavern of darkness and mounting despair that was interview room one: both Jarvis and Simms reckoned there was a fair chance Brennan was holed up in Meechan's mansion up in Mugdock.

As Jarvis recalled, they had also done some odd jobs for Meechan up at the house and got a bit nosy.

"Aye man, what a feckin' place that Tara is."

When Hardie shook his head mystified, Chico expanded:

"Aye, that's whit he calls it, Tara. I think it's somethin' to do wi' that mad Gone with the Wind film that boy Gable wiz in know? Well, it has three storeys tae it and a basement with a pool and you could get lost in it for a month.

"If you're saying Meechan would be wantin' to make sure he had control of the big giant, then there's no better place. Up there he could have chopped him into a thousand pieces and threw him into one of these lochs and no one would have known aboot it. Know whit ah mean?"

Now they were getting somewhere, and with Simms backing up what his sidekick had to say, there was certainly enough to go bothering a sheriff for a search warrant.

Jimmy McKelvie was Thoroughgood's favourite sheriff; he'd called on the retired lawyer with the huge handlebar moustache so often that the old boy barely wanted to know what his signature was for, even in the broadest terms.

"Come away in, DS Thoroughgood," said McKelvie at his front door, brown corduroy slippers matching his cardigan. "'What can I do you for tonight?"

Thoroughgood quickly explained, and before long he had his right hand held in the air and was swearing the oath required to get McKelvie's signature attached to the search warrant. With the sheriff 's moustache twitching in pleasure at the genuine joy he took from helping the police, and a "Good luck" ringing in their ears, Thoroughgood and Hardie returned to City Centre office in not much more than fifteen minutes.

Less than an hour later Thoroughgood was holding a briefing with Support and Tactical Firearms Unit officers in the muster room inside. The plan was that at precisely nine p.m. they would hit Meechan's place. The extra hour was needed to ensure the two-acre grounds had an effective cordon thrown round them so that Meechan or anybody else, be they a priest or a six-foot-five-inch Irishman, weren't able to make good their escape.

Meechan was enjoying his evening meal in the company of Brennan and Tommy Rankin when his mobile went off; a quick check of the screen showed the name Lazarus flashing. He immediately pushed his chair back and nodded to Rankin that he was taking the call in the oak-panelled anteroom he favoured for such impromptu but sensitive calls.

Soon Meechan had been put in the picture about the day's developments, a state of affairs which meant his only option was to terminate Frankie Brennan's life. He made his way back through to the dining room.

"Right Tommy, you and Frankie have got to get out as quickly as possible, we're about to be raided by CID. They're after you, Frankie," he said, jabbing his finger in Brennan's direction.

"I need you both out of here and all trace of your

clothing and your very existence gone before they get here. That bastard Thoroughgood is going to leave no stone unturned and I don't want him finding a scrap." Meechan offered Rankin a handshake and a "good luck" before doing the same to the giant.

"Thanks, boss," said Brennan resignedly.

"Frankie, you'll be all right at the office overnight, there's a camp bed that's a bit cramped, but you'll get a sleep and then tomorrow we'll have you gone. Trust me, big man," and with a wink Meechan brought to an end his last conversation with Frankie Brennan.

34

THE RED Focus pulled up to the huge jet-black iron gates outside Tara and Thoroughgood pressed the buzzer on the intercom system, easily reached from the driver's window. He would have recognised the Northern Irish accent at the other end of the intercom anywhere.

"Yes?" said Meechan.

"Detective Sergeant Thoroughgood and Detective Constable Hardie with a search warrant for the premises of Declan Meechan. Please open your gates or we will be forced to have them put in."

"Now there would be no need for that, DS Thoroughgood, when all I have to do is press a button and they open … just like that. Now come away in," said Meechan.

"I don't like this one bit, he's way too cool for my liking," said Hardie, but Thoroughgood was already signalling to the Support Services van, packed with officers in black boilersuits for the search ahead, and behind it the TFU vehicle to follow them on.

They surged up the short drive turning onto a widened forecourt, surfaced in beautiful white chuckies. Behind the imposing three-storey mansion with its twin towers, Thoroughgood could see the moon reflected on the calm surface of the small lochan behind the house Declan Meechan called 'Tara'. Standing between the twin white pillars at either side of the dark oak doorway, Meechan stood as still as a statue, watching silently as the three-vehicle police convoy drew up and stopped on his pebbles with a crunch, yards away from him.

Thoroughgood got out and walked over to the pillars; he seemed so much smaller than Meechan, who stood one step up. The menace emanating from those icy grey eyes had never been more latent.

"Nice place you have here, Mr Meechan," said Thoroughgood.

There was no reply; instead Meechan leaned against the left pillar, hands deep inside his navy pin-striped suit trousers and stared straight through him.

"So to what do I owe the honour for this so unexpected pleasure? And you've brought your mates with you! I don't know if my crockery will stretch to tea for two vanloads of coppers."

Hardie arrived at Thoroughgood's shoulder:

"Oh, we don't want tea Meechan, we've come for big Frankie Brennan and anything else that may be involved in the murder of the Browns and," Hardie held up the piece of paper with Sheriff McKelvie's signature at the bottom, "we aren't leaving until we've got what we want. So I hope you haven't been planning an early night, Meechan."

Meechan remained untroubled, not the slightest hint of emotion betrayed on his face or in his eyes.

"Well, I'm afraid you'll be disappointed, Detective Harvey."

"It's 'Hardie,' and I'm sure you won't let us down. Now I'd like you to take a closer look at the terms of the search warrant here before we enter and start to turn your house upside down. A damn shame to be messing up such a fine pad," smiled Hardie.

Meechan took hold of the paper and scanned the contents.

"I like the bit 'for the person of Francis Brennan or any other items which may be associated with the crimes for which he is wanted.' You've had a fair few bites of the cherry and I'm sure my lawyer Charles Coyle will be fascinated when I tell him on the phone.

"But as you say detective, the night is about as young as you are, so if you want to get started, I have a fine malt opened in my drawing room and a decent book by the hearth. Unless either of you would like to join me then I suggest you make a start. I'm sure Mr Coyle will be along inside the half hour mark to take up any legal matters that may concern him about the content and terms of the search warrant and/or your behaviour."

Meechan pushed himself off the pillar, turned and walked into the house where he held open the impressive oak door. With one extravagant sweep of his right hand he beckoned in the search party, his face adorned by the type of smile that made Thoroughgood realise they were wasting their time before they had even begun.

He had eight Support Services officers and a sergeant at his disposal for the search of Tara and it still wasn't enough. Milngavie and Maryhill Police Offices had each loaned him a panda with two uniform officers to keep the perimeter of the grounds under observation in the most effective manner possible. The search team split up into four groups of two with the Support Services sergeant co-ordinating his four teams and maintaining a video-recorded overview of proceedings.

To Thoroughgood's surprise, Meechan declined the offer to accompany any of the searching officers. All there seemed for him and Hardie to do was to poke their noses round Tara, like two under-privileged peeping Toms who had never before been invited to the party at the big house and had taken matters into their own hands.

Hardie descended into the basement with some enthusiasm and moments after he'd gone down the polished marble steps, Thoroughgood heard his name called. Joining the DC at the bottom of the steps, Thoroughgood's eyes swept over the brilliant aquamarine of the swimming pool, and then on out through the French windows, at the reflection of the silvery moon beaming onto the flawless surface of the lochan.

"Bastard," said Hardie.

"My thoughts exactly," agreed Thoroughgood with some disgust.

"Have we got it wrong, Gus? I mean, knocking our pans in for twenty years with the shifts kicking the guts out of your life and sacrificing everything for a pension that's like a pot of gold when you're in the middle of your service and the Holy fuckin' Grail by the time you come to the end of it. Safe in the knowledge you are never going to get anywhere near a life of luxury like this. Who says crime doesn't pay? Just try telling Meechan that."

Thoroughgood had wandered over to the full-length French windows, his mind drifting towards thoughts of his meeting with Celine at another nearby expanse of water, Milngavie Reservoir. Hardie's croaky voice broke his trance:

"You know we're going to get fuck all and the bastard told us as much. I bet he's in there, in his drawing-bloody-room, pissing himself in between the pages of his novel or was it the Oor Wullie annual he said he was reading?"

"You're right of course, faither, but he said he reckoned it would take Coyle thirty minutes to arrive, so why don't we go upstairs and have a little chat with friend Declan—as long as you promise to keep your temper."

"Scout's honour. Dib, dib, dib, dob, dob, dob, and all that, gaffer," grinned Hardie for the first time since they had entered Tara.

They returned upstairs to ground level, bypassing two of the black boiler-suited Support Services officers rifling through the pine units of Meechan's impressive farmhouse-style kitchen. Arriving back in the hall at the front of the house, Thoroughgood knocked on one of the Georgian glass panels in the doorway, according Meechan some respect before entering his "drawing room" as he had described it.

Meechan had loosened his black silk tie as he enjoyed the heat from the log fire crackling in front of him, but otherwise there were no signs he was feeling either the heat of the fire or the police activity.

"Ah, my two favourite police officers. Have you come to tell me you've found something then?"

"No, we just thought we'd be friendly," said Thoroughgood as he and Hardie parked themselves at either end of the huge leather sofa opposite Meechan's high-backed armchair.

"So who tipped you off Meechan?"

"I haven't got a clue what you mean, Detective Sergeant and, as you know full well, I can't answer any of your questions without my lawyer, Charlie Coyle, present. I'm surprised you're bothering to waste your breath, or are you finding DC Harvey's conversation a bit below par?"

"It's just that you looked so sad and lonely sitting here with your book and your malt. You could save us all a lot of bother by telling us what you've done with Frankie Brennan."

Meechan laughed; a harsh grating laugh that had something vicious about it.

"How can I tell you what I don't know? Listen, I'm just as keen to speak to Frankie Brennan as you, but thoughtlessly for both of us, the big fella has gone to ground without leaving a postal address. I've already told you you'll get nothing from your search, but then that's it, isn't it? You have to be seen to be doing something and this is an indication of how desperate you are."

Hardie could not help himself from chipping in his tuppence worth:

"Desperate? Why would we be desperate when we've got full witness statements from two of your underlings implicating you in the triple Brown murder enquiry?"

"Oh come on, Detective Harvey, if you did then you would have arrested me the minute you got here. But that's just it: even with statements from your two little boys you don't have enough to jail me. And you know that when Charles Coyle gets his teeth into your fine little mess he's going to have a field day.

"Believe me, I will be demanding a full public apology from the Chief Constable for the harassment you," Meechan pointed at Thoroughgood, "Detective Sergeant, have been subjecting me to. I just thought I'd give you fair warning of what's coming around the corner for you, Thoroughgood. When I'm finished with you, your pathetic little career will be lying in bits, and all for what?"

Meechan paused and took another draught from the dark golden liquid glowing in the crystal glass. Holding it up between him and the flames of the fire, he enjoyed the dancing patterns sparkling through the glass.

"The suspense is killing me. Come on Meechan, put

me out my fuckin' misery," said Thoroughgood amicably enough.

"This is all about who got the girl, isn't it, Thoroughgood? You couldn't handle it ten years back and you can't take it now. The truth is," and Meechan swept his left hand about him in a grand panoramic gesture, "look at everything I've achieved in these ten years. Whereas you, my pitiful little friend, are still staying in your shitty little flat in Partickhill Road, with a whole lot of nothing. Correct?"

Thoroughgood could see Hardie about to rise from his end of the elegant chaise lounge until he placed a hand on his colleague's knee.

"That's the problem with people like you Meechan, you have an annoying habit of whitewashing the past so that you don't have to face the truth. The truth is, you arranged for one of your henchmen to take me out and leave me with more fractures than I had bones. Why did you have to do that, Meechan? Do you ever ask yourself why? Like fuck! Because that would mean facing the truth and that would be just too painful for you to take. But I'm going to give you a history lesson right here, and one not according to the Gospel of Declan Meechan.

"The truth is, Celine had made her choice and she had chosen me and my shitty little flat in Partickhill Road and my pathetic little job as a copper; that was until you filled her full of all those lies; that I was on the take, corrupt and down the drag, going with the whores. You made her think I was going to be a cripple for the rest of my life, and that you were the one with the big bright future.

"Where's your future now, Meechan? One of your gang is dead, another missing and the other two are under police protection, ready to turn evidence against you. You know I don't give a flying fuck if we get sweet Fanny Adams here tonight, it's just been a real pleasure to have such a cosy little chat with you."

Meechan's face betrayed no emotion, but the anger burning with such intensity in his slate grey eyes was scorching. Hardie rose from the massive leather sofa and crossed to the elegant Queen Anne mahogany drinks cabinet.

"Why don't you pour yourself and DS Thoroughgood a malt, Harvey? And while yer at it, my glass needs a refill," said Meechan, winking at Hardie.

"For the last fuckin time, you bastard, it's Hardie. But thank you, a malt would be nice. What about you, gaffer?"

Thoroughgood nodded his head. Hardie had barely sat down when the doorbell sounded. Meechan screwed his head around over his right shoulder.

"Ah, Charlie Coyle, how inconvenient, he can wait a moment. As I was saying, finding out Celine had agreed to become my fiancée is the final straw for you Thoroughgood, and so vindictive and pitiful have you become, you will stop at nothing to try and discredit me in her eyes. Charlie is going to have so much fun bringing all that out in court."

Meechan had no time to react before he found himself dripping from the emptied contents of Thoroughgood's glass.

"Damn," said the DS, "I hate wasting a Talisker like that."

The mask of Meechan's self-control slipped and he stood up in an explosion of movement that took him to within a yard of Thoroughgood, who remained motionless. Towering over the DS, Meechan appeared

278

momentarily to be weighing up whether to strike his uninvited guest. The drawing room door opened.

"Can you introduce me to the officer in charge of this outrage?" said Charlie Coyle.

"That would be me," said Thoroughgood amicably, "but before we have a word, I suggest you calm down your boss here, he seems to have taken exception to my use of his malt."

Coyle looked nervously at Meechan, who took a step back from the still-seated Thoroughgood, with Hardie poised like an old tiger ready to pounce at the other end of the sofa. Meechan removed a handkerchief from his trouser pocket, bearing the stitched initials DAM, and wiped his face clean of the Talisker.

"Evening Charlie, if the detectives don't mind I'll take you out into the hall for a word and explain exactly what is going on."

"There's no need for that, Meechan, I'll save you the bother," said Hardie.

"Your boss is having his house searched for Frankie Brennan, who we want for the murders of Walter, Jimmy and Davie Brown, and any incriminating evidence we believe may be linked. There are nine Support Services officers making a videoed search of the premises and grounds and here," Hardie pulled out the search warrant and flashed it in front of Coyle, "is the authorisation."

Coyle took hold of the warrant and studied it closely from top to bottom:

"I see, and how long can we expect this search to go on?" asked the lawyer.

"As long as it needs to, so I'd make yourself comfortable, Coyle," responded Hardie with a grin.

After a moment's awkward silence, Thoroughgood

got up and signalled to his number two to follow. There was no point in spending any more time engaged in verbal sparring with Meechan, even if he had to admit to himself how much enjoyment he had taken from throwing the Talisker in the criminal's face.

Climbing the staircase, Thoroughgood sought out the Support Services sergeant, who was busy supervising the search of Meechan's office. A ruddy-faced individual with a friendly nature, Alan McGarvey had been at Tulliallan with Thoroughgood when he had joined up all those years back.

"How we doin' Alan?" asked Thoroughgood.

"Nothin' here. We've been through all the rooms, the cupboards, the lot and I've four of the lads out checking round the grounds, but I'd say whoever was here has gone. He's certainly had someone staying in one of the guest rooms, judging by the hurried way the sheets have been put back in place, but that's about it. You'd have to say it looks like he's had some warning we were on our way."

"Aye, you're probably right. It's funny but at times I've felt like Meechan has been one step in front of us the whole way through this investigation."

McGarvey was never one to mince his words, a habit which had followed him out of the Police Pipe Band unit.

"What if he's getting some help from the inside, Gus? You ever considered that? It's not as if it hasn't happened before."

"This isn't the Met, Alan. Who the fuck is going to go risking their career for Meechan in return for a few shekels? Naw, he's been lucky all right, but much as it hurts me to admit it, he's a clever bastard."

"Lucky or no, Gus, give it another half an hour and if

we haven't got anything from the search of the grounds then we're wasting our time and I'll come and look for you, all right?"

"Agreed," said Thoroughgood and headed off to find his shadow.

Hardie had slipped back down into the basement and out the French windows and was enjoying one of his Silk Cuts. His oval bump seemed to have been magnified by the view through the glass as Thoroughgood approached.

"Fuck's sake faither, you pregnant?"

Hardie scowled and flicked his cigarette onto the lawn. "How's it going?"

"Not a bleedin' sausage. It looks as if someone has been staying in one of the guest rooms and left in a hurry, but what does that prove? It's not as if Brennan won't have been here before. No, I'm afraid that shortly I'm going to have to go and inform Meechan that the search is over and we won't have a thing to show for it. How much is he going to enjoy that?"

After McGarvey had confirmed his search team were through, the DS rapped on the Georgian window of the drawing room and entered with his face set, prepared for a barrage of barbs.

"Ah, DS Thoroughgood, search complete and nothing to show for it?' asked Meechan.

"Much to your surprise I'm sure, Meechan," replied the DS. "But remember this, Declan Aloysius Meechan, this search may be over but our investigation is not. Sooner or later you are going to slip up and I'll be there, waiting right behind you." Thoroughgood turned round and walked out.

McGarvey and his team were already in the Police Personnel Carrier, and Thoroughgood made a point of going up to his old mate and thanking him for his help. He jumped into the passenger seat of the red Focus and Hardie did a three-point turn with just enough speed to send a shower of chuckies spraying in the general direction of the doorway, where Meechan's grin was framed in their rear view mirror.

Turning into Glasgow Road the police radio blared into life:

"DCI Farrell, please repeat, confirm, armed male inside premises is believed to be Frankie Brennan. Can you confirm he is armed? Do you need back-up, repeat do you need back-up?"

The absence of a reply suggested that Farrell did indeed and the police controller was soon barking out a help request:

"Units to assist DCI Farrell at the premises of Meechan holdings, Dumbarton Road, opposite the Western Infirmary. Armed male inside."

Thoroughgood didn't even bother replying.

"Come on Hardie, get a fuckin' move on."

35

FARRELL AND his number two, DS Andy Smith, parked up three hundred yards along from the office. Smith, a big ruddy-cheeked individual with straw for hair, had worked for Farrell for three years and for a reason no one could fathom, appeared to enjoy his role as the DCI's number two. Turning to his subordinate, Farrell delivered a final debrief:

"Nothing is more important than our safety. So although we will give Brennan fair warning, if he's looking like pulling on us then we shoot first, get our story straight second, and then ask questions third."

"Nae bother boss, I'm no intendin' taking a bullet for that bastard."

Farrell smiled: "Okay, let's go,"

They slammed the door and crossed Dumbarton Road, overcoats pulled up tight to ward off the cold chill of the late April evening. The office doors were wooden with large glass panels embossed with the "Meechan International Holdings" logo on either pane and, sure enough, when he pushed the right hand door, it swung open first time. Before Farrell and Smith entered, the DCI made sure both he and his partner had switched off mobiles and radios. The last thing they wanted was to give Brennan a warning he had company.

They took in the ground floor of the office, partially

lit by the dim glow of overnight security lighting. It was open plan, with three coffee tables, and chairs on the polished wooden floor, and a counter running the width of the ground floor. To the left there was a banistered stairway which spanned around fifteen feet from ground floor to a small landing outside an office door; Meechan's office, where Farrell had been told his quarry would be. The DCI turned round to make sure Smith was in position, Farrell putting a finger to his lips to indicate silence.

They heard a creak coming from the ceiling above: someone was home all right. Farrell pointed a finger towards the stairs then moved towards the bottom step, his heart hammering in his ears. Taking the standard-issue Smith and Wesson out of his overcoat pocket, he placed his right foot on the first step at the precise moment Frankie Brennan opened the door at the top of the stairway.

Even in the half-light the grin on the giant Irishman's face was malevolent:

"I thought I smelt pig. You'll be here for Frankie Brennan, copper?" he boomed.

Farrell kept his revolver down by his right hand-side, hoping to hide the fact he was tooled up:

"That would be right, Frankie. I'm DCI Farrell and this is DS Smith; we don't want any trouble Frankie. All we want is for the three of us to walk out of here alive."

Brennan had other ideas.

"If I walk out of here with you, copper, I'll be doin' life in some shithole like Peterheid. Now what makes you think I'd want to be doin' that?"

Farrell remained motionless on the bottom step, he could hear Smith's breathing behind him, and every fibre of his body felt like it was about to snap from the tension.

Farrell tried a reassuring smile that failed miserably.

"Come on, Frankie, what say you come down and we have a wee chat round one of the coffee tables here. There's been too much killing already."

Brennan was no longer smiling.

"Fuck off copper," he growled and raised his left hand so that Farrell and Smith could see the barrel pointing at them.

"There's only going to be one person walking out of here pig," said Brennan. "Now I'm gonnae gie yous two options. First you get out of my way and I walk down these steps and out that front door."

"You know I can't let you do that, Frankie. Come on, be reasonable. What's the second?"

It was a stupid question and one Farrell instantly regretted asking; he had been playing for time and now he knew it had been pointless.

Farrell anticipated the shot but even though he was already throwing himself to the floor the bullet only just missed his right shoulder, splintering the bottom of the stair banister as he dived off the bottom step below it.

Smith, seeing the giant aiming both his gun and all his attention at Farrell, had dropped to one knee and sighted the giant straight along the barrel of his revolver. Brennan was twenty feet above them, looming large on the small landing outside the doorway and his massive frame seemed to take up every square inch. Smith could hardly miss.

"Drop the gun, Brennan, or I shoot," Smith warned.

Brennan jerked his head towards Smith and began raising the Colt. The thud of the bullet as it ripped into Brennan's guts sent him reeling back against the office door and a loud grunt came from his mouth.

"Fuckin' pig, you'll pay for that," he roared, and as he regained his balance he quickly fired off two shots but both were wild.

Brennan ripped the office door open and dived inside, checking the damage from the bullet he had taken. It had grazed him on his right side.

"Nothing too serious, nothing that is gonnae stop me takin' care of two shitebag coppers," he muttered to himself.

He moved further into the office on unsteady feet. At the bottom of the stair, Smith checked Farrell was okay and spoke:

"Right gaffer, we can either go up and smoke him out, or radio for back up and sit him out."

Farrell stalled. The last thing he wanted was for back up to arrive and a waiting game to develop, with Brennan brought out alive. But what to do? He could hardly order Smith up the stairs with him, with the giant and a mouthful of lead waiting for them at the top. Before Farrell could answer his mate, the doors at the top of the stairs burst open,

"Tocfaidh Ar La!" roared Brennan, his voice resounding through the whole building as he hurtled down the stairs, his Colt outstretched in his huge right paw, spitting flame and lead.

This time the giant caught Farrell and Smith completely by surprise, and the second shot hit Smith in the left shoulder, throwing him back against the office wall like a ragdoll. Farrell managed to get behind one of the coffee tables in the open-plan office. When Brennan reached the bottom of the stairs and began to turn, Farrell had the giant's whole torso to aim at, and this time he didn't waste a shot. One after another, he fired three times, aiming for the area just below Brennan's heart. At a range of ten feet he couldn't miss. The first bullet stopped Brennan in his tracks momentarily.

"You fucker," gasped Brennan, as he looked down at the red liquid pumping from his body.

He took a faltering step forward trying to raise the Colt with his teeth gritted. The second bullet stopped him dead, pushing him off balance. Brennan reached out for the banister at the bottom of the steps, desperately trying to stay upright and raise his Colt in Farrell's direction. He was now swaying slightly, like some early Saturday evening drunk when the third bullet smacked into him, slamming his body back against the banister and forcing a loud gasp from his mouth. This time he dropped to the floor.

Farrell got up from behind the protection of the upturned coffee table and, training his Smith and Wesson on the fallen giant, he moved cautiously forward. Standing above Brennan, he saw that the Irishman's breath was now coming in shallow ragged bursts. Brennan's eyes were still open; he was conscious and the Colt was still in his right hand. Summoning one huge final effort, Brennan spat defiance at Farrell:

"You're never takin' me alive copper."

Almost too late, Farrell saw the flicker of movement from Brennan's right hand side and this time he pointed his revolver at Brennan's forehead and pulled the trigger.

"The end," said Farrell and watched as Brennan's head smashed open.

For a moment Farrell stood transfixed as the dark red vital liquid slowly spread from the back of Brennan's smashed head and ran across the polished wooden floor of Meechan's office. He was snapped from his thoughts by the gasping coming half a dozen feet to his left, then Smith groaned:

"Fuck me boss, that was a bit close for comfort."

Smith was propped up against a wall, his right hand clutched to his left shoulder, with blood seeping through his fingers. Farrell bent down and ripped off his tie, slipping it round Smith's shoulder and knotting it tight to try and stem the flow from the wound, receiving a grunt from his partner for the trouble.

"Been better, gaffer, but he's just winged me, so I'll live all right. Thank fuck that's the last we've seen of that maniac. How many bullets did it take to put him down?"

"Five between us, Andy. Aye, I thought he was never gonnae go myself. Good man, I'll radio for an ambulance. But I'm going to make the call as if we're requesting back-up for a live incident, then we need to get our stories straight, quick time before the cavalry arrive."

"Fine by me, boss, you know what these bastards from Professional Standards are like: if Complaints and Discipline don't get you, they'll have a bloody good try at doin' you for something."

"Exactly, said Farrell. "Now I've got a call to make, so give me a minute outside will you?"

Smith nodded his agreement. Taking a step outside into the cold, Farrell breathed a huge sigh of relief. That had been too close for comfort: he was still going to need to cover his tracks with regard to the follow-up investigation that would, as a matter of course, ensue after the discharge of a firearm by any police officer. The fact that at the end of this particular incident a man lay dead and a police officer injured would mean he and Smith had to make sure their version of events was watertight. He clutched his radio to his mouth.

"DCI Farrell requesting urgent back-up, locus Meechan Holdings Office, 225 Dumbarton Road. One male inside armed with a handgun. Repeat, require urgent assistance immediately."

The divisional controller acknowledged his call and put out the scramble for all stations nearby to attend ASAP.

Farrell took out his telescopic baton and smashed through the pane of one of the doors, before forcing the door in with the good old-fashioned shoulder charge that every beat copper learns in his probation.

He went inside to check on Smith and wait for the circus to begin. Within a couple of minutes he heard the footsteps outside and shouted:

"In here boys, it's over and we have a man down."

The uniform cops who were first on the scene were soon engaging him in a full recount of events, soon interrupted by the arrival of the paramedics. Smith was helped out into the ambulance and Farrell was about to exit the rapidly filling office when Thoroughgood and Hardie arrived.

"Well, well, well, DCI Farrell, a bit off the beaten track, aren't you?" said Thoroughgood.

"What do you mean by that, Thoroughgood? For your information DS Andy Smith is in the back of the ambulance with a gunshot wound to his shoulder and it took us five bullets to put that big mad Irish bastard down and save our skins. So what exactly is that supposed to mean?"

Thoroughgood could feel his anger rising to the surface; he was aware the paramedics and uniform cops milling about had their ears wagging, but, his frustration boiling over, he couldn't help himself.

"I'll tell you what it means. It means you have just conveniently shut up the only link we had that would lead directly to Meechan and put him right at the heart of this whole sorry mess. That's eight dead and Meechan is behind it all, and now we aren't going to be able to put a finger worthy of the name on him. So tell me, DCI Farrell, just how did you come by the information that Brennan was in Meechan's office?"

Farrell's agitation was obvious as he took out his glasses and a hanky and began to polish. The DCI realised he couldn't afford to lose face in front of the shocked audience, who couldn't quite believe what they were hearing outside the scene of a shooting that had left one man dead with his brains splattered across an office floor and a CID officer injured. Farrell jabbed his glasses in Thoroughgood's chest.

"Now you listen to me, you upstart. You aren't the only CID officer with informants capable of yielding valuable information. I had a call from one of my touts who has been active in trying to get information on Brennan's whereabouts and he placed him here for me."

Farrell was quickly into the well-rehearsed story he would deliver to the follow-up enquiry and anyone else he needed to convince.

"When we arrived the door had been forced, and as we made our way into the office Brennan came out at the top of the stairs with a bloody great revolver in his hand. He fired the first shot and we had to respond, then he injured DS Smith with a shot to the shoulder as he came crashing down the steps. I had no option but to open fire. It was either him or me so what the bloody hell would you have me do, Thoroughgood? Wait for Brennan to riddle me so full of holes I turned into a colander?"

Thoroughgood knew there was no point in carrying

on with a confrontation he couldn't win, and so did the watching Kenny Hardie.

"That's not what DS Thoroughgood means, boss. It's been a long frustrating night out at Meechan's and we have nothing to show for it. I think the frustration has got to us all. Of course it's a pity that you didn't manage to get Brennan alive, but under the circumstances it's far better both yourself and DS Smith have made it out just about in one piece. You must understand our frustration though, boss. First of all Brennan somehow manages to locate Reid, but gets out just in the nick of time, then we lose Reid to a hired killer, and now Brennan's lying inside cold as the grave and Meechan will be laughing all the way up his sleeve."

"So what the hell do you expect me to do about that, Hardie? Listen, I've had enough of your conspiracies and coincidences; if you don't mind I'm going to hitch a ride in the ambulance with DS Smith and make sure he's okay. But you," Farrell lowered his glasses and jabbed them at Thoroughgood for a second time, "haven't heard the end of this. I don't give a shit how frustrated you are about Meechan; myself and my partner have just risked our lives and I am not going to stand here one minute more listening to your bullshit. What's wrong, Thoroughgood? Don't you like it when someone else gets a share of the limelight?"

Thoroughgood opened his mouth but before he could say anything Hardie grabbed his shoulder.

"Come on, gaffer, it'll keep for another day," and turning the DS almost forcibly, the pair walked away without another word. Behind their receding backs Henry Farrell flashed a wide smile in recognition of a job well done.

"Where now, gaffer?" asked Hardie as he and Thoroughgood sat in the Focus.

"I suppose we'd better get back to Stewart Street quick and fill Tomachek in, but he's going to be swinging off the chandeliers when he hears about Farrell turning Meechan's office into a shooting gallery."

"Aye, yer spot on there, gaffer. What did you make of Farrell's little performance back there?" asked Hardie. "There're just too many convenient little coincidences. I mean, when the fuck did Henry Farrell ever run a tout?"

"That's exactly what I was thinking, faither. If he's got a tout then he must have registered him with the nosey bleedin' parkers at CHIS. Do we know anyone in there?"

"I'm sure one of the CID Aides we had in last year, Shuggie Burns, is in there now. Leave that one with me, boss, and I'll see what I can come across, because if he hasn't registered the informant then something is definitely smelly. Do we share our concerns with Tomachek?"

"I don't think we have an option there, do you?" asked Thoroughgood with a grin.

36

MEECHAN USHERED his lieutenant into the drawing room. "You know where the malt is, Tommy," he said, stoking the dying coals of the fire.

"We need to be going over a few points about the arrival of our delivery from up north. The artic should be in at one p.m. tomorrow, as they'll be taking the overnight ferry from Barra to the mainland and getting in about nine a.m. tomorrow morning. I want you to meet Morriston at Freezerland tomorrow and, after you're satisfied the gear is up to scratch and duly divvied up, bring our guest out here to Tara for dinner. I think it's long overdue that I meet Morriston, and we find out exactly what these exciting ideas are he has for expanding the operation."

"Tomorrow the first consignment resumes the Barra operation and we will hopefully have new avenues for expansion, if what you say about Morriston is right. Earlier today I closed out a deal which will make us a sleeping partner with one of the biggest undertakers in Glasgow." Meechan stopped as he saw a look of bafflement flit across Rankin's face.

"You may be surprised, but an undertaker's is a highly lucrative business venture, and one that from time to time can be very useful for conveying things from A to B in the most discreet fashion. You get my drift, Tommy boy?"

Rankin smiled at the sheer deviousness of his boss's fertile imagination:

"So where is this based, Declan?"

"In the Hardgate, very handy for us and a possible path for us to diversify into if need be. For the moment I haven't made my mind up just how I'm going to go about that, but there's endless scope. Just now I am happy to be the major but sleeping partner, while the new owner, a relative of mine, Peter Malone, I'm sure you've met, gets bedded in."

Meechan enjoyed another mouthful of his malt before continuing:

"As for that fucker Thoroughgood, I don't agree with you. Something needs to be done about him."

Thursday was a clear, blue morning and Rankin was positioned at Freezerland's back entrance in plenty of time to welcome Morriston and the delivery truck. After the Scania had been backed into the loading bay and the disembarkment of the frozen goods was well under way, Rankin treated the islander to a coffee in the warehouse office and got down to business.

"So you got down with no trouble, Ian?"

"Couldn't have been easier and I wasn't even sick on the ferry so it was a great wee trip. What's the plan?"

"Well, one of the boys will bring in the gear and I'll have a wee sample and make sure it's up to scratch. Once collections are arranged, we'll head off for a little visit to a couple of Mr Meechan's clubs and then you'll be staying at his tonight. Over dinner I think you'll be given your opportunity to bend Declan's ears regarding your plans to expand the Barra operation."

"That sounds great," said Morriston in the light dancing tone of the Western Isles.

A knock on the door and one of Rankin's underlings

wheeled in a couple of plastic sacks displaying the neatly logoed "Barra: Fresh from the Sea" packaging. Rankin dismissed the minion, placed the two freezer bags on the office desk and cut them open with a sideways slice three inches long.

The first package bled fine white powder when he opened it; he quickly took out his wallet, removing two credit cards. He stuck one into the bag and lifted it out with a covering of the white powder on top. Placing the first card with the powder on the desk top, he neatly divided the powder into two white lines on top of the mirror he had removed from the desk's drawer.

Leaning down, Rankin quickly snorted the first line up through his right nostril and, after pushing the glass bearing the second white line back across the desk to Morriston, he sat back to enjoy the rush. Morriston followed suit and after a short silence Rankin admitted:

"That's good stuff, all right. It's gonnae go down a treat at our clubs. I'm sure you'll enjoy looking around a couple of Declan's places to see just where we're selling it."

Morriston smiled back.

"All the way from Mother Russia, and so much more to come. It's good shit all right, but what did you expect, Tommy? You sampled enough up the road that weekend we had you as our guest!"

It was Rankin's turn to smile as this time he placed his index finger and his thumb together and inserted them into the second freezer bag. Removing a pinch of brown powder; he placed it onto his tongue and taste-tested it.

A frown crept over Morriston's face:

"You sure you don't want to do the chemical test on the smack? Everyone else I've ever done business with has. After all we aren't just talkin' chicken feed when it comes to money."

Rankin gave a patronising laugh.

"Naw, that's quality all right son. Let's just say when you've been doing this kind of business for as long as I have, you develop a nose for it!" Rankin laughed again and this time Morriston joined him.

"That's good stuff as well. I'm sure our junkies will lap it up. I know you're saving your full sales pitch for Declan's ears tonight, but how about expanding a wee bit for me on the Mother Russia angle?"

Morriston, enjoying both the hit from the coke and his newfound friend's curiosity, favoured Rankin with a smile.

"Fuck, that's good, but then with the sources we've accessed in Russia, it should be. I don't want to go into a big recount of the whole operation but suffice to say, through some of the Russian trawlers that put in off Castlebay we meet some very interesting types. With the fishing markets not what they were and EC quotas strangling the life out of the fishing industry, well, some of the more opportunistic and disillusioned of our fishing friends have, shall we say, decided to cast their nets further afield to land a decent catch."

Rankin shook his head in amusement and cut another couple of white lines neatly on the mirror.

"Whoever your contacts are, they know how to get quality charlie and that's good, because we don't want any crap in our clubs and this is certainly anything but." He swept down for a second snort.

Morriston grinned but before he went for his second course curiosity got the better of him:

"I'm glad you're happy, Tommy. But are you going to let me know how you distribute it?"

"Within fifteen minutes our two delivery vans will come and take away most of the heroin and after it's been packaged up into more manageable amounts, it'll be dropped off round the corner shops we have an interest in. The local dealers will come in and pick up their supplies and after that business is done the shit will, quite literally, hit the streets!"

Morriston shook his head approvingly, "And what about the charlie?"

"Roughly the same process. The delivery trucks drop off to the clubs and pubs we own, run and protect in the city centre and the West End, all of which do food, and then it's up to the management to make sure all goes smoothly when the clubbers are looking for the coke."

Morriston was impressed: "A military operation, by the sounds of it."

37

CELINE PARKED her silver-and-black Mini Cooper in the car park on the far side of Milngavie Reservoir. Her mind wandered to thoughts of Declan Meechan and the night ahead. The name of his house, Tara, brought a smile on her face.

The thought struck Celine then, how could any girl not fall in love with the type of man who would name his house after one of the greatest love stories in film history?

Shutting the door of the Mini, she pulled her baseball cap down, her hair bunched through the gap at the back, and jogged across the road, turning right and running along the first and smaller of the two expanses of water. It was three-fifty p.m. and she knew that by the time she reached the wooden bench on the far side it would be nearer four-fifteen than the agreed meeting time of four p.m. But that was a woman's prerogative.

The sky was clear blue, but how the wind stung! The uneven ruts of the footway encircling both pools were almost full with rainwater, and the splashing grimy liquid soon left her trainers wet. But as she gazed down on the valley below sweeping out over Milngavie, and as the path turned forty-five degrees, providing a panoramic vista that took in the north of Glasgow from Springburn inwards, she forgot about the damp clinging cold and began to revel in the sheer physicality of her union with the elements. The quality of the air was so much better, so pure it almost stung lungs attuned to the polluted oxygen of Glasgow city centre.

By now she was running parallel to the main road climbing out of Milngavie and through the hamlets of Strathblane and Blanefield. Turning left at the gatehouse, the pathway began to drift round behind the larger pool and she could detect the fresh scent of various bushes lining the grass bank that swept down to the path. Checking her watch, Celine saw it was now ten past four, and she knew that around the hydrangea bushes masking the next corner was the bench where she would find Gus Thoroughgood, the man she had once loved more than life itself, very nearly costing him his life as a result.

Thoroughgood had parked his RX-8 at the top end of the car park at three-thirty and taken a slow walk anti-clockwise to their bench, knowing he would probably be there, seated and shivering, at least five minutes prior to four p.m. He wanted to be early to wallow in the memories of all those beautiful spring and summer evenings they had spent enjoying a walk or a jog round the reservoir. All so long ago.

He stood for a while in front of the bench, the minutes melting away as he lost track of time, so immersed in his own mad world had he become. Transfixed by the grey breaking water, remembering the times they had kissed and embraced without a care. Eventually, as he sat down, a voice snapped him from his vigil.

"Hi Gus, I should have known you would be early, old habits die hard!"

Thoroughgood tilted his head up, smiling into the beautiful face sitting incongruously under a black baseball cap. "I could say the same about you, Celine. I just wanted time to think."

She sat down on the bench beside him. "And what did you want to think about, Gus?"

He strained every sinew in his being to avoid turning round and losing himself in those eyes. He didn't know why he said it, but when he had he was glad, because it was the bottom line and that was where they were now. "You, me and Declan Meechan."

He gave in and looked round, drinking in her features; it had been so long since he had sat close to her and he realised that the familiar surroundings and her proximity were assaulting his self-control in a pincer movement he didn't think he could fight.

Celine smiled nervously and leant back against the bench.

"But Gus, there is no 'me and you,' now there's only me and Declan."

If that was the bottom line, then it hurt, however he was not surprised by what he had prepared himself for as the inevitable.

"You've made a big decision, Celine, and I respect that. But before you throw your life away, I owe it to both of us to let you know the bigger picture. If you are going to take Declan Meechan for better or for worse one day, then you need the whole truth and nothing but the truth. Before it's too late."

Celine remained relaxed against the back of the bench but the smile was gone and her face had tightened.

"Are you the right person to give me the truth about Declan, Gus? Can you be honest with me?"

Thoroughgood turned sideways, opening up a small gap between their bodies: he wanted her full attention, for he knew this was the last chance he would get to say what had to be said.

"Yes, I believe I am Celine, because there is nobody else. But can you bear to hear the truth?"

She shot him a stare and there was nothing passive in those liquid-chocolate brown eyes:

"Try me."

"Okay. I guess that with you running his city centre clubs and pubs, you're already aware of quite a lot that is going on, but not enough you can't turn a blind eye to it: the charlie dealt around the dance floors and in the toilets and maybe a bit of smack too, but then you're only managing those clubs."

"You tell me of one city centre club that doesn't have a cocaine problem. We have CCTV installed in every one of our premises and it's still not enough. Come on Gus, you're a cop so try living in the real world, or don't you get out much?"

Thoroughgood smiled: "Aye, maybe that's my problem. Your problem is; we have information that at least half of the coke and the smack coming into the city is down to Declan Meechan. Information is telling us he's getting his supply from up north, possibly from the Western Isles. That's after the drugs are smuggled in from the continent and then dropped on the shore somewhere off the west coast."

"That's ridiculous. I've never heard Declan mention anything or anywhere in business terms that is not right here in the heart of the city. All his energy is going into building the new multiplex in the West End. This is just ludicrous, Gus."

Thoroughgood smiled, flexing his shoulders back and stamping his feet to get the blood pumping again.

"Ludicrous it may seem, but almost certainly true. Where do you think all the money has come from to finance this complex? Thin air? Funnily enough, we also have two unsolved murders involving two Teuchter brothers from the Isle of Lewis. One fished out of our . . ." Thoroughgood's anger momentarily got the better of him as he gestured out at the rippling water.

"Sorry, this reservoir, minus his limbs, and the other riddled with lead and char-grilled. But it would be too much of a coincidence linking them both to your fiancé's drugs operation coming in from roughly the same area."

"This is just fantasy now, Gus. How can you expect me to believe all that? Declan is a respectable businessman; his wild days are behind him. He told me that and I believe him."

Celine's tapping foot betrayed signs of agitation Thoroughgood couldn't miss.

He pressed on. "You might also be aware that from time to time other crime syndicates try and encroach on Meechan's turf. That's why three members of the Brown family are in the mortuary, all of them riddled with lead, one of them half-burnt and the other with most of his insides missing thanks to a gutting with a machete."

As Thoroughgood paused for breath Celine opened her mouth to protest but he quickly shot a hand up to halt her:

"That was the price the Browns paid for encroachment and the drive-by shooting outside the City Chambers."

Celine remained unmoved.

"Let's face it, Gus, the Browns had plenty of enemies. Declan wouldn't be the only one with plenty of reasons to want them removed from the scene."

"Maybe not, but he was the only one who put together a four-man gang to carry it out and guess what, when one of them decided he wanted out, he had his throat cut."

"There is no way you're telling me Declan cut anyone's throat," said Celine defiantly.

"No he didn't, but he did have Frankie Brennan sent round to try and gut him. When that didn't work, a bogus priest turned up in Stobhill Hospital and slit his throat. We know the bogus priest is a contract killer and guess what, we know he grew up with Declan Meechan in Belfast."

"Coincidence. You can't surely expect me to believe Declan is hiring hitmen to come in and take out people who worked for him?"

"Yes, I do, and it gets better. After Gary Reid was taken out we managed to get two younger members of the gang, Chico Jarvis and Ricky Simms, to come across inside the Bar-L for the promise of protection and a better life. You recognise these two names from any of the doormen or dealers you've seen round the clubs and boozers?" Thoroughgood could see from her face that she did. He went on:

"So they finger big Frankie Brennan—that name ring a bell? And mention they've met Meechan at least once for a pat on the back and a nice wedge of cash for a job well done. That means we need big Frankie but unfortunately, the big man gets rumbled inside the offices of you-know-who last night and after a shoot-out—you know, the one that's been on the news all day—big Frankie is no more and the whole case against Meechan we hoped to build by apprehending Frankie and using the evidence of the two kids, collapses."

Celine's face was now like stone and it was hard to comprehend just what was going through her mind, but Thoroughgood had not finished.

"There is one last thing, Celine: we think he's getting information from inside the force. When Hardie and I arrived at Reid's the night Brennan tried to do him, the giant had just very conveniently left, as if he had been tipped off. The night Brennan got it at Meechan's office we were on a wild goose chase looking for him up at your fiancé's mansion in Mugdock: only for one of our senior officers to get a tip off that mad Frankie was at the office. Then surprise, surprise, there's a shoot-out, Brennan has half his head blown away, taking all that incriminating information with him to his grave. Does the name Henry Farrell mean anything to you?"

Celine shook her head from side to side but her eyes were blazing and her voice crackled with anger.

"This is ridiculous, you're trying to say Declan hides Frankie in his office and then what, one of your colleagues shoots him? Then you claim Declan has this DCI Farrell in his pocket? Well, I've never heard of Farrell, and how the hell can you blame all this on Declan?"

"It seems to me, Gus, you're so desperate you would pin the Ripper murders on him if they hadn't happened in the nineteenth century. This is just a trash-talking exercise to slaughter the man I love for something he did to you ten years ago. I know what Declan did was wrong but you've got to get over it and put it behind you before your whole soul rots with revenge. Move on, Gus."

Celine stood up and for a moment she didn't say anything, looking over the reservoir which had begun to calm as the breeze had dropped.

"You know, I didn't know what I would find when I came here today to meet you. I suppose if I'm honest, I'd hoped there would still be something left from what we had together. Something I always thought was special but there's nothing left now, just the anger and hatred that has been eating you up for the last ten years. You just can't take it anymore and you had to make one last attempt to bring back what we had in the past. Well Gus, it's gone now."

She took a step forward to the edge of the path, her arms folded in front of her, and stared out into the horizon. She could feel Thoroughgood's eyes burrowing into her back but for a moment he said nothing, and the only sound was the dying breeze rustling in the bushes behind them.

"I know you're finding this all hard to take, and I can understand why you think it's some cheap shot from me to get back at Meechan. It isn't. I know now I can be far more honest about my feelings for you and that's probably because I know it's the last chance in this life I will get to do so."

Still there was not even a tremor of movement in Celine as she remained impassively scanning the horizon. Thoroughgood continued, determined he would finally get everything that had been weighing him down for the past decade off his chest.

"It took me nearly two years, between lying on hospital beds and operating tables, to be put back together again and fit to return to my job, but the scars inside me have taken a helluva lot longer to heal. That's because I love you, Celine. I loved you then, I loved you even though I thought the only thing I felt for you was hatred when you believed all the lies he told you. And I still love you now. But I guess time really is a healer and now I know I can live my life without you."

At this she turned round and took the three steps needed to reach the bench before dropping onto it like the weight of the world was suddenly on her shoulders. He stared into her eyes and at last thought he saw the anger dimming.

"For so long, when you didn't come to visit me in the hospital, or up at Castlebrae, I hated you. I couldn't understand why you didn't come. When I found out why, it gave me something to help come to terms with it all. The memories and the hurt still seem so fresh. And now I see you're about to throw your life away on what? A tissue of lies and deceit? Sure you get to live in a mansion and money will never be a worry again, but does this mean one day you will never want to scratch the surface?

"I don't know how he has convinced you to become his fiancée, that's between you and him. I just wanted to say what I needed to say, and let you know nothing has changed in the way I feel about you, and probably never will. I know now it really is too late and you were right, I have to let go and move on. At last maybe I can do just that."

He saw a tear well up in the side of her right eye and trickle down her cheek, and when she turned her face towards his he could see that she was indeed crying.

"I loved you so much Gus, and then it all went so badly wrong and I didn't know who to believe. I've probably spent the last ten years still not knowing. Now it's not about who is right or wrong, it's about making a future and a life for myself and accepting the consequences, whatever they are. I'm so glad you said all these things and I think it's the same for me but it's just too late now. Our time has gone," and with that she leant forward, cradled his face in her two hands and kissed him the way that only she could.

He could feel their tears intermingling and for a moment imagined their souls had too. She pulled back and stood up, taking a deep breath and wiping her eyes with the back of her sleeve. "Goodbye, Gus," she said.

38

THEY LOST track of the time, such had been the passion of the moment as they sat entwined on the dark green leather sofa, but the headlights from the driveway alerted them to the fact that their guests had arrived. Meechan drew himself from her reluctantly and asked:

"Does the lady of the house wish to receive her first guests?"

"Couldn't we just stay here ourselves on the sofa soaking up the fire?" she asked.

He stood up, towering over her, stopping to brush his lips over hers.

"I'm afraid not darlin', much though I'd love to."

"All right Declan, the lady of the house will do as her master commands."

"Not commands Celine, never commands, only asks."

She smiled and lithely moved off the sofa, aware that his eyes had never left her.

"What?" she asked artfully.

"I'm just wondering how I managed to survive all these years without you," said Meechan, straightening his lilac silk shirt and trying to flatten out the creases in his beige linen trousers.

Tommy Rankin was surprised to see Celine behind the opening door, but with his surprise went plenty of pleasure.

"Celine, how you doin'? It's been a while but you look great."

"Hi Tommy, always the flatterer," and as her eyes strayed over his shoulder she added:

"This must be Mr Morriston, our guest from the Isles?"

"It is indeed, young lady, so you are the lovely Celine who I have heard so much about?" said the smallish man with the darting shrewd eyes and brown wavy hair, holding out his hand and shaking Celine's in a light grip.

"I think I will like you, Mr Morriston. Now please, come in and make yourselves comfortable, Declan's in the lounge," she said, ushering them in.

Meechan, standing in front of the crackling log fire, smiled as they entered but left a brief pause as he made Morriston only too well aware he was sizing him up. Morriston had little doubt that was exactly what was going on as he felt the menace of Meechan's piercing ice-grey eyes sweep over him. Unperturbed, he strolled forward and extended his hand.

"Mr Meechan, it's my pleasure to finally meet you. Thank you so much for making me a guest in your impressive home."

Meechan's grip was vice-like, as, nodding towards Rankin he said:

"Tommy has spoken highly of you so I thought that since we are starting out on a new venture, it was only fitting we had you to dinner when you were down in Glasgow on business. I hope you like steak?"

They all laughed and after a couple of drinks the atmosphere was relaxed with an easy familiarity springing up between the company which boded well. There had been more humour when Celine presented the prawn cocktail for the first course, Meechan making a great play of extolling the virtues of the North Atlantic prawn.

By the time they had made it through dinner and a cheese board as well, Celine made her excuses and informed them that after tidying up in the kitchen, she intended to have an early night. After much good-humoured protesting and some gentle jibes from Rankin that he was amazed Meechan was not turning in prematurely as well, she headed back through to the kitchen and began to load the dishwasher.

It had been a good night. She'd always had a soft spot for Tommy Rankin, the classic lovable rogue, while Morriston had come across as an amusing down-to-earth type who was determined to make a success of his business. She was sure she had detected real pride in Declan at her presence and fussing over everyone, so it had not been a bad debut as his fiancée. But now was exactly the right time to let them talk over their business in peace with a couple of drinks. Dissecting the profit margins to be had from frozen seafood at midnight was not Celine's idea of enjoyment.

"At last we come to the business end of the evening, gentlemen. Well Iain, the floor's all yours, for the next hour you have both mine and Tommy's undivided attention, so let's hear all about these ideas of yours."

Morriston smiled, stretching his feet out under the mahogany dining table and reaching behind his arching back with his arms and hands.

"It's as simple as this, Declan; my Russian friends are wanting to up the ante in terms of the quantity of both our delivery and its regularity. I don't know if Tommy has told you about the rugged nature of Barra but there are so many coves and beaches which are uninhabited, we can take our choice of where the deliveries can be dropped. It's up to you, Declan, we could increase capacity if you want."

"I'm all for increased profit margins, what are we talking in kilos here?"

"According to my contact, Nikolai, that would be entirely up to us. But perhaps as a tester we should increase things by twenty per cent and see where that takes us, Declan. There is no point in the extra coming down if you can't shift it."

"Aye, you've got a point there, Iain," agreed Tommy Rankin.

Meechan nodded his head as he joined in their mutual accord:

"Okay, we'll do as you suggest. Now tell me, how are the Johnsons being missed up in the Western Isles?"

"Not at all is the answer there. You see Declan, they were both from the Isle of Lewis, and in Barra nobody from Stornoway is going to be popular. Put it this way, the whole operation is a lot happier now they're on permanent vacation."

Meechan's smile was soon gone.

"That's good Iain. It's important that nobody up the road thinks they can take liberties. Do you understand me?" The threat was not even veiled.

"No one at our end is going to make that mistake again, Declan, you have my word."

Meechan leaned forward and reached for his whisky glass; taking a slug, he licked his lips to enjoy the peatiness of the Lagavulin before replacing it on the table and steepling his hands.

"Now Iain, there's something else I require of you to prove your loyalty. Before you go home tomorrow I want you to help Tommy here scratch a little itch that has grown into a major sore."

Morriston, knowing he could do little else, smiled benignly:

"Anything you want, Declan."

Listening through the serving hatch in the kitchen Celine could hear the deep baritone of Declan's voice talking about market share, then thought she heard the Browns mentioned. The noise of the dishwasher, newly started, obscured sound but Celine's curiosity was stirred. What she heard she could not comprehend.

The realisation swept over Celine and left her cold. Standing in the kitchen, she was frozen still like a statue. Then as she hung the dishcloth up on a hook next to the cooker, she heard the weight of someone's foot on the polished pine floor. She turned the kitchen tap on and lifted a glass from the draining board at the side, hoping that would make her presence appear innocent enough.

"Still up, my darlin'?" said Meechan.

Turning round, Celine smiled: "There's more to clearing up a dinner party than just sticking dishes in a dishwasher, Declan, you know!"

"Of course there is, are you sure you don't want to join us in the lounge? We'll probably have one more and then call it quits." He spoke with not a sign of suspicion.

Celine moved across the kitchen floor and pressed herself close up against his body. She could smell the peatiness of the malt on his lips as she kissed him and she realised she couldn't help herself. After a while she pulled back:

"We don't want your guests to feel neglected, do we Declan?"

"I wouldn't worry about Tommy and Iain, they seem

to get on pretty well and I've even had an invite up to the Western Isles but I wouldn't want to go anywhere without you, my darling."

He held her at arm's length, staring into her eyes with a seriousness in stark contrast to the warmth of the moment before.

"Now I hope you haven't misunderstood anything you might or might not have heard through the hatch here. You know some of the people I deal with are, well, unsavoury, and the only thing they understand is the violence they dish out returned with interest back to them. What happened to us in George Square was part of a concerted effort to have me removed by the Brown family. There was only one option when it came to stopping them. I can promise you, Celine, I am doing everything I can to make all my business dealings legitimate. It just takes time. One day soon, I will be able to look you in the eye and tell you I'm straight."

Her eyes sparkled with the pleasure she took from those words:

"That's all I need to hear, Declan." This time they kissed and then held together for moments that seemed endless.

Watching her ascend the stairs, from behind the smile masking his face, Meechan wondered just how much she had heard. He would know soon enough if she could be trusted and at least it would not be too late if the answer proved negative. In Declan Meechan's world everyone and everything was expendable.

39

THOROUGHGOOD CLIMBED into the RX-8 and slammed in a CD. AC/DC, *Highway to Hell*. He sent a text to Hardie enquiring if his partner could meet him for a pint in the UB Chip at seven p.m. The answer, as if there had ever been a doubt, was yes. He turned the Rex out of the car park and immediately clicked through the gears up to third, taking solace in the powerful engine noise and the surges of acceleration. He needed a drink.

Thoroughgood was halfway through his first pint of Guinness when Hardie arrived and immediately expressed surprise at his "choice of poison." After replenishing his Guinness and buying Hardie a Furstenberg they took a seat on the raised dais to the left of the fire. Hardie didn't beat about the bush.

"How did it go? I figured you'd maybe want a chat and a pint, so I hope you appreciate how I kept my night free for you!"

"You're so fuckin' considerate it hurts. You are also right, of course. It was a disaster. She basically told me she didn't believe a word I'd said, that I've become eaten up with hatred of Meechan and that I need to move on before there is nothing good left in me. What worries me is she might be right."

Hardie took a large mouthful of Fusty, as he tenderly called it.

"Well, there was always a chance it was gonnae go that way. After all, she has just become engaged to the bastard."

Hardie took great delight in venomously drawing the profanity out for as long as possible. Hardie didn't do subtle, what he did do and do bloody well was straight talking, and he knew that was precisely what Thoroughgood needed right now: no bullshit.

"Look, you've given it your best shot, Gus, and she's made it clear it's over. Now you really have got to move on. What about Sara? I thought that was going really well. For fuck's sake, Gus, how many birds have you come across in the past ten years who were prepared to watch that shite up at Firhill?" Hardie's attempt at drawing a laugh just about raised a smile from his mate.

"Shite it may be but at least we don't have a bloody clue what is going to happen from one week to another under Campbell Paton. Where's the interest in going to Ibrox and being bored shitless by a team built by a manager who hasn't got a Scooby Doo what the Scottish game is all about and is too arrogant to admit it?"

"Ah, there is life, thank God," said Hardie in mock relief. "Well, mon ami, I have no doubt that Monsieur Le Gronnais will get it right and the Queen's eleven will soon vanquish the tatty howkers and take their rightful place back among the elite of the Champions League. Now while you were away making a desperate effort to salvage your love life, I had a long chat with our man in the Central Informants Unit. It's just like we thought; Farrell has no informant registered with them whatsoever. So whatever he is up to, it's something smelly all right and he doesn't want anyone to know about it. The question is; how are we going to find out just who his informant is?"

"I think you're looking at it from the wrong angle, Kenny, it's not about us trying to draw his informant out, it's more a question of us setting Farrell up and letting him draw Meechan out. The problem is how."

Hardie belched and then slammed his half-empty pint pot down on the table, drawing a withering look from the two middle-aged blondes sitting at the table next to them; he winked wolfishly at them. They turned away in disgust immediately. Thoroughgood observed his mate's behaviour with amusement:

"Aye, I can see you've not lost your touch, faither!"

"Better out than in as the saying goes. Anyway it's simple: Jarvis and Simms. We'll get Tomachek to feed Farrell with some duff information that they've been moved to a new safe house, and then we sit tight there and wait for the cavalry to arrive."

Thoroughgood nodded his head in approval.

"That's not a bad shout and it wouldn't take much to do. I'm sure Tomachek would go for it. Gary Reid would still be alive if Farrell hadn't fucked about getting uniform protection sorted, and then how the hell did Brennan find out where Reid was holed up? Nope, Farrell's in it up to his ears, and this way we can expose him for the dirty bent copper he is and hopefully get Meechan to do something stupid into the bargain. First thing in the morning we'll go and see whether Tomachek will agree to it, and then it's game on."

"A 'Thanks, my dear faither,' would be nice, mon gaffeur, but I'll accept your gratitude in kind," said Hardie, raising his empty glass and pointing to the bar.

Friday morning dawned cold and grey, and as he opened his curtains and looked out onto Partickhill Road, Thoroughgood reckoned by the way the trees were swaying there was a nasty biting breeze in the air as well.

By nine a.m. he was turning the ignition on in the RX-8. Turning left, Thoroughgood headed down Gardner Street, the steepest road in Glasgow and one more like a ski jump than a road, such was the severity of the gradient.

Coming to the first junction, about a hundred feet down, he put his foot on the brake and felt it to be a bit soft and unresponsive, but the Rex ground to a halt and he continued down Gardner Street unconcerned. However, when the red Royal Mail van pulled out, he slammed on the anchors for a second time, nothing happened and the RX-8 sailed on with gathering momentum, straight towards the red van.

The driver saw that the car coming down the hill was not going to stop, and Thoroughgood could see the look of sheer panic on Postman Pat's face. He could also see the driver mouthing some kind of expletive before he began to manically yank hard left on his steering wheel in a desperate attempt to take avoiding action.

Gardner Street was as narrow as it was tight, and with cars lining either side of the roadway, there was very little room for manoeuvre. The mail van slammed straight into a parked people carrier nestling innocently alongside the kerb while the RX-8 and Thoroughgood continued their descent, missing the van by inches but ominously gathering speed with every yard that passed.

The car continued to pick up frightening momentum and no amount of dabbing at his brakes worked. The handbrake was so loose it felt like it was hanging by a thread. There was no response. His brain feverishly processed the information relayed to it by the failure of his brakes and there could only be one conclusion: someone had tampered with them overnight and that someone could only have been Meechan or one of his cohorts. But he had no time to digest the thought as the second junction loomed up ahead of him.

This time, out of the corner of his eye he caught sight of the green Range Rover coming in on his left hand-side, and he furiously pumped his steering wheel to blare his horn into life. The white lines of the junction were almost upon him when the driver at last turned her head in recognition of the strident tones of the RX-8 horn, sheer horror filling her features. Her mouth opened and even above the sound of his horn he thought he could hear her screams and those of the two tiny children he had just noticed in the kiddies' seats in the back.

Thankfully, screaming was not her only response to the sight of the RX-8 hurtling straight for the side of her vehicle, and the Range Rover jolted forward in response to the driver slamming her accelerator to the floor. Still it seemed certain a crash was imminent and Thoroughgood attempted to slow his own progress by twisting his wheel one way then the other to introduce a slalom effect which would at least cause a minimal diversion from the straight route to oblivion his vehicle was on. It was the only thing he could think of.

As the RX hit the junction the Range Rover was almost but not quite clear, when its rear bumper was caught with a crack. Although the RX-8 shuddered from the jolt of the impact, the Range Rover drove on with only slight damage.

Thoroughgood had hoped to get lucky and receive enough of an impact to stall his vehicle's uncontrolled descent, but it was not to be. As the bottom of the hill approached, so did the junction with the area's main route, Dumbarton Road. Thoroughgood knew the chances of him getting through that junction without disaster were virtually non-existent. He was almost at the bottom of the huge hill when his mind jumped into flashback mode as he relived the hit and run which had almost done for him all those years ago.

He could feel the searing pain caused by the multiple smashed bones in his broken body, and taste the dripping blood as it ran into his mouth. Then his mind fast-forwarded to the here and now, and he could feel the cold beads of sweat forming on his forehead and running down his back. His hands were clammy on the wheel as he gritted his teeth and prepared to meet his Maker.

The traffic was flowing freely along either side of Dumbarton Road and he felt hope growing inside him as he hit the junction and a gap miraculously opened up before him like the parting of the Red Seas.

Maybe, said the voice in his head, the big man is on my side at last.

He began to feel a surge of relief sweeping over him as the RX-8 left the junction, but a new danger loomed ahead and this time he knew he had used up all his luck. The giant metallic hulk of a City Council rubbish truck was pulling out from the side of the road ahead and Thoroughgood watched as the driver continued shouting out instructions to one of the binmen on the opposite side of the road.

He hit the horn again and again and again, and slowly the driver turned his head just in time to see the Rex smash straight into the front of his vehicle, the brilliant blue of its bonnet disappearing underneath the front of the huge truck.

As the Rex ploughed underneath Thoroughgood threw his hands above his head in an automatic gesture of self-defence. The impact was sickening and he was thrown about, first backwards, then forwards like a ragdoll. The airbag saved him initially. Billowing out from the steering wheel, it enveloped his body in life-saving padding, leaving him winded and with a searing pain on the left hand-side of his ribcage. It could not save him from the truck crushing his vehicle.

The wheels of certain death surged over the bonnet and then inexorably on, smashing the RX-8's windscreen and chewing up the roof, which started to collapse on top of him. Thoroughgood looked up, waiting for the inevitable to happen. The vehicle roof above the passenger side began to buckle and broke in half as one of the dump truck's wheels smashed through it. He looked directly above him, waiting for the same to happen at his side; holding his breath, he shut his eyes and uttered a silent prayer, asking the man upstairs to make it quick. Then, realising nothing else had happened he opened his eyes.

The car roof above him was still intact; a form loomed over the space where the driver's side window had been and began yanking at the crumpled door. It was the truck driver, and he wasn't happy.

"What the fuck do you think you're playing at, you bleedin' maniac?" shouted the binman.

"It wasn't a suicide bid that's for sure," was the best he could do before he passed out.

40

WITHIN AN hour of his admission to Accident and Emergency at the Western Infirmary, Thoroughgood had been x-rayed, the scan showing he'd fractured a couple of ribs. By the time Hardie and Detective Superintendent Tomachek visited, he was sitting upright in a bed in one of the general wards upstairs.

Tomachek, immaculate in one of his trademark tweed suits, was first through the ward door but only after he had stopped at the nurses' station to avail the duty sister of his usual words of wisdom. Hardie, standing at his side, looked like some reluctant schoolboy brought along in punishment for some trivial misdemeanour. Drawing up a couple of chairs, the pair took up position either side of the patient.

"Well Thoroughgood, you'll go to any measure to avoid doing a shift, won't you?" said Tomachek in a standard senior-officer-type attempt at humour.

Thoroughgood nodded and offered a thin smile by way of an answer. Fractured ribs weren't the only things causing him pain. Despite the best efforts of the airbag he had suffered some whiplash, while his head was throbbing for all it was worth.

Hardie, seeing his mate was in obvious discomfort, attempted to fill the awkward silence:

"Your brakes were cut, Gus. The fluid was all over the

road where you parked the Rex. The boys from the garage at Helen Street, where we had what's left of the car taken, have already been on the blower to confirm somebody had tampered with them all right. So who do you suppose was behind this?" asked Hardie, rolling his eyes to the heavens in answer to his own rhetorical question.

Thoroughgood cleared his throat and took a sip of water from the glass on the locker next to his bed:

"And not a bloody grape between the two of you?"

Tomachek smiled and seemed to let a sigh of relief go in the same movement:

"Good man, Gus. Bit of a sore one mind you about the car, complete write-off you know."

Thoroughgood winced as he tried to adjust himself to a more upright position.

"Bastard! If I don't do anything else in this life I'll nail that fucker Meechan. Now what are we going to do about setting the trap, sir? With respect, this can't wait anymore. Meechan obviously thinks he is above the law, and we can't let this go unpunished."

Tomachek raised a hand. "My dear boy, I can safely say the time has come to take matters into our own hands. A spot of summary justice is what is required, and Hardie and I have spent the run over from Stewart Street discussing exactly how we are going to set and spring our little trap."

Hardie spoke. "We think we have the ideal place to act as a safe house and see what we can lure out. Obviously it needs to be somewhere we can take observations on, and somewhere the public aren't going to get caught in the middle of a firefight if it all goes tits up."

"I don't know if you remember the old King's Stables boozer out on the Forth canal just before you come to

Kirkintilloch? Well, it's gone to the wall and the place has been bought by an old mate of mine, John Kennedy. I've made the call and as long as we foot the bill, he's quite happy to let us use it for our little job. It's ideal because there's only one road in and out and you get a pretty good look at it from the first floor of the building which surprise, surprise, was an old farmhouse and stables."

Tomachek continued with the outline of their plan: "The whole thing will be set in motion tonight. I'm attending a meeting with ACC Crime Cousins at Pitt Street this evening and DCI Farrell will be there. I'll feed in our plan there and we'll hopefully be off and running."

A look of concern soon knocked the smile from Thoroughgood's face as he began to assess the implications of the plan springing into action with such immediacy:

"But who are you intending to use as the stand-ins for Jarvis and Simms sir?"

"That'll be myself and Ross McNab," said Hardie. "Gus, there is no way you're going to be fit by Sunday night."

Tomachek continued. "We need to bring this one to a head, and as soon as possible. It's going to take us a couple of days to have the stables and farmhouse shipshape, but Farrell will be made aware that Jarvis and Simms will be relocated there on Sunday at five p.m. and then we'll just have to wait and see how long it takes Meechan to try and get to them."

Thoroughgood looked far from happy and it had nothing to do with his ribs: "Can I ask what arrangements you've made for DCI Farrell, sir?"

"You can indeed Gus. Naturally DC Hardie here has put me in the picture regarding your full suspicions, and it does seem there is a chain of events here that go beyond the mere realm of circumstance. This morning I had a very interesting chat with Detective Superintendent Moira Gary, who is head of the CHIS; she assured me that they have no informant at the present, or at any time, registered by DCI Farrell.

"As you know I've no time for the man, and I will be taking a personal interest in his movements over the next few days. Arrangements, as you could call them, are already being made to have his mobile phone records secured. But you have my word Gus, if Farrell is involved he will end up behind bars, enjoying a fate that may well end up worse than death."

With that, Detective Superintendent Valentino Tomachek pulled himself up to every inch of his impressive six-feet-three-inches, arched his back, stretched out his right paw and administered the Masonic handshake he insisted on giving the non-Masonic Thoroughgood from the first day he had met him. Then Tomachek turned to Hardie:

"I expect you'll want a couple of words with Gus? Radio for a uniform car to pick you up when you're finished."

Tomachek held out his hand for the car keys to the Focus they had arrived in. Hardie couldn't help his scowl, but Tomachek clearly enjoyed pulling rank and smiled benignly:

"Remember Kenny, an ace beats a king every time, as I think you will find out at Parkhead this weekend when the glorious Bhoys vanquish the Forces of Darkness in convincing fashion."

Turning his back on both of his junior officers, Tomachek exited whistling the Celtic anthem The Fields of Athenry. Never one to let another enjoy the last word, Hardie shouted after him:

"I look forward to taking your tenner off you, boss."

Tomachek's index finger shot up behind his back in a single eloquent gesture.

"For fuck's sake, faither, you've got as much chance getting a tenner of Tomachek as he has off you!"

Thoroughgood let out a groan as he attempted to re-adjust his position in the hospital bed. His gaze wandered out into the corridor just beyond Ward Ten: standing there, staring straight back, was Sara Spencer. She walked in and took his previous bedside companion's place in the cheap and slightly rocky bedside seat. She smiled at him and placed her hand on top of his:

"Are you okay, Gus?"

"I've been better, Sara, but now your beautiful face is here sitting beside me, I feel a whole lot better."

She leant forward and kissed him on the lips and he couldn't help but detect a sense of sadness, which she seemed to be wearing like some old item of clothing, one you couldn't bear to be parted with while knowing that it had to go.

"Are you sure everything is all right, Sara? You seem a bit down."

This time her smile seemed to dissipate like the fading of the sun on a cold winter's day. She lowered her head for a moment then gradually lifted it until their eyes met:

"It's my job Gus, the opportunity I told you I was hoping would come my way to run my own show has finally arrived."

Thoroughgood smiled: "That's great news, Sara, whereabouts?"

"Sierra Leone."

The smile was gone from his face almost as soon as it had settled. His look of surprise and then disappointment could not be hidden by the many years of police training he'd had to conceal his emotions.

Eventually Thoroughgood managed to find some words:

"Sierra Leone, bloody hell, it's not exactly around the corner, Sara!"

"I guess not but I did tell you there was always a good chance I would be moved abroad sometime in the next year. It's just that the end of next month is a bit sooner than I'd expected. But it's a huge opportunity in career terms, and if I turn it down then I'll set myself back at least five years. Basically if I don't take it, Gus, then they'll leave me behind."

"Yeah, I know all that, I guess I just thought we would have more time together to see where things would take us. I know it's been early days but I thought we really had made a connection. I mean Sierra Leone, it's not as if I can pop over for the odd long weekend, is it?"

"That's true, but just where were we going anyway, Gus? After Tuesday night you've hardly had time to reply to my texts, never mind give me a call. That's not exactly the way to go about letting a girl know you want to make a future with her, is it?"

Thoroughgood knew she was right. He'd sent out negative vibes to Sara and now her dream career ticket had arrived, and what was there keeping her in Glasgow?

Sara's ran her fingers through her long brown locks; clearly she felt guilty about having a go at him when he was confined to a hospital bed.

"Look, I'm sorry Gus, I'm being unfair. I know you've been through a lot today and it's not right for me to be taking potshots at you, it's just that you've been so hot and cold. I guess I don't really know where I stand with you, and that's why I've got to take the job in Sierra Leone."

He knew there was only going to be one conclusion at the end of this conversation, but it didn't stop him trying to mount a desperate salvage operation.

"I know I've been a bit erratic, but it's the job. This week has been something like I've never experienced in my whole career. We've had seven murders and an eighth fatality by shooting in one week, and I nearly joined them all in the city mortuary this morning. I could go through the remaining eighteen years of my service and never experience anything like it again but, as they say Sara, shit happens, and it certainly hit the fan this week. I hear what you are saying. Your job is every bit as important to you as mine is to me. I guess what I'm wondering is, does that mean, we're going to be apart for a while or that I'll never see you again?"

"It's a twelve-month posting with options to extend, depending on how it works out, but the Civil Service are very good to their employees and they subsidise the purchase of a home back in the UK, if you want to buy. I like Glasgow and I think I might want to come back here when I've finished out there."

Sara paused and watched a slight smile creep back onto Thoroughgood's shellshocked face.

"Maybe it's for the best Gus, because I think you still need time to work out if you really are over Celine. That's what's behind all this, isn't it? It's not the shootings or your job, you just haven't moved on, have you?"

For fuck's sake, was it that obvious? He asked himself. But this was no time for the truth:

326

"Nope, that's not true, Sara. Sure it wasn't nice seeing her with Meechan like that the other night, but that was always going to happen at some stage. I can tell you this is a helluva lot harder to take. You said you're due out by the middle of March, so where do we go from here?"

"The sooner you work out what your priorities are in life and where you stand with the whole Celine business, the sooner you'll know if there is going to be an 'us.'

"I just don't want to get into a situation where I'm putting everything into a relationship and it isn't coming back, Gus. I'm thirty-two now and I want a family, but I don't want to make a mistake with a guy who isn't sure what he wants in his life. It's okay for you but the clock is ticking for me. Quite frankly, taking the job in Sierra Leone is the safer option."

Thoroughgood could see how tough it was for her to get these last few words out; the tears that had been gradually welling up in her eyes now burst their dam and were running down her face. He reached out a hand and stroked the side of her face.

"Listen, I understand, but would you mind if I write to you?"

"That would be great Gus, but only when you're clear in your mind where you're going. I'm sorry, but I've been hurt once and I just don't want to go through that all again."

She stood up and leaned over him, kissing him on the forehead, and he could sense the subtle difference from the kiss she had given him when she had first arrived. He watched as she walked away and as she exited the ward, she turned and blew him a kiss then walked out of his life and he knew it was probably forever. He mouthed the words, "Goodbye Sara," but they were wasted.

Lying in his hospital bed, he realised tears had been running down his cheeks for some moments and immediately tried to wipe them away, embarrassed. What for? There was no one there to see him for the ward was empty:

Just like my life, thought Thoroughgood.

41

BANDAGED, BRUISED and with two broken ribs, Thoroughgood winced his way out of the Western at lunchtime the next day. Waiting in the car park below, Hardie pushed the Mondeo's door open and gave his gaffer a welcoming smile:

"How are the busted bones today, gaffer? You sure you're doing the right thing?"

"Judging by the encouragement I got when I told the sister I was intending to leave today, I'd say she agreed with my decision."

"Aye, it's a bit of a thought that gaffer, but here's another one that will maybe cheer you up. I see Thistle are at home today, against Clyde in the derby, so since the Old Firm game isn't until tomorrow how about I come along with you to Firhill to watch the Jags get another stuffing?"

The laugh which escaped caused Thoroughgood to grimace in pain, and his hands shot up to his fractured ribs and the support bandaging coiled around his middle:

"You at Firhill? Is that some kind of joke?"

"Not at all, I just thought there wasn't much point in leavin' you wallowing at home when you could go and do it at Firhill!"

Thoroughgood shook his head and pointed to the road ahead:

"Speaking of home, can you get me there sooner rather than later? More importantly, what's happening with the safe house? Has Tomachek slipped Farrell the bait?"

Hardie smiled. "Yeah, it's all in hand. They had the meeting with ACC Cousins yesterday and I spoke to old Val when he got back to Stewart Street. Farrell has all the details, and we just need to wait and see if he's bitten. Tomachek will fill you in himself, because after we've dumped your stuff at the 'hoose' we're meeting him for a liquid lunch in the Rock."

"Excellent, that will be the first time I've ever been debriefed by a Superintendent on an ACC's meeting in a boozer! How the fuck did you manage to organise that, faither?"

"To be fair to the old boy it was his idea. You never know, he might even join us at Firhill and then you'd have a Billy on one side and a Tim on the other!"

"You're okay, Kenny, I don't think I could stand the embarrassment."

But as he sat in the passenger seat and contemplated the afternoon ahead, Thoroughgood's spirits rose visibly. Maybe his life wasn't as empty as he had thought less than twenty four hours back as long as he had his friends, and old faither, although he would never admit as much to his face, was certainly one of them.

"My dear boys, how nice to see you both. I hope you've both got hearty appetites to set you up for the big game? What's your poison?" boomed Detective Superintendent Valentino Tomachek.

"Kronenburg," was the chorused answer.

They selected a seat next to the window. Thoroughgood had always wondered what Tomachek would be like when he was out of his working clothes, as apart from on duty and at the odd re-trial do, he had never seen his superior officer in casual wear and found the idea hard to get his head round. A pair of brown brogues, deep green cords and a thick deep red Pringle jersey was not the look he had imagined his boss would go for.

After making themselves comfortable and ordering two scampi and a rump steak, all accompanied by the compulsory serving of chips, the conversation soon settled down to Tomachek's meeting with ACC Cousins and DCI Farrell.

"Farrell is one cold fish all right," said Tomachek. "Never once did he display the slightest bit of emotion or surprise the whole way through the meeting. Just kept cleaning those bloody glasses. But he's got all the information he needs to make sure Meechan bites. In fact, the cheeky bugger's only query was why we needed to shift Simms and Jarvis in the first place. Can you believe that? He's getting information fed to him which will no doubt help line his bank account, and he has the cheek to complain! I'll have that bastard's balls before this is all over."

By two p.m. they had finished their grub and a second round; when Hardie offered to head to the bar for a third, Thoroughgood placed a restraining hand on his wrist.

"Sorry Kenny, I'm going to leave it. The other thing is, gents, I don't think I am quite ready for Firhill. I've got to be honest and say it's a bridge too far, and admit I need my kip. So if you don't mind, I'm going to head back over the road and get the head down."

It was hard to say who was the more shocked, Hardie or Tomachek. The latter was first to articulate his thoughts:

"Well done, dear boy, well done. It's good to see you letting common sense prevail. I thought it was asking a lot of you so soon after being through a major smash and with the broken ribs and all. No, I've absolutely no problem with that at all. I'll bell Mrs Tomachek and say I'll meet her at the shops and win some much-needed brownie points."

Hardie, swilling the remains of his pint around the bottom of his glass, added:

"Nae bother, gaffer. It's understandable, plus it means I can save a few bawbees for the Old Firm game at noon tomorrow."

Tomachek was taken by surprise for a second time within minutes:

"My dear Hardie, you're not telling me you're going to Parkhead only six hours before a major operation?"

"Look at it this way, boss, it might be the last time in my life I ever see the 'Gers gub your mob on their midden. How can you expect me to pass up on that?"

All three of them laughed but there was an edge to the laughter.

When they reached the front of Thoroughgood's tenement, Hardie was soon enquiring as to just what was behind his gaffer's decision to take it easy:

"So what about tomorrow night, Gus? You heard the old man say he was keeping it tight, it's gonnae take some work to get you inside."

Thoroughgood turned and offered his hand to Hardie.

"Let's just say I'll sleep on it, but if there's any way I think my presence would jeopardise the operation I won't be near the Kings' Stables. I'll call you at ten-thirty a.m., I assume you won't have left for Parkhead by then."

"Okay, Gus, that's a fair call, I hope you get a decent kip." Thoroughgood opened the security entry and headed into the close, aware that the call he was going to make in the morning was likely to end in an answer he didn't want to give.

He must have slept for a couple of hours when the doorbell rang, for it was almost four-thirty p.m. His room in total darkness except for the red figures displayed on the clock radio, he debated the need to get up and answer it. Who was it going to be? Morse, having decided he couldn't live on egg and chips at the Hardies' forever? Hardie himself come to check up on him like some clucking old mother hen, or maybe Meechan come to finish the job his henchmen failed to complete?

After what seemed like an eternity in which the doorbell rang twice more, he decided he might as well answer it. Pulling on his black Thistle robe to provide some cover for the Rush t-shirt and boxers he slept in, he headed out into the hall, shielding his eyes against the daylight flooding through the blinds into the hallway.

He reached the door, disregarded the spyhole, so ignoring the first rule of crime prevention. After all, what did it really matter if Meechan himself was standing outside the door waiting to gut him? Thoroughgood removed the chain and unlocked the Yale before pulling the inside door open: it was not Declan Meechan who was standing in front of him but his fiancée.

His mind failed to register the view his eyes presented in front of him and he rubbed at them furiously, annoyed that his befuddled brain was playing tricks on him in some painful quirk of fate. Celine spoke:

"Hi Gus, are you okay?"

Words deserted him, and he opened the door as far as it would go, gesturing for her to come in. They headed into the lounge in silence, for Thoroughgood still wasn't sure he could trust the vision before him. He made straight for the comfort of his Chesterfield, as if it would help provide some kind of comprehension check. No, she was still there and he dug his fingers into its arms, determined that he would wake up and find this was all a cruel dream. There she was, wearing a cream raincoat, jeans and knee-high leather boots:

"Gus, speak to me, are you okay? Gerry texted me what happened, and when I called him he gave me the full story. I hear your car is completely totalled and you were lucky to escape with a couple of broken ribs and whiplash."

Despite himself it all came out wrong.

"But why should any of that bother you, Celine? You made it all too clear up at the reservoir that you'd found happiness and that everything I had to say to you was a pack of lies. I'm rotten with hate, remember?"

She took a seat on his sofa and crossed her legs, swinging a boot to and fro in an involuntary glimpse of her inner agitation.

"I didn't mean it that way, Gus, but I know now you were right." Celine lowered her head and stared at the cream carpet.

"I'm sorry?" was all he could say.

"I said you were right. The other night Declan had a couple of his friends round for dinner and when I was in the kitchen, I overhead some of their conversation. You were right about the Browns and the drugs. In fact, I think everything you told me up at the reservoir was spot on. What can I say? I just didn't want to believe any of it. When Gerry sent me that text, I just knew I had to come and see you and tell you, you were right. I'm sorry Gus, so sorry."

He could see the tears forming in her eyes and before

he had time to think about what he was doing, he crossed the lounge and sat down next to her, putting a comforting arm around her. All the indecision and shock were gone:

"Why is it that whenever we are alone, one of us seems to end up crying? You've nothing to apologise for. I knew full well you had to back yourself and the decision you had made when you agreed to become Meechan's fiancée. He's more than capable of making someone believe that black is white. Unfortunately his track record—and I include myself in that—and the city mortuary, paint a different picture. I must admit Celine, when you told me he was determined to go straight eventually, I just about threw up. But that's not important now, now you know I was telling the truth."

His words were of little comfort and as he pulled her close, he could feel her body wracked by great sobs, as all the bottled-up hurt and pain of being betrayed by the man she had convinced herself was her future, exploded in raw grief. He'd never seen Celine like this, so vulnerable and utterly desolate in the final acceptance that the life she had been intending to live was based on a work of fiction.

Eventually he removed his arm and headed over to the drinks cabinet to pour a couple of glasses of Courvoisier. He moved to the CD player and selected a disc, Tears for Fears, The Hurting. Sitting back down beside her, he handed her the crystal glass with the dark brown liquid sloshing invitingly.

"Here, drink some of this and stop beating yourself up. It's supposed to be me who's in need of a brandy, not you."

At last she raised her head and shared those beautiful brown eyes with him and he stroked her tear-stained cheek with a gentle caress of his hand. Slowly, like the sun breaking from behind storm clouds, a smile crept onto her face. Celine took a deep breath.

"I'm so sorry, Gus, it's all such a mess and because I didn't believe you, wouldn't believe you, you nearly lost your life. How can I ever forgive myself?"

He could not help himself; maybe it was her vulnerability in such close and delicious proximity, but he cupped her face in his hands, leant forward and kissed her with all the tenderness he had in him.

The kiss lingered on their lips and in a move that surprised him as much as anything he had ever done, Thoroughgood recovered his self-restraint. Gradually he pulled himself clear but his eyes never left Celine's.

"Look, this isn't going to solve anything. There is nothing I want more in this world right here, right now, than to make love to you but that wouldn't be right for you, me or my smashed ribs."

Her tears started to flow freely once more, and this time he attempted to dab at them with his fingers.

"I know you're right, Gus, but I just don't know what to do anymore. Where do I go from here? My life is ruined."

"No it is not," he said, a little too forcibly. "I won't allow it to be. But we both need clear heads to think through how we are going to play this whole thing."

"What do you mean," she asked through the fingers now covering her face.

"I mean that Declan Meechan must be brought to justice. I mean he can't go on leaving the city littered in a string of bodies every time someone upsets him. I mean he must, and will, be stopped, and that hour is not far away. But for all of that to happen, and for him to be put behind bars, you must go back to Tara and play the part of the adoring fiancée for a little while more. Can you do that for me, my darling? Can you trust me?"

She smiled once more and this time the air of hopelessness had gone:

"I trust you with my life, Gus. But you called me darling? Does that mean you forgive me, Gus? Forgive me for choosing him and his lies over you for a second time?"

"I love you Celine, that's all that matters."

42

AT TEN-THIRTY on Sunday morning Thoroughgood called Hardie as promised and prepared to lie:

"All right faither, any pre-match nerves then?" He tried to sound at his most buoyant: "Anything other than a tanking is a bonus surely?"

A cough sounded at the other end of the phone:

"Aye, and get it up you, with all due respect, of course gaffer. Anyway, what about you, are you match fit?"

"No, I'm afraid I've failed a fitness test and won't even make the bench. You're going to have to lead the attack on your own, if that's all right."

Hardie couldn't quite believe his ears.

"Are you sure about that, Gus? Meechan's bound to be in on this with Farrell singing like a canary to him. It could be your one and only chance to settle the score legitimately with that evil bastard."

"No faither, I'd be a liability to you and McNab and there is no way I would ever forgive myself for putting the two of you in jeopardy because I couldn't cut the mustard. What's wrong, don't you think you can get a result on your own without me there to hold your hand?"

Thoroughgood had known his final remark would get Hardie's hackles up because it was a tack he had used many a time before and it had never failed yet. A sound, something like a Volkswagen on a cold morning, came from down the line:

"What do you mean by that? Twenty-three years on the job and I've never let a bloody sod down. Don't you worry, we'll have Meechan banged up by the time you can say Celtic 0 Rangers 2."

"So that's your prediction then? Is that the one you've got a tenner on with old Valentino?"

"It is indeed, and I have every faith in the Queen's eleven delivering said tenner into my back pocket."

"If you say so, faither. Now listen, you take care out there tonight. Meechan is a dirty bastard and I wouldn't put it past him to have a trick up his sleeve. One other thing, what's happening with Farrell?"

"We're sorted there, apparently some of his mobile calls have been traced to a number registered to a Mr D. A. Meechan. No, gaffer, friend Henry will be banged up by early Monday morning, and that one is definitely worth a flutter."

"Excellent. Now just take care out there tonight faither, after all you're no getting any younger. I'll give you a call in the morning once I've had my beauty sleep but promise me there'll be no heroics."

"You have my word, gaffer, on that and Declan Meechan being in custody by Monday morning."

"Good man," said Thoroughgood even though he knew this was one promise Hardie would not be able to keep: he didn't know Meechan the way Thoroughgood did.

He dozed off again and by the time the dull ache coming from his fractured ribs had become so painful it had woken him, it was nearly two p.m. Washing down the twin Co-codamol capsules with his cold coffee, he headed for the shower. He phoned for a taxi and was driven down to South Street where he hired a car from the

Arnold Clark rental office. A Mazda, this time a six series; he could have wept the way some of the familiarities in the dashboard reminded him of his treasured Rex.

He parked the Mazda about half a mile from Tara's gates and waited for the dying of the light. Checking through his old squash bag, he located bolt-cutters, insulated rubber gloves, a can of shaving foam and a balaclava. His fingers curled round the handle of the familiar service revolver his grandfather had brought home from the RAF at the end of the Second World War.

He had cherished the revolver as one of the strongest links to the man who had been the closest thing to a father he had had as a kid. Its chamber was filled in each one of its grooves, and he stuck the handgun inside the specially elongated poacher's pocket of his Barbour jacket.

While the search of Meechan's mansion had failed to provide either Frankie Brennan, or any tangible evidence, it had allowed Thoroughgood to familiarise himself with the layout inside and, after a chat with the Support Unit cops who had completed the sweep of the grounds, the twin areas where the perimeter fence was vulnerable to uninvited guests.

Watching the rotation of the CCTV camera, Thoroughgood estimated he had roughly twenty-five seconds to cover the thirty yards of ground leading to the wall, cut the wire and then cover the camera head in shaving foam. He would then try to haul himself over the wall and make the four-foot drop into Meechan's private domain.

As the camera swivelled past the trees and circled north, he broke cover and made the wall, counting to himself, in less than ten seconds. Wincing in pain, he used the wrought iron to haul himself up onto the sill of the sandstone basewall and let out an involuntary gasp as the pain cranked up another couple of notches on the Richter scale. Quickly he pulled the bolt-cutters out of his back pocket and cut a three foot gap in the razor wire.

Looking up to the pillar where the camera was mounted a further three feet above his head, he realised he needed to get himself up onto the top of the column if he was going to foam the camera and the seconds were ticking fifteen, sixteen, seventeen … The pain was almost unbearable by the time he made it onto the top of the column. On his knees, he tasted the salt from the beads of sweat dripping from his brow, but, just before the camera swept round to face him he sprayed it in foam. Turning his body so his back was facing inwards, he dropped down off the column onto the sill on the inside of the wall, in one agony-racked movement.

Gritting his teeth as the waves of pain threatened to induce imminent nausea, he let go and dropped the four feet onto the lawn at the base of the wall, then strained his ears for the sound of any alarm. There was none.

The distance from the wall to the French windows which encased the swimming pool was, Thoroughgood guessed, around one hundred feet, and with shrubs and fir trees running down the right hand side, he had perfect cover to reach within twenty feet of them. The night sky was conveniently dark now, but Thoroughgood could make out the shape of two security lights perched above the windows. Searching amongst the foliage he uncovered a couple of broken branches, one of which he decided would be strong enough to angle the lights upwards.

He approached the first light from the right, taking care to make sure there were no lights going on inside. When he was almost underneath the first light, he pushed the branch up and connected with the rim, sending the light's encasement in an upward direction, uselessly gazing out into the almost pitch black of the sky above. The second security light was easily manoeuvred, and Thoroughgood gave thanks that both were newly installed, not rusted onto their brackets and as such immovable.

The French windows were the next obstacle to overcome and Thoroughgood was relieved when he examined them closely, to see they were externally beaded. Pulling the Swiss army knife from his pocket, he began to scrape the beading free from around the perimeter of the outside glass frame.

Thoroughgood had been at plenty of break-ins where entire window-panes were found discarded in front gardens after the housebreaker had removed the beading and then popped the frame out. It gave him particular amusement that Meechan of all people had his French windows secured in such a slipshod manner. When he had completely de-beaded the outside window he applied some slight pressure and saw the frame tilt, then lifted it out and placed it against the wall immediately to his right. Ten minutes later the second frame was also out, and a check of his watch showed it had just gone seven p.m. He made his way into the pool area, taking care with every step not to send a shockwave of noise upstairs which would alert Meechan to the presence of an intruder. The lights were low, and the noise of the generator regulating the pool's temperature meant any noise from his movements was muffled.

He reached the stair leading to the ground floor and took a deep breath before climbing it, one painstaking step at a time. For the first time he could hear the muffled sound of music coming from the lounge, he assumed. He recalled the lounge was to the left of the front door, just inside the reception hall, while Meechan's drawing room was opposite. That put the lounge on his right and as he hovered on the landing at the top of the stairs which had taken him out of the basement area, he thought he could hear voices.

There was a corridor, perhaps fifteen feet long, that ran alongside an adjacent wall belonging to the kitchen, and then he would be out into the reception hall with the glass-paned door to the lounge no more than ten feet away.

Taking a deep breath, as much to try and break the tension wracking his body as anything else, he started to make his way to the lounge door just as it opened. Celine walked out and barely managed to stifle the gasp of sheer astonishment that emanated from her open mouth. Thoroughgood put his index finger to his mouth in an act of habit, praying she would have enough composure not to give the game away but also wondering whether she might well elect to do so out of design rather than accident.

After the briefest of moments she nodded and pointed back down the passageway he had just come from. He descended the steps with a good deal less care than he had climbed them with Celine immediately behind him.

"What the hell do you think you're doing, Gus?" She spoke in a whisper that scarcely managed to conceal the shock at what she obviously viewed as an act of lunacy.

"I don't have time to explain, Celine. What I need you to do is get back into the lounge and act as if nothing has happened. You've got to trust me on this one, Celine. Believe me, I know what I'm doing."

In the glow of the wall-lights around the pool he could detect the tears welling up in her eyes, for she knew as well as he did the danger that was just around the corner. Wrapping her arms around him, she pulled him close. The action spoke more than mere words, and then she pulled free and turned to walk up the stairs.

There standing at the bottom of the steps was Meechan, his shadow rising up like a giant out of the dancing reflections of the water thrown up by the dimmed lighting.

"How very cosy. I could ask, 'to what do I owe the pleasure?' But the warmth of your embrace has provided me with my answer. So touching, and yet such a great pity that two's a party and three's a crowd."

43

HARDIE HAD to admit his gaffer's decision to not see things through at the King's Stable had taken him by surprise. After all the personal enmity between Thoroughgood and Meechan, Hardie could not believe the DS had decided to let him and McNab finish the job.

The briefing at Stewart Street City Centre office, held by Detective Super Tomachek, had gone well and everything, Hardie was sure, was watertight. The armed cordon formed by the Tactical Firearms Unit around the King's Stables, meant there would be no escape for Meechan and his men. The plans he had secured provided the layout of the building in great detail, and an earlier reconnaissance visit made that morning with McNab meant the layout was fresh in his mind. There was only one way in via road, and there was now only one solitary entrance into the building; the front door. Everything else was boarded and sealed up in the metallic casing that encapsulated half of the dwellings in Glasgow's run-down schemes.

On top of that, Rangers had recorded their first victory in an Old Firm derby at Parkhead that season, and Hardie smiled as the thought swept over him: if that wasn't a good omen, what was? Tomachek had also been in buoyant spirits, despite Celtic's loss, particularly when he took Hardie and McNab aside and told them a mobile phone call between Farrell and Meechan lasting nearly fifteen minutes had been monitored at nine p.m. the previous night. There could be no doubt then that Meechan knew exactly where the two remaining members of his gang were due to be relocated to at six p.m. the following evening.

By five-thirty Hardie and McNab, resplendent in a red Berghaus jacket and black beanie hat and navy blue hoody respectively, were climbing into the rear of an unmarked white Citroen van, borrowed from Scenes of Crime/IB branch and parked in the rear yard at Stewart Street Office. As the doors were shut tight by one of the two uniform officers who would convey the pair to their destination, Hardie peered out of the blackened rear window and watched the red Mercedes sports car belonging to DCI Henry Farrell pull into the yard.

Farrell parked the Mercedes opposite the van and as he climbed out of it, took more than a passing interest in the white Citroen, usually resident at Force HQ, Pitt Street. Hardie prayed the two uniform officers climbing into the front of the vehicle would lead the DCI to guess this was indeed the motor being used to convey Simms and Jarvis to their new safe house.

The van headed along the M8, turning up into Springburn and then through Bishopbriggs. The conversation between Hardie and McNab was almost non-existent to start with but slowly, as they began to tune in to what lay ahead, both of them attempted to iron out the little kinks causing them concern.

McNab had been chosen to back up Hardie, as the enquiry had originally been in East Division and Tomachek was acutely aware that all the glory couldn't go to Central CID. The fact McNab had been on the original MI for the Browns was also a big positive; while it had been Thoroughgood's recommendation, because McNab had spent three years seconded to 'V' Support Services as a firearms-trained officer, his expertise would be essential. Not slow to realise the positive effects a successful outcome to the night's work would bring to his career, McNab had jumped at the chance.

Pulling out the plan of the King's Stables he had tucked inside his Berghaus, Hardie went over the whys and wherefores once again.

"They've got to come through the front door, and we have a ground floor or a first floor to lie in wait for them. You're the firearms officer; should we split up, one on either level, or stick together?"

McNab curled his mouth at either end as he considered the possibilities.

"I like the shot we would get from the balcony on the first floor. They're going to come charging in expecting us to be sitting playing cards on the ground floor or shit like that, so they aren't gonnae be looking for two revolvers trained on them one up one down. We'd have the element of surprise on our side and however minimal and fleeting that would be, it's one you want with you when shooters are involved."

"Aye, I'm all for that!" said Hardie.

They arrived at the derelict country pub just before six, safe in the knowledge that a ring of armed steel had encircled the location almost ninety minutes previously. The building was a fine stone edifice dating back to Victorian times. The Forth and Clyde canal ran along the front of the building, with a pathway and an area once used for seating in the warmer weather.

"No' a bad place to enjoy a beer on a pleasant summer's afternoon, is it, Hardie?' said McNab.

"Aye, I enjoyed a few here all right, son. I had a spell out at Kirkintilloch office in the late Eighties and we used to finish our early shift and head for the Stables; a couple of pints on a sunny afternoon was as good as it got when it came to unwinding after seven early starts."

Hardie's reminiscing was ruined by the sharp blast of a chill April breeze that threatened to cut them both in half.

"Let's get the fuck inside before we both turn hypothermic," suggested McNab as he wrung his hands together in a futile attempt to bring some warmth into them.

Inside, the bar ran three-quarters of the length of the ground floor. At one end were the toilets, at the other a stairway up to the first floor which had been used for dining. Apart from a few rotten tables and chairs, it was now home to a couple of single beds where Hardie and McNab would take it in turn to catch some shuteye.

The electricity had been re-installed for the duration of their operation, and the fridge behind the bar filled with milk and beer that morning. McNab headed around behind the bar and scooped a couple of cans of Stella Artois out before handing one to Hardie, who had just applied a match to the fire he had laid in preparation for their arrival, earlier that morning.

Hardie took a long draft of lager, his gaze trained on the fire as it slowly sparked into life beneath the superb mahogany fireplace.

"A crying shame this fireplace is being left to rot with the building. I wonder if I'd get away with ripping it out and taking it back to mine when this is all done?"

"I won't tell if you don't," replied McNab helpfully before joining Hardie in a mock salute with his can of Stella.

"I suggest we finish these and take up our positions. You had any further thoughts on where you want us to deploy, Ross?" asked Hardie.

"One up one down would be best. That way we can catch them in the crossfire. If you want to go behind the bar then I'll take the balcony diagonally opposite the door. Just remember, we're duty bound to give them the benefit of a warning that we're armed polis. After that, fuck 'em!"

Tommy Rankin guided the speedboat along the Forth and Clyde canal enjoying the remains of the day and the cool air gliding gently over the surface of the canal. He had done his homework late last night within hours of Farrell's call to Meechan, and established that taking a vehicle to the pub along the single-lane road which could so easily be stoppered up would mean there was no chance of an escape if the polis had set a trap.

A Maryhill boy, he knew all about the Forth and Clyde canal and its twisting route out of Glasgow and into the countryside towards Kirky. He'd had the speedboat stolen from its mooring on the shores of Loch Lomond early on Sunday morning, and now here he was behind the wheel with Morriston and two henchmen armed to the teeth, determined to ensure that Simms' and Jarvis' wagging tongues were stilled for good.

Three hundred yards away from the pub, the canal turned into a gentle bend and Rankin switched the engine off and listened for a moment to the sounds of the night. Apart from the rustling foliage lining the banks and the sound of occasional traffic coming from the main road to Kirky, the silence was delicious.

Rankin turned round, leaned against the steering wheel and dished out the final instructions:

"All right boys, it's not rocket science. I'll pull up at the berth just down from the pub, you get the jemmy out, fuck the door open and then nobody lives. Do you understand me?"

The collective nod of three heads made it clear they did; they pulled down their black balaclavas and pulled out the Kalashnikovs, ready to blow away whoever they met behind the front door of The King's Stables.

Rankin started up the speedboat engine, pulled down his balaclava and reached inside his pocket to pull out the Luger that was his favoured handgun. He laid it lovingly down on the dashboard next to the wheel and put his foot down. The speedboat revved into life, leaving a trail of white spray behind them. They were fifty yards away from the makeshift jetty extending ten yards out into the canal opposite the stables, and there was no sign of life apart from the smoke pluming out of the chimney. The boat surged past the jetty and slowed before Rankin turned it neatly and brought it to rest, watching as his three colleagues vaulted over the prow and onto land.

For some reason Rankin turned off the engine, breaking the getaway driver's golden rule of always having the motor running when a job was in progress. Watching as the first of his hooded mates levelled the jemmy against the door and brought all his force to bear, there was a sharp crack as the metal casing around the doorway was sprung.

In the same moment that Morriston and his two sidekicks burst through the door, Rankin heard a voice pierce the night air and he did not like what it said.

"Armed police! Throw down your weapons."

The warning from the Police TFU armed incident commander came too late: no one had taken into account the possibility the intruders would come via the canal and because they had been ferried almost to the front door of the pub, below ground level, the armed officers ringing the King's Stables were taken completely by surprise.

It was McNab who got the first eyeball on their three guests as they burst through the door and he knew immediately as he took in their Kalashnikovs, that a shouted warning would be a complete waste of time.

Raising his revolver he sighted the first man through the door and shot to kill. The bullet hit the balaclavaed male an inch to the right of his heart and he dropped like a stone. But with his first shot McNab had given away both his position and the element of surprise. The balcony was now being splintered into bits by high-velocity rounds of lead from twin machine guns.

He ducked just in time. But Hardie was downstairs behind the old pub's bar, and immediately in the path of the gunmen and the line of their withering fire. The firestorm died down and McNab heard the sound of the first footsteps on the stairway; another single shot rang out followed by a groan.

Hardie had kept his position concealed for as long as possible, and when the two blackened figures had started their way up the stairs he unloaded as many rounds as he could into the shadowy duo. He felled one immediately, while it looked like he had clipped the other in the shoulder. With two of the three gunmen down and the other one winged, the odds had swung dramatically in the detectives' favour.

McNab, guessing what had happened below, made his way to the top of the stair where he saw one figure sprawled in a heap over the first step and a second lying face down on the floor in a pool of blood. The other male was backing out towards the front door with his Kalashnikov trained on Hardie, who in turn was crouching behind the bar with his revolver aimed at the gunman. But the male had caught the flicker of movement at the top of the stairs, and it was enough for him to let his control of the weapon waver.

Hardie seized his opportunity, pumping three rounds at the doorway. Another grunt and the male staggered back through the door and outside. As Hardie began to make his way out from behind the bar, the Kalashnikov spat lead furiously in his direction, before rifling the top of the stairway. The detectives heard the receding footsteps of the gunman making good his escape. They both bolted for the door.

"You okay, Kenny?" asked McNab as he came hurtling down the steps and vaulted the prone figure lying in a heap at the bottom.

"Never better Ross," said Hardie with a triumphal smile.

Morriston made it to the speedboat just as Hardie and McNab exited cautiously out of the front door; the black boilersuits of the TFU officers were materialising round either flank of the pub but it was too late. Morriston lowered himself in with a helping hand from Rankin, and the speedboat revved into life and shot along the waterway.

"Bastard," shouted Hardie, his brief moment of triumph ruined.

There was no way he was letting them escape, and as the sound of the speedboat engine dimmed, the noise of a second engine filled the vacuum, providing Hardie with the answer to his prayers. As soon as the detective saw the TFU four-by-four come into view, he grabbed

McNab and received a knowing nod by way of answer.

The two of them sprinted for the vehicle and Hardie opened the door and uttered one word to the driver:

"Out."

Initially the driver thought about putting up an argument but a glance at the gnarled features in front of him made him think twice. McNab was already in the passenger seat and immediately they turned right; Hardie took the Land Rover down the banking and onto the towpath running parallel to the canal. The speedboat had almost disappeared from view but Hardie knew about a quarter of a mile along from the pub was a lock, which also had a car park adjacent to it, and he reckoned it was there the two escaping gunmen would leave the boat and jump into a waiting car.

While the towpath was wide enough for the Land Rover to make its way along with either wheel straddling the side of it, it was not suitable for a foot-to-the-floor pursuit. Hardie had to concentrate fully, his cause not helped by the darkness. Eventually he could see the gates of the lock and the ladder at the side of it. The speedboat was almost there and Hardie gave the accelerator an extra squeeze.

Rankin helped Morriston out of the boat and onto the bottom rung of the ladder, then attempted to push him up. The islander had taken two bullets, one in the right shoulder and the other in the guts, and was losing plenty of blood. By the time Rankin got Morriston to the top of the ladder he was aware of the droning of a diesel engine; as he turned to squint over his shoulder he saw the cause of the noise was a marked police Land Rover.

Rankin turned round, leaning his body weight back against the ladder while he sighted the Kalashnikov in the direction of the oncoming vehicle; he let it rip into life and saw at least three strikes on the bonnet of the Land Rover, which slowed and then ground to a halt.

Satisfied he'd bought some vital time, he followed Morriston onto the bank and helped his injured mate in the direction of the waiting Vauxhall Vectra, all the time conscious of the growing engine noise coming from the Land Rover. They were nearly at the Vectra when Morriston spoke.

"Listen Tommy, get going on your own, there's no way you'll make it with me holding you back. Besides, I need treatment and quick. Let me take the motor and divert them, and you can make it out over the fields on foot."

"You sure?" asked Rankin, aware that Morriston would be lucky to see another dawn if he didn't get urgent medical attention, never mind escape. Morriston nodded, opened the driver's door of the Vectra and threw the Kalashnikov inside.

Rankin sprinted over to the fence enclosing one of the cornfields running along the side of the canal. Swinging himself over the top rail, he saw a spark jump off the rail, three inches from where the bullet had impacted. Ducking low on the other side, he could see his pursuers had not been fooled by his attempt at a diversion.

He ran into the cornfields, making for the direction of a clump of trees that would at least provide a semblance of cover. It was a strange sensation letting the corn stubble brush through his hands as he ran through the field; somehow, Tommy Rankin found it liberating and his mind returned to the distant sunshine of his youth. Memories of summer holidays as a kid spent on his favourite uncle's farm in Ayrshire warmed him against the chill air. His silent reverie was quickly brought to an end when a harsh voice barked from behind him:

"Armed police! Stop or I shoot!"

The realisation hit that here in the now he was running for his life and all his plans, all his hopes, rested on what happened next. The trees were ten yards away and he turned, slowly slipping his right hand inside his black ski jacket and wrapping his fingers round the Luger. In the remnants of the dusk's half-light, McNab could only make out one of the gunman's hands from the shadowy silhouette fifteen feet away. Guessing where the other one was heading, he opened fire.

Rankin felt the rush of air shoot past his cheek as the first bullet missed by inches, and drew the Luger but as he levelled it at his pursuer the impact of the second projectile on his forehead threw him back and laid him out, his corpse flattening the corn. McNab walked over to the body, his revolver still cautiously aimed at the prone figure.

Pulling the balaclava back over the head of the gunman, recognition swept over his face.

"Fuck me, it's Tommy Rankin," he said out loud.

The sound of heavy breathing at his shoulder alerted him to Hardie's presence:

"Aye, it's Tommy Rankin all right, minus half his brains."

44

MEECHAN SWITCHED the lights on, and the pool and its surrounds were suddenly bathed in floodlight.

"What's that expression when a married man is betrayed by his wife? Ah, of course, it's come back to me: cuckolded, isn't it? I promised you the world, my world, and this is what you've given me back, Celine. I suppose I should consider myself lucky the truth has been revealed before we went down the aisle. Christ, I might have even been playing at happy families and the doting daddy, bringing up a copper's baby. Maybe I've been lucky."

He took a step forward, pointing at Thoroughgood.

"But you, Detective Sergeant, your luck has just run out. For tonight, for this," he swept his arm before him, "for this I will finally end your life."

Thoroughgood knew he was in no state for a physical confrontation with Meechan, nursing two broken ribs, but he couldn't draw the revolver from inside his jacket with Celine standing between him and the man who had just promised to kill him. Realising he had to put Celine's safety first, Meechan had just offered him the perfect out.

"But that's just it, Meechan, Celine is pregnant and the baby belongs to her fiancée."

Meechan's Northern Irish Belfast accent became almost guttural in his rage.

"You lying bastard, you think your lies can save you or her now?" A sadistic smile lit up Meechan's face:

"What have you got to say to this, my darling whore?"

"It's true, Declan. I came down to the pool to get my robe and that was when I discovered him. I don't know why but I felt I needed to tell him, I didn't want any trouble between the two of you, but it's true. You remember the night we had together after Jimmy's 'do'? I just wanted to be a hundred percent sure before I told you and to find the right moment, but it's true Declan, as God is my witness."

It was Thoroughgood's turn to frown. His mind raced and panic set in: she was far too bloody convincing for this to be an act, or was she? Right now there was no way he could find out without putting her life in jeopardy.

"A likely story. No. We will finish this here and now."

Meechan glared at Celine with a burning hatred and she shivered with the fear it induced in her.

"And then, bitch, I'll deal with you."

Meechan took another step forward and Thoroughgood knew the moment for caution was long gone. He reached inside his jacket pocket and pulled out his grandfather's revolver.

"Take another step, Meechan, and nothing in this world or the next will give me as much pleasure as blowing your fuckin' brains out."

Meechan halted and let go a short harsh laugh.

"Very brave, with a pistol in your hand, copper."

He bent down and dipped his hand in the edge of the pool, swirling his fingers around in the water. Thoroughgood, still enveloped in the uncertainty of Celine's words, looked at her, searching for some kind of confirmation.

At the side of the pool a metallic chain, used to fasten the cover, dangled loosely. Meechan unhitched it, deftly balling it in his hand and then rising slowly. He lashed it out at Thoroughgood's arm, knocking the revolver out of his hand and quickly side-footing it into the pool.

"You were saying, copper?"

Slowly, with a deliberate delight, Meechan rewound the chain and then smashed it off the tiled poolside floor for good effect. Celine screamed, her panic raw:

"Stop it, Declan, for God's sake, it's all true."

"An unlikely truth dearest, wouldn't you say? Nevertheless, it matters not."

He closed to within five feet of Thoroughgood. The DS, clutching his stinging right wrist, backed off, but he was running out of space in which to retreat.

"No, Thoroughgood, we finish this right here."

Meechan made his way over to a rack at the side of the pool stocked with barbecue equipment, and removed two long sharp knives that bore a strong resemblance to machetes. He tossed one in Thoroughgood's direction.

"Pick it up, pig. In that blade lies your only hope of salvation, to be sure. But I warn you, carving up pork is my speciality." Meechan laughed, plainly enjoying himself.

"Stop it Declan, I beg you stop it, for the love of Jesus," cried Celine.

Meechan waved his hand in her direction as if she was an inconvenience so minor she barely registered on his consciousness. In one languid stride, reminiscent of a big cat stalking wounded prey, he closed on Thoroughgood and threw out the chain.

"Take hold of it and wrap it round your free hand. We'll finish this like men."

Thoroughgood coiled the end of the chain around his right wrist, lifted the blade and watched the light glint off it. Maybe not a machete but with a broad six-inch blade, it was as near as damn it. Switching the blade to his left hand, he knew he was going to need all his strength to keep Meechan at bay, just as he realised that tonight he must surely die.

The first yank almost took him off his feet, and the searing pain from his ribs brought bile to his mouth as he kept his eyes on Meechan's right hand. He saw the arc of the blade as it came down in a brutal swipe that missed his left hand by an inch. Already unsteadied by the force of Meechan's pull, he stumbled down onto one knee, the sweat dripping off his brow and his breath harsh and rasping.

The chain loosened as Meechan advanced. Thoroughgood had exaggerated his vulnerability and when Meechan got within two feet of him he lunged with the blade, slashing at Meechan's groin. Meechan let out a roar of anguish and pain. Looking down he saw a flap had been cut loose at the top of his denim-clad leg and from it blood beginning to seep.

Touching his wound to check on its severity, Meechan realised it was only superficial and this brought the cruel killing smile back to his face. He rewound the chain round his left hand, pulling sharply.

"It will take more than that, Thoroughgood. Is that the best you can do?" mocked Meechan as he gesticulated with his blade for Thoroughgood to come to him.

Thoroughgood's face was contorted with fresh pain. The lunge had tugged hard on his injured ribs, but, still on his left knee, he was determined not to show any vulnerability:

"Why don't you come and find out, bastard?"

He attempted to raise himself up and as he did so everything went dark. Celine had aimed the ceramic flower pot with deadly accuracy, and as she watched him crumple on the tiled floor in front of her from the impact of the blow she had landed so deliberately to the back of his head, her face was awash with emotion.

Meechan's eyes blazed as he tried to read something from the expression on her face while being denied the opportunity to finish his feud with Thoroughgood once and for all.

"What the fuck do you think you are doing?"

"If you would just give me the chance I'll tell you, Declan. The game is up. He told me just before you came down to the pool. The safe house Simms and Jarvis are supposed to have been relocated to was a ruse to draw you into a police trap. Thoroughgood guessed you would send others to do the job and that's why he came here to finish this madness between you two once and for all. I swear he is every bit as crazy as you are, but he told me there's no way any of your boys will get out alive from, what was it he called it, the King's Stables. Who did you send?"

As she looked into his face she could see from the flicker of concern that the answer was Tommy Rankin. Meechan dropped the chain, tossed away the knife and pulled his mobile from his pocket, quickly punching in series of digits. Holding the mobile to his ear, he waited for an answer and got one which confirmed the awful truth.

"Well, well, if it's not Declan Meechan. I've got some bad news for you: your friend Tommy is lying in a field pushing up the daisies and now we're coming for you," said Hardie.

Meechan cut the mobile without saying a word. For a moment his self-control deserted him and his eyes glazed over, moisture escaping them and spilling onto his face against his iron will. Quickly he cuffed away the tears. Celine raised a hand to try and comfort him but he slapped it away.

"Look Declan, you've got to go. If you stay here, what's going to happen? You'll go the same way as Tommy. Please, while there's still time, just go."

He looked into her eyes and all the certainty in him had gone.

"Answer me one thing, Celine: the baby. Are you lying? Are you pregnant with my child? I must know."

"Yes, I'm telling the truth. I only told Thoroughgood because I thought it would make him go but it was too late. Now please, while there's still time you must go. When you're safe somewhere you can get a message to me somehow."

He leant forward and kissed her, then pulled back.

"Whatever has happened, whatever does happen, Celine, always remember I love you."

She smiled: "It's the same for me, Declan."

Hardie was standing leaning against the cornfield gate, staring at the body of Tommy Rankin.

"So what do we do now? A pint would go down a bloody treat, Kenny," said McNab.

Hardie's mind was already busy working out the connotations of his brief conversation with Meechan's silent mobile.

"I wonder where Meechan is right now? If I was a betting man I'd say there is a fair chance he'll be at home congratulating himself on a job well done, but not for much longer. No Ross, we have work to do … if you're up for it?"

"What did you have in mind?" asked the DC.

"Well I'm just a bit concerned about where Gus is. I thought there was no way he'd miss tonight's show, but I'll bet he knew Meechan wouldn't dirty his hands trying to shut up Simms and Jarvis. I'd put decent money on him deciding to pay Meechan a visit. Now that visit is maybe still to happen, and if we're quick enough we can get there before it all goes pear-shaped and save Gus from himself."

In less than ten minutes they found themselves sitting at the traffic lights that would take them, with a right turn, onto Strathblane Road and the route leading to Meechan's house up in Mugdock. As they waited for the green light, a black Range Rover bearing the private plate DAM shot through the lights, heading for Glasgow at speed.

"Fuck me," said a disbelieving Hardie, "that's Meechan's motor and wherever he's going, he's in some bloody hurry."

"Well what're you waiting for, Kenny? Let's get after him," said McNab.

They turned into Milngavie Road with the Range Rover all but out of sight, opting against shouting for back-up. Meechan was obviously unaware of their pursuit, and slowly they began to close on him. By the time they hit the Switchback dual carriageway, the pursuit had begun to pick up speed, and it was then McNab decided the time was right to call for help.

"I reckon he's heading for the Clyde Tunnel, Kenny. If we can get the Armed Response vehicles positioned on the north side we'll have him nicely bottled up."

Hardie nodded in agreement and McNab was soon sending out the radio request:

362

"Code 44 car pursuit, Detective Constable McNab in pursuit of black Range Rover registered mark DAM 1. One male up, direction of travel: south along Canniesburn Switchback, possibly heading for the Clyde Tunnel."

By the time they had reached the end of the Switchback dual carriageway, Meechan was aware of the marked four-by-four drawing closer in his rear view mirror and flattened the accelerator. He broke the first set of lights at amber but the second set, running across Great Western Road, he went through at red, missing the back of a green Rover 620 by inches. After he shot through, he quickly checked the rear view to see the police four-by-four slowing dramatically to avoid slithering into a giant Asda artic ploughing its way relentlessly onwards up the Great Western Road.

There was no time to lose, and Meechan rammed his foot hard on the accelerator as he shot towards the Clyde Tunnel. Traffic was light and allowed him to spot the two marked police cars with lights flashing, blocking the entrance to the south tunnel but with the four-by-four in his rearview once again reducing the gap, he kept going, his mind surveying the ever-decreasing options ahead of him.

Two hundred yards from the police roadblock, Meechan could make out the faces of the cops training firearms on his Range Rover from behind the safety of their vehicles, having already deployed the stinger device used to burst tyres across the road in front of them. However, they had only blocked the south side of the carriageway, and at the last minute he pulled his steering wheel hard down right and smashed through the stationary swivel barrier used to block the tunnel during repairs.

The barrier smashed his windscreen and splintered,

then he was through and onto the north carriageway, on its outside lane. He had gambled the traffic would be so sparse at that time of the night he might at least have time to prepare for the first oncoming vehicle, and his gamble looked like paying off.

The blaring of horns sounded, a silver Ford Mondeo, the first vehicle coming on in the inside lane, but as the tunnel started to dip into its lowest section, halfway under the River Clyde, he continued at sixty mph unopposed.

Meechan spotted the headlights in his rear view and realised his was not the only vehicle speeding underneath the Clyde the wrong way; as he heard and felt the first metallic crack, he realised his pursuers were armed. He had no time to dwell on what was behind him, for four hundred yards ahead the giant form of a Scania was heading his way in the outside lane and worse still, the inside lane was taken by a red Citroen.

Assessing the situation, Meechan realised he had one shot at survival and quickly changed lanes into the inside track, heading straight for the Citroen. He was gambling everything on its driver slamming on the brakes and a gap opening up between the rapidly slowing car and the Scania, which he guessed would continue to plough straight on, its driver confident he would be safe within its size and bulk.

Sure enough, the Citroen began to fall back from its previously parallel position with the Scania and by the time Meechan was passing the artic there was a gap for him to swerve into before he rammed into the saloon car. But the manoeuvre had cost him time, and the pursuing police vehicle continued to close.

Meechan knew his most vulnerable moments were still ahead as he continued to climb up the steep side of the north end of the tunnel leading back out onto the open roadway. The rise was such that the oncoming traffic would have no view of his Range Rover until it was almost on top of them.

The matter was taken out of his hands when he felt a shock juddering through the spine of the Range Rover as a bullet thudded into one of his rear tyres. Trying with all his might, he attempted to wrestle control of the steering wheel, but it was not enough to stop the violent swerve that took the Range Rover into the inside lane just as a motorcycle began its descent into the tunnel. The driver didn't stand a chance and the bike ploughed straight into the bonnet of the Range Rover, throwing his body over the top of the roof and landing with a dull thud on the roadway behind Meechan.

He kept the Range Rover going relentlessly, heading out of the tunnel. As he crested the lip of the entrance to the northbound carriageway, he pointed the vehicle as best he could in the direction of the sliproad diagonally across from him, which led off the southbound carriageway into Govan. He could feel the grinding of the wheel rim jarring on the tarmacadam of the roadway. Putting all his strength into his bid to keep the steering wheel stationary, he smashed back through the swivel barrier and attempted to cross the twin carriageways on the southside of the tunnel.

With ten yards to go before he reached the relative safety of the sliproad, the headlights of two cars lit up the side of the Range Rover and he missed the outside vehicle by a couple of feet before he shot into the relative safety provided by the massive concrete wall which shepherded the off-sliproad on its route into Govan.

At the top of the slip-road Meechan opened the Range

Rover door and jumped out; he ran up to the Saab that had stopped behind him and hauled the door open, levelled his Colt at the head of the startled middle-aged male sitting in the driver's seat.

"Get the fuck out and I don't blow your brains out."

The driver did as he was bid. Moments later the silver Saab was back on the dual carriageway on the southside of the Clyde Tunnel heading for the M8. This time there was no pursuit and Meechan knew that his only worry would be how quickly the driver could report his vehicle as stolen and the cops alerted to look out for it. Within ten minutes he was crossing the Erskine Bridge and sweeping back into Hardgate.

The prone figure of the shattered body that belonged to the motorcyclist had forced Hardie and McNab to slam on the brakes of their four-by-four at the lip of the tunnel. While Hardie radioed for assistance and an ambulance, McNab cradled the driver's head in his arms looking for signs of life.

Removing the visor, the trickle of blood from the side of the mouth and the vacant glare from staring eyes confirmed that his search was almost certainly futile. After completing his calls for an ambulance and police back-up to a background chorus of blaring horns from the jammed traffic backing up at the entrance of the northbound carriageway, Hardie returned to his partner. When McNab gave him the thumbs down he could think of only one word to say:

"Bastard."

45

THOROUGHGOOD'S VISION was blurred and his head was throbbing. All he could remember was Meechan approaching, and then it had been lights out. He tried to pick himself up off the tiles but found his legs would not obey the commands being sent from his brain. He felt a pair of hands press down on his shoulders and he was looking into Celine's eyes.

"Take your time, Gus, you've just had a bang from one of Declan's ceramic flower pots," she pointed at the ornate blue pot lying on its side three feet away.

"I should know, since it was me who landed it."

She helped him shuffle into one of the nearby wicker chairs at the top end of the pool and he watched as she made her way to one of the chest freezers lining the wall opposite him, returning with a bag of ice which she made him place on the spot where she had administered the flower pot with such effective impact.

Slowly, as the pain and burning subsided, Thoroughgood once again found the strength to look into her eyes

"Why, Celine? Why did you lie to me? Then this?" he pointed to his head. "You try and split my skull open?"

"God help me Gus, I didn't know what else to do. It was all I could think of to stop him. If I hadn't, what would have happened? He would have cut you to pieces;

surely a sore head isn't too high a price to pay for your life?"

He attempted a smile that just wouldn't form.

"What about the baby? Is it make-believe or the real thing?"

It was Celine's turn to look away. After a short pause she once again met his glare:

"It's true, Gus. I'm pregnant. When you told me all those things up at the reservoir I didn't know what to do, I didn't want to believe them about Declan, especially since I'm now carrying his baby. When Gerry McIlroy told me what had happened to you, I knew it had to be Declan who was behind it and that you'd been telling the truth and not just trying to split us up. When you came out and said I was pregnant like that, to try and stop Declan from hurting me, I didn't know what to do. I thought I was going to throw up, but I knew why you were doing it and at that stage it seemed the only way to stop him taking my life and my baby's too."

Thoroughgood remained unconvinced.

"What about the rest, Celine? Was that all true as well? Do you love him?"

"There is a part of me that will always love Declan, just as there is a part of me that will always be in love with you. What's happened over these last few days has brought that home to me, and I just don't know how much more of it I can take. That's the God's honest truth. The only way I could get him to leave without bringing harm to me and the baby was to tell him what he wanted to hear."

Thoroughgood's shoulders slumped and he let the ice fall to the tiles; the pain inside his head was far more severe than that on the outside. He stared glassily into the pool, aware that her eyes were still trained on his face, and eventually he found the strength to ask what had to be asked:

"So where does that leave us this time, Celine? You know that Declan Meechan's life is finished in Scotland, there's no future for him in Glasgow other than in a cage. You have to make a decision Celine, once and for all, about the baby, about you, and who you want or don't want to be with in this life."

She looked shocked and angry at the same time.

"What are you suggesting I do? Get rid of the baby? The baby is my future, Gus, and that means whether I am with or without someone else."

He began to shake his head but the movement nearly severed it from his shoulders.

"No, you misunderstand me, Celine. I mean I'm here for you and the baby if you want me. I know there'll be tough times ahead, but nothing would be as bad as losing you again, Celine, forever."

This time she cared not a bit about his sore head and threw her arms around him.

"Oh, my darling, to think that for the last ten years I shut you out of my life; I know I don't deserve you, Gus, but thank God for you."

He only just managed to blurt out the words from the confines of her embrace.

"You just have but first you must tell me where you think Meechan has gone, because this has got to end and the only way that's going to happen is with him behind bars."

"I really don't know. He didn't say where he was going. I don't think he'll be headed to the usual places. He has business interests in Whiteinch with a frozen food company called Freezerland. I've also heard him talking about an undertaker's business he was interested in but I don't have a clue where that is, maybe the Hardgate. I think the whole Freezerland thing could be a front for drugs. As you know, I heard a few things at dinner the other night, when I was in the kitchen, that made me wonder. I think if he's going anywhere it will be there. We had a man called Iain Morriston staying with us and he's from the Isle of Barra. I think he's definitely involved in it."

Thoroughgood smiled. "No, that's great Celine; that gives us a starter all right."

He took out his mobile and quickly keyed in Hardie's number. The gruff voice at the other end was instantly recognisable:

"Gaffer, where the fuck have you been? I've been trying you all day."

"Listen Kenny, I'm up at Meechan's place and I haven't got time to fill you in with the details, but suffice to say I know Meechan wasn't at the Stables but I've got a pretty good idea where he's headed right now and I want you to meet me there."

"Roger that, where is the rendezvous?"

"The Freezerland warehouse in Whiteinch. Think you can find it?"

Hardie laughed. "Gaffer, you know me; I'm convinced I was a taxi driver in a previous life! But Whiteinch, that's a funny one, 'cos we've just lost Meechan after chasing him down the wrong way on the southbound carriageway of the Clyde Tunnel. Maybe he was trying to lead us on a little detour."

"What? What kind of mess did you leave behind?"

"Aye, it's no' pretty, we've got one motorcyclist dead,

a couple of smashes and the tunnel is shut. Mayhem, in short."

"Listen, watch what you're doing. Meechan's armed, and let me know the minute you're there."

"Ach, don't worry gaffer, I've got McNab here to help me."

With that, the call was over and Gus turned to Celine and said his goodbyes:

"Listen, you lock the doors and don't let anyone in until I get back. If you see anything unusual happening you call me on the mobile."

She smiled and they came together in an embrace he did not want to break.

It took Thoroughgood fifteen minutes to find the Freezerland warehouse in Whiteinch. Hardie and McNab were already there, the marked TFU Range Rover sitting just outside a twelve-foot-high wire mesh perimeter fence. Thoroughgood greeted his colleagues.

"I gather you've had quite an eventful night!"

"I'm no' sure the old ticker can take much more," said Hardie with a short laugh.

"It doesn't look like there's much chance of Meechan being round here, Gus. On the way over we got word of the driver of a silver Saab being held up at gunpoint by a man matching Meechan's description on the Govan sliproad off the Clyde Tunnel. Guess what? A hundred yards away was his personalised Range Rover with the flat back tyre I made a hole in. Uniform have put a lookout for the Saab and hopefully we'll get something back on that soon. But there's fuckall sign of a silver Saab in the yard or round here."

"That's disappointing, but you can fill me in on it after we take a quick look in the back of that container truck."

Thoroughgood pointed at the large artic emblazoned with the "Barra: Fresh from the Sea" logo sitting in the loading bay.

"Cos I've a funny feeling we might find something we shouldn't in there."

Hardie spotted a large metallic pole he could use to jemmy the back of the container truck open. Taking care to cover up the security cameras with a helpful coating of shaving foam from the can Thoroughgood kept for such necessities in his Barbour pocket, they made their way to the back of the truck, and, after three or four attempts, the padlock eventually gave way and they hauled the doors open.

Thoroughgood was first to climb in, wincing as he went at the pain the movement had induced from his ribs. The back of the container was full, unsurprisingly, of bags of frozen seafood, from prawns to cod. Thoroughgood grabbed one of the bags and split it open with his Swiss Army knife. It revealed exactly what the label on the packet said it would, frozen prawns.

McNab ventured further into the middle of the container, passing the section divided off for prawns and frozen cod until he reached the section reserved for salmon.

"That's weird. I didn't know you could get salmon up in Barra?"

Thoroughgood looked at Hardie and shrugged his shoulders, for in truth he hadn't a clue where salmon could or could not be found.

"Open it and have a look. You never know, you might find it's something fishy!" he laughed.

"Aye, very good Gus, now throw me over that fuckin' Swiss army knife and I'll have a butchers."

McNab cut the bag with a diagonal slice and watched in wide-eyed disbelief as a succession of individually cellophane-bagged packages fell out, each one filled with brown crystallised powder, undoubtedly heroin. He threw one of the bags over to Thoroughgood, who caught it and, using his teeth, ripped open the cellophane wrap. The DS dabbed his finger inside and applied the crystalline-coated digit to his mouth:

"No doubt about it: smack."

It was Hardie who asked the obvious question:

"So, gaffer, what are we gonnae do about Meechan?"

McNab provided the answer. "Did Celine give you any other pointers as to where he might be?"

Thoroughgood nodded his head in the affirmative.

"The only thing she could come up with was some undertaker's business he has an interest in, maybe in the Hardgate. But I don't have any more than that."

"I'll radio control and see if a little bit of local knowledge won't sort that out. While we're waiting on a steer on that, I'll request local uniform to send over a Panda to stand by here. As soon as we get a green light on things, I say we take my hire car and head in the general direction of Hardgate. As far as I know there is only the one undertaker's over there called Malone's, so we might as well make for it and see what develops."

There was no argument, and a short while after McNab had made his radio request they were on their way to Hardgate in Thoroughgood's hired Mazda.

Meechan had wasted no time en route to his eventual destination, Malone's Funeral Parlour. The hands-free in the Saab's black leather interior allowed him to make two calls before he got there. One was to Henry Farrell and the other to his old friend Father O'Hare, a.k.a. Brendan O'Driscoll.

Having satisfied himself that he had ironed out the loose ends he made a third and final call to Peter Malone, the man whose old and failing family undertakers he had bankrolled and breathed new life into. He knew his second cousin would meet his every request with the kind of phlegmatic unflappable realism that had so impressed him when he had broken one of his golden rules not to fund relatives' business ventures.

On arrival at the back of the parlour, Malone was already waiting at the rear entrance used to bring in "new arrivals." Malone, a grey man in the black garb of the undertaker, respectful, reserved and understated, his smile nondescript, beckoned Meechan in.

"Hello Declan, everything is ready as you instructed, if you want to come in I will show you the casket I had in mind for your journey."

Meechan shook his proffered hand, releasing the tepid grip he had been offered.

"What did you call it, Peter? The Last Supper, was it? How appropriate!"

Malone led him into an antechamber which functioned as a showroom for a range of coffins. Skirting past the lighter pine versions, Malone came to a dark mahogany casket and opened the lid, standing back and basking with some satisfaction in the quality of craftsmanship now going to be used to secure Meechan's escape from Glasgow.

"As you see, Declan, the scene from the Last Supper is carved inside the lid and the interior lined with the finest silk. Obviously, I have added breathing holes to filter the air in and installed a light. There's enough room to allow you to eat the sandwiches I'll put inside for you. All in all it should make for a very comfortable ride, and with this level of padding inside, potholes are not going to be a problem for you."

"Excellent," said Meechan, his slate-grey eyes resting on Malone, who seemed to shrink under the intensity of their gaze.

"Now Peter, I've made myself clear regarding the rest of my instructions, there is no time for a repeat. If I'm right, the polis will be in possession of the information that will allow them to track me here. You take me to the destination I have arranged and wait for my man, and then you're free to return and enjoy the fruits of your labours and the fifty grand inside this envelope."

Meechan fished out a crushed manila envelope from the inside of his leather jacket.

"Make no mistakes, Peter, for I will be in touch and as God as my witness, I will be back in Glasgow someday."

Malone gave him another one of his washed-out smiles:

"For all you have done for me, Declan, you have my loyalty for the rest of my days, be assured. What about the polis?"

"Don't worry about them, Peter, you stick to the story we talked over on the phone and you'll be fine. Now I think it's time for us to get going."

Malone stood back, lowered the trolley the casket was sitting on and Meechan hopped inside. Rolling his shoulders from side to side and flexing his legs, he found he had more than enough room, even at six-feet-plus, to lie fully extended. Meechan tested the interior light and felt the silk lining and smiled with satisfaction.

"Excellent, Peter. Now as long as your driving is up to the mark, I might even get some shut-eye."

"I think you'll find it very restful in there all right, Declan," said Malone, and shut the casket.

He wheeled the trolley out to the side door of the parlour, where the rear of the Daimler estate was already opened, and smoothly he pushed the coffin into the back of the vehicle. Inside, Meechan laughed out loud and, hearing the muffled sound of his laughter coming from inside of the coffin, Malone felt a chill run down his spine. He jumped into the driver's seat and turned the ignition on, and within a couple of minutes they were on Great Western Road heading north.

The Mazda pulled into the drive at the side of the road leading to the car park at the rear of Malone's Funeral Parlour. Thoroughgood had completed his account of his latest run-in with Meechan, and Hardie was suitably dumbfounded by his gaffer's bloody-mindedness.

"Fuck me gently, gaffer, you took a chance there with your busted ribs, did you no'?"

The conversation ended when they noticed the silver Saab parked discreetly at the rear of the undertakers.

"Okay, boys, my revolver is at the bottom of Meechan's pool, so you'll need to tool up, looks like the bastard is here," said Thoroughgood, as Hardie and McNab followed him out of the motor as quickly as they could.

Hardie made his way over to the Saab and checked to see if he could get inside, but the doors were locked. Placing his left hand on the bonnet, he found plenty of heat still coming from the engine.

"It's not been stationary long, gaffer, bonnet's hot all right," he said in hushed tones.

Thoroughgood and McNab were at the rear door,

which the latter had found locked; looking over at Thoroughgood, McNab's glance confirmed that entry would have to be forced and the DS handed his mate the metal pole they had found so useful at Freezerland. A couple of minutes later the steel shutter was forced up and they smashed the glass panel above the handle in the interior door it encased and made their way inside the premises, showing complete disregard for the activated alarm bell reverberating through their bodies. A comprehensive search of the interior revealed absolutely nothing.

"Bastard's gone, gaffer, we're too fuckin' late."

"I'd say so, faither. Still, with an all-stations and all-ports lookout request, he won't get far. It's not as if we have been left empty-handed, boys. A drugs haul worth over a million quid, the end of Meechan's criminal activities and the gangland war he has been waging, and the exposure of a corrupt cop should be enough to keep old Valentino puffing away in perfect happiness. You never know, we might even get a drink out of him."

The background silence was broken by the James Bond theme tune from Thoroughgood's mobile.

"Fuck's sake, Gus, that's a bit cheesy, is it no'?" said McNab, shaking his head in mock disgust.

"Anyway, even if Tomachek doesn't take you both for a bevvy I will. Cos you've finally got that bastard Farrell off my case and I forgot to tell you my entry into the Serious Crime squad has been confirmed in writing, as of Friday's appointments in the bulletin."

"I'll drink to that," said Hardie with a broad grin but as he looked over at Thoroughgood, who was on his mobile, he could see an expression of sheer horror cross his gaffer's face. It was soon obvious who was on the other end of the mobile and just why Thoroughgood was so concerned.

"What's that Celine, a car has just pulled up?" Thoroughgood listened avidly.

"A red Mercedes, what does he look like?" Another pause while Thoroughgood listened to her description, then he repeated it for his colleagues' benefit.

"Small with dark hair, a raincoat and gold-rimmed square glasses."

"It's Farrell!" exclaimed a startled Hardie.

Thoroughgood attempted to continue his phone conversation with Celine:

"Hello, Celine are you still there? Celine?" but at the other end the line was dead.

46

THE BATTERY in her mobile was lifeless and she'd hardly been able to hear a word Thoroughgood had said. Initially Celine had decided not to open the door, just as Thoroughgood had ordered her, but looking through the peephole, she had seen the flashed warrant card. Her fears allayed, she opened Tara's large oak front door to a smiling middle-aged man immaculately dressed in a black Hugo Boss suit, and whose lively eyes were only partially hidden by gold-framed square lens glasses.

"Detective Chief Inspector Henry Farrell. Miss Lynott, I guess?"

"Yes, that's right. To what do I owe this pleasure?"

Again that sickly smile. "There's no other way to put this than to get straight to the point, Miss Lynott, surprising as that may be. Declan has sent me to help get you out of here. We're to meet him outside the city, and then the two of you are to leave Scotland together and make a fresh start."

Celine was too stunned to say anything, and an awkward silence developed that dragged on. Recovering her composure, she invited Farrell inside.

"Let me get this right: you, a Detective Chief Inspector, are going to smuggle me out of Glasgow under the noses of your colleagues to join up with the man they have been pursuing. Surely there's something not right there, DCI Farrell?"

Farrell followed her into the lounge, and after she had gestured to him to take a seat, he did so and promptly took his glasses off and began to buff them with his handkerchief.

"Mmm, I can see why it might look a bit, shall we say incongruous, but over the years your fiancé and I have developed an understanding. There's no way I'm going to see a good man go down because Strathclyde Police and one particular colleague of mine are pursuing a vendetta against him. Declan has asked me, as someone he trusts, to get you out of Glasgow and to meet up with him, and it's as his friend I'm here to do as he has asked. I'm sure you didn't for one minute think he would leave you behind?"

Celine was caught off-guard once more, because that was exactly what she had thought had happened. She knew she needed to play for time, and her mind turned over the options as she attempted to come up with a decent stall. She also knew that Thoroughgood would come back to Tara for her as soon as he could. After another uncomfortable silence in which she was increasingly aware of Farrell's furtive eyes assessing her, Celine made her play for time:

"Well, Detective Chief Inspector Farrell, I did hope Declan would make some kind of contingency arrangement, but he left in such a hurry it didn't seem like that was going to happen. This has all caught me off-guard so I'll need time to get some stuff together, at least get an overnight bag sorted."

Farrell's smile oozed insincerity.

"I'm sure you will understand, Miss Lynott that time is of the essence here. It will not be long before my overzealous colleagues are knocking at your door, and then your opportunity to join the man I assume you love, will have gone, maybe forever. By all means go upstairs and get a night bag together but I must stress we have a very limited window of time available to get you out. After that you will be left on your own, facing a future of God knows what."

Celine flashed her sweetest smile:

"Thank you for being so understanding, DCI Farrell; there are some things a girl can't leave home without. It'll only take five minutes and then we can go." She stood up and added:

"Perhaps you want to fix yourself a quick drink while I go and get my things together?"

The sickly grin reappeared on Farrell's face.

"That would be most conducive, Miss Lynott. A gin and tonic would go down very nicely at this moment in time."

"It's all here, DCI Farrell, help yourself. I'll be five or ten minutes, tops."

"Please, no longer than that."

Celine nodded her head reassuringly and left the room. The grace with which her body moved was not lost on Henry Farrell as he savoured the sight of her shapely curves from a rear view. A minute later he was leaning on the superb marble fireplace, sipping his Gordon's and tonic, and considering how things were likely to pan out once Meechan and Celine had left Glasgow.

The second instalment of one hundred thousand pounds he was expecting in his account made the future appear very rosy for him although he had begun to wonder if he was under suspicion from Tomachek, never mind those bastards Thoroughgood and Hardie. A subordinate had tipped him off that Hardie had been sniffing about the

CHIS Unit trying to find out the identity of the informant who had housed Frankie Brennan for him, and of course there was nobody registered.

At the meeting with ACC Cousins, Tomachek had gone out of his way to make sure he knew all the details concerning the safe house, and it was that over-elaboration which had ensured Declan Meechan had not gone on the abortive raid on the King's Stables, and just as well. But what could they prove? Once Meechan and Celine were gone there was nothing and no one left to point a finger at him, he thought.

Farrell took another mouthful of G&T. He checked his watch: Celine had been gone five minutes. He placed the G&T on the mantelpiece and decided it was time to hurry her up, but the sound of the door bell interrupted his train of thought. Farrell wondered if Thoroughgood had made it back already; if so, he had some talking to do.

Making his way out into the hall, he walked up to the door. The lens in the peephole meant he had to take off his treasured glasses and when he looked through the glazing, relief swept over him as he saw his worst fears had not been realised. It was not Thoroughgood on the steps outside the door, but an insignificant sort in a navy blue suit. He opened the door, immediately putting his glasses back on, and saw it was a black-haired male in his early thirties clutching a Bible under his arm, his dog collar evident at the top of his navy jacket.

Ah, pissing priest, thought Farrell dismissively. But this priest was different. In his left hand he held a handgun with a silencer snugly fitted on to the barrel, and now it was pointing straight at Farrell's forehead.

"Time to meet your maker, Lazarus," said the priest.

Farrell didn't even have the time to admonish himself

for his stupidity before the bullet was pumped into his forehead at point-blank range. He crumpled on the steps, his life immediately extinguished.

O'Driscoll bent down and hauled Farrell's body into the hall. That was the easy bit. Now came the part he had almost baulked at when Meechan had issued him instructions over the phone. He had always thought Meechan was essentially the most ruthless gangster he had ever come across, and that included his IRA associates. After the brief telephone conversation he had absolutely no doubt that was the case.

He checked the downstairs rooms systematically, calmly and quietly, but his ears soon picked up the sound of a wardrobe door closing upstairs. Slowly he climbed the stairs, the handgun with the fitted silencer clasped in his left hand and hanging down at his side. He reached the first floor landing and as he took a step, a floorboard creaked from under the carpet runner. The noises coming from the master bedroom across the hall stopped, and the door opened.

Mother Mary, thought O'Driscoll, she's a beauty all right.

Celine had heard the footsteps coming up the stairs and assumed it was Farrell come to tell her to get a move on; there was no way she was going to let some creepy little copper on the take bully her. She opened the door resolved to let him know he had no right to come barging upstairs.

"I thought I told you I'd ..." her words trailed off when she saw the man in the navy blue suit with the dog collar and the jet black hair.

A hint of warning shot through her mind and she placed it. Wasn't it a priest who had murdered Gary Reid, the man Gus had told her Meechan had hired, known from his days in the IRA before he made the crossing from Belfast to Glasgow? It meant only one thing: Meechan knew she had betrayed him. Celine felt herself freezing, framed in the doorway, her heart pounded and her body was wreathed in a cold clammy sweat. Her eyes locked with those of the male and she thought she noticed a hint of sorrow in those eyes.

"Has Declan sent you?"

He nodded and then he spoke.

"I'm sorry."

The bullet thudded home, straight into her heart. She collapsed on the landing. O'Driscoll walked over to her body, placed the pistol to her head and pulled the trigger. There was no place for mistakes, no room for sentiment in his line of work but by God, at that moment, he had to apply every shred of detachment he possessed to keep it that way.

He stood up and took a step away, pulling the silencer off the barrel of his handgun and looked down at the beautiful contorted face in front of him.

My God, thought O'Driscoll, how could Meechan live with himself? Still, business was business.

Hardie hammered the Mazda, foot to the floor at every opportunity, desperately trying to get to Tara as quickly as possible. As the vehicle flew along Strathblane Road, passing Milngavie Reservoir on its left, the only sound that could be heard inside was deafening silence. McNab, Hardie and Thoroughgood all had no doubts at the reason behind Farrell's appearance at Tara, and they knew time was against them.

They reached the Mugdock turn-off and passed a purple

Mondeo as it pulled out onto the main road. So intent were they on reaching their destination, the raven-haired male driving the vehicle and wearing the clergyman's dog collar escaped their notice. Within minutes they reached Tara's open gates and Hardie accelerated through them and up the driveway, skidding to a halt that threw a shale of chuckies up in the air.

Hardie noticed the front door was slightly open, as had Thoroughgood, and before either McNab or Hardie could say anything, he threw open the passenger door and sprinted through the oak doors of Declan Meechan's mansion. As they followed him they heard Thoroughgood shout one word:

"Celine!"

The elements of despair, torture and sheer hopelessness in that haunted single word would stay with Hardie, he knew, until the day he died.

In through the open door they ran, noticing the red gelatinous liquid sticking to the steps; both of them had enough experience to realise that this could mean only one thing. Death was inside.

The sight of Farrell's body propped up against the banister at the bottom of the stair, and the telltale circular black scorch mark synonymous with a point-blank shot to the forehead was evident, but the last thing either Hardie or McNab had expected to see. McNab was first to put his thoughts into words:

"Jesus H Christ, what the fuck does this mean?"

Realisation dawned on Hardie, as his mind struggled to dissect and then associate the information his eyes had relayed to it on the way in to Tara:

"It means we're way too fuckin' late."

McNab was incredulous.

"Meechan has set up Farrell? What about Celine?"

The look on Hardie's baggy features was one completely without hope. They both knew the answer to that question.

"I think we'd better get our arses upstairs, Gus is going to need us."

They climbed the stairs in stony silence, Hardie first; they could already hear the sobbing coming from above. Sitting on the landing floor cradling Celine in his arms was Thoroughgood, too distraught to notice the arrival of his colleagues. Over and over he repeated one word;

"No, no, no."

"My God," said McNab.

Hardie seared him with a withering look.

"Why don't you radio for back-up and an ambulance and then you'd better call Tomachek," he added pointedly, "from downstairs. While you're at it, Meechan has a drinks cabinet in the lounge, I think we need three large brandies quick."

McNab nodded his head, unable to take his eyes off the broken figure of Thoroughgood holding the lifeless corpse of the woman he had always loved but never had the chance to love. Rocking back and forward, all the time he held her head next to his in a world all of his own. A world that McNab could not, and had no wish to comprehend.

Slowly he turned and walked down the stairs.

Hardie circled around Thoroughgood. Facing his friend and colleague, he knew there were no words in his or anyone else's vocabulary that could bring solace to Thoroughgood and instead he placed his hand on his shoulder.

"Come on, Gus, you've got to let her go. It's over."

Thoroughgood looked at him his eyes glazed.

"How can it be over before it has even begun?"

Malone pulled into the small side road leading into one of the vast forests that chequered the road north to Crianlarich and opened the rear of the Daimler estate, sliding the coffin out onto its supporting shelf and edging the lid open. Meechan's face smiled up from underneath.

"We're here, I take it?"

Malone nodded his head in the affirmative.

"Yes, Declan."

Twenty minutes later a purple Mondeo pulled into the same side of the road and a jet-haired male jumped out. Meechan did likewise and led O'Driscoll away from the vehicles, for the conversation they were about to have was for no one else's ears.

"It's done then?" asked Meechan.

O'Driscoll met his friend's eyes and held them and Meechan could see the reproach burning in them.

"Yes, Declan, it is done; all your loose ends are tied up."

Looking down, he checked his watch.

"Now, if we are going to catch our Russian friends on the trawler we'd better get cracking."

O'Driscoll started to turn away in the direction of the Mondeo. He was stopped by Meechan's grip, and slowly in the semi-dark he turned back.

"Tell me, Brendan, how did she die?"

O'Driscoll's face was almost blank, bar a semblance of what Meechan thought was perhaps contempt. Barely audible, he spoke:

"Declan, my friend, there are some questions that should never be asked," and O'Driscoll walked away.

COMING IN 2016 THE PREQUEL TO PARALLEL LINES

THE SHIFT

Chapter 1

THE wind howled as it administered a series of stinging slaps to his recoiling features. It had been a long, hot summer and September had, until now, stayed warm and balmy, but it seemed that autumn was at last making its presence felt.

"What's wrong with you, Uni boy? A wee bit of wind and you are burrowing into your tunic like a ragged-arsed mole digging for his life. Tell me, what the fuck did you join the Glasgow Polis for anyway?"

Before Thoroughgood could reply, and the thought had already taken root that it was a question he couldn't have answered even if he had wanted to, his inquisitor's voice made itself heard once more above the icy gusts that seemed to slice through their woollen 'monkey' suits.

"You fuckin' students are all the same, think you can turn up with your bloody degrees and run the show before the ink has dried on your warrant cards but . . ." The voice stopped and Thoroughgood ground to a halt, aware that his tormentor was no longer parallel with him, turning slowly to stare into taunting grey eyes.

The senior cop's index finger jabbed out into his rookie's shoulder and a breath of stale alcohol washed over Thoroughgood. He found himself mesmerised by a mouthful of rotten teeth that resembled a blown fuse box.

"It don't work that way out here you wanker. It is what I say that goes and it is me who calls the shots. When I say jump, you ask how high? 'Cos what I say is the only way you are gonna stay alive on these streets. Do you understand me, Uni boy?"

Thoroughgood attempted to provide an answer but found words hard to come by for a second time and settled for a nod of his head.

Davidson's contemptuous eyes remained locked on Thoroughgood's features, but the probationer, a mounting anger at his treatment at the hands of his tutor cop rising inside him, met the older man's spiteful gaze with a seething resolve that he would not be cowed.

Their close proximity brought home the sense of latent violence that accompanied Davidson like some imminent threat of impending menace promised and relished. "Now, listen good,…boy," hissed the senior cop, emphasising the last word before adding, "I don't like middle class sponging student scum and I couldn't give a fuck whether you make it out the other side of your probation dead or alive, but what I do care about is keeping my own hide in one piece. So while you are with me, you play by my rules. Your education, Uni boy, starts right now."

The peak of Davidson's uniform hat, which he wore at an angle that slightly covered a headful of straw hair, and those cruel grey eyes, only added to the intimidation oozing from every word.

Yet Thoroughgood attempted to subdue his own raging disgust that a male in his late thirties, whose physique was far from imposing and inclined to strain the silver buttons of his tunic, was indeed doing a very good job of intimidating him.

Physically, Davidson was no threat; it was his experience and know-how gained on two tours of Northern Ireland during the height of the Provinces' problems, and a reputation spawned from his spells in the Emerald Isle for dealing out brutal and systematic beatings, that kept Thoroughgood's mounting anger in check.

Davidson took another step closer. "Rule one for any beat cop is 'know where you are'. Stay sharp, stay alive. You may have all the brains in the world, Uni boy, but now we are gonna find out if you have the wits to go with them, 'cos wits is what keeps you safe 'n' sound on the street."

The senior cop's lecture was ended by the chimes of an ice cream van and within seconds, a golden-roofed, blue-sided vehicle emblazoned with the words 'Mojito's Ices: Satisfaction Guaranteed' came into view at the top of Braidendmuir Street.

"Move it," spat Davidson out of the side of his mouth and immediately set off up the hill towards the van.

About 50 yards from the vehicle, he turned left into the doorway of a derelict tenement close and gestured to Thoroughgood to do likewise. Still staring at the van Davidson eventually spoke. "You never know what is drawn out of the woodwork by the icy. Did you know that junkies have a sweet tooth and that ice cream, chocolate and all that shite helps them fight their cravings?"

"Nope," said Thoroughgood taking his hat off and running the fingers of his right hand through a mop of black hair.

"Junkies equal warrants. So you stay awake and we might just get ourselves a body here," said the senior cop.

Within seconds the deserted street was teeming with kids and mothers as highpitched chatter and shrill cackling filled the air but Davidson's hopes that any of the criminal fraternity would oblige him with an appearance were left disappointed.

As the last of the van's customers left, the senior cop barked, "Stay here," and made his way towards the vehicle, leaving Thoroughgood framed in the tenement doorway and puzzled by Davidson's actions.

The rookie watched in fascination as the former soldier engaged the driver of the vehicle, a young dark-haired male who Thoroughgood put in his early 20s, in an increasingly heated conversation which ended when Davidson grabbed him by the scruff of his denim jacket and half dragged him out of the vehicle's sales hatch.

A combination of the blowing gale and distance meant, infuriatingly, that no matter how hard Thoroughgood strained his ears, he could not hear a word of the exchange.

Having clearly made his point, Davidson propelled the shaken ice cream man back through the window and, as he did so, a brown paper envelope quickly found its way onto the service counter before being scooped up by Davidson and shoved into his tunic breast pocket.

Ten yards from the tenement close Davidson shouted, "Time to move out, Uni boy," and without waiting for a reply, began to stride off as the ice cream van surged down the road in the opposite direction.

Chapter 2

They continued to pound the concrete pavement, lined by grimy, graffiti-stained tenements, some shuttered up with steel casing, others showing signs of life that looked anything but human. Desperate though he was to ask his senior cop what had just taken place with the van driver, Thoroughgood decided he would be dammed if he would give Davidson the chance to slap him down with one of his vicious rebukes. Besides, in Thoroughgood's eyes, it was obvious enough what had just taken place.

The only sound breaking the silence of the once more deserted streets was the metallic chink of Davidson's whistle, which he wore chain entwined through the silver buttons of his woollen tunic. The thought slipped through Thoroughgood's mind that it was almost like the sound of spurs clinking, such was the noise produced every time Davidson's footfall made contact with the pavement.

Thoroughgood had noticed that none of the rest of the shift cops tended to bother wearing the whistle, which seemed to be strictly for ceremonial occasions, unless you were a probationer or Davidson. Now he knew why his senior cop persisted in wearing his; Davidson wanted to send out a warning that the sheriff was in town before he was even seen. With the ex-soldier's reputation for handing out summary justice already having reached Thoroughgood's ears, Davidson's strutting only added to the impression that this place they called Lennox Hill was more like the Wild West than a slumland on the outskirts of Glasgow. The area was widely regarded as the arse end of the North of

Glasgow and one in which the heroin problem had turned half the population into feral zombies who would sell their grannies for a 'tenner bag' of dust, as it was called by the natives, to feed their deadly habit.

Divisional HQ at Bayne Street was only a few miles away from the sub divisional station at Lennox Hill, or 'The Hill', as it was dubbed, which seemed to exist in a parallel universe to newly commissioned Constable Z325, Angus Thoroughgood.

Having graduated from Glasgow University at the beginning of July 1989, Thoroughgood was now in the fourth month of his police service, having negotiated his disastrous basic training course at the Scottish Police College by the skin of his teeth.

Already his university life seemed like some kind of surreal dream from where he had been snatched and landed into a company of wolves who were intent on administering their version of "justice" however they pleased, on a sub species who hated and despised the police in equal measure.

The Lennox Hill station was a five man affair with one elderly officer detailed as station constable and four others rotating on two-man patrols. The fact that the radio reception in the area was erratic and that there were several blank spots where there was no coverage, had already led to the local cops being ambushed on more than one occasion by the natives.

When the residents of Lennox Hill did not seethe in silent resentment, they indulged in their favoured role of the 100 yard hero, brave enough to hurl abuse on a passing patrol only when the gap was big enough.

While he knew that Davidson, or 'Dangerous' as he was known to everyone in Zululand, as 'Z' Division was nicknamed, was only making a valuable and potentially life-saving point, something he was wont to do at least once an eight hour shift, it was his constant sniping at Thoroughgood's former status as a student that really got under the latter's skin. That, and Davidson's persistent assertion that the rookie cop was an "information plant for the brass".

After they had checked a row of shops, front and back, at the top edge of The Hill, Thoroughgood had found it increasingly hard to concentrate, his mind drifting back to the West End where most of his mates would be out on the piss while he pounded the streets with Glasgow's answer to Wyatt Earp. His mind already longing for the 3am piece break, Thoroughgood couldn't help himself checking his wrist watch. He knew it was a mistake.

"Bored? Good old-fashioned honest coppering not what you were promised when they signed you up, you smug little fuck? Never mind the fuckin' time, where are we?" demanded Davidson.

Thoroughgood had switched off and the furtive glance he made around him for confirmation of his whereabouts revealed as much. He felt the impact of Davidson's right forearm ram across his chest and gasped in astonishment as he saw the glint of the knife he grasped, which had appeared from nowhere and was now just inches below his chin.

Again, the fetid alcohol-laced breath billowed over him as his senior cop's fury emptied over Thoroughgood. "What did I tell you five minutes back, Uni boy? Know where you are at all times. Here we fuckin' are and you've switched off already. What happens if we get jumped and need to put out an urgent assistance call and you don't know where the bleedin' hell we are?"

The pressure on his throat and the glinting menace of the knife just below his chin, ensured that Thoroughgood remained silent, but in truth he had been left speechless by the actions of the man who was supposed to be tutoring him in the art of the beat cop.

Slowly, a smile of malicious relish spreading across his face, Davidson drew his forearm back off Thoroughgood's throat but quickly manoeuvred the knife point into the flesh just under the probationer's chin.

"Where we are is the old gas works, and your grave . . . if I want it to be, Uni boy. What happens if I slit your throat and leave you for dead, bleedin' out and dumped in one of the old tanks? A smart-arsed graduate who wouldn't listen to his senior man, stormed off and got his throat cut for his troubles by our friendly locals? All of which would mean I have one less headache to worry about."

Thoroughgood eventually found words, but when he delivered them he realised that he did not recognise the hoarse rasping of his own voice. "You're a fuckin' madman, Davidson. You can't be serious . . . you're my tutor cop for Chrissakes . . ."

The point of the blade remained lodged against the underside of Thoroughgood's chin and Davidson's piercing, hate-filled gaze continued its relentless stare into his shocked features. "Jesus Christ can't save you, Thoroughgood, but I can . . . or not . . ." Davidson let his words fade into an ominous silence.

He added. "You know how I survived two tours of duty in the Province, Uni boy? By staying switched on and relying on my wits every minute of every fuckin' day. You walk the streets with Billy Davidson, then you stay switched on, 'cause I ain't gonna take a blade in the back for some smart-arse book worm who is still wet behind the ears."

The pressure from the blade increased to the extent Thoroughgood thought his skin would give way. His ear drums seemed about to burst as the noise of his heart hammering went into overdrive and he almost stopped breathing.

Davidson pulled the knife back, flicked the switchblade's button, recoiled the four inches of gleaming steel into its ivory handle and slipped it snuggly into the poachers' pocket that had clearly been custom-made, inside the left breast of his tunic. A feral smile swept across the senior cop's features and the blown fuse box reappeared in his mouth, then he spat contemptuously onto Thoroughgood's immaculately polished shoes.

"Better get that gob cleaned off before the Sergeant catches you . . . Uni boy."

But before Thoroughgood could react, the noise of a diesel engine approaching filled the previous still of the night. Looking past Davidson's lacerating smile, Thoroughgood saw a Mark III Ford Escort approach, liveried in the white with red side stripes adorning all Strathclyde Police vehicles; a design that had them nicknamed 'jam sandwiches'.

"Sergeant Rentoul is a stickler for the smart uniform, Thoroughgood, and he won't be happy with the bull on your boots being covered by a huge gob," said Davidson, and filled the air with harsh laughter.

The police vehicle drew to a stop some yards away and the hulking shape of the senior shift sergeant, Jimmy Rentoul, hoisted itself out of the car and ambled towards the two cops.

The creases in the sleeves of his tunic and fronts of his woollen trousers were razor sharp, the army service ribbon fixed to his uniform breast seemingly stood to attention, while the peak of his cap reflected Thoroughgood's features in it, such was the gleam of its shine.

"Well, well. Davidson and Thoroughgood. I'm delighted

to see you are not dossing your way through the night shift," began Rentoul before stopping in mid-sentence as his eyes, which had been scrutinising Thoroughgood's appearance from top to toe, located the slimy green substance on the probationer's right Doc Marten.

Immediately a giant index finger bore into Thoroughgood's chest. "What the fuck is this, son?"

Realising that whatever explanation he offered would be pointless, Thoroughgood played it straight. "I'm sorry, Sergeant Rentoul, I must have caught it round the back of the gasworks. Thought I'd heard a noise back there but it was nothing, and missed the gobshite on my boot on the way out. I'll clean it off immediately."

"Not before I've finished with you, son. Now listen to me, and listen good. If I ever see the uniform of Her Britannic Majesty's police service soiled in such a manner again, I will have you up on a charge of neglect. Do you understand me?" demanded Rentoul.

"Yes, Sergeant," stammered Thoroughgood.

"Remember, I know your story, Thoroughgood. A smart-arse just out of Glasgow University with a degree in, what was it again . . .?" stumbled the Sergeant.

"Medieval History, Sarge," offered Davidson helpfully.

"Aye, that's it, thanks Billy Boy. Medieval fuckin' History, that's right. You tell me what bleedin' use that's gonna be to you out on the streets of The Hill?" Rentoul paused, but before Thoroughgood could answer, he supplied his own. "Absolutely no fuckin' use, is the answer you are searchin' for. But then we both know that, just like we both know the reason you are here, son." Again, Rentoul left the comment hanging in the air.

"Sorry, Sergeant, I don't know what you mean," replied Thoroughgood, befuddled at this new line of questioning from his superior officer.

This time the palm of Rentoul's left hand rammed into Thoroughgood's chest and propelled him back into the crumbling brick wall behind him. The probationer barely managed to keep himself upright. No sooner had he regained his balance than Rentoul was in his face.

"The reason you are here, you son-of-a-bitch, is that you are a grass for the brass. You've been sent here to inform on my shift and try and get some of the toughest cops in this man's army busted out of it. But let me tell you this, you snivelling little arse-wipe, that ain't gonna be happening any time soon. You are almost five months into your two year probationary period and you know who is going to have the biggest say in whether you make it out of it and make the grade as a cop?" demanded Rentoul.

Thoroughgood knew the question was rhetorical and produced a resigned grimace.

"Jimmy bloody Rentoul is the answer you are looking for. Do you think I'm gonna allow one of my veterans to lose his uniform for a nancy boy university graduate who is touting to the bosses? No way son, no way. I will be watching you and having you watched every step of the way. I will know, before you do, when you need to take a shite. Let me promise you, arsehole, there is no way you are going to make it through the box of delights I have waiting for you, Thoroughgood." Rentoul took another step forward, his face millimetres from the rookie's.

"Now get your fuckin' notebook out, shit-for-brains, and let your sergeant sign it," bawled Rentoul.

Thoroughgood tried to keep his emotions masked as he shakily flicked the breast pocket of his tunic open and pulled out the notebook, opening it at the day's tour of duty page. But before he could hand it to Rentoul, the sergeant ripped it out of his grip.

In the background Davidson helpfully piped up, "You not

going to fill the location of the sergeant's sign in before you hand it to your superior officer, Thoroughgood?"

Rentoul took a sideways glance at the senior cop and gave a disgusted shake of his head, before returning the black, plastic-covered notebook emblazoned with the words Strathclyde Police back to Thoroughgood.

"Well . . . fill the location in here . . . Constable Thoroughgood," snapped Rentoul, his last two words dripping in sarcasm.

"Blackmill Gas Works, Blackmill Road, Sergeant," answered Thoroughgood lamely as he wrote the date, location and time in a quivering hand and proffered the book back for his gaffer's supervisory signature.

Rentoul penned his name, opposite the time and location of the sign and slammed the book into Thoroughgood's right shoulder.

Turning to Davidson he asked, "How long you give him, Billy Boy? You think he'll make it to six months?"

Davidson's icy grey eyes peeked out from underneath the tilted lid of his police hat and met Rentoul's gaze before locating Thoroughgood's shell-shocked features.

"I wouldnae be betting your money, or mine, on that, gaffer," said the senior cop gleefully.

Also available from R.J. Mitchell

The Hurting: The Glasgow Terror

The Longest Shadow